DAUGHTERS, SONS AND SHADOWS

Bill Cariad

This edition published in 2014 by
Andrews UK Limited
www.andrewsuk.com

DAUGHTERS, SONS And SHADOWS

Prologue

Bordeaux region of France, village of Créon, a mid-July evening, 1942

In the house where she had once known great happiness with her husband, Matthew, and from the window of the room where she had given birth to her only child, Chantal saw the Gestapo coming for her and instantly knew three things. The first thing she knew was that one of the two men who should have been here to meet her tonight was a traitor. Since neither had shown up, *which of them had sold her out?* Her now wildly beating heart refused to accept her racing mind's thought that both men might have been united by the Judas coin.

The second thing she knew was that she would be unable to withstand Gestapo torture without giving them what they wanted. Himmler's thugs would want names, locations, codes, other precious lives in fact. *And none more precious to her than that of her own son!* Therefore the third thing she knew was that she must deny them what they wanted. She must deny them by ending her own life, by her own hand, before they reached her.

Chantal swiftly calculated the time it would take them to breach the front and rear doors; climb the stairs; break through the stout bedroom door, and figured she had ten more minutes of freedom left to her. The shock was like a cold physical force, gripping her limbs, squeezing her lungs, threatening to paralyze her where she stood fighting for breath with the bitter-sweet taste of betrayal drying her mouth. Her trembling hands fumbled for the pen and paper she would need for her message. She could hear their excited voices now, like baying hounds closing on helpless prey, as she quickly wrote *Cherie... I have been betrayed... not much time left... they won't get me... I'm using a bullet...*

They were getting nearer; she could hear them on the stairs as she suddenly realized which one of the two men had betrayed her. She hastily added to the note then stood on the wooden chair to reach the wooden beam. In the beam's secret compartment crafted by her son, she concealed her message. Her son would, she knew, come here eventually and he would find her message. And he would know she had denied them their prize and protected him by doing so.

They were shooting the lock away from the bedroom door when Chantal stepped down and kicked away the tell-tale chair and put the gun in her mouth.

County of Surrey, England, town of Carshalton, Friday 3rd January 1992

Tentative birdsong and a misty damp dawn were combining to birth the new day upon which Jonathan Teale's life ended. He died as he had mostly lived: quietly and without fuss. Right up to the day before his demise, the seventy-four years old founder of Teale & Lewis, a Carshalton-based firm of solicitors, had shown every sign of defying the grim reaper for a few more years despite the heart diagnosed as weak in 1939.

Destiny had decreed that it be his devoted housekeeper who found him. When she finally telephoned Jonathan's son, Andrew, at 7am, it was to calmly state that she had been unable to waken mister Teale. Only when she requested that Andrew *'Please come'*, did her voice begin to falter. When she had delivered her news and re-cradled the phone, propelled by blind routine the housekeeper then went into the kitchen and put the kettle on.

An explosion will normally make itself heard immediately, its impact instantly felt by something or someone. In a split second it can destroy, or irrevocably alter, whatever stands in its path. Some explosions are detonated by remote control, their unseen initiators themselves unable to see or, arguably, even remotely regret the end result of their actions.

Then again, there are those forms of explosion predictably associated with matters of the heart. Like love and romance, lust and sex, volatile forces in the making, their emotive ingredients often blindly mixed by those who believe they merely play with fire. Blind to the hidden fuse sparked by the vagaries of human nature, they are unable to foresee how long it might take for their emotional time bomb to explode...

Chapter One

*For a tear is an intellectual thing, and a sigh is the sword
of an Angel King.*
(Blake)

**County of Kent, England, Town of Shorncliffe, Monday, 22nd
February 1943**
The police constable silently cursed his undoubtedly warm and
dry absent sergeant, the German Luftwaffe, and the water which
had found its way down his neck. Caped against the driving
rain, his back to the wall of the building, the unhappy man stood
facing an unlit road and a miserable night. Fifteen feet to his left,
the public were denied entry by the damaged door which had
earlier resisted the grunted efforts of several men; the blast-waves
had shifted the door's framework. A head-turn to his right, the
hastily assembled blackout curtain ended in sodden ground-level
folds; the improvised shield completely covering the arched roof
and normally open ends of the porch walkway running the gable-
end length of the building. Tonight the porch walkway served as
both makeshift workplace for the ticket staff and access to the
platforms of Southern Railway's Shorncliffe station.

The police constable was there to ensure that anyone leaving
the station didn't turn left towards the misshapen structures
barely visible in the rain-filled dark; his sergeant had classified
those buildings unsafe following the prior evening's damage.
Consequently, the already overstretched Folkestone Fire Brigade
would hopefully come tomorrow to control the demolition of
houses already deemed to be on the point of collapse.

Newspapers had dubbed this recent spate of bombing which
had started the previous month, as *'The Little Blitz'*. A title
which had done nothing to lessen the impact. Enemy bombers
over-running their primary targets invariably released their

lethal cargo, regardless of what lay below, before turning and running for home. Last night Shorncliffe had lain below such a bomber and had paid the price of proximity to the main ports of Folkestone and Dover.

The gear-change sound of an engine engaging the incline approach to the railway station, carried to the policeman's hearing and he turned to his right to watch the military 'three-tonner' labour into view. The army driver brought the transport to a halt outside the station's entrance as the vehicle's tailgate was released from inside and men of The Royal Artillery Regiment began jumping to the ground. The policeman called out to them, explaining the situation, and without demur the soldiers began filing past him and into the porch walkway. Before the last man had disappeared behind the blackout curtain, their transport had turned and was on its way back to the nearby Shorncliffe army camp.

The shivering sentinel was thinking about a lovely hot cup of tea when the two women approaching on foot came into his view. He recognized them, so, timing it to perfection and with the flourish of a matador, he parted the blackout curtain and directed them through the opening. The older woman ignored his pantomime, but he had the satisfaction of seeing her younger companion grinning her appreciation. His rapid movements had caused the rainwater to run down his neck again and with a heartfelt groan the constable released the blackout curtain and allowed it to fall behind the women.

Once inside the porch walkway, Margaret Creacey gripped the free arm of her companion as feet carefully found their way and eyes adjusted to wartime's pre-requisite dim blue lighting bathing the scene before them. Her grip was briefly disengaged to allow for the transaction with the blue-faced ticket collector who still clutched in one hand the sheaf of rail warrants bequeathed to him by the departing soldiers, the last of whom courteously held aside another blackout curtain for the two women as they stepped onto the platform.

Following the soldiers, the two women immediately turned left to access the arched tunnel which would lead them to the London platform on the other side of the station. The light was

4

better in the tunnel, and, seen close together, the two women were unmistakably mother and daughter. Both were tall and despite their outer rain-wear garments still somehow managed to appear elegantly slim in build. It was in the faces that the lineage was strikingly evident.

Framed by the headscarf which had allowed some of the dark hair to escape in curls now flattened by rain to her forehead, the face of twenty-three year old Elizabeth Creacey might have inspired the Raphaelite painters of centuries past. Her pale complexion perfectly contrasted the naturally dark eyebrows over clear blue eyes, and, despite the enforced absence of makeup, the finely sculptured nose and high cheekbones seemed to glow just enough to shadow the sharply defined jaw-line. The determined set of the mouth was the only outward sign of the tension within her as they neared the London platform.

Beside her, though similarly featured, Margaret Creacey's face bore the marks of time and sorrows past. A once inspirational English teacher and happily married woman, to those to whom she was known she was now a shadow of her former self because the fallen always leave their mark on those still standing. She had already outlived some of those she had taught when they'd been boys bursting to reach the threshold of manhood and in her mind's eye they had still been no more than boys when they'd been sucked in and swallowed down by the madness of war. The same madness which had claimed the lives of the two men she had loved in her life; two hospital surgeons, one her father, the other her husband.

Now, as she reached the platform and could see an approaching train, Margaret Creacey was racked with emotions she was struggling to conceal. She hated stations and crowds but was determined to be with her daughter up to the last possible moment. Since being widowed she had, she realized only too well, increasingly depended upon the woman who had inherited a father's strong character. Elizabeth's maturity belied her years, but Margaret's guilt lay in the knowledge that for too long she had leant heavily upon the young shoulders.

The incoming train was drawing near and, behind her set facial expression, Margaret's fractured thoughts raced on;

'Elizabeth has never once complained... so I mustn't do so now. She has been interested in nursing for as long as I can remember... Had it not been for me, she probably would have left home long ago for a larger hospital where she could learn more... Her father, bless his memory, would have been proud of her now.'

Margaret swallowed hard with her next reflection. She hadn't even been aware that Elizabeth had applied for a place with the government-sponsored Cadet Nurse Corps, but, when the acceptance arrived and she'd finally been told, she had realized it was time for her to let go. She hated goodbyes, but would shortly be forced to watch her child leave for London and her well deserved place with the teaching hospital.

The train arrived, doors swinging open even before it came to a halt, suddenly telescoping around them the demonstrably contrasting emotions which heralded safe arrivals and the quiet uncertainty of wartime departures. Margaret fought back the tears as she turned to her daughter. Despite her attempt to sound normal, she heard the tremor in her voice and thought she might choke on the words before she could get them out.

"Well then, you'd best get on and find yourself a seat, darling."

Elizabeth embraced her forty-three year old mother, over whose shoulder she could see the moving canvas of uniformed men and their loved ones. A strangely painful reminder that the woman she held had been widowed for two years now. Her mother had said goodbye to her husband on this very platform; never to see him again. *'I've tried to help her make a new life without a husband, but have I tried hard enough?'* She ended the thought feeling unsure. Pretending not to see the pain in her mother's eyes, Elizabeth kissed Margaret's cheek and kept her tone light as she spoke. "Try not to worry, Mum. I'll write as soon as I'm settled in. I love you, Mum, take care of yourself now."

The shrill of a whistle and the noise of slamming carriage doors filled the air, intruding on the senses and nullifying the tenderly spoken words. An on-board and battle-dressed young man displaying the cap-badge of The Royal Sussex Regiment, reached down to help Elizabeth board the train. She remained at the open carriage door's window, waving to her mother until finally a bend in the track cut off her view.

Almost oblivious now to her surroundings, Margaret Creacey slowly retraced her steps back to the station's makeshift entrance. The emotional floodgates had finally opened, permitting now the release of tears which streamed unchecked down her face. She pushed aside the blackout curtain and emerged onto the street. Immediately to her right some kind of disturbance was taking place and voices were being raised. Her weary soul ached for a quiet path and instinctively she turned away from the noisy melee. Eyes blinded with tears, she headed off to the left.

Later that evening, the still shocked police constable's report to his sergeant would confirm for the record that he had been on duty outside the railway station to prevent members of the public leaving the station in the direction of the bomb-damaged and still unsafe buildings. A fight had broken out between two soldiers, just off to one side of the temporary station entrance, and he had proceeded to break up said fight. To do so had meant leaving his post. A witness, ironically the woman the soldiers had been fighting over, said she had called out to Mrs Creacey, whom she knew, in an attempt to stop her heading towards the danger area. Mrs Creacey had either failed to hear, or had chosen to ignore the warning.

The police sergeant's report to his inspector, included the information that earlier that day parts of the damaged buildings had been seen collapsing. His report went on to praise his constable, who had risked his own life in a vain attempt to save Mrs Creacey.

The police inspector had known the Creacey family for much of his adult life. Two years ago he had personally, unforgettably, delivered to Margaret the news that her father and her husband had both been killed by the same bomb. Now the daughter must be told that she had lost her mother, and the inspector was privately relieved that this time he wouldn't be the one to break the bad news. He asked his assistant to telephone London's Scotland Yard and whilst waiting to be connected, began searching in his desk for Southern Railway's timetables. As he did so he was mentally calculating just how long it might take for Elizabeth Creacey to discover that she was all alone in the world.

South London, England, Battersea district, Monday 22nd February 1943

The Thames was running high between her banks tonight. *'In more ways than one'*, thought the head-bent hurrying woman. The pungent smell of the river running alongside, carried to where she walked on the Battersea Church road.

One gloved hand tightly clutching the handbag held across her chest, the other hand being left free to maintain her balance, Patricia Swan was on her way home, on aching feet, to the Battersea flat she shared with two cats. The rain which had been falling steadily since she'd left the pub, forced her to tuck her chin hard against the collar of the thin coat covering her small, spare-framed body. A woollen hat, already sodden, concealed and protected her from the worst of the downpour and with her head down her face was barely visible. Occasionally she stopped, before carefully picking her way round some of the deeper puddles. She was anxious to get home and feed the cats. Normally, after standing all day long at the assembly line of the Morgan Crucible factory, she would have been home by now with her feet warmly soaking in a basin. The birthday, and the letter, had altered her routine.

When today's shift on the searchlight components line had whistled to a close, Patricia had accompanied Sally, her best friend and co-worker, to the coincidentally named Swan pub for a glass of shandy in celebration of Sally's fiftieth birthday.

"Can't see us doing this again in fifty years time," had been voiced by Patricia.

"Don't see why not," Sally had replied with a thigh-slapping cackle, "If someone carried us in here, we could manage the rest."

"Speak for yourself," Patricia had responded, "In fifty years time it would take more than a shandy to revive this old bird."

The letter had come from Patricia's daughter, Katherine, carrying the news that she had landed a place with a London teaching hospital. Patricia and Sally had downed another shandy in celebration of Katherine's news.

Three years younger than her friend, Sally knew how hard the years had been on Pat since losing her husband, Albert, in 1918, two years after Katherine had been born. Having never remarried,

Pat had gone on to raise Katherine by herself. In Sally's privately held opinion, Katherine was a right little cow. Even recently, the selfish cow had left her mother on her own while she gallivanted up town with, she'd been told, some kind of so-called artistic crowd. The idea of Katherine becoming a nurse was a mystery to Sally, but she wouldn't say so to Pat. Her friend would never hear a word said against her daughter and Sally understood that. Besides, having kept her counsel all these years she was not about to spoil her own birthday by saying anything now. So, in their opposite directions for home, the two had left the pub still friends.

The Banshee wail of the air-raid siren caught Patricia still short of her flat with its familiar communal shelter. A veteran of raids past, she knew exactly where she was and didn't panic. With barely a pause she decided to head for the church hall cellar which, she knew, was only two minutes away. Rounding the corner, she could see others already converging on the hall a few yards ahead of her. She remembered the last time she'd used this place to take shelter; the limited cellar space had been filled so she'd just sat with others in the hall itself and had had a good natter to chase away the fears. She reached the entrance to the church hall when the idea came to her; this time she would sit out the raid by having another read of Katherine's letter. She passed through the doorway of Saint Patrick's church hall, glad of the respite from the rain.

It was later reported that the bombers had been after the Battersea Power Station, which was why the surrounding area had taken such a pounding. The fire crews, police, and local people, toiled long into the night over many badly damaged locations. Among those places seriously damaged, with some loss of life, was the Saint Patrick's church hall.

Following laid down procedures, for later identification purposes the firemen gave to the police whatever personal effects they had managed to salvage. On this occasion, amidst the rubble of a church hall, one of the victims had made their task easier. She had still clutched in her hand what they had identified as a letter from a relative.

Chapter Two

He jests at scars that never felt a wound.
(William Shakespeare)

Carshalton, Surrey, England, Monday 6th to Wednesday 8th January 1992

The Monday funeral of Jonathan Teale was well attended; the solicitor had been a popular man, attracting friends from both within and outside his profession. He was laid to rest beside his wife, Violet, who had died giving birth to their son, Andrew, in 1960.

Jonathan had never remarried, instead devoting all his spare time to raising his son to manhood. Later, when the young Andrew had firmly decided to follow his father's legal footprints, had come the invaluable coaching and patient guidance through the learning tunnel towards eventual qualification and a place in the family firm. The day following the funeral found a listless Andrew aimlessly pottering about the house he and his father had shared before Andrew had acquired his own flat a short drive away.

On the Wednesday morning Andrew telephoned the office and spoke to Bob Lewis, now the firm's senior partner. They briefly discussed the re-distribution of current commercial and domestic business which Jonathan had been handling. A number of the commercial clients had been dealt with by Andrew's father since their joint early trading days and the initial feeling of the partners, expressed by Lewis, was that Andrew should sustain the Teale connection where he felt able to do so.

Andrew closed the conversation by advising Lewis he would stop by the office to remove his father's personal effects. Lewis assured him he would be undisturbed whilst in his father's office, and the pair disconnected.

East London, England, Tuesday 23rd February 1943

Within the area's architectural mix of the grand and the gaudy; some of the streets were busily filled with night people. Some law-abiding, some not. In Aldgate street, four middle-aged male night shift workers amiably traded anecdotal grumbles about 'the wife' as they trudged to wherever their factory might be. In Leadenhall street, to avoid the passing local 'Beat Bobby' as he quietly padded his turf and dreamt of bed, a burglar sank into shadow with his newly liberated haul of blank ration books. In Eastcheap, still on display in the doorways of darkened and sandbagged shop-fronts, prostitutes discreetly flashed their wares and softly voiced price to passing uniformed soldiers too young and frightened to cross the sexual Rubicon.

In West Smithfield Street, in the middle of a direct line between the bustling low-level sprawl of Smithfield meat market and the lofty elegance of Saint Paul's Cathedral, stood the East London Teaching Hospital of Saint Bartholomew. More commonly referred to as 'Bart's'. For the twenty women carrying small suitcases and shiveringly assembled outside the security conscious main entrance as February wintered towards its close, the hospital would be their home and workplace for the next two government-sponsored years. Provided of course they stuck it out as the student nurses they'd chosen to be, before fulfilling their pledge to join the services or take up civilian nursing in return for their training.

Below the arch of the main entrance where they huddled, some of the group shielded a shared torch to read the informative plaque which told them that above the arch was a statue of King Henry VIII flanked by two figures representing sickness and lameness. The plaque told its readers that Henry VIII's statue commemorated his decision to allow the hospital to continue; following his earlier and less obliging decree to close down the hospital's 15th century Priory Church of Saint Bartholomew The Less.

To the relief of all present, the chubby pink-cheeked and cheery woman who had introduced herself as Mrs Evans and had been tightly shepherding their group as it steadily grew, announced with an accompanying tick on her hand-held clipboard that everyone was present.

"Now, if you will just follow me, ladies."

Obviously a veteran of these encounters, Mrs Evans's bright smile might have been acknowledging their lack of choice in the matter. She appeared to be clad in several layers of clothing under her overcoat, but legs which were encased in white woollen stockings looked more than capable of supporting the bulky ensemble. She led them off at a canter, taking the group through the arched main entrance which those at the front could see led into open space.

The group was led into an open square fringed by the shadowy shapes of Plane trees. The centre of the square was commanded by a large fountain, which in turn was cornered by four sheltered seating booths. Their guide faced the dryly silent fountain as she spoke again, forcing the group to divide on her flanks in order to hear what she was saying.

"Not surprisingly, ladies, this area is called The Square. In more clement weather, some patients are able to sit out here."

Mrs Evans pointed off into the gloom on her left to inform the group that the building they could see on that side was the East Wing, swung her finger to the right and someone obligingly said '*West Wing*' Their chubby-faced guide beamed approvingly before pointing straight ahead to an imposing looking building she identified as the King George the Fifth block.

"Now, if you will just follow me, ladies," cried Mrs Evans again, unaware of the expressive mix of looks exchanged by her charges as they trod after her along the East Wing side of The Square.

Their guide bypassed the King George the Fifth block, instead turning the group left at the end of the East Wing. Ahead of them, another building towered in grey relief against the darkened skyline. They could see countless windows but no warm welcoming lights beckoned; the blackout curtains were cheerlessly doing their job.

"And before you, ladies, is The Queen Mary Nursing Home."

Once again the cheery and for some now irritating tone of Mrs Evans drew little audible response from student ranks. Which shouldn't really have surprised; the building destined to be their new home looked so bleak and uninspiring, as if designed to dull even the brightest spirit.

"Round to your left, ladies," continued their undaunted guide, "is the Nurse's Gate. You will in future use only *that* gate to enter and leave the hospital." She paused to glance over the collective faces, "I do not however expect anyone will wish to use that gate just at this moment. So now, if you will just follow me, ladies."

As if entertaining second thoughts one or two of the group held back to gaze thoughtfully at the corner which concealed the Nurse's Gate, before hurrying to catch up with the others who were already pushing their way through a blackout curtain draped across the entrance to the nurse's quarters. Inside, the student ensemble silently followed Mrs Evans through a labyrinth of corridors before finally being ushered into a room just big enough to accommodate the now perspiring group. Open-faced shelving units, crammed with variably coloured linen items, occupied most of the room's wall-space. Separated from the students by a waist-high wooden counter, stood what appeared to be a facial replica of Mrs Evans atop a slimmer torso. Their guide clapped her hands together to draw their attention.

"Now then, ladies, this is Miss Brownside and she will issue you with two uniforms before I show you to your rooms. Just form a queue, ladies, and be ready to tell Miss Brownside your size. Be sharp now, we haven't got all night."

A short time later the obedient group stood holding their suitcases along with what had been described to them as 'first year' grey uniforms. If Mrs Evans heard some of the comments on the colour, she gave no sign of having done so. Finally the fully laden students were led back into the maze of corridors and up some stairs which brought them to another corridor, narrower and dimly lit, with a seemingly endless number of doors stretching ahead on either side. At this point, their guide brought them to a halt and turned to face her weary looking group. Mrs Evans quickly explained the drill which was to be followed, then began walking slowly backwards as she read out names and room numbers from her clipboard. After a few minutes and now facing a diminished audience, she abruptly stopped. Her attention had been drawn to the figure who had quickly squeezed past the remaining students to reach her and whisper in her ear. Those students nearest to her heard Mrs Evans's *'Dear Lord'* as she quickly consulted her clipboard before looking up again to address her curiosity-aroused audience.

"Elizabeth Creacey and Katherine Swan. Would you both please accompany Mrs Trotter. The rest of you will continue with me."

The two students detached themselves from the main body, glancing quickly at one another before turning all their attention on Mrs Trotter. Who smiled briefly, before quietly commanding them to follow her. They were taken downstairs and led through yet more corridors before being brought to a halt and presented to another woman who wore the distinctive uniform of a Ward Sister.

"Elizabeth Creacey?"

"That's me," responded Elizabeth, warily observing the serious-faced Ward Sister.

"Come with me please, Elizabeth," said the Ward Sister, turning towards a closed door.

"We'll go in here, Katherine," said Mrs Trotter, indicating another closed door.

Throwing each other a last flickering glance, the two students obeyed and separated.

The following morning, when the remaining student nurses were once more re-assembled by Mrs Evans, they were quietly told of the circumstances which had caused two of their number to be returned home immediately. The general sympathy expressed was genuine enough but was collectively overwhelmed by the chief preoccupation of selecting, from the widely differing backgrounds, a kindred soul to share whatever trials of their own lay ahead.

Chapter Three

What's bred in the bone will come out in the flesh.
(Late 15th century)

Carshalton, Surrey, England, Wednesday 8th January 1992
Andrew Teale parked his BMW in the 'gold-dust' space at the rear of his firm's premises.

Dark heavy looking cloud threatened rain as he stepped from the comfortably heated car, shivering reactively to the cold air which struck his face. Tall like his father before him, the wide shoulders suggested power within the slim body. He was casually, though still soberly, dressed in a dark polo-necked jersey and matching coloured slacks which fell on his highly polished black shoes. Thinning hair topped an otherwise young looking face and gold-rimmed spectacles were the worn testament to the price he'd paid for the accumulative years of peering proximity to text and figure-work.

He wanted to avoid the main reception area, so, carrying the empty suitcase he had brought, he entered the premises by unlocking a door at the rear of the building. Selecting from his father's key-ring as he moved, he reached his objective without incident. Outside the door he paused for a moment, as if expecting to hear a voice from within the room. Sighing with regret he unlocked the door, pushed it open, and stepped inside the room.

His father's *Aura* was immediately felt in the room; everywhere he looked. He placed the suitcase on a vacant chair, marshalling his thoughts with an effort. *There would be the photographs, of course, spread liberally around the room, occupying space wherever space had been found. And the desk; a magnificent piece of furniture that had been a gift from a grateful client whose name he couldn't recall right now. Undoubtedly the desk would contain personal effects he should remove.*

Once again selecting from the key-ring, Andrew approached the desk.

London, England, Monday 1ˢᵗ March 1943

It was perhaps inevitable that when Elizabeth Creacey and Katherine Swan returned from their unhappy journeys, they would be drawn together. Their second encounter began with tears.

Having failed to find a taxi in the smog-filled street outside the Holborn Viaduct rail station, Elizabeth had returned inside the concourse. Wherein she had obtained reassuring advice and obligingly gesticulated directions to Bart's hospital from a railway porter.

"You'll be quite safe out there, Miss," he'd said, before emphasising his assurance with a double negative which would have made her late mother scream, "Won't be no air-raid sirens tonight. Bleedin' bombers won't find London in *this* pea-souper."

Later, having walked almost the entire length of the High Holborn thoroughfare in her bid to reach the hospital, Elizabeth was reminded of the porter's words. Visibility was so poor she could hardly see anything at all. Nevertheless she was unafraid. She had encountered uniformed nurses on their way to the station who had helpfully confirmed she was on the right course for her destination. Suddenly, in the gloom, she saw that someone was standing still in the middle of the broad pavement. Drawing level, she realized the figure was that of a sobbing woman.

The woman's right hand gripped the suitcase she was carrying, whilst her left hand was scrabbling furiously in the shoulder bag pulled across her front. Elizabeth was *almost* certain as she silently held out her handkerchief, but, when the woman interrupted her search to look up, the recognition was confirmed. The *Thank you* was sniffled unseeingly as the woman used the handkerchief to rub her eyes.

"That's all right," replied Elizabeth, quietly, while her visual appraisal took in the plumpish figure before her. The woman had short hair, cut straight and light brown in colour, and, noted

Elizabeth as the head came up again, dark coloured eyes now studying *her* face.

"You're Katherine," ventured Elizabeth, "From the student group at the hospital, right?"

"Yes," responded a tremulous voice conveying obvious surprise, "Are you from Bart's?"

Half her mind still elsewhere, Elizabeth merely nodded in response. Suddenly, inexplicably, she was annoyed with herself for feeling disappointed that the woman obviously had not remembered her. Katherine's sobs erupted again and Elizabeth watched the head being lowered to the borrowed handkerchief.

"Shall we put our suitcases down?" Posed calmly by Elizabeth, the unexpected question brought the woman's head up again.

"What? Oh, yes," agreed Katherine.

As they bent in unison to ground the cases, tentative smiles were exchanged. Straightening, Katherine suddenly plunged her right hand into her coat pocket to produce, along with an embarrassed look, her own handkerchief. "I thought I'd done all my crying on the train," was voiced in a high-pitched tone, "I've just come back from my Mum's funeral...," she trailed off, leaving in the smog-filled air between them the suggestion she'd intended saying more.

"As it happens, *my* mother was buried today," responded Elizabeth, her quiet deep voice sharply contrasting that of her companion. She saw the surprise in the dark eyes.

"So you know how it...," began Katherine, stopping as she saw the tears start down Elizabeth's face, then continuing in a rush, "She was *killed in a church for God's sake!* "

An instants silence was followed by their joint collapse into brief but helpless laughter, which quickly became flooding tears as they clung to one another. Moments passed as they individually recovered from the outpouring of emotional stress. Neither of them noticed the disapproving stare levelled at them from the thin-faced and uniformed woman who limped past them in the gloom.

"Here, use mine," offered Katherine, "I've practically ruined yours."

Accepting Katherine's handkerchief, Elizabeth explained through her tears. "I couldn't cry on the train," she wiped her eyes, "Too many people."

"I couldn't stop," confessed Katherine.

"I couldn't cry for Dad, either," resumed Elizabeth, involuntarily plunged back in time, "Two years ago now, but I still remember not being able to cry properly. Mum cried buckets, so I had to be strong for *her*." She stopped abruptly, then added, "I've never told anyone that."

"I don't even remember my Dad," responded Katherine, "He died years ago. It has only been me and Mum... "

Once again, realized Elizabeth, the woman had been about to say more but had stopped herself. She noticeably startled Katherine by asking what else she'd been about to say.

"I'm not really sure about nursing," blurted Katherine in surprising reply.

"You're just upset," said Elizabeth, "Let's start walking, it's getting colder."

They picked up their cases in concert and side by side began walking in the direction of the hospital. "I keep thinking," shrilled Katherine, "If I'd been with her, it wouldn't have happened."

Elizabeth looked straight ahead as she responded, "I know what you mean," she said, her voice resonating with feeling.

And so began the relationship between Katherine Swan, aged twenty-seven, and the twenty-three year old Elizabeth Creacey. A relationship that was destined to influence events in ways neither of them could have imagined at the outset.

The woman who had passed Elizabeth and Katherine on High Holborn wore under her overcoat the uniform of a hospital Ward Sister. She limped into the administrator's office at Bart's hospital, gave her name as Mary Reynolds, and waited rigidly upright as the clerk checked her papers. The clerk thought that despite her stern countenance, the woman was not unattractive. Behind the clerk a door opened and two white-coated doctors emerged. The older man, obviously unshaven, wore his tie askew under his wide-open coat. As they passed the waiting figure at the admin desk, the dishevelled man stumbled and was grabbed by his colleague to prevent him falling.

Watched by Ward Sister Mary Reynolds, the duo continued on their way out of the admin area. *'Discipline was certainly lacking in some areas here'*, was her reproving thought.

The clerk unknowingly curtailed any further thoughts on discipline by returning her papers and smilingly directing the Ward Sister to the Matron's office. His smile was not returned.

On the outside steps of the King George the Fifth block, the two junior doctors stood breathing the night air. The slightly younger but considerably fresher of the pair spoke first.

"You'll end up *joining* the patients if you carry on like this."

"Worth it, though," riposted the older man.

"You scraped an exam you should have sailed through. *Would* have sailed through if you'd spent the night in your own bed, instead of sitting beside someone else's."

"She made it, though," persisted the unshaven man.

"We've got nurses to hold hands."

"I felt... responsible."

"You can't be responsible for all of them, Peter."

"I can try," came the quiet response.

"Oh, I give up. Are you coming in?"

"You go ahead, I just need a minute."

Left alone, the unshaven man gazed out onto the darkened square thinking about what his friend had said. The echoing words *You can't be responsible for all...* unavoidably reprising his memory of that day on the river. The unforgettably fateful day ten years ago, when the holiday boat had capsized and sent three non-swimmers and himself under the choppy waters. He had rescued one of them but had failed to save two, one of them his own brother. In the midst of their own grief, bolstered by their religious convictions, his parents had attempted to console him with the words *You can't be responsible for all God's creatures, Peter.*

The knee injury he'd sustained that day had been destined to rule him out of joining his contemporaries answering the call to arms in '39, but had given him his first close encounter with a hospital. So many times since, had he privately wondered if his choice of profession had been motivated by a subconscious search for some form of atonement. And so many times since, he had told himself that such introspection was pointless.

Supported in his choice of career by wealthy parents who had indulged him with financial backing, he had vindicated their faith and had seemingly achieved his own objectives.

'So why was he so... dissatisfied?' he silently wondered now, staring into the dark, and from somewhere in the night a response arrived and floated through his head. *'He had seemingly arrived at a point in his thirty year old life when he was realizing that no matter how many he saved, he was perhaps destined to remain... unfulfilled...?'*

Abruptly, he reined in his thoughts, too tired to think any more. With a heartfelt sigh, the introspective man named Peter Corder turned back into the hospital. Back towards those who provided his *raison d'être*. His limp was barely discernible.

Carshalton, Surrey, England, Wednesday, 8th January 1992

Andrew's suitcase was already filled with the photographs and numerous other personal effects harvested from cupboards and desk drawers. He was seated behind the desk now, quite comfortable in the swivel-chair, his thoughts leapfrogging from past to present. Idly, he stroked his father's key-ring. There were six keys on the ring. The small label, also ringed, clearly stated *Office*. Andrew continued fingering the keys as he mentally matched; *One for front door, one for rear door, one for office door, two for desk, one for...?* He looked around from his vantage point, remembering how his father's mind had sometimes worked, when the thought struck him. *'Was it a safe key?'*

Perplexed, Andrew came to his feet. *'Surely he would have known of a safe in his own father's office? Must be something else'*, he told himself.

He began looking.

Chapter Four

Fain would I climb, yet fear to fall.
(Walter Raleigh)

If thy heart fails thee, climb not at all.
(Elizabeth 1)

Saint Bartholomew's Hospital, East London, England, May 1943

For Elizabeth Creacey and Katherine Swan the months of March and April had passed in a back-breaking blur of seemingly endless physical toil, frequent lectures, and nightly study.

Despite the individual character differences, evident from the beginning, the cementing of their relationship had strengthened daily. Due in no small part to Mrs Evans, who had shrewdly arranged for them to share a room. Unbeknown to the duo she had also spoken to Ward Sister Martin, who was in charge of the incongruously named 'Harmsworth' Ward. It was perhaps understandable that nobody would have suggested the title might be off-putting to those entrusting their lives to the Ward. Not while the family name of *The Daily Mail* and *The Daily Mirror* proprietors still freshly gleamed on the wall plaque commemorating them as worthy Bart's hospital benefactors. Two students only were assigned to a Ward per-shift, and, as a result of Mrs Evans's *quiet word,* Elizabeth and Katherine had been paired on Harmsworth Ward shifts since the beginning of March.

The daily regime was relentless; they rose at 6-30am to attend to their personal ablutions before struggling into the 'first year' grey uniforms which had eighteen buttons, six hooks, and five studs to be done up. Finally donning caps and aprons, they were rushed from their annexed quarters to the basement canteen of the King George the Fifth block. Where they soon learned that an established 'pecking order' had to be observed when choosing where to sit and eat their quickly taken breakfast.

At breakneck speed, *but*, as dictated by Ward Sister Martin, *without unseemly haste*, they then proceeded to bedpan duties. This was immediately followed by the serving of breakfast to the patients, invariably complicated by extra fetching and carrying. Cleaning duties chased hard on the heels of breakfast, the detritus of which still had to be cleared away.

After scrubbing and polishing things until backs ached and fingers were numb, they were galloped back to the canteen for a hastily scrambled lunch. Lectures; which had to be attended in 'Off Duty' times such as so-called 'free evenings' and lunch periods, were noticeable for the sound of protesting digestive systems. Virtually flying from lunch and lectures, they then actually served lunch to the patients. Which once more involved the time consuming additional fetching and carrying. Bedpan duties rushed them around again, to be remorselessly followed by yet more cleaning and polishing.

Each day it always seemed as if they suddenly found themselves back in the cheerless basement canteen to gulp another tasteless evening meal, hurriedly followed by more lectures, before being catapulted round the Ward with the patient's evening meal. Bedpan duties forced their way back on the agenda before finally, mercifully, the students collapsed back in the privacy of their own rooms. Wherein tired limbs willed themselves to pick up the books that weighed a ton, for bleary eyes to study. Katherine would be asleep as Elizabeth tiredly recorded the day in her diary before using the last of her strength to turn out the light at the stipulated 10-30pm.

Lying in the dark each night before sleep claimed her, Elizabeth would think of the lost parents who had positively contributed so much towards bringing her to this current point of her uncertain career. She thought of the father she had adored; the softly-voiced but strong minded surgeon who had awakened and stimulated her interest in the world of medicine. Never having discouraged her dreams of accomplishing something worthwhile in the field of nursing, he had died before she'd had the chance to tell him of her ambition to do something in the field of convalescence for ex-servicemen and women, but she felt sure he would have approved of the idea. Just as he would have pragmatically advised her that the first step towards the realization of her ambition, would necessarily include the experience and qualifications she now sought to acquire. She thought of her mother; not the disheartened widow-woman but the vibrant person who had nurtured a daughter's love of life and language. The beautiful and intelligent person who had taught her the value of common sense; the person who had shown her how she could retain respect for her body and her spirit whilst still enjoying those first breathless schoolgirl and schoolboy sexual fumbles. The woman whose impulsiveness had often shocked and delighted both husband and daughter in equal measure. Each night, before sleep finally closed down her thoughts, Elizabeth silently pledged to live up to the memory of the two people who had believed in her. They were physically lost to her now; but were still with her in spirit every waking moment.

As the relentless routine continued, one day in the canteen a fellow student was overheard reciting a legend apparently coined by those with more knowledge of the cultures within London's teaching hospitals. "Guy's to flirt, Bart's to work, and Saint Thomas's if you're a lady," the student had quipped. Upon hearing it, Katherine had groaned and wailed, "Why couldn't we have been told this before we chose the workplace?" Elizabeth had become accustomed to Katherine's constant grumbling and knew her room-mate had mixed feelings about nursing *anywhere*. Despite this, for the most part, Elizabeth thought Katherine was fun to be with and enjoyed her company.

The last few days of May remained between the probationary nurses and their next pay day as Elizabeth and Katherine savoured a rare break in their room. Elizabeth was writing up her diary, whilst a restless Katherine threw aside the newspaper sporting a bold headline proclaiming '*Italian Campaign Going Our Way!*' Katherine had other matters on her mind. "That Doctor Corder's quite dishy," she said, unperturbed by Elizabeth's silently shrugged response.

Despite the age-gap, it was the younger Elizabeth who had quietly assumed the dominant role in their relationship and Katherine had proved to be willingly compliant with the unspoken arrangement. Basically insecure beneath the brash exterior, Katherine had naturally sought, and had found, comforting support in the maturity which belied Elizabeth's years.

"I'll be twenty-eight soon," announced Katherine suddenly, making it sound like death, "Do you realize that?"

"That won't excuse you from bedpan duties," parried Elizabeth behind a smile.

"I want to have a bit of fun before it's too late," persisted Katherine.

"Yes, you can forget all about fun when you're twenty-eight," responded Elizabeth then deflected the thrown pillow with her diary, which she abandoned. Now realizing where this conversation was going, she knew her room-mate would continue until she got what she wanted.

"Shall we," asked Katherine in her false *I don't care* voice, "go to hear Lou Preager, then?"

Elizabeth knew it wasn't the band leader neither of them had heard of before which interested her room-mate; it was the men who would be at the dance hall. She sighed; personally she would have preferred a film but knew that Katherine, in her own fashion, was signalling she didn't want to go to the dance hall alone. "Yes, all right," she resignedly replied.

Katherine squealed with delight and Elizabeth had picked up her diary again when her room-mate spoke once more.

"Shame about Sister Martin leaving."

"Mmm," sounded Elizabeth. Katherine was referring to the fact that the Ward Sister was being transferred to another hospital. The woman had been well liked; *firm but fair,* her accorded accolade within the student fraternity.

"Wonder who," queried Katherine in the *not bothered* voice, "we'll get in her place?"

"I heard Corder say it's to be a Sister Reynolds," murmured Elizabeth.

Katherine had now lost interest in the comings and goings of Ward Sisters. With a mischievous grin on her face she finger-tapped the spine of Elizabeth's diary. "I know it's days away, but what shall we wear to the dancing?"

Carshalton, Surrey, England, Wednesday 8th January 1992
It was in one of the filing cabinets, at the back of a half-filled drawer, that Andrew Teale found the wooden box. He guessed it to be one of the 'hardwoods'. It was dark in colour, about eighteen inches long and no more than eight inches deep. He hefted it in one hand:

'Papers inside, and something more substantial', he silently deduced. Half-amused, but wholly intrigued, Andrew settled down again behind the desk and inserted the rogue key in the keyhole set into one end of the box.

Bart's Hospital, East London, England, Saturday 29th May 1943
On the morning destined to be her last day in charge of the 'Harmsworth', Ward Sister Martin was able to confirm that Elizabeth and Katherine would have a duty-free afternoon and evening. Aware of the duo's planned social adventure, she reminded them that they had to be back in the nurse's quarters by ten that evening.

The two women began their free time by cleaning and tidying their 15ft by 12ft shared room. Cleaning of the end-of-corridor communal bathroom was carried out on a rota basis, but today wasn't their turn. The bedroom itself was sufficiently challenging: Two single beds; two bedside lockers and a shared wardrobe inset with a precious mirror, left little space for manoeuvre. When they had finished, what remained of their afternoon sped by as Katherine continued to fuss over what to wear and Elizabeth caught up on her studies.

"How do I look?" asked Katherine for the umpteenth time.

"Devastating," assured Elizabeth.

"I wish we had nylon stockings," grumbled Katherine, already discarding the devastating outfit in favour of another. "What are *you* wearing?" she asked for the fourth time.

"Haven't really thought about it," replied Elizabeth, her attention elsewhere.

"*Haven't really thought about it*," mimicked Katherine, her exaggerated facial expression matching the sarcasm.

A little later, finally acknowledging her room-mate's frustration, Elizabeth helped Katherine choose shoes to go with a figure-hugging dark skirt, and merely raised an eyebrow at the woman's insistence upon a low-cut white blouse which left little to the imagination. '*She's certainly dressed to thrill*', observed Elizabeth, surprising herself with the thought. Watched closely by Katherine she then dressed herself quickly, finishing with a high-necked cream-coloured blouse and black slacks. She opted for flat shoes to offset her height.

"You don't even try," griped an envious sounding Katherine, "and you still look like a film star."

"Don't talk rot," responded Elizabeth, "In any event I'm dressing for myself, not for a man. I'm not really interested in men at this point in my life."

"I'm not talking rot," said Katherine, "Anyway, *you* might not be interested in men but they'll still flock to you. I'll just hit one of them over the head as they rush to get you," she declared.

They both smiled at that whilst donning coats and shouldering the mandatory gas-masks, but Elizabeth was now more aware of her room-mate's lack of confidence whenever the subject of men arose so she selected her next words with care. "Anyway, a man should appreciate you for what is inside, not just looks."

"Just let me get a man inside *me*," responded Katherine, "He'll appreciate it all right."

Laughing at the ribald remark as they made to leave, Elizabeth bumped into the back of Katherine who had stopped in the opened doorway of their room. Together they caught the full glare of the passing figure in a Ward Sister's uniform. The now silent students observed the departing back view of seesawing shoulders as the stranger limped along the corridor.

"She looked a bit fierce," whispered Katherine.

"I'll say. Come on, let's go," urged Elizabeth.

Outside the nurse's home they turned right for the short walk to the Nurse's Gate, passing through the arch under the watchful eyes of the uniformed man who stood inside a tiny booth. Then they were out into the street known as 'Little Britain', and, arms linked, they set off on the walk to Holborn Viaduct and the train which would carry them to the district of Hammersmith and the *Palais de Danse.*

Alone in her room, Ward Sister Mary Reynolds sat at the small table which supported the flickering oil-lamp. One hand distractedly massaged her troublesome thigh as she anxiously checked the staff list before her. She was looking for any name that might have an association with her last post. To her profound relief there did not appear to be one. Her painstaking scrutiny passed over the names of Creacey and Swan without the pause of recognition.

Elizabeth and Katherine reached the underground station without incident, where they purchased their tickets and joined the slow moving throng of people carefully walking down the dimly lit and motionless escalator steps. Puzzled as to why she could see the moving escalator carrying people upwards, Elizabeth politely quizzed the sailor abreast of her.

"All part of the war effort, love. Saves fuel, and it's easier to walk down than up."

Amused by the simple logic, Elizabeth thanked the sailor. She then edged closer to Katherine as they reached the bottom of the steps, to be moved by the human tide on the dimly lit Piccadilly line platform. Almost immediately the tube train noisily slid into position alongside the crowded platform and as the room-mates were among the last to board their selected carriage, they had to stand. Elizabeth's height made it easy for her to hold on to one of the rubber hand-grips suspended from the carriage roof whilst Katherine, too short to reach the support, steadied herself by holding on to the strap of Elizabeth's gas-mask. Elizabeth was suddenly startled as another hand enveloped her own on the rubber grip. To her relief, through the dim interior light she saw that the hand belonged to the sailor who had spoken to her on the escalator steps.

"Not 'urting you, am I?" he asked, sounding concerned.

"No," Elizabeth assured him, "I just got a fright."

"Wouldn't be 'ard in 'ere," he chirped in response.

Elizabeth readily understood what the sailor meant. The inside of the carriage was, she thought, decidedly eerie in appearance. The combination of dim blue lighting spaced along the length of the carriage and the dirty yellowish netting which covered the windows and doors, had the effect of giving the faces of the passengers a deathly pallor. Her shifting glance took in others similarly sharing the suspended rubber grips, their bodies swaying around like multi-coloured wraiths in the poor light.

"There seems to be a shortage of these hand-grips," she impulsively remarked to the sailor.

"Believe it or not," replied the sailor, "some blokes pinch 'em to make coshes out of 'em."

Now sandwiched between her room-mate and the sailor, Katherine tugged at Elizabeth's arm as she spoke. "You're not supposed to be interested in men."

To Elizabeth's ears, Katherine's attempt at a stage whisper sounded like a pistol shot. She could have strangled her colleague right there and then. Those other passengers easily within earshot were, to her dismay, demonstrably amused. The sailor's voice sounded then and was obviously intended to be heard by all.

"I prefer something beefy to get 'old of. Bit like yourself darlin'," and so saying he released his hold on the hand-grip and squeezed a clearly surprised Katherine.

As those nearby passengers erupted in delighted cheers, the train came to a halt. The doors rattled open and with a brightly smiled "Cheerio then," the sailor was gone.

"Serves you right," a grinning Elizabeth told the chastened Katherine.

The remainder of the journey passed without any further drama, ending at Hammersmith where they eventually re-surfaced on to street level. Despite the hour and the inky darkness, the area they found themselves in was bustling with human activity. A passing air-raid warden helpfully pointed them in the right direction.

When they finally reached the blacked-out dance-hall entrance, two posters drew their immediate peering attention. The first of those confirmed for them that tonight's music would be provided by *The Hammersmith Palais de Danse resident band leader, Lou Preager.* The second poster told them that the admission price was half-a-crown and that alcohol was not sold inside. They then spotted other couples entering a building beside the theatre and a still discernible sign proclaimed it to be a public house called *The Laurie Arms.* Katherine said a drink would do them both good and Elizabeth allowed herself to be led into the pub.

Inside the pub, despite her height advantage, all Elizabeth could see was people jammed together in a small, cigarette-smoke-filled space. There was no sign of a bar. "It's no use," she attempted to convey to Katherine over the babble of voices, "We'd best leave." Then she saw that Katherine was speaking to a soldier who promptly shouted a drinks order over the sea of heads to an unseen bar. As Katherine gaily chatted to the soldier, Elizabeth stood feeling like a fish out of water. Minutes later, back over the heads, a chain of seemingly willing hands passed two filled glasses until they reached the soldier who passed them to Katherine.

"One shandy," announced a gleeful Katherine as Elizabeth was given her drink, "courtesy of The Royal Corps of Transport."

Despite her discomfort, Elizabeth couldn't help laughing at that. They both drank thirstily and were soon ready to leave, but Elizabeth paused in the doorway as Katherine again spoke to the helpful soldier. When her friend finally made it to the door, her face was beaming.

"He says the drink will cost me a dance," she explained, giggling.

As they bought their half-crown tickets in the dance hall's foyer they could hear the sound of the music. The cloakroom queue was slow-moving and the impatient Katherine persuaded Elizabeth they should keep their things with them. So with coats, bags, and gas-masks held over-arm, they walked into the ballroom and the wall of sound. People arriving immediately behind, forced them further into the squash of watchers on the edge of the dance floor.

Elizabeth had never witnessed anything like the scenes before her; so instantly infectious was the mood of the place, she realized she was grinning inanely. To her right she could see the band, led by a beaming figure she assumed was Lou Preager. Above the musicians, draped form end to end of the stage curtain, a brightly coloured banner screamed its message 'Write a Tune Competition... Win £1000!', and Elizabeth thought of what she could do with a fortune like that. The band stopped playing and applause quickly followed, becoming briefly louder as the crowd evidently recognized the tune the musicians now began to play. The band's vocalist then stepped up to the microphone and called out the title; Lou Preager waved his baton, and to the catchy up-tempo sound of *The Blackout Stroll,* the dancers were on the move again as the band's vocalist led them off: *'There's no more cuddling in the moonlight. There's no more petting in the park. But why let's worry over moonlight, for when we're strolling in the dark...* "It's lovely," roared the crowded dancers. *'Laugh and drive your cares right up the pole, whisper see you later to your baby doll. For now we change our partners* (and all the lights went out) *in the blackout stroll.*

As the lights came back on the whole thing began again and at that moment, beside Katherine, appeared the grinning figure of the soldier who had engineered their drinks in the pub. Elizabeth couldn't hear the verbal exchange between them, but suddenly a bag, coat, and gas-mask were dumped in her arms and a laughing Katherine was being swept away on to the dance floor and out of sight. Feeling foolish, she naively looked around to see if there was anywhere she could sit down, and, as her eyes suddenly locked with those of a man her father would have called a *Spiv,* the lights went out again and the vocalist's lyrics pierced the darkness. *'For now we change our partners in the blackout stroll.'*

The lights came back on again and the stripe-suited *Spiv* was right in front of her!

"Want to dance, Poppet?"

Elizabeth smiled in response then immediately wished she hadn't. She could smell the drink on his breath and his words had come from thin lips in a face which wore an expression she interpreted as a sneer. Perversely, at that precise moment the band abruptly moved straight into *'You Were Never Lovelier'* and she couldn't suppress yet another smile even as she replied, "No thank you." Trying, as she spoke, to block the sudden mental image of her dancing with this creature and an armful of coats and bags and gas-masks.

"Why not, then?" challenged the man, his tone belligerent now.

"I'm waiting for someone," she blurted, wondering if he was too drunk to notice how laden she was. Feeling the perspiration on her face and hoping he wouldn't notice *that* either.

"Who's that, then?" persisted the man, his beery breath closer now.

"The lady is waiting for me. Now push off, there's a good chap, before I forget my manners."

The new voice, which she realized had actually started just behind her, was still speaking as the figure moved to place himself between her and the *Spiv*. She registered the fact that he was as tall as herself, because she was looking levelly at the iron-grey hair on the back of his head. Her eyes also took in the Captain's pips on the narrow uniform-clad shoulders. She couldn't make out the Spiv's spluttered reply but saw him walking away, then her rescuer turned to face her. Elizabeth was instantly transfixed; her head swam and she could suddenly feel her heart hammering in her chest. His face was that of a man she judged to be in his thirties; the hair colour she didn't understand. His face was thin, the skin roughened and lined. A tough looking face, and, she instantly decided, also a kind face. The eyes looked green*ish,* she couldn't really tell. Her mouth was dry and she could feel the heat in her own face as she suddenly realized that he had spoken. *'God, what did he say?'* she thought, and knew she was blushing furiously now.

"...anyway he seems to have lost interest."

She could hear him now and saw him smile as he spoke, and she thought it made him...

"Are you okay?"

He still smiled with the question but the eyes had narrowed slightly, suggesting concern, and she was now sure they were green. "Oh yes, thank you," she struggled for composure and heard the croak in her voice. *'Oh God, I sound like a frog.'* She cleared her throat to continue, "and thank you for... "

"Thank you for what?" intruded a suddenly re-appearing Katherine, her soldier firmly in tow. The captured soldier's rapt gaze was directed towards Katherine's ample cleavage and Elizabeth's first and uncharitable thought was that her room-mate's ploy of dressing to thrill had obviously succeeded. Her second thought, no less critical, was that apart from his uniform the man appeared to be a slightly chubbier version of the *Spiv* she had only just encountered. Quickly dismissing these thoughts she promptly returned Katherine's belongings to her as she explained, "I was having some trouble and this gentleman arrived just in time. I was just thanking him."

"What kind of trouble?" queried Katherine, her curiosity obviously aroused.

Elizabeth didn't really want to answer the question, but in any event was saved from doing so by the officer who offered both a hand-shake and a smile with his words.

"I was glad to help. My name is Jack Matthews."

Elizabeth shook his hand and almost dropped her coat.

"Permit me," said Matthews, gently relieving her of the coat, "And you are...?"

Elizabeth gave her name to the man with the calm looking green eyes.

"Why don't you and your friends," responded Matthews, "join me for a drink in the bar?"

"Bar?" echoed Katherine, "What bar?"

"Members only bar," contributed Katherine's suddenly attentive soldier.

"Members and friends of members," said Matthews, smiling amiably.

Elizabeth was then taken aback further when her room-mate suddenly enthused, "Well, I'm Katherine, and this is Tom Ball, and we'd love to join you in the bar." Elizabeth inwardly cringed at her colleague's manner, at the same time as she saw the good humour fade from Tom Ball's chubby face to be replaced by an expression of unease. As she briefly pondered the reason, Jack Matthews merely nodded to Katherine and directly addressed her uniformed companion.

"Pleased to meet you, Tom. What say *you* we dispense with rank for the evening?"

Tom Ball's face clearly registered his surprise, but a grin slowly re-appeared as he shook the proffered hand of the officer. "Suits me, sir, sorry, Jack," he corrected himself with a nervous sounding laugh.

A fresh round of applause greeted Lou Preager's announcement that led the band into *'There's a Harbour of Dreamboats'* as Elizabeth was steered by her coat-carrying grey-haired rescuer towards the other end of the Ballroom. Where she could see now the construction which outwardly resembled a pub. Inside it was crowded, but luckily a foursome were vacating a table which the opportune Katherine pounced on without pause. With female requests duly noted, Tom Ball accompanied Jack Matthews to the bar area. Katherine didn't waste any time.

"He's very dishy, your Jack."

"He is *not*," refuted Elizabeth, "*my* Jack."

"He looks even older than *me*," Katherine gleefully opined.

"His age is a matter of indifference to me," declared Elizabeth, unconvincingly.

"Pull the other one," began Katherine, dismissively, "You might be Miss Prim on the outside, but underneath you fancy him like mad," she ended firmly.

Elizabeth couldn't control her burst of laughter.

"That's better," said the smiling Katherine, "You were looking far too serious."

Elizabeth looked at her room-mate, somewhat surprised that the normally self-absorbed woman had even noticed her reaction to the man in question, and wondering now why it was she always found herself thinking of Katherine as merely a room-mate or a colleague. *'Why do I not yet think of her as a friend?'* she silently asked herself, unable to conjure an answer and deciding she should say something to break this train of thought.

"What about you and Tom?"

"He's dishy too," replied Katherine, "In his own way," she enigmatically added.

"Looks like," said Elizabeth, carefully, "he's out for a good time."

"He's on compassionate leave. His brother is ill. They thought he would die, but he pulled through. So Tom has got something to celebrate before he rejoins his unit."

"When will that be?"

"He doesn't know yet."

"Where is he staying?"

"Right here in Hammersmith, with his brother's wife."

"Which hospital is his brother in?"

"Guy's."

"Well you two certainly seem to have done a lot of talking with the dancing."

"Mmm," agreed Katherine, sounding smug.

"You really like him, don't you?"

"I think he might just be what the doctor ordered." Katherine broke off the laugh accompanying her second enigmatic response as the men returned bearing drinks.

"What were you laughing about?" queried Tom, settling himself at the table.

"Me being a cow," replied a straight-faced Katherine.

Tom Ball's puzzled look was spread between Katherine and an equally bemused Elizabeth.

"Actually," said Jack Matthews into the small silence, "In its time, this place has seen its fair share of cows."

Elizabeth saw that Tom was frowning whilst Katherine just looked blankly at Jack, each of them obviously unsure how to take this remark. She caught a glimpse of Jack's smile as he waved a hand around at their surroundings.

"This whole place," qualified Matthews, "began its life as a dairy farm."

As Elizabeth and Katherine looked around them in disbelief, a suddenly enlightened Tom Ball picked up on the other man's cue.

"Didn't know about the dairy farm," said Tom, "but I remember our Mum brought me and the brother here when it was an ice-rink. I must have been about ten at the time."

Jack Matthews nodded his head, "They turned it into a dance hall ten years ago," he paused, smiling slightly as he resumed, "Of course during the first world war, the Air-force used it as a hangar. So this place has had a fairly interesting... "

34

"Okay, okay," interrupted Katherine, punching Tom's arm and smiling at Matthews, "Thanks for the history lesson. Now, can we," she implored, "just get back to enjoying ourselves?"

Tom Ball flashed a quick grin at Matthews before turning his attention to Katherine, whilst Elizabeth suddenly found herself the sole focus of a smile from the man with the green eyes. Because of the noise levels all around them, she had to lean in close to him to hear his softly spoken words. "Tell me about yourself," he invited, "What do *you* do in these troubled times?"

Competing with the babble of voices coming from adjoining tables, together with the sounds of boisterous dancers and Lou Preager's band, Elizabeth began to tell him about her current occupation and her nursing ambitions. She did so slowly at first, then more freely as he gently fanned her enthusiastic flow with the occasional encouraging remark. At some point she was aware of Katherine saying she and Tom were *'Off to attack the dance floor again'* but was still talking to this utterly charismatic man who by now, she realized with mild alarm, was actually holding one of her hands in his own.

Gradually he drew her out on the recent loss of her mother, and she saw him nod as if in complete understanding of how it had affected her. *'This is ridiculous,'* she thought, suddenly angry with herself and withdrawing her hand from his, *'I'm talking to this man as if he was some kind of priest.'* She forced herself to ignore the smile; the greenish eyes; the kind looking face, and regarded him critically. He was sitting perfectly still, calmly watching her, seemingly unperturbed by her changed demeanour. She quietly drew breath and posed her question.

"Is there a Mrs Matthews?"

'So here we are then,' thought Elizabeth, *'I've finally asked,'* and sat now dreading the reply. She saw him look over her shoulder, and heard Katherine's shrill vocals reaching the table even before the woman came into view. Jack's calm green eyes found her own again as he finally responded.

"No. Would you like to dance?"

"I'd love to," she replied, the relief, evident in her voice, coupled with curiosity because she'd heard in *his* voice the unmistakable sound of a French accent.

Katherine and Tom sat down as she and Jack got up and made their way on to the crowded dance floor, and Elizabeth blew Lou Preager a mental kiss as he led his band into the beautiful melody of 'As Time Goes By' just as Jack Matthews held her in his arms for the first time. Neither of them spoke as they slowly moved to the music and Elizabeth wondered if he could feel her trembling slightly to his touch. She closed her eyes, allowing her other senses free rein. In her mind they were alone with the music, and she could smell maleness and mothballs. She opened her eyes and the words were out before she could stop them.

"You smell of mothballs."

"Hibernation," he replied into her ear without any hesitation.

"You live in the dark?" she joked, and felt his body stiffen in her arms. She moved her head to see his face and saw something fleeting there before it became a smile as he responded.

"The uniform spends most of its life in a wardrobe. I very rarely wear it."

"What *do* you wear?"

"Something that doesn't smell of mothballs," he replied smoothly, "but wouldn't be suitable for splendid occasions like this."

Elizabeth moved her head back to his shoulder and closed her eyes again. The tension she'd briefly felt in him had gone, and she felt good in his arms. She glanced down at the insignia on his tunic. "Signals badge, I see, what do you do, exactly?" she asked, wanting to hear his voice again, lifting her head to look into the green eyes, wondering how old he was, wondering about the French accent. She saw the smile which prefaced his easily delivered reply.

"Boring desk job. Shuffling paper mainly."

"Oh, I see, you were bored so you came here to pick up a woman?" responded Elizabeth, hoping she'd made the challenge sound light-hearted. She was drawn closer by him then, her head once again on his shoulder and his voice felt like a caress against her ear.

"I came here tonight," he began, pausing to chuckle quietly, "in my mothballed uniform, to hear the music which I enjoy and to simply relax." He paused again, before softly adding, "Meeting someone like you was the last thing I expected, believe me."

Snug against his shoulder, Elizabeth felt the blood rush to her face and was glad he couldn't see the effect of his words. The mood was abruptly broken by a couple bumping into them, and she drew back to look at him then. She saw the question in the green eyes to which she nodded in understanding and they began to move off the dance floor. She suddenly had the irrational feeling that she'd known this man forever, yet her mind was a whirling jumble of the unknown and the untried. She wondered what it would feel like to be kissed by him. She was remembering the hardness of the body she'd been close to on the dance floor, and the calloused hand which had earlier clasped her own in introduction. *'Not the hand of a mere paper shuffler,'* her father would have concluded. She told herself she must learn more about him. They rejoined Katherine and her partner to find fresh drinks awaited them. A serious-faced Tom Ball proposed a toast *'to absent friends'* which was echoed by the others, and, as Elizabeth leant forward to replace her glass on the table, her tutored ear caught the last sounds of whispered French coming from the man who had held her on the dance floor. She saw him glance at her, stopping the question on her lips as she saw in his eyes what she interpreted as an entreaty for silence. It was quickly followed by the smile she was coming to know. He leaned in towards her and once more she felt the toughened skin of the hand which gently covered her own on the table.

"Will you have dinner with me? Soon?" he asked softly.

"Will *you*." she parried, "tell me more about yourself?"

"Whatever you want to know," came the smiled response.

"Elizabeth!" exclaimed Katherine, "The time!"

Elizabeth's responsive glance at her wristwatch told her it was already after nine-o'clock.

'God help us,' she thought wildly, *'we'll never make it. It took so long to get here...,'* and then a calm sounding voice cut into her panicked thoughts.

"What time do you have to be back?"

"Ten o'clock," interjected Katherine.

Elizabeth's gaze was held by Jack Matthews as he continued speaking calmly, "I have a car outside, I'll run you both back. Don't worry," he assured her, "You won't be late."

Elizabeth exchanged relieved looks with Katherine whilst noticing that Tom Ball's face was wearing its 'surprised' expression again. Jack suddenly excused himself, saying he had to make a telephone call. Bemused, she watched him go over to the bar and saw him exchanging words with the barman who nodded him through a door which stood to one side of the bar. Putting aside her puzzlement about *that*, she rounded on Tom Ball. "What's wrong, Tom?"

"What do you mean?" he responded, sounding surly.

Katherine, scrabbling in her handbag, chimed in, "You did look as if you were having a turn a moment ago, love."

"It's something to do with Jack giving us a lift, isn't it?" pressed Elizabeth.

"Well, you know," began Tom, shifting in his seat and looking decidedly uncomfortable, "With the petrol rationing and all that, you have to be a bit bloody special to even *have* a car. Let alone," he hesitated, "be able to run a bloody taxi service."

"Well he *is* an officer," contributed Katherine, "That's special enough, surely?"

Feeling strangely resentful of his manner, Elizabeth watched Tom Ball receive this statement of the obvious from Katherine and saw him shrug his shoulders. His expression told her he was obviously far from satisfied.

"There's something else bothering you," she persisted, "What is it?" she demanded, and saw his first response was to look at her room-mate.

"Go on, love, get it off your chest," urged Katherine as she began scribbling something on the piece of paper she'd finally extracted from her handbag.

"He's wearing the uniform of a Royal Signals Captain," resumed Tom in a reluctant sounding tone, "but he doesn't come over like any officer *I've* ever known."

Elizabeth watched him sit back in his seat, his body language clearly indicating he'd said all he was going to on the subject. She stared at him as her thoughts chased one another. She had little experience of dealing with army officers, but thought that Jack's behaviour had been what her mother would have described as exemplary. She thought that perhaps Tom was simply jealous of Jack's rank, or just resented his easy manner and good looks, or the fact that Jack, and not himself, was about to resolve what could have been a problem. So, on balance, her mind was unwilling to share Tom Ball's scepticism yet was stimulated enough to ask its own question. *'Who was Jack telephoning?'* she wondered.

"Well, anyway," pronounced Katherine into the silence gap, "he said he'll get us back on time and that's all we need to think about."

Sensing something indefinable, Elizabeth looked up towards the bar area and saw Jack approaching their table. She felt her face reddening and knew it wasn't just because she'd been talking about him whilst he'd been gone. He didn't sit down when he reached their table, moving instead beside her chair to gather her coat and gas-mask which he held for her as she rose compliantly from the seat. His voice was a whisper in her ear as he slipped the coat over her shoulders.

"What's bothering young Tom?"

Taken by surprise she turned to face him and answered truthfully, "The car. The petrol. And *you,* a bit, I think." He surprised her again by smiling and *she* surprised *herself* by immediately feeling reassured. The other couple had moved to stand beside them and Tom Ball was looking down at the slip of paper Katherine was pressing into his hand. Jack's voice-tone served to bring the other man's head up quickly.

"Do you have a billet for the night, soldier?"

Whilst Elizabeth was trying to understand how Jack Matthews could *sound* so different when he looked exactly the same to her, there was, she noted, no mistaking the other man's reaction. Tom Ball was responding to the voice of authority.

"Yes sir, my brother's place. I've had a bit of compassionate leave, sir...," he trailed off.

Elizabeth watched Jack Matthews place a hand on Ball's shoulder as he spoke again, "Don't feel awkward about being suspicious of someone you're not sure of, it may save your life before this show is over. Part of your job, in any event. Tonight, soldier, I'm fortunate enough to have the use of a car," he paused, smiling as he went on, "with the right coloured petrol, and I will be escorting these ministering angels back to Bart's. Now is that okay with you, soldier?"

"Yes sir," Ball meekly replied.

"Okay then," said Matthews, "Let's start by trying to get out of here."

Elizabeth's arm was gently held by Jack as he began guiding the group back through the still revelling crowd towards the exit. As they left the dance hall, a seemingly inexhaustible Lou Preager was leading a chorus of *'Praise the Lord and pass the ammunition.'* Once outside, they were led a short way through the dark until they reached a parked car which Jack identified as their transport. Elizabeth enviously saw Tom Ball kiss her room-mate before Katherine climbed into the back of the car. Elizabeth settled herself into the front passenger seat as Jack prepared himself beside her. He didn't ask for directions, and, using the moonlight to find his road, steadily eased the car through its gears as he commenced their journey.

'Like a man who knows what lies ahead,' thought Elizabeth, her head buzzing with questions she didn't want to ask while Katherine was so close within earshot. She hadn't a clue where they were and could see only solid looking shapes looming skywards, anonymous in the inky blackness. Aware of Jack's concentration on his driving, she was reluctant now to speak at all. They journeyed in silence for some time, occasionally sighting other slow-moving cars. She silently marvelled at how Jack could see anything at all; his mostly covered headlamps, designed to reduce the amount of ground-level light in the blackout, permitted the thinnest beam of light imaginable to her own straining eyes. Then she suddenly recognized the shape of things outside the car. "This is Piccadilly Circus," she voiced, her reluctance to speak forgotten.

"That's right," confirmed Jack, "Not too far to go now."

"Is this *your* car, then, Jack?" was suddenly voiced from the back seat.

"Belongs to a colleague," he answered simply.

Inwardly cringing at what she thought to be Katherine's rudeness, Elizabeth released a soft cough of embarrassment before quietly addressing the man. "It's really good of you to do this."

"My pleasure."

'He sounds sincere', thought Elizabeth, wanting to ask *Who did you phone?*

"What did you mean," shrilled Katherine, "back at the dance hall, about the colour of the petrol?"

Elizabeth silently cursed her questioning room-mate, curbing the impulse to tell Katherine to get out and walk. To control herself she peered outside the side window and thought she now recognized the Holborn road she'd used for her walk towards Bart's when returning from her mother's funeral. That memorable night she'd first heard the voice she wished now would just be silent.

"Black market petrol," began Jack, calmly, "actually looks like petrol. Officially issued petrol doesn't," he ended succinctly.

"Oh," said Katherine, "Well, I never."

It *was* Holborn, realized Elizabeth. Through the gloom she could just make out the shape of the Giltspur street corner. *'Where he will turn at any moment and the journey will be over...'* Jack's voice cut across her dejected thought and she turned her head to him.

"When I told the owner of this car who I was transporting, and why, he said the petrol was a small price to pay for looking after people who might look after *me* some day."

Elizabeth saw him glance her way as the car rounded the corner, and thought she saw the smile as he ended with the words, "That's who I was calling from the room behind the bar."

'God, he can read my mind' she thought, trying to suppress her own smile.

Their driver brought the car to a halt opposite the main entrance to the hospital and Katherine immediately redeemed herself in Elizabeth's mind.

"I'll wait outside the Nurse's Gate, Elizabeth. Thank you very much, Jack. God bless."

As Katherine stepped into the street and closed the car-door quietly behind her, Elizabeth suddenly felt miserable. This evening wasn't ending how she had imagined it might. She suddenly sensed Jack's movement; turned her head, and all at once he was kissing her. As her head swam and her heart pounded, he pulled back to hold her face between his hands as he spoke.

"We don't have a lot of time. I must see you again." His voice was commanding in its intensity.

"I'd like that," she responded, feeling almost breathless.

"The day after tomorrow," he resumed, "Right here, seven thirty pm. Can you get away?"

Elizabeth didn't know whether she could get away, or not. "Yes," she replied.

"You'd best leave," said Jack, "Before I change my mind and drive off with you right now."

Elizabeth saw him smile as he released her face. Barely controlling her excitement she turned to the door, was holding it open when the impulse seized her. She turned back to face him again. "Jack...," she hesitated, then plunged on, "Why is your hair so grey?" She saw the smile, and watched his finger reach out to touch her just under her chin; *Just like father used to'* she recalled instantly, and heard again the French accent with his reply.

"Some of the paperwork I shuffle is frightening. Now off with you."

Giggling, Elizabeth obeyed, stepping out into the street to watch him lean over and quietly close her door. She saw him give a brief wave before he drove off into the night. Rejoining Katherine, they passed through the Nurse's Gate with minutes to spare and silently made their way to their room. Each busy with individual thoughts, neither of them really said much as they undressed in the dark and slipped into their beds.

Still young enough to wonder about the life ahead of her, and already old enough to imagine how lonely it might be, Katherine Swan lay in her bed, eyes wide open, staring into the dark of an uncertain future. Knowing she wasn't attractive enough to be able to pick and choose men. Remembering the last bitterly humiliating experience; when she'd been stupid enough to believe the romantic writers who subscribed to the notion of 'following your heart'. When she'd believed in love, and had followed to London the self-worshipping painter. The man who, whilst ridiculing her own meagre talent for sketching, had used her body as a subject and a plaything before offering her to his friends. 'No,' she admitted to herself, *'I must finally come to terms with the fact that I'm just a plump and plain woman with a bit of personality and time is running out. I don't want to end my days alone like Mum, God rest her soul. Neither do I want to spend them like she did, grinding away for pennies and the company of cats. The original lure of an allowance, with uniforms and books and tuition provided for, in return for a pledge to join the services or go into civilian nursing, brought me here with the half-baked idea that I could latch on to one of life's innocents .I'd entertained the illusion of attracting some naive young doctor with a gleam in his eye and money in the bank. Driving my thoughts back then had been the misguided notion, a wildly desperate idea, that I might somehow be more attractive in a uniform. But I've already lost sight of whatever it was I'd hoped to find by coming here, and I certainly hadn't anticipated the slog of studies which I know in my heart of hearts I will never successfully complete. Tom Ball has said things to me tonight that struck home. He said that life was for living, and should be enjoyed. He said he has savings tucked away and that he has plans to make more money when the war is over. And I just know he fancies me. He's not particularly good looking, but I've tried 'good looking' before and where did that get me? And I recognized Tom Ball's loneliness; a mirror image of my own. Had I not approached him in the pub I would have remained unknown to him, but I can't spend the rest of my life approaching men in pubs.'* Katherine's thoughts hardened: *'No, the time was now. Had to be now, I may never get a better opportunity. I don't want to be cleaning bedpans and scrubbing floors as a so-called nurse for the rest of my life. So I will have to be determined. See it through. I'm sure I'll be good for him. Could she love him?'* She briefly considered the question; *'Too soon for that. Plenty of time for that later.'* she decided. She remembered now the way he'd looked at her, and knew she could make it work. Her mind was made up.

Before Tom Ball's compassionate leave was over, she was going to use every trick she knew. She was going to marry Tom Ball.

Elizabeth Creacey's eyes were closed as she replayed the evening in her mind. She could see his face clearly; see the lines etched into the tough looking skin; see the slow beautiful smile accompanying the voice echoing in her head. She could still feel his touch. When she tried to recall exactly what she had learned about him, and what she hadn't, the film in her head refused to focus there. Instead reeling itself forward to the kissing scene in the car. She wanted to feel that kiss again. She lay in the quiet dark wanting more than a kiss; wanting the unknown. She lay in the dark; wanting Jack Matthews.

In the basement of the anonymous Baker street building, the SOE duty officer logged the call which had informed him that one of the pool-cars was back on base. He hoped the driver had enjoyed himself. *'Lord knows,'* he thought, *'the blighter deserved whatever good times he could find. Shortly now,'* he mused, *'the man code-named 'Shadow' would be sent back to pick up the pieces of a shattered and demoralised network. The man himself was brilliant, no question, and it had been readily acknowledged that the network couldn't be rebuilt by anyone else, not at this stage. But Hitler's Gestapo,'* reflected the duty officer, *'wanted the man very badly. They had almost got him the last time. Could he continue to successfully evade them?'*

The basement room was warm but the 'Special Operations Executive' duty officer mentally shivered as he pushed away the answer favoured by the odds.

Carshalton, Surrey, England, Wednesday 8th January 1992

The discovered wooden box, empty now, stood to one side of the contents which he had spread over the desk. Andrew Teale sat behind his father's desk contemplating the haul: Which appeared to comprise; several hard-covered writing journals; some faded newspaper clippings; a few old black and white photographs of faces he didn't recognize; a small, glass-framed, head and shoulders sketch of an unknown man; and a file folder containing typed letters and a neat bundle of filled envelopes held together by a stout rubber band. The top envelope was marked '1949' and a rifling examination confirmed that each envelope bore a similarly marked date, with the one at the bottom of the bundle showing '1944'. The dates had been handwritten, unmistakably by his father's hand. A cursory glance inside a couple of the envelopes told him they contained letters written in a hand unknown to him. He left them unread.

On the numbered covers of the writing journals, again in an unknown hand, the neatly legible legends declared them to be *The diaries of Elizabeth Creacey*. The name meant nothing to him. Inside the journals the same neat hand was evident, and the entries appeared to relate to wartime events. He moved the diaries aside and continued his trawl. He returned to the file folder, glancing through several sheets of A4-size type-faced business correspondence. Some of them were recognizably file copies of outgoing letters, the letterheads proclaiming *Teale and Lewis* but not in a design he'd seen before. '*So quite old, then,*' he silently deduced. "Brilliant, Sherlock," he muttered to himself with a smile.

He checked a couple of the letterhead dates; saw 1950 and 1952, and then felt his smile give way to a frown. A frown caused by the realization that he was looking at letterheads which evidently had emanated from *Ramsay and Shields, Private Investigators.* They seemed to be reports of some form or another compiled on behalf of Elizabeth Creacey, the apparent owner of the carefully preserved and carefully concealed diaries. The name Creacey suddenly triggered a distant memory... when he was a boy? '*Now what...?*'

"All right in there, Andrew?" The voice of Bob Lewis accompanied the knock on the door.

"Come on in, Bob."

The door opened enough to allow Teale and Lewis's new senior partner to poke his head and shoulders into view. "I'm just off," said the florid-faced and white haired solicitor, "Just thought I'd check on you. See you were all right, I mean," he ended awkwardly.

"Yes, well I'm fine thanks, Bob. Lost track of time, but I'll pack up myself in a minute or two. I think I've got everything."

Lewis opened the door wider and stood in the doorway as he spoke again, "Will we be seeing you tomorrow?"

"Absolutely. Lost too much time already."

"That was to be expected."

"Thanks for covering for me."

The senior partner shook his head and his tone was sincere, "Andrew, had it not been for your father I wouldn't have a firm to cover for," he paused, shook his head again, then smiled, "Anyway, I'll be off. Goodnight, Andrew."

"Goodnight, Bob."

Andrew remained seated but now inactive behind the desk; stilled in remembrance of the respect his father had commanded. Recalling now also, some of the signs of the loneliness he knew his father had borne without complaint. He glanced at the material on the desk, sighed quietly, then began carefully replacing it all back in the wooden box. He would take it home with him and go through it properly later.

Chapter Five

The ruling passion, be it what it will,
The ruling passion, conquers reason still.
(Alexander Pope)

Bart's Hospital, East London, England, Sunday 30th May 1943
Elizabeth and Katherine came awake to the sound of rain insistently beating on their room window. A noisy portent of what the day had in store for them. On top of everything else they would have to cope with on the Harmsworth Ward, Sundays meant visitors under their feet.

Katherine appeared to take everything in her stride as the day progressed and the Ward Sister surprisedly noted that none of the usual grumbling accompanied student Swan's performance of her various tasks. Not that Elizabeth paid much attention to her fellow student; she was too busy trying to fight her way through the mental fog in which she found herself. The Ward Sister observed, and indeed was periodically moved to comment upon the fact that student Creacey was having an unusually clumsy day.

On several occasions throughout the day, Elizabeth was embarrassed to discover herself being addressed by visitors and completely unable to concentrate on what was being said to her. So her semi-professional smile was wearing thin by the time she reached the last lecture period, where the combination of a virtually airless room, and boringly presented information, simply compounded her torpor. Nevertheless she was aware of Katherine's absence.

By the time the mandatory lecture had finished, Elizabeth had convinced herself that she had magnified out of all proportion the events of the previous evening. On the end-of-day trudge through corridors leading to her room, she wearily told herself that Jack Matthews, a man she didn't even know, was hardly likely to be feeling the way she herself had felt all day. Reaching her quarters, she found the note on her bed from Katherine informing that her room-mate had gone to see Tom Ball.

Too preoccupied to consider this information, Elizabeth lay on her bed and made herself face the probable fact that Jack Matthews; with his captivating smile; with his charm polished smooth from experience of dozens of girls, wouldn't even have given her a second thought today. To such a man last night would probably just have been another casual encounter and she told herself it was silly to imagine she might have meant any more than that to him.

Later that evening, with still no sign of Katherine, Elizabeth unsuccessfully attempted to study. Neither could she find any coherent words for a diary entry. She finally undressed and lay in bed feeling thoroughly miserable, no longer sure in her mind that Jack Matthews would even turn up tomorrow. She fell asleep imagining herself standing outside the Nurse's Gate for hours.

Waiting... waiting...

Monday 31ˢᵗ May 1943
Elizabeth woke to the sight of her room-mate already dressed and the sound of her own name impatient on Katherine's lips. Reluctantly she hauled herself out of bed, her limbs lead weights protesting every movement. Making her solitary and bleary-eyed way to the communal bathroom, she recalled now the fitful tossing and turning throughout the night. She joined others already busy with their ablutions at the row of hand-basins and was horrified at the reflection staring back at her from the mirror. *'God knows how much sleep I've had, but I feel awful.'* The mirror didn't help; merely telling her she didn't look any better than she felt.

Back in her room she discovered that Katherine had already left without her. She dressed quickly, pondering why her room-mate hadn't waited for her, glancing at the woman's bed and wondering if she had actually slept in it. Dismissing the thoughts as quickly as they had come, she rushed from the room. She had other things to think about; yesterday's doubts still uppermost in her mind.

Her basement canteen breakfast was, did she but know it, about to set the tone for the rest of her day. For some inexplicable reason, Katherine hadn't saved her her usual place. So she was forced to sit beside a group of students who accompanied their meal with earnest discussion of the anatomical merits of the various 'Housemen' they had thus far physically encountered. Elizabeth disgustedly abandoned her unfinished breakfast, ignored their ribald laughter, and made her way on to the Harmsworth Ward.

She arrived on the Ward to find Junior Doctor Corder trying to communicate with a new patient while Sister Mary Reynolds looked on from the foot of the bed. The patient, heavily swathed in bandages and immobile, had, Elizabeth knew, suffered injuries to both arms and one side of his face. Coming upon the scene, she immediately realized what the problem was and her reaction was instinctive. "He can't hear you, Doctor," she said, moving quickly to the head of the bed, "His hearing aid has fallen out." She smiled at the patient as she retrieved the aid which had slipped to the mattress and was hidden by the pillow. Gently replacing it, she was rewarded with a wink from the undamaged side of the patient's face.

"Thank you, nurse, I hadn't realized," said Peter Corder as he thumbed through the file he held, "Doesn't seem to be," he continued with a smile, "any mention of it in the notes."

She was still basking in the sound of being addressed as *nurse* when the voice of Ward Sister Reynolds whip-lashed over the length of the bed and into her ears.

"Student nurse Creacey, you are, or should be by now, aware of the regulations. If you wish to bring something to Doctor's attention, you do so through me. Is that understood?"

She was then subjected to further criticism in front of the speechless patient and a clearly embarrassed looking Junior Doctor Corder, before she was finally dismissed by the Ward Sister with the instruction to get on with her work. Perversely, what might otherwise have proved to be an incapacitating experience instead served to galvanise her for the rest of the day. So determined was she that the Ward Sister should find no other reason to chastise her, she submerged herself in the Harmsworth

Ward routine. On the occasions when she and Katherine had to physically assist one another, the necessary dialogues were confined to the tasks in hand. Which seemed to satisfy her room-mate as much as it suited herself. As a consequence of this fierce focus, she found herself thinking less about the forthcoming evening and its still to be discovered outcome.

Just to round off her day with unwanted high blood-pressure, the six o'clock lecture over-ran and Elizabeth found herself skipping the evening meal and rushing back to her room to change for her date. She was surprised to discover the discarded uniform evidence that Katherine, who had once more missed the mandatory lecture, had already left.

Removing her own uniform was like shedding the protective skin which had covered her throughout the day, and she suddenly felt her doubts about Jack Matthews rushing back to the forefront of her mind. Sighing with frustration she moodily elected to wear a dark green flared skirt and a white blouse. Whilst quickly dressing, and to divert the unwelcome uncertainty of her immediate future, she briefly pondered her room-mate's behaviour of the past two days. Then a glance at her watch drove Katherine from her mind. 'Jack Matthews', she thought wildly, 'might not even turn up, but Elizabeth Creacey wasn't going to be late.'

Thus, on the impetus of her confused logic, Elizabeth Creacey stepped through the Nurse's Gate at seven thirty sharp. She saw immediately that Jack Matthews, looking wonderful in his army Captain's uniform, was standing right outside waiting for her. She silently rejoiced whilst choking back the sob of relief. She wanted to rush to him but her legs disobeyed and she faltered. He came to her instantly, his hands steadying her. His grip was strong and she felt herself give in his arms, her head resting on his shoulder, her eyes closed, her body involuntarily trembling.

She opened her eyes, finally registering the scene over his shoulder. She saw the legislated white-rimmed hats of passers-by, starkly back-dropped by the wall of sandbags fronting the shops across the street. It all looked so unreal to her at that moment and she felt light-headed. Jack still hadn't spoken a word, but, even as she realized that, he was guiding her across the busy street to the car she recognized. He wordlessly helped her inside, closed the door, rounded the front of the car and seconds later climbed in beside her.

"Well," he said quietly, sitting perfectly still in the car, "You've already answered one question."

"What...?" she began, feeling the warm tears on her face.

Elizabeth saw him move then, a blurred shape through her tears and the darkened interior of the car. He pulled her towards him until their foreheads touched and in her ears now was the English speaking voice with the French accent.

"You haven't been out of my mind for two days," he began, "I've been telling myself repeatedly not to hope. I've tried convincing myself you couldn't possibly have felt the way *I've* been feeling since I last saw you."

"Oh Jack...," she tried, but was stopped by his finger on her lips.

"I'm taking us to a district called Knightsbridge. I have an apartment there." He produced a handkerchief and began gently dabbing her face as he continued, "We can talk there. I think we've got a lot to say to one another."

As he gave her the handkerchief and swung round to start the car, Elizabeth struggled to contain her emotions *and* her curiosity concerning his French accent. The vehicle moved off and she leant back in her seat with the contented thought that she had him to herself for a time. Her questions could wait, she told herself, but the words were out before she could stop them.

"How old are you?" *'So much for waiting*, she thought.

"Is that important to you?" he responded quickly.

"Not really, I just wanted to know," she heard the words tumble out again, "I want to know everything about you."

"The birth certificate," he began calmly, "makes me thirty-two." He paused, chuckling, "Some mornings it feels more like sixty-two."

"I'll keep you young," she spontaneously voiced, then looked for but couldn't see his eyes before hurriedly adding, "I didn't mean that to sound so... "

She was interrupted by Jack, his eyes still on the road, reaching out a hand and squeezing her shoulder as his reassuring words reached her ears like soothing music.

"It sounded fine to me."

Elizabeth firmly decided to sit in silence for a spell, composing herself as Jack concentrated on finding his road solely with the aid of moonlight. Twice he stopped to turn his lights on briefly as he peered along the thin beam of light legally allowed by the heavily covered headlights. She began to feel more clear-headed. "You haven't asked me how old *I* am," she said.

"Twenty-three," he responded instantly, "You told me in the dance hall."

'So much for a clear head,' thought Elizabeth, unable now to stop the giggle escaping.

"What's the joke?"

"I just felt like giggling," she replied without thought, feeling utterly foolish now.

"Best time to do it," he responded simply.

Elizabeth relaxed even more then and resisted the urge to lean over and kiss him. "I couldn't stop thinking about you, either," she confessed softly.

"We'll soon be there," he informed her in reply.

Not much later he brought the car to a halt alongside a solid unbroken row of shapes she saw to be tall, column-fronted buildings. Elizabeth joined Jack on the pavement and had a quick visual impression of grand looking surroundings. She was led up to the top of some steps, where she waited impatiently while he unlocked an imposing looking door. Immediately they were inside they embraced one another, becoming locked in a kiss with her back pressed against the door. She broke away from him, catching her breath before she managed to speak.

"You must," she began, awkwardly trying to smother her embarrassment with flippancy, "think me terribly forward, sir."

"Absolutely shameless, my lady."

Elizabeth saw him smile as he spoke but she felt her face flush and he must have noticed because his response was immediate.

"And quite the most beautiful woman I have ever kissed."

"You've kissed many women, I expect," she retorted, watching him closely.

"Dozens at least, today," he said, smiling and holding her stare "Let's get out of this hallway."

Elizabeth's earlier external impression of 'grandness' was fully confirmed when she entered the beautifully furnished rooms he identified as the lounge area. He briefly sketched a verbal picture of what she now realized was an enormous and elegant looking apartment. He took her coat, draping it over a chair as he said he could offer red wine if she would like a drink. She smiled her acceptance and watched him open the doors of a highly polished piece of cabinet furniture to reveal sparkling crystal glasses and a well stocked bar. While he poured the wine, she gazed around the room. She was thoughtfully observing the obvious signs of what her father would have described as *a woman's loving touch*.

"Do you actually live here?" she asked, trying to sound politely interested.

"Sometimes," he replied, enigmatically.

Distracted now, Elizabeth simply nodded her thanks as she took the glass of wine he proffered whilst she carefully considered her next words. "You said you weren't married," she reminded him, hearing her failure to conceal suspicion.

"That's what I said," he agreed, his voice calm.

In response, Elizabeth eyes slowly traversed the room as she sipped at her drink.

"My mother," he paused, smiling into her eyes, "lived here for a time. Up to now I just haven't found any need to change anything. A part-time cleaning woman keeps everything ship-shape."

She couldn't meet his gaze, afraid he might see the indecision in her eyes, and tried not to blush as she sipped again at her wine. Then he gently took the glass from her fingers and placed it beside his own on a low table which stood in front of a *chaise-longue*. He took her hand, guiding her down to sit beside him.

"You wanted to know all about me," he reminded her quietly.

"Yes," she replied, completely unable to read the expression on his face now.

He began calmly, telling her he was the only son of a French mother and an English father; both of whom were now dead, he quietly told her. He paused fractionally, before going on to say he would tell her more about his parents at another time. He told her that he had been born in France, and had been brought to England by his parents when he was two years old. He paused again, this time to retrieve and re-present her wine glass. Which she accepted with a smile, her attention rapt, merely holding the glass as she silently willed him to continue.

Jack went on to tell her that his mother had taken him back to France in 1920, where he had remained for eighteen years before returning to England with his mother in 1938. He told her he had enlisted soon after arriving back in England. He then looked directly into her eyes, gave a *Gallic* shrug of his shoulders and told her that, yes, of course, there had been girlfriends but no serious relationships in his life to date. He said that whilst he'd been in France, his work had taken all his time and energies. Another *Gallic* shrug prefaced his reminder that then of course had come the war.

Intrigued by his account thus far, Elizabeth placed her glass back on the table as she asked him about his work in France. He responded by saying that he had simply helped to run his mother's factory, adding, *with a sadder looking smile,* she thought, that he would tell her more about that period at another time. She had watched his face throughout the narrative and had seen the familiar signs of strain, which she was partly, hopefully, attributing to their meeting again tonight. She very much wanted to ask him more about his parents, but her longing to be kissed was overwhelming her curiosity.

'*He must be reading the message in my eyes,*' she thought, because he leant towards her and took her in his arms and began kissing her. Gently at first, until she felt his embrace become stronger as she responded. She eagerly explored him with her hands, daringly gripping a thigh with one whilst her other hand caressed with abandon the hardness of muscles covering his stomach and shoulders. She was conscious of the loud sound of their breathing in the quiet room as his lips moved to her neck, then her ears, before coming back to her mouth. A hand suddenly brushed across her breasts, sending the fire through her body, and she closed her eyes to savour his touch with her other senses.

Then the heady mix of thoughts and sensations coursing through her mind and body was abruptly disturbed as she felt him release her, and became aware of him pulling away from her. She reactively opened her eyes and saw so much raw emotion on his face she was startled into closing them again. Her rapid thoughts were in disarray; *'Have I done something wrong to make him stop?... That was a wonderful sensation... that felt so natural... so loving. Was this how you knew you had found real love?... Was this what mother had meant her to save herself for? Was this how it had been for her parents?... This has been much further than I'd ever dared to go with awkward, fumbling boys... the need to know never fully realized... never satisfied...'*

She heard him move and re-opened her eyes to see him lighting a cigarette. She waited, not speaking, confused beyond words, her heart still pounding in her ears, blood hot in her body, her lips swollen to the touch of her dry tongue. He reached out suddenly and grasped one of her hands, raising it to his lips, holding on to it as he began speaking.

"Elizabeth," he didn't look at her as he spoke, "If we are to go any further, there is more I must say first."

'His voice sounds different again,' she thought, *'The mix of languages more obvious now. He sounds older, somehow, and as strange as the iron-grey hair on his young head.'* She forced herself to breathe steadily, and, when he finally turned to face her, she silently looked the question with her eyes.

"These are," he resumed slowly, "difficult times we live in, as you know. Your own work provides you with daily evidence of this... "

She saw his expectant look as he broke off, as if inviting a response, and, unsure as to what reaction he sought, she simply nodded and he seemed satisfied enough to continue.

"My own work is...," he hesitated, "of less importance than yours," he paused to stub out his cigarette, "but still I am unable to say much about it. To share."

She was about to respond but he sighed loudly and pre-empted her, his voice suddenly firmer as he resumed,

"I will be going away soon," he shrugged, "Army business. Shuffling paper in a different place."

She saw his chest expand as he drew in more oxygen to go on.

"I had not planned on meeting a beautiful nurse and being struck by what my Italian friends call the thunderbolt."

His grip on her hand now was fierce but she didn't flinch, trying to smile as from somewhere she found her voice and asked, "The thunderbolt?"

"You get hit by the thunderbolt," he explained with a smile, "when you meet someone who stops your heart for a moment and then captures it entirely."

Elizabeth could again feel her own heart pounding. He now held both her hands in his own as he resumed and she sat perfectly still, mesmerised by the passion in his voice.

"I know you feel something also. I have seen that tonight. I wanted you to know just how I feel about you, before you say anything to me, before we go any further."

She saw the green eyes look directly into her own as he smiled and said, "But you English, I believe, prefer things to be simple. So, quite simply, Miss Elizabeth Creacey, you have captured my heart and it is yours now until you have no further use for it."

"I can't believe...," she began.

"Believe me," he implored.

She could feel her tears now and gasped through a throat which felt constricted, "No, it's not that. I just can't believe how fast this... this is all happening," she qualified, and was unable to stop the sudden choking sound which she released before adding, "I just can't believe that *this* is happening to *me*." Once more her hand was raised to his lips, and then she saw his eyes close as he held her hand against his face. She almost whispered the words which opened his eyes. "I have *never* felt like this, so I must also have been struck by your thunderbolt. My heart has also been captured." Then she incredulously heard herself say, "I must have fallen in love with *you*, Mister Jack Matthews."

She was drawn closer to him by the strong arms, and her head nestled on his shoulder as she struggled to rationalise her feelings and put them into words. "I still can't believe how fast this is happening to me, to *us*. I hardly even know you and yet I seem to know, with absolute certainty, that I love you. That I will always love you." She moved in order to see his face, and suddenly felt strangely empowered. "Kiss me, Jack," she commanded, unembarrassed by her boldness. They kissed passionately for what seemed like an eternity, until her sudden thought forced her to pull away. "When do you have to go away?" she asked.

"Probably next week," he replied quietly, "We can see each other again. There's still time."

"I'm afraid...," she began.

"There's no need to be," he interjected, misunderstanding.

"I've never made love before," she quietly qualified.

She watched him become perfectly still for a second before he once more gently raised her hand to his cheek. Then he rose from the *chaise-longue* to pull her to her feet.

"In many ways," he began, smiling, "tonight will be the first time for both of us, my love."

"I don't want to disappoint you," she told him.

She let out a gasp of surprise as he effortlessly lifted her off her feet and into his arms, and she instinctively clasped her hands around his neck.

"You won't disappoint me," he said.

"You might drop me," she said, unable to stop herself giggling like a schoolgirl.

"I won't drop you."

"I saw Clark Gable do this once in a film," she told him, smiling nervously now as she looked into his green eyes.

"Tonight, *Mon amour*," he replied, carrying her across the room, "we will make our own film."

Ten minutes before the stipulated 10pm, Jack kissed Elizabeth outside the Nurse's Gate and she watched him drive off before making her way to her room. Katherine Swan was waiting for her.

Carshalton, Surrey, England, Wednesday evening, 8th January 1992

The combative tone was loud on the car radio: The Royal British Legion, represented by a war veteran's righteously insistent voice, was hammering home its grievance point to a smooth sounding civil servant of London's Ministry of Defence. The subject of debate was the latter's insensitive policy concerning the widows of war heroes.

'David without a slingshot and Goliath without mercy,' was Andrew Teale's conclusive thought as he killed the radio and parked his car. When he reached the entrance to his flat, the medium-height blonde and curvaceous reason he'd acquired it was struggling outside the door with her briefcase atop an armful of shopping. Jenny Murray, the love of his life, was grinning as she saw him approach.

"Good evening, Sir Galahad," she greeted him, rolling her eyes in mock-distress, "Just in time to rescue the maiden."

"How many times...," he began, reaching past her and unlocking the door.

"I know, I know," she interrupted, "My master's voice need say no more. I should have the key in my hand *before* I pick up anything else."

Jenny made a face at him as she went through the doorway, and, grinning himself now, he followed her. They deposited their individual loads on the kitchen table, exchanged a brief but happy kiss, and he went back outside to his car for the suitcase. Jenny being Jenny, had already started three tasks in the few moments it took him to return. The unpacking of shopping had begun; a saucepan was over gas, and she was finishing pouring him a drink. He took it gratefully, already feeling better just by being in her company.

"Dad's stuff?" she enquired, indicating the suitcase visible in the hallway.

Andrew nodded. Jenny had also loved his father, and had called him Dad from the first week she'd met Jonathan. His father had adored her.

"I will help you with it, later," she said quietly.

"Thanks," he replied, lifting her briefcase from the table when the thought struck him, "Ever heard of a firm of investigators named Ramsay and Shields?"

Andrew watched as she furrowed her brow and tapped a fingernail against her wineglass. She was wearing a figure-hugging brown woollen dress and he thought she looked stunning. He also thought the time was rapidly approaching when he would be proposing marriage to the woman standing before him, and fervently hoped her answer would be yes. They were good together, he reckoned, two of the blessed, he felt, happy with each other and with their work. Jenny was making a name for herself in the claims department of a large insurance company which often employed external investigators. He saw her finally shake her head.

"Don't think so. Why?"

"Oh, just some stuff I found in Dad's office. You can see it later."

"Hungry?"

"So-so," he replied, unhelpfully.

"Would Sir Galahad prefer his so-so cold, or hot?"

Andrew laughed, releasing some more of his tension, stated his preference, and together they proceeded to help one another prepare the evening meal.

Bart's Hospital, East London, England, Monday evening, 31st May 1943

Elizabeth's mood was shattered within minutes of entering her room. The waiting room-mate had clearly been drinking and was obviously impatient to impart her news. *'Or perhaps,'* thought Elizabeth as she listened aghast, *'she simply needs to share her burden of guilt.'* She noted that Katherine couldn't seem to stand still; the woman was restlessly pacing the room's cramped space as if her body was unable to be at peace with the words spilling from its host.

Elizabeth was shocked by the calculated approach which Katherine seemed intent upon adopting towards marriage. As she listened to the woman outlining her plan to become Tom Ball's wife before he was returned to his unit, Elizabeth could hardly believe her ears. The determination she saw etched on the older woman's face stopped her from fully voicing her opinion. She tried instead reminding Katherine that she would be dismissed if the hospital discovered she was married. Which was when a waspish sounding Katherine told her she would be leaving nursing behind just as soon as she sorted out something else to do until Tom Ball came home for good and looked after her. Unable to mask her own feelings at this point, Elizabeth wondered if this was in fact the real Katherine Swan she was seeing for the first time.

Observing her room-mate's reaction had sent Katherine to bed in tight-lipped silence. Only later, as she too lay in bed, did

Elizabeth reflect that the woman hadn't even asked how her own evening with Jack Matthews had fared. It already felt like hours, she realized miserably, since she'd watched him drive away. Now she was wondering how she would bear not seeing him again until Saturday, which was when he'd said he would meet her again. At the time he'd told her, she'd thought *that* was bad enough. But now, to cap it all, she had returned to find herself facing a Katherine who was decidedly not the Katherine she thought she had known. Finally pushing aside the despairing mixture of her thoughts, Elizabeth fell asleep savouring the memory of Jack's lovemaking.

The following morning brought confirmation of the shift in the Swan/Creacey relationship. Katherine returned from the communal bathroom, finished dressing, and left the room without a word. Elizabeth followed soon after, trying not to think of the fact that it would be four whole days before she would see Jack again. Trying not to wonder how long they would have together when she *did* see him. Unable to *stop* wondering about several things; such as his parents, the opulent apartment, his work, what *was* his work? Trying not to feel afraid.

The non-stop routine of hospital life on the Harmsworth Ward still continued apace: The canteen 'pecking-order' seating rituals for the hastily scrambled meals; the increasingly didactic lectures; the feeding and tending to of patients, and the endless cleaning. Including of course the countless trips down 'bedpan-alley', as that particularly odorous chore had been labelled. However, energy-sapping routine notwithstanding, the emerging difference now was that Elizabeth seemed to find more time to spend with patients. Even a few words exchanged whilst fluffing a pillow, or checking a temperature, or holding a drink to lips that said *'Thanks, nurse'* was helping her to feel she was actually doing the job she had come here to do in the first place.

With her watch telling her one hour of her shift remained, and having avoided her room-mate all day, Elizabeth moved towards the bed of a beckoning young pilot whilst pretending not to see Katherine who was only two beds away. The incredibly young airman simply wanted the window-curtain opened a little more; he told her he liked to see as much of the sky as he could. The window in question overlooked 'The Square' and as Elizabeth glanced out she was reminded that earlier that day, heralding another intake of students, she'd seen the redoubtable Mrs Evans leading a baggage-laden group of women towards the nurse's quarters. Recalling now her own arrival day and of how it had ended for her, and Katherine, she looked now to where her room-mate stood and considered making a conciliatory approach there and then. Until she saw the Ward doors swing open to admit a trolley. A nurse she'd never seen before, wearing a uniform she didn't recognize, walked alongside the trolley carrying various items which Elizabeth knew would belong to the recumbent patient.

Moving patients around between hospitals was a practice Elizabeth was becoming increasingly aware of. Casualties requiring different surgical or other treatments were often 'sent-on', thus creating space again for those in need of a particular hospital's speciality. So she wasn't surprised, as her shift drew to its close, to be called upon to assist with such a switch. As always, the nurse accompanying the incoming patient would return to her own hospital with a new patient. Which on this occasion was clearly destined to be one from the Harmsworth Ward.

Elizabeth quickly discovered this particular nurse was from Saint Thomas's. They chatted to one another now as they worked together, even though Elizabeth still felt uncomfortable talking over and around a patient as if he wasn't there.

"I hear you have Ward Sister Reynolds here," remarked the transfer nurse.

"Yes, that's right," confirmed Elizabeth, cautiously adding, "Do you know her?"

The woman nodded emphatically as she replied, "Bit of a sour-puss. Or has she changed?"

Elizabeth's expression must have conveyed the expected answer because the transfer nurse nodded again as if confirmation had just been provided.

"She was my Ward Sister at Saint Thomas's," confided the woman.

"What was she like there?" asked Elizabeth, only mildly interested.

With one leg heavily bandaged the incoming patient was now contentedly tucked up in his new bed. In response to Elizabeth's signal, a porter hurried over to take charge of the trolley now supporting its new occupant. This left the transfer nurse free to carry the small case containing her new patient's personal effects along with a large envelope which held copies of his treatment charts. Elizabeth walked alongside her, wondering if the woman had simply decided to ignore her last question. She hadn't. Pitching her voice so low that Elizabeth strained to hear, the transfer nurse finally answered.

"She was okay to begin with, but there was an almighty fuss and she left. Transferred, they said, but we weren't told where to."

"What happened?" queried a now intrigued Elizabeth.

They had reached the swing doors through which the trolley had already disappeared. The woman looked around anxiously, giving every appearance of being torn between the need to follow the trolley and her obvious desire to pass on a good story. Desire triumphed.

"She was involved with a young doctor. Well, to be fair, *involved* doesn't sound right I suppose. We actually heard she was expecting him to marry her."

One hand on the door, looking through its small glass window to see the trolley still reassuringly in sight, the woman paused theatrically. Clearly enjoying her drama, perceived the watchful Elizabeth. "What happened?" she asked, fascinated now.

"He was much younger than her," resumed the woman, "and he jilted her for a student nurse. She made life hell for students after that." She paused, shaking her head, "For everybody, come to think of it, but young doctors and student nurses particularly. Which didn't leave a lot," added the woman, giggling before visibly controlling herself as she pushed open the swing doors before delivering her final words. "Still, I suppose you've got to feel sorry for her, really. You know what men are like. Must go now. Thanks for your help."

The Ward shift change was beginning as Elizabeth, still preoccupied with thoughts of Ward Sister Reynolds, stopped at the unit used to deposit dirty crockery. She found a tearful

Katherine being comforted by one of the oncoming shift students. Seeing her, the fellow student didn't wait for Elizabeth's question.

"Ward Sister's just hauled Katherine over the coals," she volunteered.

The words were out before she could stop them, "Somebody has to keep us on our toes, I suppose." Katherine's head turned and tear-filled eyes glared at her. Elizabeth took a deep breath before continuing into the silence, "It must be a rather lonely job, being a Ward Sister, I mean. At least we students have got each other," she ended quietly.

Katherine immediately, and silently, trounced past her and out of the door. To be followed by the other student who was muttering as she went, "I'd best get on the Ward."

Her reasoning dramatically ignored, Elizabeth divested herself of the dirty crockery which had led to her unhappy encounter. With a sigh of regret she left the room thinking of how her words must have sounded to Katherine. Thinking about Ward Sister Reynolds. Thinking about the lecture she must soon attend with an alert mind. Feeling miserable, feeling alone, and feeling far from alert.

On the other side of the closed hatch separating the crockery unit from a small storage room, Ward Sister Reynolds had overheard the exchange. Her face was expressionless as she left the store room.

Elizabeth's diary entry that evening reflected her state of mind, but as usual she felt better after writing it.

Carshalton, Surrey, England, Wednesday evening 8th January 1992

The meal over, Andrew agreed it was Jenny's turn to toss the half-crown piece. It was the same old coin that he and his father had used to decide who washed and who dried. Jenny, delighting in the story, had insisted the pre-decimal coin be transferred from Jonathan's kitchen to hers. Andrew lost the call of the toss and rolled up his sleeves. When they had finished the washing up, they opened the suitcase and began spreading its contents over the lounge floor. Jenny went straight for the wooden box and

Andrew passed her the key along with a brief explanation of how he had unearthed the object of her attention. Opening the box, Jenny zeroed in on the writing journals, reading aloud the legend written on the front of the journal numbered 'One' which she now held.

"The diary of Elizabeth Creacey?"

Andrew fielded the question with a frowned response, "I don't know who she is, yet somehow I feel that I should."

"Should I read it?"

"Could I stop you?"

"Not really," replied Jenny, grinning as she settled herself down and began reading.

Chapter Six

Where both deliberate, the love is slight;
Who ever loved that loved not at first sight?
(Christopher Marlowe)

East London, England, Saturday 5th June 1943

Her feelings comprising a heady mix of frustration, puzzlement, exhilaration and concern, Elizabeth Creacey paced up and down outside the Nurse's Gate. It was 10-30am, the time scheduled for their meeting, and Jack Matthews was nowhere to be seen. For days now she had carried the mental image of running into his arms immediately she came through the gate.

'*Like a bloody schoolgirl,*' she silently berated herself.

The disappointment was sharply felt; following as it did three days of she and Katherine not speaking to one another. She *longed* to speak with Jack, hoping *he* would be equally thrilled by her news. She could still hardly believe it herself; wondered wildly if she should move away from the gate in case someone came to her saying '*Sorry, there has been a mistake.*' But she couldn't risk moving for fear that Jack would miss her. '*10-32am. Where was he?*'

Like a sentry, she had adopted her own drill within a drill to keep her mind occupied. Four paces one way, stop, glance around, turn, four paces the other way. The street noise around her was almost deafening. At one end of her self-imposed perimeter, a cheerfully loud costermonger was doing a brisk trade from his fruit-laden barrow. At the other end of her impatiently measured stretch of ground, in evident vocal competition with the costermonger, a news-vendor was shouting headlines whilst exchanging copies of *The Daily Mirror* for coins being thrust into his hand by chattering people either hurriedly entering or leaving the hospital. Leaning against the wall behind the news-vendor, dramatically captioned Billboards still proudly proclaimed the end of last month's campaign-altering news: *German Afrika Corps Defeated! Rommel Routed!*

Seemingly everywhere she looked she could see uniformed soldiers and sailors, some with shouldered kitbags, jostling for pavement room with anxious looking civilians and distinctively clad porters from the nearby Smithfield meat market. Across the street, towering above the human traffic, a magnificent looking shire horse snorted steam through its nostrils as it patiently stood to allow the draymen to unload their cargo of filled-sandbags. Under the direction of two stridently voiced Air-Wardens, the sandbags were being strategically placed to reinforce those already fronting the glass-windowed shop-fronts. A policeman's whistle was being well exercised as he attempted to bring order to the road traffic chaos being caused by the stationary and amazingly even-tempered horse.

At 10-34am the recognized car swept into her vision and within moments was parked a street width away from where she stood. She saw him get out of the car. He was in uniform, but, in *her* eyes, still stood out against the other uniformed men on the street. She saw his smile of recognition across the street separating them and she didn't stop to think; she just ran to him. She saw now his head move quickly left and right before facing her again, but she *still* didn't think and just continued running. He caught her, laughing with her, swinging her off her feet until her shouldered gas-mask case swung round to connect with a *thunk* sound against his side.

"Ouch! I need a nurse," he cried, smiling as he set her down on her feet.

"You've got one," she responded, breathing hard.

"Next time look before you run, please," he admonished whilst leading her round the front of the car to the pavement, "My heart was in my mouth for a second, there. Anyway, you look wonderful," he continued, smiling as he opened the passenger door, "Your carriage awaits."

She returned his smile and got in the car, settling herself as he walked round to the driver's side of the vehicle. As soon as he was seated beside her with his door closed, she blurted out her news.

"Jack, I've got the whole weekend free," and her heart sang as she saw the delight on his face.

"How on earth did you manage *that*?"

"That's the wonder of it," she replied, "Ward Sister Reynolds, of all people, said I could have it."

"Well, anyone who gives you a weekend pass gets *my* vote of thanks," said Jack, starting the car.

His knowing glance registered the tension beneath his passenger's euphoria, and saw the fingers nervously twisting a webbing buckle on her gas-mask. "Had a rough few days, have we?" he asked quietly, and saw her nod her head as she blew through pursed lips. "Want to talk about it?"

Elizabeth expelled an audible sigh of relief and opened up the emotional dam she'd built inside her since she'd last seen him. She told him all about Katherine's behaviour change. About what her room-mate intended doing with Tom Ball, and of her coldness when she'd talked about marriage and her future. About their subsequently not speaking to one another. She told him of her own clash with the new and already feared Ward Sister Reynolds, of how she had been humiliated by Reynolds in front of Junior Doctor Corder and a patient. She almost breathlessly related to him what she had subsequently learned about Reynolds, whilst also recounting the reason behind her own last encounter with Katherine.

"I didn't want to tell her about what I had learned," qualified Elizabeth, "but I was trying to communicate an understanding of the loneliness of command faced by the Ward Sister."

Elizabeth didn't see the narrowed eyes of Jack Matthews signalling his reaction to her words *the loneliness of command*. She was too intent upon describing her amazement when she'd been told, only this morning, that she could have the whole weekend off because, in the Sister's stated opinion, student nurse Creacey had worked twice as hard as anyone else on other shifts. Lastly, she touched upon some of the thoughts about *him* which had occupied her mind over the period they had been parted. Till finally her words ran dry and the narrative ceased.

"A fairly ordinary four days, then," responded Jack, quietly, his tone neutral.

Elizabeth looked at him in surprise and saw the corners of his mouth twitch in the beginnings of a smile. She began laughing and couldn't seem to stop, until finally she was too weak to laugh any more.

"Better?" Jack kept his tone light, hiding his concern.

"Much." replied Elizabeth, feeling practically breathless again but strangely content.

"I've missed you too," he told her, sensing the need.

Still feeling drained from the release of emotional tension, she was aware of her body silently drawing strength from his words. She wondered if this was what writers of romance referred to when they wrote of *love's emotional rollercoaster,* and she couldn't even *begin* to imagine what her parents would have thought now of their hitherto 'mature beyond her years' daughter. An exasperated sigh escaped her lips whilst a glance out her window rewarded her with a view of strange surroundings.

"Where are we going?" she asked now, feigning a calmness she didn't feel.

"To the apartment," he replied, adding firmly, "But first we have a stop to make."

She waited for more information, then, realizing none was forthcoming, settled back in her seat and began to look at the scenes outside. Scenes she didn't recognize at all. Scenes which suddenly made her feel unsettled, all at once crystallizing her thoughts, making her uncomfortably aware that her driver had awakened forces seemingly outside her control. Forces which were taking her in a direction she'd never planned to take. 'Forces', said a small voice inside her now, *'which could weaken her strength of purpose and dilute her ambition... '*

"Where are we?" she asked abruptly, forcibly curtailing her thoughts just as the car was steered into the pavement's edge and brought to a halt by her unresponsive driver. She turned to him and saw him smile.

"What's the date today?" he suddenly asked.

"The fifth of June," she automatically answered.

"A date to remember, then," he said.

She stared at him uncomprehendingly, her thoughts in disarray. She saw him grin at her blank expression, then he reached out and clasped her hands in his own as he spoke again.

"Today, *Mon amour*, will become the anniversary date of our engagement," he paused, "Once we go into the shop just here and you choose the ring," he ended calmly.

Lost for words, Elizabeth looked back outside to the street and couldn't see anything that resembled a jeweller's shop. The small voice of suspicion was whispering in her mind as she turned back to Jack. "Is this because I told you about Katherine?" she challenged.

"Not really," he answered calmly, seemingly unperturbed by her tone, "I had already considered taking a chance on the ring size and then surprising you later in the day," he shrugged his shoulders, "I couldn't decide," he confessed, "but I *had* planned on getting it today. You've been wound up since you got in the car, and not just about Katherine, I think, so that's what tipped the scales and has brought us here now."

Elizabeth attempted a smile, inwardly searching for words to express her thoughts, then Jack squeezed her hands as she heard again the underlay of French in his voice.

"This is of course a well known madness, Elizabeth, this thing which is sweeping us both off our feet. This thing of which poets write endless verse, and the Gods of chance have decreed should be known as love. When it happens we mortals lose ourselves to it, and the heart takes us to where it will. For some, it leads to happiness. For others, sadness. For us, I hope, happiness will overcome whatever sadness we may encounter along the way."

Her hands were released and she silently watched him move to rest his arms on the car's steering wheel. He rested his head on his arms and turned to face her as he continued.

"But we need not lose our minds on the journey, you and I, and nor shall we. Together we face an unknown path, and at the onset the seeds of doubt will naturally emerge." He smiled in the pause, before adding, "Perhaps you carry some of those seeds in your pocket right now."

Reprised now by his words, she was reminded of her previous thought about his reading her mind. She felt the heat on her face then his voice was filling the car again.

"When you spoke to me in the dance hall of your plans and ambitions for your future, I heard the same strength of purpose I used to hear in my mother's voice. She taught me many things, Elizabeth, some of them complex but some of them quite simple. Such as the importance of respecting and supporting a partner's hopes and aspirations. I would never stand in the way of your ambition to succeed. And I believe that what we could share would only strengthen your resolve, not serve to weaken it. The seeds of doubt would find no place to grow."

Elizabeth realized that he had finished speaking, even though his words still reverberated in her mind. A mind which suddenly felt clear. Her own mind, perfectly aware of the change which had occurred in her heart and at peace with that change. Recognizing it for what it was, a change for the good. She no longer felt as if she'd lost her way, was instead feeling that she had discovered a better way to reach wherever she was going. His voice sounded again as he moved and her hands were once more clasped.

"I will not ask you to be my wife until this war is finished," he said, "But I *am* very definitely asking you today, Miss Elizabeth Creacey, if you would care to become *engaged* to be my wife." He stopped, one eyebrow raised in question, the smile in his eyes.

"Mister Jack Matthews," she began formally, adopting a serious sounding tone, "I think that this would be a perfectly acceptable date for our engagement." She saw his puzzlement at her phrasing just as she felt her smile uncontrollably starting, "And after we choose the ring, you can take me to the apartment and make love to me." She giggled at his surprised facial expression and leant forward to kiss him, "I do so love you, Jack," she ended simply.

The relief was evident in his voice as he smiled and said, "Let's go and get that ring."

Elizabeth was to remember the weekend that followed for the rest of her life. Once through the door of an unrecognizable shop-front, and inside the most glamorous establishment she'd ever experienced, Jack laughed and teased as she agonized over her choice of ring. When she couldn't decide between a final two, he threatened to buy both and the jeweller beamed. Finally she made her choice, and even the jeweller laughed because it had been the first one she'd selected almost an hour before. She floated from the Bond street jewellers on a cloud of happiness, completely oblivious to her surroundings now, lost in thoughts of her wonderful *Fiancé*, and driven to the apartment all the while staring at her ringed finger.

She was carried over the apartment's threshold by Jack as he whispered in her ear, *'Consider this to be an undress rehearsal,'* and taken to the bedroom where they made love. She was absolutely amazed when the lovemaking turned out to be even better than the first time. Later, she cooked him a meal for the first time. Which didn't go exactly to plan; they were both naked at the time and she found it extremely difficult to concentrate. She then made love in a kitchen for the first time also, but didn't find that difficult at all.

Later still, she didn't know what time it was as her wristwatch had been discarded, they sprawled together on the *chaise longue* listening to a gramophone record of a wonderful singer whom Jack said was named *'Al Bowlly'*. The mellifluous Bowlly sound floated around the lounge and she thought the man's voice was wonderfully soothing. Her languorous thoughts conjured an image of her dancing with Jack, but she couldn't seem to bring herself to move. She contented herself instead by snuggling closer to the man who, no matter which way she moved, seemed to fit her like a comfortable glove.

She suddenly thought of her mother and father and found herself wondering what it might have been like for *them* when they'd met; when they'd realized they were falling in love. She wondered now where *their* memorable 'first time' had occurred. Had there been weekends like this for them? Had it been a weekend like this which had led them to conceive their daughter? She wondered what they would have made of their very English, and very unmarried daughter now lying in the arms of a Frenchman who had made love to her twice in one day. Their very English daughter who, even now behind closed eyes, was imagining that Frenchman making love to her a third time. She wondered, as his hand now cupped one of her breasts, what it would be like to have his child.

At some point Jack slipped from her arms, put a finger to her lips, and motioned her to remain where she was. Through heavy-lidded eyes she watched him move to a small *escritoire* and sit down. She saw him pick up a fountain pen...

Elizabeth came awake to find Jack sitting beside her, quietly watching her. He kissed away her apology for falling asleep, and, when she returned from the bathroom with her face wiped of sleep, he silently handed her a sheet of paper. She sat down to read his offering.

To Elizabeth, from Jack, 5ᵗʰ June 1943

For You... For Us... For Life.
When the race begins and I'm on the line
A man needs to know his direction
I will start with you
In a world gone mad, when things are bad
A man needs companionable silence
I will sit with you.
When flattery, the food of fools
Threatens to turn the head that rules
You'll be frank with me
When a sense of humour seeks a mate
And some are slow to appreciate
You can laugh with me.
Whilst bureaucrats reign and we workers rage
A man can feel frustration
You can encourage me
When the chips are down and those around
Cast doubts on one's ambitions
You can support me.
When a sense of reason disappears
And my moods could move a saint to tears
May you tolerate me
In company's throng, the supper song
Sounds better by far by two

May you compliment me.
When the race is run and it's time to rest
With more time to feel and taste
I look forward to you then, my love
As I look forward with you now.
My love, this is designed to be prophetic, insofar as I
foresee the influence I expect you to have on my life.

Elizabeth finished reading, and, moved beyond words, was unable to immediately voice her thoughts. Her eyes were held by the words he had seemingly penned while she had slept. She suddenly wished her parents had lived to meet their author, knowing they would have been impressed by the man who sat now before her, his green eyes steadily regarding her, and she felt the warm tears blurring her vision. She was held then by Jack, and her hair was stroked while she fumbled for a handkerchief. Drying her eyes, she finally found her voice. "It's so beautiful, Jack, I shall keep it with me always."

She gazed into the face of the capable looking Frenchman, and recalled now the account of his background. "Did your mother influence your writing ability?" she asked, and his quickly responsive smile accompanied his telling her that apparently his father had been the artistic half of his mother's marriage. She heard the wistfulness in the voice which told her of how his mother had described her husband as a gentle but proud man, whose memory had been constantly kept alive by her telling of stories about the man she had obviously loved very much. The memory of her own father was then reawakened when Jack put his finger under her chin before tilting her head back till their eyes were level. "*Ma vie est ta vie,*" he said, his voice husky with emotion, and he saw her failure to understand, "*My* life is *your* life," he quietly translated.

They went to bed, then, where he slowly undressed her and caressed her until she thought her body would catch fire from the heat of anticipation. She took him inside her with an exultant cry of passion that seemed to reverberate around the room even after she had climaxed in wave after pounding wave of swirling, sensational pleasure. When they were both finally spent, she lay in his arms unwilling to surrender to sleep. Wanting to prolong her consciousness of what had been the most incredible day she had ever known in her young life.

Elizabeth awoke on the Sunday to find she was alone in the bed. Worse still, the bedside clock showed her half the day had already slipped away. The faint ticking sound of the timepiece brought to her the realization that she couldn't hear any other sound. She closed her eyes again and lay perfectly still for a few more moments, revelling in the almost forgotten pleasure of a peacefully quiet start to the day.

The reality of her situation suddenly struck her like a blow, re-opening her eyes and stimulating her enough to sit upright in the bed. *'Mornings start days,'* she silently rebuked herself, *'So this is certainly not the start of the day.'* She swivelled her hips and placed her feet on the floor, bringing the cooling reminder that she was naked. *'This is now the afternoon,'* she silently berated herself, *'of the last day I may have with Jack for heaven knows how long and here I am sleeping away precious hours.'*

She rose to her feet and spotted Jack's robe lying on a chair. Throwing it around her shoulders, she went in search of its owner. The bedroom door led into the hallway, from which, she remembered from her previous evening's tour, she was looking at other doors which accessed a spare bedroom; the bathroom; the kitchen; a storage cupboard, and the lounge. As her eyes scanned the carpeted hallway she was again struck by the bareness of its walls; reminding her that she hadn't seen a single picture, or photograph, anywhere in the spacious apartment. Last night's questioning probe had unsatisfactorily elicited Jack's casually delivered response about 'wartime storage', and, unwilling to appear rude, she had resisted the urge to press him further.

She still couldn't hear a sound anywhere, but saw that the lounge door was ajar and she padded silently on bare feet to the doorway. She peered round the door and saw Jack seated at the *escritoire*, so she pushed the door open a little more and moved further into the room. For a few moments he was unaware of her presence as he carried on writing, then he suddenly looked up and she was immediately alarmed by the sombre expression on his face. He stood as she approached him, his expression softening as he smiled, and she reached him and kissed him on the nose, surprising him, and he laughed and hugged her. Looking over his shoulder and down at the writing table, she could see several sheets of paper lay covered in his now recognizable handwriting.

"I feel awful," she confessed, stifling a yawn, "Me fast asleep, and you toiling away."

"No matter," he replied quietly, leading her away from the *escritoire*, "You needed the sleep. Now, first you must eat before freshening up. Then we will drive to where we will hear birds sing. And we will walk, and we will talk," he ended with a smile.

His smile was *different*, perceived Elizabeth, and the word *Guarded* came and went in her mind as he deftly evaded her question as to why he appeared so solemn, instead leading her into the kitchen and insisting that she eat. Soon after, when she had eaten her supervised meal, he 'small-talked' her all the way to the bathroom. Where he left her, saying he would finish his writing while she washed and dressed. Left alone, she performed her ablutions quickly, fretting all the while she dressed that she might have disappointed him in some way.

When she re-entered the lounge, again seemingly unnoticed, Jack was posed like a statue in the middle of the room. A quick glance told her that all traces of his paperwork had been removed. He wore his full uniform and his hands were buried in the trouser pockets, and his head was bowed in what she assumed was serious thought.

"Jack," she began, worriedly, "What's wrong? Have I...?" she began again but was stopped by his reaching her in quick strides and grasping her shoulders as he spoke.

"One or two matters on my mind," he said flippantly.

"Is it me?" she persisted, unable to disguise the concern in her voice. Her face was held in his hands and she looked into the green eyes as he replied.

"Nothing you have said, or done, is in any way responsible for my current frame of mind."

Her face was released as she was still trying to understand the meaning behind his words. Meanwhile she found herself being handed her coat and handbag and guided towards the street door as he continued speaking.

"Ever been to the County of Surrey?" he casually asked.

In the act of struggling into her coat she was momentarily thrown by this sudden switch of dialogue. She had to stop and think. "Once," she replied, perplexed now and trying to gauge his mood, "When I was much younger."

"Thought we'd walk on your England's green and pleasant land," he said enigmatically, smiling as he added, "You told me in the dance hall that if you had money one day, you would like to open a convalescence home for ex-servicemen and women."

They had reached the doorway, but his words stopped Elizabeth in her tracks. '*I don't remember telling him...,*' was her immediate and half-formed thought. Then she recalled that night and his gentle encouragement which had seduced her into divulging her nursing ambitions. '*Telling him,*' she remembered now, '*how her darling of a father had fuelled those ambitions by ensuring she received a good education, in addition to unselfish helpings of his own valuable time. Time which he had used to broaden her knowledge by imparting informative parts of his own...*' "Yes," she replied, regaining focus, "Yes, but why...?"

"There is," he interjected, smiling again, "something in Surrey I'd like you to see." He paused to steer her through the doorway, "We'll talk about it in the car."

Outside the apartment Elizabeth looked skyward, using a hand to shield her eyes from a bright sun. As Jack unlocked the car she glanced along the street, which she saw now was in fact crescent-shaped. Sunlight was splashing its rays over the stone-columns fronting buildings which curved away from her, and she suddenly recalled her father using the word *Georgian* to describe this particular form of architecture. Along the street, a short distance away from where she stood, two women sat on a small wall of sandbags as they animatedly chatted. Behind the women were the doors they'd left open, and the strains of Glen Miller's *That Old Black Magic* reached her ears and she began humming the tune as she seated herself in the car. As Jack drove past the women, she smiled and waved at the women and they cheerily responded in kind. She then turned to Jack with the words '*I feel like a Queen*' in her mind and the words died on her lips when she registered his facial expression.

"Jack, what's wrong?" she began in alarm, "You look as if...," she broke off, unsure of herself, suddenly unable to find words. She couldn't see his eyes but did see his lips tighten and heard the strain in the words which pierced her senses.

"I was going to tell you when we got to Surrey. Elizabeth, I had a telephone call this morning while you were asleep. I've been told I must leave tonight. I can still get you back to Bart's for ten, so that's not a problem."

She thought she saw a glint of moisture in the eyes which quickly glanced her way before returning to the road ahead. She heard herself ask when he would come back and heard him say he didn't know, and told herself not to cry.

"We've been very lucky, haven't we?" she began, and a hand reached out and squeezed her shoulder, "To have had," she continued, "this time together, I mean."

"Lucky, yes," he responded firmly.

"Jack," she took a deep breath, "Is what you do... in any way... dangerous?"

"No more so than your own occupation," he replied, "We are after all, in a war." He paused, then went on, "I suppose a paperweight could fall on me and damage a toe."

She heard his calmly flippant tone and smiled at his casually made joke, and tried to relax. Tried to believe him. "Where will you go?" she asked, unable to stop herself looking at him.

"Scotland," he answered immediately, "Can't say exactly where, though."

She relaxed a bit upon receiving this information, Scotland didn't sound dangerous. A fresh thought emerged. "Will you be able to write?"

"I will when I can," he replied.

"Jack?" Her tone made him turn towards her, but she looked straight ahead as she made her request. "Can we go back to the apartment now?" She sighed with relief when she saw him unquestioningly check his rear-view mirror before executing the turn which set them back on course for the Knightsbridge apartment. "Sorry about Surrey," she tentatively offered.

"Surrey will always be there for you," he replied quietly.

Elizabeth heard something in his voice which made her want to question him, but his next words stopped her from doing so.

"I'm going to leave you a key to the apartment," he announced, "It's yours now, as much as mine, and I want you to use it whenever you want," he ended with a smile.

She considered his words, reluctantly attempting to imagine herself in the apartment without him. She glanced down at the ring on her finger, and the words were out before she could stop them. "You *will* come back to me, Jack, won't you?" she said, instantly wishing she hadn't.

"I will come back to you," he replied.

His reply had been immediate and firm, but Elizabeth suddenly had a mental picture of her mother on the Shorncliffe station platform. She was silent for the rest of the journey which finally brought them back outside the apartment. The women who had waved her off were gone, their doors closed. Outside the car the street was empty of life, and she wondered if children had ever played in this street before being evacuated along with their peers to the comparative safety of the countryside she herself had left behind. She wondered, fleetingly, if she and Jack would ever have children of their own. She climbed the steps to the apartment with her thoughts in turmoil, wondering now if she would ever come here on her own, impatient to get inside and regain the sanctuary of their own private world. Immediately they were on the other side of the door she sought his embrace, and he stroked her as he spoke.

"Would you like a drink?"

"I just...," she began, faltering, "I just... want you to take me to bed and hold me."

He dipped slightly at the waist and effortlessly lifted her up into his arms. She clasped her hands around his neck and he carried her to the bedroom. Much later, after they had made love, they lay in each other's arms and talked quietly of the things they might do when the war was over. Silly things, everyday things, as if their light-hearted conjecture might hasten the end of the conflict which was about to separate them. She consciously quelled the more serious questions she had in her mind, determined against breaking the spell they were allowing to dull their senses to the reality which lay ahead. At one point she requested he read aloud to her the poem he had composed, and had the word *Chips* explained to her. She failed to stop the tears as he said that life itself was a gamble, but that he was looking forward to running the race with her forever.

Inevitably the time came for them to leave, and the drive back to Bart's was made in thoughtful silence. Elizabeth thought of the poem he'd written, folded carefully in her purse, and remembered the line about *companionable silence* as she fought back more tears. Her heart lurched as she recognized the hospital buildings, and she thought it might stop completely as did now the car. Jack passed her a bulky looking envelope she hadn't even noticed.

"This is for you," he informed her quietly, "Key to the apartment, address and directions, and some money. You might need it, so don't argue," he ended firmly.

"I don't think I can move," she responded, her voice sounding hollow in her ears.

"It's easy," he said lightly, "once you take the first step."

She was then surprised by the speed with which he exited the car and appeared on her side of the vehicle holding open her door. Reluctantly she climbed out and Jack drew her close and kissed her softly on the lips. A finger touched the underside of her chin and her heart ached.

"Look after yourself," he said firmly, "Remember everything we've said we will do when I return. It will help you to run the race."

She gasped in alarm as he moved away from her and walked back round the car. She saw his smile as he waved briefly before getting into the car, and then she couldn't believe she was watching him drive away into the night. But he was gone.

With no memory of how she had arrived, she reached her room to find Katherine already in bed and apparently asleep. She undressed slowly in the dark and climbed into bed. Where she lay thinking of things she would say tomorrow in her diary. Thinking of Jack Matthews until sleep mercifully released her tortured mind.

Carshalton, Surrey, England, Early hours of Thursday, 9th January 1992

The sensation of coldness awakened Andrew Teale and he felt the stiffness in his limbs as his eyes opened. He slowly realized he was lying on the floor of his lounge. The soft groan escaped his lips, as he shifted his body slightly in response to Jenny's voice directing his bleary-eyed gaze to where she sat in the armchair.

"You looked so peaceful," she told him, "I decided to leave you where you were."

Andrew watched her put aside whatever she'd been reading, then peered at his wristwatch. "Judas Priest, it's past one o'clock!" he exclaimed.

Jenny came to her feet, stretched, and stifled a yawn as she responded. "I lost track of time," she confessed, moving towards him where he lay.

Andrew made it to his knees before asking, "Have you been reading all this time?" He was on his feet as she reached him, and he saw his father's stuff spread all around where Jenny had been sitting. Then he was suddenly bear-hugged.

"Hold me, please," requested Jenny, quietly.

Andrew caught a glimpse of reddened eyes as he responded by returning her hug. "I fell asleep," he said, stating the obvious in a surprised sounding tone.

"Mmm," came the muffled agreement.

He looked over Jenny's shoulder and saw the wooden box. Saw too the writing journals, and remembered. "Must be riveting stuff in those diaries," he said through a yawn.

Breaking away from their embrace, Jenny moved around the room and began switching off lamps as she spoke. "C'mon, lover, bedtime. I'll tell you tomorrow about what I've read so far."

"So what, basically," he asked through another yawn whilst indicating the spread of material with a waving hand, "is it all about?"

"A remarkable woman," replied Jenny as she switched off the last lamp and took his hand.

Chapter Seven

But men must know that in this theatre of man's life it is reserved only for God and Angels to be lookers on. (Francis Bacon)

West London, England, 2300 hours, Sunday, 6ᵗʰ June 1943

In the Baker Street basement of the organization entitled *Special Operations Executive*, final preparations were routinely proceeding. In a shower room at one end of the basement, Jack Matthews had stripped naked to body-wash. Using a brand of French soap available only to the local population of his intended destination, he was now thoroughly removing any aromatic traces of England's capital city.

Watched now by 'Jock' McGowan, the surly Scottish duty officer who was known to worship the God *Detail*, he emerged from the shower to dry himself on the bath-sized towel which had been 'liberated' from the Paris Ritz hotel by an SOE operative at the beginning of the war. All outgoing operatives now ritualistically used the towel, though none would hear any mention of the word *superstitious*.

Jack Matthews hadn't shaved. Nor had he brushed his teeth, but he did grit them as he gingerly stepped into the dirty underwear. Following that unpleasant stage of his willing compliance with 'Jock' McGowan's attention to detail, he sat in front of a mirror whilst a woman old enough to be someone's grandmother expertly applied the quick-drying dye to required areas of the distinctive hair on his head. When the treatment had been completed, he recommenced dressing. First to be pulled on were the well-worn smelly socks, then he eased his arms into a carefully damaged and poorly repaired shirt before climbing into grimy trousers ingrained with stains. To encase his sock-covered feet, he put on the stout walking boots with the 'doctored' left heel. Despite knowing he would shortly be removing it, but to re-test the fit, he donned a heavy work jacket which he himself had acquired in France many months before. The jacket had not been cleaned and he could already smell the farm from which it came.

Still being carefully watched by McGowan, who clutched to his chest the habitually carried 'check-list' which some within SOE claimed had emerged with him from his mother's womb, Jack Matthews began his selection from the material assembled atop a wooden trestle table. He slipped off his jacket to put on the shoulder harness containing the Browning automatic pistol, carefully checking the gun's load and its action and ensuring the safety catch was on before re-holstering it. Putting his jacket back on, his glance fell on the table. Still there, awaiting him, was the tiny clip designed to affix to the underside of his shirt collar. The clip contained his cyanide pill. He had always carried one before, but this time made the snap decision not to. He couldn't, he realized now, couple the thought of Elizabeth with the thought of taking his own life. When he quietly informed McGowan of his decision, the surprised looking duty officer held his gaze for a second but said nothing before marking his check-list accordingly. The decision as to whether or not a pill was carried was entirely at the discretion of the individual operative.

Finally, under Scottish scrutiny, into his various pockets went the assortment of artfully contrived personal effects and all-important identification papers which declared him to be a farm labourer from *Villagrains*, a small village in the *Bordeaux* region of occupied France. As was customary, the duty officer gave him a current summary sheet which would be studied on the way to the airfield. The summary would update him on recent events within his target location, thus enabling him to have the right answers to questions it was hoped would never be asked. A bulky envelope remained on the table, but McGowan had been briefed on its destination so made no comment.

The duty officer then watched the now dark-haired, scruffily dressed and smelly farm labourer walk up and down the basement 'dragging' his left leg. McGowan had seen it all before, but the transformation never failed to impress. He was almost tempted to compliment the man, but a lifetime of habit held sway over the impulse.

As expected, and right on time, Matthews and McGowan were now joined at the trestle table by a third man who wore the uniform of a Royal Signals Corps Major. The new arrival was Simon Rawlings, the ruddy-faced and sturdily built deputy director of SOE and not a man to be trifled with. He simply nodded in greeting to his colleagues as the hazel-coloured eyes which missed nothing narrowed enough to make McGowan nervous. The duty officer sensed that something other than the pill-clip had been spotted by his Boss's personal radar. McGowan quietly began driving himself crazy trying to figure out what it was.

The presence of Rawlings in the basement at this hour was not unusual; he frequently escorted his operatives to airfields. But on this occasion his interest was a mix of the professional and the personal; over the past four years a strong bond of friendship had developed between himself and the man who stood before him now kitted out and ready to go.

As always, the weather had dictated the date and time of the operation. This time Rawlings would drive them both to 'RAF Tempsford' in Bedfordshire, and the Halifax plane which would drop Matthews under a full moon and over a field just outside *Pellegrue* in the *Bordeaux* region of occupied France. Rawlings knew that some operations could, for a variety of reasons, be seriously handicapped before a plane had left the ground. Tonight, two such reasons were worrying him now. One of them he had spotted on arrival, the other was known only to himself and the man now regarding him steadily through green eyes.

"You've decided against drawing your pill, I see."

"Cuts down on the weight," replied Jack, smiling as he picked up the bulky envelope from the table and gave it to the deputy director. He then winked and nodded his thanks to the watchful McGowan before moving towards the stairs leading to the car-pool compound.

Enclosed by high stone walls, their tops jaggedly embedded with broken glass, the SOE car-pool compound was basically a patch of open ground at the rear of the headquarters building.

Separating the HQ from its bricks and mortar neighbour, and providing access and egress, a sufficiently wide passageway ran between the main street and the improvised car park. Ignoring the nearby screeches of combatant cats, Rawlings and Jack clambered aboard their transport as Anti-aircraft searchlight beams criss-crossed the night sky off to the south of the city. The touching hands of the dashboard clock silently signalled midnight as the car began its familiar route through darkened London streets, which eventually led to a road enabling a faster speed. Knowing the highway ahead like the back of his hand, knowing also he would practically have it to himself, Simon Rawlings moved up through the gears and accelerated. He drove in silence for the period of time it took his passenger to read by torchlight the provided summary sheet. That done, the summary sheet joined the bulky envelope now residing in the car's dashboard compartment and Jack Matthews began talking.

Rawlings remained silent for the most part, interjecting only when he had a question, unable to shake off the feeling of foreboding as he listened to the man seated beside him summarise the contents of the envelope being left in his charge. Finally, solemnly, he made the solicited promise to his friend. When he'd made his promise, a heavy silence briefly reigned inside the car. Rawlings was now uncomfortably aware of the difference between the man who had been brought back from France, begrudgingly, and the supposed same man he was sending back there. Forcing aside his disturbing thoughts about *that*, he quietly began voicing his other concerns regarding this current operation. "Frankly, Jack, I'm worried about the lack of good quality intelligence coming from where you're headed."

"Today's quality," responded Jack with a shoulder-shrug, "could be tomorrow's rubbish."

"And whilst I remain," resumed Rawlings, determinedly, "privately supportive of the personal reasons which motivated you, I think that last stunt you pulled over there may have done more harm than good."

Ignoring the barbed reference to his having not consulted Rawlings before providing the German Gestapo with irresistible bait, Jack instead voiced his question, "So the Colonel still doesn't know?"

"No, he doesn't. I creatively edited my notes of your last debrief before reporting to him. If he ever did find out, he'd have *my* balls for starters and yours for dessert."

"He would never get to mine," said Jack, "He would choke on yours first."

The tension which had earlier occupied the space between them, instantly evaporated in the sound of their shared laughter. Nevertheless, Rawlings forced them back on track. "We've heard nothing," he persisted, "from either of the two to whom you revealed your identity before I brought you back without realizing what you had done."

"You know as well as I do," responded Jack, "that sometimes it's safer *not* to communicate."

"Either one of them," said Rawlings, doggedly, "could have passed on details of not only your identity, but complete descriptions of the disguises you use. Like the one you're using right now. Stinking out my car, may I add."

"Listen," replied Jack, "I realize it's going to be difficult over there. I'm not exactly expecting flowers and a red carpet. Unfortunately, as far as the *Créon* connection is concerned, you just pulled me out at the wrong time... "

"Thanks for reminding me," interjected Rawlings.

"I was going on to say," resumed Jack, calmly, "that whilst I was angry about it at the time, I want you to know I will always be grateful to you for ordering me back to London. Had you not done so, I would never have met Elizabeth."

"I'm not your bloody matchmaker, sunshine, but I'm happy for you. And worried about you for the same reason. This romance of yours has maybe softened what used to be the rough edge which has kept you alive. You've changed, Jack, you're not the man I brought out. I'm sending a different man back, and it worries me."

"You're beginning to sound like a mother hen," said Jack behind a chuckle.

"I'll bloody mother hen you... you excuse for a Frenchman... "

Rawlings allowed the man's laughter to close him down, and made no attempt to continue the exchange. He had made his points. He had cleared his chest, but not the unease which remained in his mind. His passenger had meanwhile closed his eyes and assumed a 'catnap' pose, so he silently conversed with his own troubled thoughts for the remainder of the journey which finally brought them to their destination. The pre-departure drills at Tempsford airfield went smoothly and quickly. Normally such flights carried two or three SOE operatives at the same time but on this occasion, and as further proof of the importance attached to this operation, Jack was travelling solo. Rawlings accompanied his agent and friend part of the way towards the plane, until the man stopped and held out his hand. His own responsive hand was gripped firmly and there was steel in the voice of Jack Matthews.

"You would keep your promise?"

"It won't be necessary," he unhesitatingly replied, "But yes, I would."

In the same instant that Jack Matthews smiled and turned towards the waiting plane, and for the first time since he had been performing this task, Simon Rawlings was seized by an almost overwhelming desire to cancel an operation. But his awareness of what was at stake provided the necessary resistance to the impulse, and moments later he watched the Halifax climb into the sky. '*In the final analysis*,' thought Rawlings now, '*I am simply observing the departure of one of many such agents who willingly go wherever I send them.*' The thought was dismissed as quickly as it had come. In his heart they were none of them 'just agents'. They were all flesh and blood individuals who had volunteered to do whatever was asked of them in the currently justifiable service of their country. Regardless of whether that country was England, Scotland, Wales, Holland, or France, they were all putting themselves in the front line.

'*And maybe that*,' he thought, '*is at the root of this bloody unease. Maybe I'm simply reacting to my role of desk-bound planner. Maybe I'm just uncomfortable with the thought that Jack, and all the others, might see me as the person who merely looks down on a plot-board before choosing the pieces who will play what Conrad called 'the great game'. Maybe they just see me as the dispassionate controller who winds them up, sends them running, and then sits back to watch from on high and await results...*'

Summoning back his self-control, Rawlings wriggled his powerful shoulders under the uniform jacket and cursed under his breath. Knowing that Jack would have laughed away such thoughts had he voiced them to his friend. Knowing he was bloody good at his job. Knowing he wouldn't want anyone else looking after his agents. Knowing he cared.

With a clear head now, and purpose in his every step, Rawlings turned and made his way towards the Nissan hut from where he would contact Baker Street. From there would go the coded signal to the waiting Frenchmen at *Pellegrue* in the *Bordeaux* region of their embattled country. That signal, when decoded, would tell them the time they could expect *The Shadow* to fall over their land.

East London, England, Bart's Hospital, Monday 7th June 1943

Upon waking in the darkened confines of her shared room, Elizabeth's thoughts had been on the move even before her feet had made contact with the floor. Her resolve strengthened by her weekend with Jack, she was determined to effect a reconciliation with Katherine. Regardless of her own unchanged opinion of Katherine's coldly articulated intention towards Tom Ball, her innate common sense told her that if they were to go on sharing a room and continue to work effectively together on the Harmsworth Ward, the intolerable atmosphere which had been allowed to develop between them had to be cleared.

Still emotionally basking in the new-found glow of a *Fiancé's* love, and its attendant compliments to the physical attributes she had grown to take for granted, Elizabeth had been moved to remind herself that her room-mate had never considered herself to be attractive to men and consequently suffered from low self-esteem. A reminder reinforced by the fact that up until recently, Katherine had frequently voiced her fear of never finding someone willing to share her life. Her methods might very well be questionable but who, Elizabeth had reasoned, could blame the woman for actively seeking to change that?

So within seconds of their returning from the communal washroom and beginning to dress in awkward silence, Elizabeth quietly drew her room-mate's attention to her engagement ring. Katherine promptly *finessed* her with a wedding ring! A stunned Elizabeth watched as the triumphant looking woman, obviously aware that hospital regulations forbade married nurses, concealed the ring held by a neck-chain back down inside her uniform tunic.

"When," she asked incredulously, "did you get married?"

"Saturday, at the registry office," said Katherine, obviously relieved to be on speaking terms again and grinning as she rushed out her explanation, "Tom fixed it, he's got the gift of the gab, and I think he paid extra. We were given special treatment because he had to go back to his unit on Sunday night."

Elizabeth was still inwardly reeling as a brief silence fell between them. A silence immediately followed by her trying not to categorise as an afterthought, the question put to her by Katherine as to when she herself had become engaged. In response she indicated they should be on the move, and, as they negotiated the corridors, she verbally sketched a carefully edited version of her weekend with Jack.

"He sounds special," acknowledged Katherine, "I'm really happy for you, Elizabeth. I'm really happy for both of us," she added, a warm accompanying smile transforming her features.

Acutely conscious of how very different her newly married room-mate looked and sounded; '*Mrs Katherine Ball oozes confidence from every facial pore*' thought Elizabeth, she smiled politely. Silently acknowledging that Katherine's artfully arranged rush into marriage certainly seemed to have induced a new persona, whilst briefly pondering what kind of future might lie in store for the woman at her side.

"Sorry I've been such a cow," offered Katherine.

"Katherine, I may have disapproved of the way you talked about marriage," began Elizabeth, quietly, "But I don't begrudge you whatever happiness you can find with your new husband. Not talking to one another, even if we disagree over something, is silly. While we share a room and a workplace, we need to communicate. Otherwise, what do we have?"

"We have our men," whispered Katherine, giggling as she nudged Elizabeth with her elbow, "Don't go all serious on me now," she pleaded, "I just want us to be happy."

They were smiling together as they walked into the basement canteen and the start of another week.

Bordeaux region of occupied France, Vicinity of Pellegrue, early hours of Monday 7th June 1943

It was generally acknowledged within their ranks that moonlit 'drops' in this area were now dangerous undertakings. Inclusion in this form of activity was therefore never normally the personal choice of those who found themselves in any receiving party. This particularly awaited drop was different however, and its participants had been carefully chosen.

The small group of nervously waiting Frenchmen, listening now to the drone of the approaching plane, were spread along two sides of the designated field which had been marked out as the 'drop-zone'. Assuaging their frayed nerves to some degree was their knowledge of the pre-arranged diversion already underway some distance from here; its hoped-for result the reduction of the German presence in this area. They also drew comfort from their knowledge of *The Shadow's* skill with a parachute. If anyone could land on this pocket-handkerchief of a field, it was him. One of their group had even voiced the opinion that *L'ombre* had probably *chosen* to use this accursed devilish moonlight *because* he had the luck of the devil.

Aside from the issuing of careful instructions, and despite the fact that he had personally hand-picked people he trusted, Claude Dubois, the leader of the waiting group, had said little to his men and had kept his currently turbulent thoughts to himself. He was of course aware that the others would be attributing his brooding silence to a specific reason, and wondered now what they would say if they knew that the man they waited for had been the catalyzing agent of the stigma of suspicion which had been attached to the Dubois name for weeks now.

Dubois sighed into the night; a great deal had changed since he'd last seen the man they called *L'ombre, 'The Shadow',* the man to whom, perversely, he owed his life. The man *for* whom he now feared. Nothing had dimmed Claude's memory of their shared discovery at the house in *Créon.* The images from that terrible night remained sharp in his mind; the ambush which would have robbed Lucille Dubois of her husband had it not been for Jack Matthews saving his life; the hasty retreat which had taken both men to the *Créon* home of Chantal.

Together they had found the devastation wrought upon *L'ombre's* birthplace, and the hellish sight of the blood and brains they couldn't marry to a body. Because the place had been empty, and they'd made themselves believe she had shot and killed one of the Gestapo before they had taken her. Had made themselves believe that her captors had deliberately removed their fallen man to deny satisfaction to whomsoever would arrive to stand where *they* had stood that unforgettable night; being made to face the thought of Chantal in the hands of her torturers.

The aftermath images were clearer still in Claude's mind. Jack had devolved a plan to root out the traitor who had given Chantal to the Gestapo. A plan not seen through to fruition before Jack had been recalled to London, but which had seen two names fall under suspicion. That one of those names had turned out to be Claude Dubois, had shaken the resistance movement to the core and divided opinion within its ranks. What was *not* disputed, was the inescapable fact that the *Boche* [1]were still being fed information by someone inside the resistance movement.

So Claude Dubois watched fearfully as the man suspended beneath his silken canopy landed in this field filled with bastard moonlight. He doubted that London really appreciated how difficult it was to operate effectively here anymore. He watched his men run to gather in the parachute and wondered if his friend might have put a name to the person who had betrayed Chantal; wondering if his own suspicions as to the identity of the traitor might be confirmed. He saw his men bringing *L'ombre* towards him, and braced himself to be the bearer of bad tidings.

Claude embraced the man who had saved his life and had triggered the events which had cast the shadow of dishonour over the name Dubois. Wondering if London had told Jack Matthews that his hitherto unknown description was now known to every German in the *Bordeaux* region.

---

[1] *Boche: French word for 'Germans'*

East London, England, Bart's Hospital, Wednesday 9th June 1943

It was mid-way through that second week of June that the incident occurred on the Harmsworth Ward. Throughout Elizabeth's tenure on the Ward, which had seen the steady influx of additional patients, the noise levels had noticeably increased. Space too was now at a premium, as a result of the extra beds which had been squeezed into what had already been a crowded area. The resultant combination of cramped working conditions; noise; and the massed body-heat of more patients demanding attention, was inevitably adding to the strain on medical and nursing staff striving to maintain their own high standards of care.

At 4pm that Wednesday afternoon; as trolleys noisily trundled back and forth; as the external street traffic sounds reached through windows opened to combat the heat; as bedpans audibly clattered here and there; as two patients could be heard arguing over just when the Allies would finally invade Italy; as another patient's radio transmitted at ear-shattering decibel levels the Glen Miller Band's robust version of *Oklahoma*, the Harmsworth Ward was a human pressure cooker waiting to explode.

Elizabeth was bone weary from lack of sleep, the consequence of consecutive torch-aided late nights studying for her fast approaching practical exam. Her back and arm muscles ached from such tasks as carrying heavy equipment to and fro, and the lifting and turning of patients unable to move themselves but requiring re-positioning to prevent bed-sores, to aid blood circulation, or to prevent muscles atrophying.

Watched now by the hearing-aided patient she had befriended following her 'dressing down' by Ward Sister Reynolds, she concentrated on preparing to change his bandages. The man was steadily recovering from the injuries to his face and arms, and mobility had already returned to his right hand. His vocal cords were still weak but he'd winked his good eye in response to her request that he hold one side of the crepe. His other eye was heavily bloodshot but he looked on with interest as she began working.

Elizabeth cut the memorised shape of the four-tailed jaw bandage, scissored off the old dressing and began applying the fresh one. Spread out prior to application, the new dressing looked like a four-legged creature with a hole for a mouth; which was how she had memorised it. The wide part, with the cut out hole, she gently placed over the patient's chin. Then she wound the forty inch length of bandage below his ears and around his head, where she crossed the ends. She was in the act of carrying the ends obliquely across the sides of his head when, at the edge of her vision, she saw Doctor Corder push a trolley through the swing doors and towards her.

Elizabeth moved slightly in order to keep the bandage taut, preparing now to fasten it over the patient's forehead. Her vision now took in Ward Sister Reynolds, a patient's arm around her neck, trying to walk him back to a bed. She saw the woman's foot strike something and her leg give way under her. She heard the Ward Sister cry out as she began falling, taking the patient with her to the floor. Then Elizabeth saw Doctor Corder push *his* patient's trolley against the end of the bed where she was working, and saw him rush towards the stricken Ward Sister and her downed charge.

Elizabeth immediately recognized the patient on the abandoned trolley as the young pilot who had gone into surgery earlier that afternoon. She deduced he was still under the anaesthetic as his breathing was noticeably laboured. In the same instant she registered the laboured breathing, she saw his face turn ashen-grey and was suddenly aware *she now couldn't see him breathing at all!* She rapidly took hold of her own patient's good right hand, placed his fingers over the unfastened ends of the bandage and quickly moved to the side of the pilot's trolley. She froze then; couldn't think what to do. Priorities silently screamed in her mind.

Pulse... check for a pulse... head and arms should be supported... The relevant textbook passages flickered in her head as she found the pulse. It was weak, and it was slow. The word *Bradycardia* thought-flashed and was gone as under her fingers the pulse stopped. *Cardiac arrest*, she realized, *three or four minutes to prevent brain damage!* She glanced across the Ward, saw Reynolds still down and Corder struggling to support the man he was lifting to his feet.

Elizabeth looked back at the pilot on the trolley. *'God, how many minutes left?'* she wondered wildly, *'I'm supposed to mark the time the arrest starts,'* her mind told her as she fought down the panic. She *saw* the mental pictures of her textbook; *heard* the lecturer in her head, *'Rhythmical sternal compression should be started at once.'* She began pressing down on the pilot's sternum and then *heard again* the lecturer's voice; a sweet voice, no longer dull, *'After every ten pressures on lower end of the sternum...* she shifted her hands slightly... *the patient's lungs should be re-inflated. If no equipment available... use mouth to mouth.'*

Elizabeth reached the end of her first ten-count, moved to the pilot's head and began breathing air into his mouth. *'I can't remember how long I should do this... I've lost count!* She moved back to his chest and began again compressing *and counting.* She suddenly heard Doctor Corder's raised voice but silently continued counting, *seven... eight... nine... ten...* before moving back to the pilot's mouth... and then unseen hands pushed her away. Those same hand she saw now rapidly affixing the life-giving oxygen bag to the pilot's face.

Elizabeth saw Doctor Corder compressing the pilot' s chest when she heard a voice saying, "We've got him back, it's okay, steady now."

She saw the trolley being pushed to where other hands moved swiftly to connect more life-support systems. She then heard a familiar sounding voice seeking reassurance, and realized it was her own. She received that reassurance from Doctor Corder, his face huge in her vision for a second before returning to its normal shape as he spoke.

"He's going to be all right now, nurse. Thanks to *your* quick thinking. Well done indeed."

She heard the tiredness in Corder's voice and could see now the exhaustion clearly stamped on his sallow-complexioned face. "I panicked...," she began, stopping in surprise as his hand gently touched her cheek.

"You reacted decisively and you saved a man's life," his hand moved from her face and squeezed her shoulder, "And you certainly saved *my* bacon, because I shouldn't have left him in the first place." He smiled wearily and released his grip on her shoulder, "I must return to him now," he said, turning away from her.

Elizabeth felt her legs trembling and sat down on the bed she'd been working alongside what suddenly seemed a lifetime ago. She took several deep breaths as she glanced around the Ward. She looked for, but couldn't see, Ward Sister Reynolds. Katherine was at the other end of the Ward, attending to someone else. Everything looked the same, and sounded the same, and yet somehow it all seemed very different to her. She turned around to see her own patient still holding in place his unfinished jaw bandage. She looked into his good eye, and he winked at her.

On the Friday of the following week, Elizabeth passed her practical exam and received her first letter from Scotland.

Carshalton, Surrey, England, Sunday 12th January 1992

Deep in thought, Jenny Murray sat at the dining table which she and Andrew had purchased as an engagement present to themselves. The table was currently covered by the black and white footprints of other lives from a bygone era. Having now assiduously followed those footprints, Jenny's thoughts were centred on motherhood; her recent reading having served to remind her of its surprisingly variant forms. She was wondering what kind of mother she herself would make when the time came, but was in no doubt whatsoever that her child would have a good father.

Andrew Teale's wife-to-be was, and always had been, a self-confessed sucker for romantic movies. A natural 'loner' in her early teenage years, she'd been too shy to mix with peers who traded boyfriends like lipsticks. So all her fantasies about a loving relationship had been brought to her via the silver screen in whatever location she'd found herself.

Jenny Murray had been the sole child of two 'flower power' youngsters masquerading as adults in the crazy days of the 60's. Immediately dumped upon the only and reluctantly available outlet, she had been blowing out the three candles on her birthday cake when the fatal news of her 'Hippy' parents reached the only place she'd known as home. She had been five years old when her no longer reluctant grandparents had explained why her classmates were calling her an orphan. She had reached the age of ten when old age had taken from her the couple who had loved her as their own. The years which followed had introduced her to a succession of foster parents, and occasional 'permanent settlements' which had never gelled.

The last of those temporary 'permanent placements' had enrolled her in a residential college and the bright girl imbued with the determination to succeed, *to belong,* had never looked back. She had emerged with qualifications, savings from holiday work, a ready-made rent-sharing female flatmate, and had launched herself into the commercial mainstream.

Blossoming beauty in her twenties, and a head for figures, had seduced the male recruiters of a major insurance company. Her subsequently observed organisational skills and capacity for hard work, allied to a sharp mind and a steely resilience in the face of whatever obstacles were placed in her way, had brought her to the attention of the Claims Investigation Director. The once natural 'loner' had gone on to prove herself an equally natural claims investigator.

Also proving the adage that success breeds confidence, Jenny had happily accepted the social invitations which had taken her to all kinds of commercially sponsored functions. She had also gone on three or four personal dates, each time firmly but not always politely declining the offers which had ranged from 'no-strings-sex' to 'threesomes, or bondage sex'. Sexually, she had still been a virgin at thirty, one of that rare 90's fraternity which men either joked about or dreamed of, when she'd attended the function which had introduced her to the man who had thrown her hormones into meltdown. She had been smitten from minute one, and the last eighteen months had been everything the silver screen of her teens had promised it would be.

'How very different, yet in some ways similar,' thought Jenny now, *'had her own rites of passage been when compared to those of the other women, and men, she'd been reading about.'*

She had carefully arranged the assorted material on the table into the order she was advising it should be read by Andrew. He stood now beside her, silently absorbing her precisely phrased instructions. He was to start with the numbered diaries of Elizabeth Creacey, and read up to where Jenny had placed the marker. Then he was to read the letters, except for the one already marked *Returned Unread*, before returning to complete the diaries. Only *then* should he read the letter marked *Returned Unread*, before finally going through the last reports which had been compiled by the investigators *Ramsay & Shields*.

Jenny merely smiled at Andrew's grumbling about her being fussy, and bossy to boot. She readily agreed to his request that the reading library be moved to their lounge, and, without losing the smile, helped him transfer the material.

Knowing her man as she did, Jenny was concerned as she watched him settle down in the lounge to read as directed. She now knew that once he had finished that reading, he would be faced with a mind-boggling dilemma. She also knew that his normally incisive approach to problems would, on this occasion, be difficult for him to adopt.

But Jenny Murray wasn't at all sure how her man would react when he read the diary entries concerning his late father. Not to mention the notes which revealed the contentious nature of matters relating to decisions which had evidently been taken by Jonathan Teale.

West London, England, SOE Headquarters, Friday 25th June 1943

Day and night, no matter the hour, the Baker Street edifice housing the command structure of *Special Operations Executive* was constantly manned and never slept. Providing readily available secure communication channels was of paramount importance to all reliant upon the organization charged by Prime Minister Winston Churchill to mount covert strike missions in enemy occupied territories and to supply, train, and support indigenous resistance movements.

On one floor of the building, the incoming and outgoing communication conduits in human form modestly comprised four specially selected female stalwarts. They were in complete control of their fiefdom, and almost anyone who entered it, and

Emily Pankhurst would have been proud of them. Working their twelve hour shifts in pairs, without complaint, the thoroughly efficient WRVS quartet professionally fielded telephone calls from every level of officialdom as if they'd been doing so all their lives.

In addition to the cool handling of sometimes heated phone calls, nimble fingers which had previously held nothing but knitting needles now tirelessly pounded Remington typewriters. Proudly producing the required reports and correspondence which either discreetly flowed out of the building by special messenger, or was quietly filed away for posterity's readers.

Located on another floor, the radio-signals room provided quick access to mission controllers who might suddenly be called upon to make life or death decisions. An essential shift system ensured communication by means of the ether was permanently monitored. The ever vigilant and multi-lingual operatives hunched over vital equipment in this room had been trained to recognize the difference between the unseen 'hand' of the field agent transmitting a genuine message, or doing so under duress. They could also instantly spot the 'foreign hand' attempting to use a captured radio to transmit time-wasting and potentially damaging disinformation.

The signal which was destined to impact upon several currently unsuspecting lives, was received on the cusp of a shift change. The 'hand' was immediately recognized. The transmitting agent had made no telling omissions, nor had he used any of the key phrases which would have indicated he was under duress. The message was regrettably acknowledged to be genuine, and the deputy director was summoned. Simon Rawlings arrived quickly, read the transcribed message, and immediately telephoned his director.

By the time the tall figure of Colonel Harry Roberts re-entered the Baker Street building, he was in a foul mood. His recreation periods had been few and far between of late, and he valued them. Currently, a deep frown was refusing to leave the pale face with the sunken cheeks and tired eyes. He was unable to stop thinking about the size of the 'pot' he'd been forced to leave behind. He had held a fine Port in one hand and a 'full-house' in the other when the club steward had called him to the phone. He reached the sanctity of his office to find his deputy already waiting for him and one look at the face of Simon Rawlings wiped Port and Poker from his mind.

"You look terrible, so this must be worse than just bad."

His deputy grimaced in response as he extracted the *flimsy* from a file on his lap and silently pushed it across the desk. Squeezing past the single cot-bed which he regularly used when going home wasn't an option, the Colonel moved around his desk to face his deputy and the signal. He read it quickly, then re-read it slowly, and a moment of further silence followed as the two men stared bleakly at one another.

Finally Rawlings spoke, quietly, his tone edged with bitter self-recrimination. "He knew the risks, of course, but I blame myself for pulling him out last month. He was here too long, and, as *you* know as well as I do, it's always dangerous for an agent returning... "

"Your decision had my full consent," interrupted Roberts, "because it was the right one at that particular time." He stared across the desk at his deputy and saw the doubt. Carefully choosing his next words, he commenced his counter-measures. "We've lost a good man, but there's nothing to be gained from your blaming yourself. The network was shaky, we knew that. *He* knew that." He softened his tone as he continued, "The man ran out of luck, Simon. He'd had his share, as we both know."

The Colonel saw his deputy's slow nod of acceptance; prompting the follow-through, "He was a personal friend of yours, so you're bound to... " He broke off as he saw the head of Rawlings drop, and silently cursed himself for taking the wrong tack. *'Give the man something else to think about,'* he silently decided before continuing briskly, "There's a *fiancée* in the picture now, isn't there?"

"Yes sir," replied Rawlings, lifting his head to stare across the desk.

"Mail has gone through the usual, I trust?"

"Yes, usual GPO divert. The *fiancée* believes he is in Scotland... *Damn!* "

"What's wrong?"

"Just remembered, sir," responded Rawlings, consulting his file, "I posted the first letter to her only last week."

The Colonel produced his pipe and busied himself filling the bowl as he pondered his deputy's words. "Oh well, can't be helped," he said dismissively, "You'll have to think of something, of course. Accident, or some such thing," he ended, lighting his pipe.

Rawlings thought of the promise he had made on the way to Tempsford airfield. "Yes, sir, I'll handle it personally."

The director had his pipe on fire now and spoke through smoke wreaths, "Wealthy family behind him, as I recall. Remind me, any surviving?"

"All dead, sir," replied Rawlings flatly.

"Ah well, perhaps that's best," intoned the Colonel, "No loose ends." Completely oblivious to the effect his opinion was having on his deputy, the director emitted an exasperated sigh as he realized his pipe had gone out.

Simon Rawlings looked at his chief and bit back an angry retort. *'Fiancée's obviously didn't count with the Colonel,'* was his bitter thought. "What remains," he began instead, "of the *Créon* network would appear to be still intact." He drew a deep breath, "Otherwise we would have known by now," he ended quietly.

In response, the Colonel abandoned his pipe and rose from his chair. He moved to a metal filing cabinet, pulled open a drawer, and returned to the desk bearing a whisky bottle and two glasses. He poured without consulting and silently pushed a generously filled glass across the desk as he spoke in a tone laced with meaning. "Yes, Simon, we would have known. He refused his pill, but he obviously didn't break."

The drinks remained untouched during the short silence which followed the director's words. A thought provoking silence, filled only by both men reluctantly contemplating the horrors which would have been endured to preserve the freedom of comrades in the field.

"To Jack," said the Colonel, raising his glass.

Harry Roberts waited until his deputy's glass was replaced on the desk. When eye contact was remade between them, he carefully began speaking again. "It's not *that* long ago since that other *Créon* debacle occurred." He paused to hold the stare of his deputy, then resumed before the obviously intended objection could be made, "I may be long in the tooth, Simon, but I can still read between the lines of edited debriefing notes. Now *I* don't know, *you* might, but *I* don't know how much his judgement had been impaired by whatever the hell he was up to before you pulled him out. I suspect that he broke some rules trying to find his rotten apple. Which would explain," he continued behind a smile designed to ease his deputy's patent discomfort, "his reticence when you debriefed him. Perhaps whatever action he took *before* he came back, was destined to compromise him later."

Harry Roberts decided enough was enough. He'd made his point, and had no wish to rub an inordinate amount of salt into the wound of a man he still valued as a deputy.

"Our problem *now*," said the Colonel with a sigh, "is who the hell do we have to replace him?"

Rawlings briefly considered telling Roberts about what he had learned at the referred to debriefing, but baulked at the idea. *'Sleeping dogs'* he silently decided, cautiously steering the conversation, "Before we send anyone else in, sir, providing of course we can actually find someone, we need to learn more about what went wrong this time. We need to find out, to establish without doubt, how they got on to Jack so quickly."

Involuntarily prompted by his deputy's sobering words, Harry Roberts found himself looking thoughtfully at the cot-bed which would probably accommodate him again tonight. Trawling through the files in search of Jack's hoped for replacement was a daunting prospect, because he already knew he would be attempting to replace the irreplaceable. Venting a sigh which carried across the desk, he grasped and raised his whisky glass again.

"You do the finding out your way, Simon, and I'll do the files. We might both get a result."

Simon Rawlings raised his glass and swallowed some alcohol and heard the dead voice of friendship burning in his brain like the whisky in his throat. He was thinking of his promise to a man he would never see again. Thinking of a woman he had yet to meet. Thinking of a nurse.

Chapter Eight

If you have tears, prepare to shed them now.
(Shakespeare)

Carshalton, Surrey, England, Sunday 12th January 1992

Having already 'walked the walk' herself, Jenny Murray had accurately gauged how long it would take her man to read through the assembled material. Knowing also which parts would be likely to jolt his system, she had pre-empted dry-mouthed shock by the silent provision of hot drinks at those periodic moments which she had judged to be appropriate.

As Andrew Teale finally pushed aside the last document of his allotted task, just such a drink was placed within his grateful grasp. "Thanks, Jenny," he acknowledged, his quick smile becoming a frown as he added, "I see now what you meant."

"Meant about what, exactly," she asked, watching him sip his drink and run fingers through his hair. He looked, she was reminded now, even thinner on top when he mussed his hair. The gesture itself she recognized as a sure sign he was undecided about something.

"About *whom,* actually," he corrected, indicating the diaries, "A remarkable woman, you said. Three nights ago, wasn't it?" He paused, sighing as he added, "Remarkable woman, remarkable story." He paused again, avoiding eye contact, "Remarkable times," he ended softly.

Jenny mentally noted that he still hadn't mentioned his father, and, kneeling in front of him where he sat, she leant on his knees and looked up at him as she spoke. "Dad's decisions, and his actions. Have they...," she hesitated... "shocked you?"

"A bit, I suppose," he responded quickly, "Oh, *I* don't know," he added, the irritation so obvious in his reply that he reached out a placatory hand to touch her as he went on, "Just thought I knew everything about him," he qualified, pausing to add softly, "Seems I was wrong."

"I've had more time to think about it," offered Jenny, "Don't judge him too... quickly." She saw his fingers prowl through his hair again. "What will you do?" she asked quietly.

Deliberately avoiding eye contact with Jenny, his thoughts now moving at 'warp speed', Andrew Teale furrowed his brow and worried his hair as he considered what reply he might offer. His restless gaze took in the wooden box which had brought him to this unforeseen point in his life and he was perversely reminded of an old television programme his father had enjoyed watching. He suddenly found himself wondering; if the situation he faced now had existed *then*, how might he have responded to Hughie Green's *Take Your Pick* catchphrase *'Would you like to open the box, or come back next week?'*

Andrew pulled his gaze away from the box and looked inside himself. Looked to the knowledge he already possessed, now added to by the revelations which the box had revealed, and knew that *next week* wasn't really an option he could choose. The more serious game currently being played out elsewhere dictated that the luxury of delay was denied him. Because legally, and morally, one of the game's key players needed to be immediately appraised of facts which had been withheld from him. From that particular player's business standpoint, not to mention the personal one, the potential ramifications were staggering.

Andrew sighed with frustration; his imagination couldn't conjure a picture of that player's reaction to the French connection, nor his response to disclosures rooted much closer to home. "I've already told you what's going on there," he slowly began, "and you've met the people for whom knowledge of what we have here, will undoubtedly be devastating." He stopped, eyeing Jenny steadily now and waiting for her response.

Refusing to oblige, Jenny remained mute. Knowing the decision had to be his own. She could hear the ticking of the Grandfather clock in the hallway and silently began counting off seconds.

"I have to tell him," declared Andrew, quietly, rewarded by Jenny's slow nod of agreement and her quick grin of approval.

He reached sideways for the telephone and began finger-tapping the numerals which would connect him to the home of Compass Designs' Managing Director.

East London, England, Bart's Hospital, Thursday 1ˢᵗ and Friday 2ⁿᵈ July 1943

The previous day's staff notice board had messaged the changes to Harmsworth Ward shift rotas, therein and thereby gifting the names Creacey and Swan a free Thursday afternoon. In their shared room, Elizabeth was studying a medical textbook when Katherine broke her news.

"But that's...," began Elizabeth, her mind working at speed, *'Do I say wonderful?'* but her thought was stopped cold by her room-mate's facial expression. A room-mate who then dolefully added to the already surprising news.

"It's not Tom's."

"I don't understand," responded Elizabeth, slowly, hoping she really didn't.

Katherine then explained how, on her wedding night, Tom and his brother had got drunk. So drunk that they'd both been bundled into the same bed to sleep it off, and, like the trooper he was, Tom had snored the night away. The following morning he'd been roused early by his disapproving sister-in-law, and had left to rejoin his unit stationed on the Kent coast.

"So who is the father?" asked Elizabeth, then listened in growing amazement to Katherine's grumbling about *'not having any fun'*. For the first time, she heard about the serviceman's club Katherine had been going to. *'Just to dance, and have a laugh'* she said. Elizabeth thought now of all the times her room-mate must have lied; leaving her to study alone; saying she was going to see Tom's sister-in-law.

The club was where she'd met Larry, explained the Katherine who was unable to meet Elizabeth's eyes when she said she didn't know Larry's last name. The Katherine who looked everywhere *but* at Elizabeth when she said *'We went into an empty storeroom. Just for a cuddle, and some fun'*.

Feigning calmness in the crushing silence which followed, Elizabeth willed herself to be non-judgemental and tried to think of what she could possibly say.

"Are you absolutely sure?" she managed, only to see the answer stamped on Katherine's face. Elizabeth was silent for more awkwardly felt moments, not liking where her thoughts were going. She began again, slowly, "I suppose... you could just say... that Tom... "

"Won't work," anticipated Katherine, shaking her head, "His brother's wife made me up a bed in *her* room. She knows Tom could never have got near me that night. She doesn't like me, so she'd tell him if I tried to call it his, I know she would."

"Oh *Katherine*," Elizabeth snapped in exasperation, "How could you be *so stupid?*"

The sudden knock on the door startled them both, but Katherine quickly recovered and gave every appearance of welcoming the interruption as she moved to open the door. From where she sat on her bed, Elizabeth could only glimpse the uniform-covered legs of a man and for a split second she wondered if... until she heard the voice of a stranger.

"Good afternoon, my name is Rawlings," the voice paused, "I was told I would find Miss Elizabeth Creacey here."

Katherine obligingly invited the man inside and offered to leave the room. When the uniformed man said it might be a good idea if she stayed, and as he stepped further into the room and glanced her way, Elizabeth's blood ran cold in her veins. *She knew* from the moment she saw his eyes. The stranger more fully introducing himself as Major Simon Rawlings looked straight at her and *she knew*. Paralyzed by fear, she couldn't move. Quickly, silently, she began begging for mercy but just as quickly his voice forced her to abandon hope.

"I'm afraid it's bad news, Miss Creacey. I'm so dreadfully sorry."

Had she not been sitting, she would certainly have fallen. As it was she felt her limbs dissolve and became aware of Katherine beside her, holding her as the stranger's voice continued through the roaring in her ears. She heard the words *tragic accident,* unbelievably followed by *swept out to sea... body may never be recovered, I'm afraid.* She couldn't be sure but thought that, through her own tears, she could see those of the stranger's as she heard the words *Jack was a personal friend.*

The man calling himself Rawlings tried to put something in her hand; through her blurred vision it looked like a calling card but her lifeless fingers wouldn't accept it. She watched passively as he gave it to Katherine instead. She heard the voice say *If there's anything you need, anything at all...* as she dimly saw the man pass something else to Katherine. She saw the uniform-covered legs leave the room, looked down at her finger wearing the engagement ring, and blacked out...

Elizabeth opened her eyes to Katherine's anxious looking expression and the faraway voice of her room-mate telling her she had fainted. She realized she was lying on the bed and she felt sick. Katherine must have recognized the signs because she was rolled on to her side while she emptied her stomach. She then felt the cold cloth pass over her face and saw Katherine's nose wrinkle as she wiped at the mess. She heard movement in the doorway and Katherine stepped aside to be replaced by the figure of Doctor Corder. She mutely returned the gaze of the tired eyes looking down at her as her pulse was felt for. She then heard Corder's voice saying *'Going to give you something,'* then he said something else but his voice was too far away...

Elizabeth opened her eyes to dim light and Katherine silhouetted against the blackout curtain. Her room-mate came to her when she stirred, sitting on the bed to hold her hand. She croaked the question and was told that she'd slept for four hours. Water was offered, and gratefully sipped as Katherine supported her head.

Gradually, haltingly, Elizabeth began to talk. Telling Katherine about the letter she'd had from Scotland. Held back the tears to tell her that in the letter Jack had said he was fine, up to his knees in paperwork, and missing her. She wondered aloud to her room-mate *'How could it have happened?'* before asking the woman to remind her what the man, Rawlings, had said.

She listened intently to the story of accidental drowning, squeezing Katherine's hand until the recital was finished. Then, in a voice she hardly recognized as her own, she told Katherine she had already seen her period and how much she wished she could have had Jack's child. Elizabeth heard her unfamiliar sounding voice break as she told Katherine she didn't even have a photograph of Jack. She couldn't seem to cry. Couldn't seem any longer... to squeeze Katherine's hand... couldn't keep her eyes open...

Elizabeth came awake to darkness. She instantly knew where she was and could hear Katherine's sleep-induced steady breathing. She thought she could hear *'voices-off '* somewhere and lay unmoving as she quietly tried to concentrate. Trying to identify the voices. Which she finally did. She then lay in the quiet dark listening to the voices of her father and her mother. And the voice of Jack Matthews...

When Katherine awoke next morning she found her room-mate already up and washed and dressed for the Ward. When she herself was ready she handed Elizabeth the two items which the man Rawlings had left with her. Wordlessly affording them a cursory glance, Elizabeth tucked the contact-card and sealed envelope inside her tunic as she followed Katherine from the room.

Later that day, when Doctor Corder asked Elizabeth if there was anything he could do to help her, she showed him the slip of paper bearing the Knightsbridge address. Corder volunteered to drive her there that evening.

Throughout Elizabeth's day the gruelling routine of the Harmsworth Ward had served as an emotional sponge, soaking up her grief and enabling her to minister to others. When her shift had finally ended, however, so too it seemed had her inner strength. A canteen meal had been half-heartedly picked at; a lecture had been ignored; she hadn't changed out of her uniform; and it was a mentally drained passenger who now sat in Doctor Corder's car.

She was unable to shake off the feeling of *strangeness* brought on by sitting in a different car, with a different man, on her way to the apartment where she and Jack had made love. She was also awkwardly aware that she was barely responding to her driver whenever he spoke. When they eventually stopped outside the achingly familiar column-fronted buildings, she too remained immobile. Sill trying desperately to find the words she wanted to say without being misunderstood, or sounding ungracious. Thankfully, the problem was solved without her having to say a word.

"I'll wait for you in the car," said Corder, quietly, and knew he'd got it right when he saw her wan but grateful smile.

Elizabeth slowly mounted the steps; key already in hand and turning effortlessly in the door. Once inside, she closed the door behind her and stood stock still for a second before slowly leaning backwards until her body met the door. She closed her eyes, remembering the first time she had leant against this door. Eventually she willed herself to move into the deserted lounge and when she switched the light on, the still-closed blackout drapes bounced the glare into her eyes. She wandered aimlessly around the room, touching things, until finally focusing on the *escritoire* where he'd sat when she'd disturbed his writing... *Writing what?* she wondered vaguely. She sat down at the writing table, looking at her surroundings from a different vantage point. The walls sported framed countryside scenes; an exotic looking vase stood atop the drinks cabinet; and the mantelpiece above the large fireplace supported a variety of ornaments. But there was still no sign of a photograph.

Propelled by restlessness she stood up and glanced at the *chaise-longue,* picturing them both there as he had memorably aroused her in mind and body, the physical part of her now aching for a reprise it knew could never be, whilst the cerebral part recalled her tantalising glimpses into his background. Leaving her on both counts, she dejectedly concluded, ignorant of so much more she would never learn.

The restless urge moved her into the kitchen, where she stood unable to imagine herself ever cooking another meal here. She gazed around the ordinary looking work area, emptied now of the warmth which they had both brought to it. Seeing in her mind now them both naked, giggling like children, and making love on the table which now stood before her innocently baring its own state of undress. Her legs suddenly felt shaky, and, fighting the tears, she sat down at the table feeling physically and mentally washed out.

'*Was this how it had been for Mum?*' she wondered sadly, the tears escaping as memories of her mother flooded her mind. '*By continuing to live in the house they had shared, by constantly doing the simple everyday things like sitting on a couch where they had cuddled, or cooking a meal which had been her husband's favourite, or touching something he had touched, had she also been tortured by daily reminders of the man she had lived with and loved?*'

She sat unmoving for a while, stunned by the belated and unwelcome understanding of the difference between mourning as the daughter of a lost parent, and grieving as the widow of a lost husband and lover. She sat and wished she could have done more for the mother who had smiled and comforted her daughter, whilst silently enduring her own terrible loss. She sat and cried, until the thoughts were swirling around in her head and losing focus, before finally stirring herself to scrabble in the handbag still slung over her shoulder. She carefully extracted the sheet of paper entitled *For you... For Us... For life* and slowly began re-reading the words Jack had written. Images of the writer came and went as she read, until she finally finished with the miserable thought that words were all she had left of him.

Elizabeth suddenly remembered the sealed envelope that Katherine had given her; the one from Rawlings. Ignoring in her head the whisper that she hadn't really forgotten the envelope; she'd been aware of its closeness to her body all day. She had felt it on the occasions when she'd bent down to pick something up, and admitted to herself now that she had just wanted to put off opening it. She had irrationally told herself throughout the day that the very act of opening it, and reading its contents, would lend official credence to the fact that Jack really wasn't coming back to her. Feeling foolish now, knowing her procrastination wouldn't alter the fact that he would never return to where she sat now, alone with just words and splintered memories which might never heal for *her* as they had never healed for her mother. With trembling hands fumbling at the uniform she still wore, she took out the sealed envelope and opened it. She carefully removed the letter and slowly unfolded it to read:

My Darling Elizabeth,

You will be reading this if something has gone wrong, and fate has ruled against us. Simon Rawlings can be relied upon. Should you need help at any time, for anything, call him. Others will contact you before long to explain the arrangements I've made to cover this hellish eventuality. To explain many things I would have told you in time.

I loved you in life, and if there is a heaven I will love you there also. Now, as I write this, my heart breaks with the knowledge that, should you ever read this, your own heart will also be broken. Because you also love me in life, I know that, and will have taken that wonderful certainty with me to whatever end I must meet. But you must continue to live your life, Elizabeth. You must be strong, you must go on, you must run the race to the finish line, and never lose sight of all you wish to achieve. I will be forever with you in spirit.

Adieu Amour... Jack.

The words still struck like hammer blows when she read them a second time. She simply couldn't take in their meaning; they were so totally unlike anything she had expected.

'*Did all men,*' she wondered, staring at the words in disbelief, '*prepare like this before going away these days?*' Her thoughts ran on, '*What did he mean by 'others contacting me?*' Then another disturbing thought pierced her mind, '*When did he write this letter?*'

Completely off-balanced by the letter, she wearily pushed the questions away. Wanting suddenly, irrationally, to recapture her earlier mood before she had read it. She was returning the disturbing missive to its envelope when she remembered the business card which was still in her uniform pocket. She took out the card and looked at the printed name and rank of the man who had said he had been a friend of Jack. Below the name was a telephone number. Looking at the card was making her think again about the letter, so she put both items in her handbag.

Still feeling dazed, she stood up from the table and slowly made her way to the bedroom. She lay down on the bed where they had made love; and ached for him. A fresh sensation suddenly engulfed her; the feeling of anger. She was angry because she still didn't know much about him and now she was lying on their bed feeling cheated. Absorbing her anger and her grief; the room echoed her lonely and frustrated sobbing.

Sensing her mood, Corder made no comment when she finally returned to the car. He drove in silence for some time before hearing the voice of his passenger.

"Thank you very much, Doctor," she said, her tone subdued.

"Given the circumstances," he said, "feel free to use my Christian name, Peter."

Following his invitational response, Corder kept his eyes on the road but was aware of her silent scrutiny. He found himself mentally check-listing what little she could possibly see in the semi-darkness of the car. He knew she was taller than he was, and he knew *he* was older. But what else could she actually see? *'Well,'* he silently told himself, *'she'll see the sandy-coloured hair which is probably untidy but I can't very well check myself in the mirror at this point. She'll see a face with too many worry lines and tired looking eyes...,'* and then her voice cut into his thoughts.

"Was I very long... Peter?"

"Well let's just say," he replied, forcing the chuckle as he glanced her way, "that you won't be going through the Nurse's Gate tonight." He wasn't asked how she would enter the hospital, and silence filled the car again until he decided to break it. "You okay?" he asked.

"I suppose so," she replied.

"Have to press on, don't we," he tried.

"Run the race to the finish line," she responded, her tone solemn.

"That's the ticket," Corder quietly replied, pondering the words she'd used.

Two days later Elizabeth unwrapped the package presented to her by Katherine along with a shoulder-shrugged comment about hidden talent. Inside the newspaper wrapping was a framed and glass-covered head and shoulders sketch of Jack Matthews and the incredible likeness took Elizabeth's breath away.

"Just from memory, obviously," began Katherine, "Hope you..."

Elizabeth was hugging Katherine before she could finish, and, through tears of gratitude, managed to get out the words "Thank you, Katherine, I will never forget your thoughtfulness."

Enraptured, Elizabeth stood holding her gift. She looked at the sketched face with the green eyes and familiar smile brilliantly captured. She looked until she saw the eyes behind the glass begin to glisten with her own falling tears.

West London, England, SOE Headquarters, Monday 5th July 1943

Three hours remained until midnight but Simon Rawlings was already experiencing fatigue. Fatigue which was manifesting itself in the form of tired thoughts: Almost a month had passed since Jack Matthews had shared a car ride with him and had unwittingly cut close to the bone with his poultry insinuation. Because whenever he felt like this, he privately empathised with mother-hens in general. He was likening now his current feeling to that of an anxious example of the species; who having safely reared her chicks must eventually send them out into the world to fend for themselves.

The deputy director of SOE allowed himself the grimace at these thoughts. He had just returned once more from Tempsford airfield and seeing his agents off always left him feeling drained and introspective. He reflected now on the three chicks, *because they were so damn young,* he had sent out tonight. They were off to Italy, and, with the invasion of Sicily imminent now, would need to fend for themselves very carefully indeed.

Somewhere off in the dark outside his office window, the medley of fire engine and ambulance sirens was interrupted by the dull *Krrump* sound of an explosion. A sound which was in complete contrast to the noise of celebration he could hear as it happily bubbled its way along the corridor and seeped through the frame of his closed door. A birthday party, he remembered now, for one of the night-duty staff. His own invitation lay somewhere on his desk, but popping corks and laughing company was not on his agenda for what was left of tonight. Or any other night for that matter, he wearily acknowledged, unable to recall the last time he'd been to a party, painfully aware he had missed the last two birthdays of his own infant son.

Rawlings sat at his desk, staring with indecision at the unsealed envelope. His only companions a troubled conscience and the sour taste in his mouth. Mentally he searched again for the options which had been available to him, only to find the same bitter conclusion that there really hadn't been any.

He couldn't forget the stricken face of Elizabeth Creacey when he'd delivered his dreadful news. His message of half-truths. Dissatisfied with the memory, he shifted in his chair and silently cursed the official secrets act. And telling himself that Jack would have done the same thing had their roles been reversed, wasn't making him feel any better.

He picked up the envelope addressed to the solicitor, Freemantle. Knowing that once he had sent it, as per Jack's instructions, Miss Elizabeth Creacey would learn a great deal. Wondering how on earth she could be expected to cope with certain parts of that knowledge, which would undoubtedly startle her to say the least, he suddenly decided to *create* an option.

He reached for a pad and pen and began writing a cover letter to Freemantle. Telling himself as he mentally phrased, that Jack had understandably set this arrangement up in a hurry and wouldn't want Elizabeth Creacey to learn *everything* in such a fashion. In the act of writing, he felt his conscience ease slightly as he silently resolved to return to Elizabeth Creacey as soon as he was able to. *'To explain why they'd had to...* but his pledged thought was broken by the remembered image of her heartbroken face. The sour taste stronger now in his mouth.

Redhill district of Surrey, England, Home of Matthew and Alicia Sands, Sunday evening 12th January 1992

Matthew Sands reluctantly opened the French doors accessing the garden. His earlier relaxed and philosophical mood had waned as the evening had worn on and Alicia had gone upstairs to bed. *He* had of course remained. Until finally, inevitably, the bitterness had wormed its way inside. Busily burrowing in his mind, making the body restless and bringing him to his feet.

Bringing him to where he stood now, with the lounge light streaming past him to pinpoint dazzled insects and the fringes of tree and leaf. The same worm of discontent bringing him here, as always, to the view of Alicia's garden and the memory tapes demanding another reprise. *To think* of his unhappy wife who spent most of her time in this garden. Constantly planting new life to nurture and lovingly tend, Alicia poured into her garden all the care and attention she would have lavished on the child she had lost, and on the children they couldn't have. *To think* of his unfulfilled wife, possibly asleep upstairs. Another early night introduced by *Messrs headache and spare room selection.* The demarcation line firmly established.

The life-force deeper inside him suddenly surged against the rancour. Reminding him he was still three years short of the big 'Five-O' and kept his stocky five foot ten body in good shape. Others had even flattered, telling him the flecks of grey in his hair made him look distinguished, and, in his own clear blue eyes, the shaving mirror consistently reflected a regular face full of Roman-nosed strength. So he could still turn a head or two.

Then he felt his shoulders sag, and the life-force ebbing, as the *worm* reminded him he'd told himself these things before but the marriage bed still remained the same cold place. He moved position slightly, and the tentacles of light picked out the fox. Glowing yellow eyes locked with his own for a moment before backing down, the tendrils of light colouring as the animal moved to dissolve into darkness. Stimulated by the pseudo Mexican stand-off with the fox, the memory tapes spooled forward to goad him. Telling him he could have done *something* had it been another man. He could have backed *him* down. *'He just couldn't compete with a garden',* mocked the frustration-worm. Matthew mentally shuddered as he surrendered to the past in his mind and let the tapes run on to spill their unforgettable history:

Alicia had progressively withdrawn into both herself and her garden since losing the baby that hellish night, seven years ago. The hospital had said it was a million-to-one chance factor which the scan had missed. Whatever the odds, the umbilical cord had choked to death the baby Alicia had never even held. Bad enough, *God, yes,* but then they had told her she couldn't have any more children. Something they'd found: *'Not life threatening, Mrs Sands,'* they'd said. *'Just life preventative',* stabbed the guilt-worm.

An inconsolable Alicia had blamed herself, and the numerous health officials had failed to reason with her. *'At least they had tried,'* prodded the truth-worm. Matthew had submerged himself in work that first year, limiting his time spent with Alicia. Leaving her instead to the glib female counsellors with impressive sounding titles proclaiming their expertise, whilst never having themselves borne children.

His own title of *husband* had lamentably disappointed. Consequently bringing too late the realization that it had been then that he had begun supplying the bricks she had used to build the wall which now stood between them. At the end of that first year when he'd broached the subject of adoption, she'd refused to even discuss it.

The memory tapes rolled on relentlessly; the worm becoming a snake, hissing in his ears and refusing the omission. About the early part of that first year with its unplanned and certainly unexpected night of release. When the words had poured out and the body-juices had mingled; two souls in need, finding each other to give and take. Leaving him the adulterer's coin of never-ending guilt. But nevertheless delighting the company's shareholders, the only real winners from his purging himself with yet more work.

Then had come the mind-numbing shock of the woman's news. The result of their frantic coupling had been... *a life!* The very oxygen needed to save his *own* marriage, had become a life to be nurtured by someone else. A life in exchange for a garden, and Matthew hadn't needed a worm to tell him it certainly wasn't the best deal he'd ever made.

Not for Matthew Sands the avenue of counsel, expert or otherwise, because apart from the female catalyst there had been no-one he could have confided in. No other person he could have trusted with potentially damaging knowledge. No impartial advice he might have respected. No wise and welcome sage to replace the mother who'd died some twenty years before he'd been confronted by a death in childbirth, and a living child he must deny.

Enervated by the night air, Matthew's physical extremities tingled. Whilst predictably, as on past occasions, he suddenly felt mentally restored by the catharsis. The memory tapes were no longer running, the worm stilled. He turned in the doorway to look back into the lounge, his eyes drawn to the paper-strewn desk. He decided a large brandy and another hour would cover his study of the marketing reports, his cleared mind already selecting the passages he must mark for discussion. The move into European markets had to be handled carefully, and as Managing Director it was *his* job to ensure that Compass Designs maximised the potential. Always providing of course, that he could resolve the problems dogging the proposed merger. Not to mention plugging an information leak within 'Compass' by finding the company's informant.

He poured the brandy on auto-pilot, his mind now totally focused on the work ahead of him, the irony lost on him that he was focused on his own form of garden. He was therefore slightly annoyed when he was interrupted ten minutes later by the ringing telephone, and *more* than slightly surprised to discover that it was Andrew Teale on the other end of the line.

City of London, England, Friday 9th July 1943 (in the cluster of legal buildings known as 'The Temple')
When the news of yet another enforced move filtered down through the Temple's ranks, the gnashing of teeth could be heard throughout the warren of rooms housing the smaller firms. To complain officially was pointless, and might even have been construed as unpatriotic by those who considered their file-shifting response to such directives as their personal and vital contribution to the war effort. Every field of endeavour has its heroes. So the Solicitor's Clerks upset by this latest edict muttered and spluttered, but they moved. A corridor difference *here*, a room or two difference *there*, no matter, they moved because in the final analysis 'theirs was not to reason why'.

Arthur Freemantle could barely *see* his Clerk; a consequence of the stroke which had pushed his eyesight into retirement some weeks before the rest of his body would follow suit. He painstakingly peered at the documents he must allocate to the appropriate files, his thoughts wandering. He was thinking about Jonathan Teale, feeling gratified by the fact that the mantle of responsibility would shortly be handed over to someone he had personally guided. Denied entry to the armed forces on medical grounds, his brilliant young protégée had been self-driven towards full qualification. A professional status which Jonathan should officially acquire very soon now, mused his short-sighted mentor.

Throwing in the mental towel, Arthur Freemantle paused his thoughts to call in his Clerk. He politely informed the woman that some assistance was required because he really did fear he was getting into an awful muddle with these files.

Chapter Nine

Almost all of our relationships begin, and most of them continue, as forms of mutual exploitation. A mental or physical barter, to be terminated when one or both parties run out of goods.
(W.H. Auden)

East London, England, Bart's Hospital, Remainder July through to December 1943

Sweeping changes and sweepstakes more or less consumed the month of July on the Harmsworth Ward. Between the time of Allied forces spring-boarding from the newly taken North Africa to invade Sicily on the 10th, and the King of Italy sacking his Prime Minister Benito Mussolini on the 25th, various forms of contraband moved from Harmsworth sickbed to sickbed quicker than the official eye could follow.

Wounded servicemen from every previous walk of civilian life fully occupied the Ward's beds, defying incapacity to fully exercise their unquenchable spirit for healthy competition. *Music, The Women's Ward,* and *Headlines,* had been the chosen subjects for the enthusiastically placed wagers. Thus, as July finally surrendered, it was the hearing-aided patient who duly collected his cigarettes for correctly guessing that *'Two o'clock Jump'* would finish top of Band leader and trumpet player Harry James's five entries in the top twenty chart.

A one-legged sailor received his bottle of rum for successfully penetrating the 'off-limits' Women's Ward, despite literally falling down *beside* a bed instead of falling *into* the arms of the bed's reportedly willing incumbent. Escorted by two attractive nurses, his triumphal return to Harmsworth with a lipstick-smeared face had swung the vote his way.

In the *Most Popular Headline* stakes, the young pilot who owed his life to Elizabeth Creacey won money for choosing the Daily Mirror's *'Benito Banished!'* which had succinctly signalled the beginning of the end for the Italian dictator.

The month of August saw the student nurse body constantly switching heads, as those who couldn't stay the course were replaced by others it was hoped would prove to be more durable. To enhance communication between senior and junior staff, and to improve morale by giving students a voice, the suggestion of Ward Sister Mary Reynolds was adopted and Elizabeth Creacey was chosen to be the spokeswoman for her peers.

Mary Reynolds took it upon herself to spend more time with student nurse Creacey, freely imparting the wisdom of her experience, and often found herself in agreement with sound organizational suggestions put forward by the impressively articulate young woman.

With Jack gone, Elizabeth strove to replace the emotional armour she'd worn before he'd entered her life. The grief was always there of course, hidden behind the calm exterior which both gave and took from the daily balm of patient care. Attempting to heal *herself* in the process. For a time the anger would come in unexpected waves, crashing against her mental barriers and penetrating the chinks in her armour. Forcing the rage she couldn't reason with and the disjointed questions she couldn't answer. *'Why hadn't she received a telegram, like anyone else in this stupid bloody war? Why a visit from Rawlings, a senior officer? Such a stupid way to die, how could he have been so stupid? He said in his letter that people would contact me to explain. What people? Where were they? To explain what?'*

The anger would invariably turn to illogical resentment of the fact that she hadn't even had an opportunity to write to him. To talk to him in a letter. Towards the end of August she found a way to dissipate the recurring anger and to keep the questions at bay. She found a way to talk to Jack, and she did, every night. She spoke to him in her diary.

On the 3rd of September, Allied forces stormed into mainland Sicily as heavy rain weathered in against London's Bart's hospital windows. In Italy, from their differing geographical and ideological starting points, British and American armies raced to be the first to claim the prize of a liberated Rome. Whilst on the Harmsworth Ward, a more tentative form of advance was launched by a Doctor with romance in his heart and Elizabeth Creacey on his mind.

Peter Corder made his first move in the basement canteen; where he'd contrived to be at the same lunch table as Elizabeth. His planned objective was to engage her in conversation, hopefully make her laugh, and withdraw leaving her with pleasant thoughts of an encounter which could naturally re-occur at some future date. The conversational part of his strategy began well enough and she *did* laugh, but only because his trousers took the full brunt of his upturned soup bowl. So in London, on the 7th of the month, Peter Corder tactically withdrew under the flag of temporary surrender whilst in Italy, on the 8th of the month, the Italians declared *their* surrender to be permanent. It was reported that in Italy the Germans were continuing to fight, despite their setback. Whilst in London, Peter Corder privately resolved to do the same.

There was however a more peaceful and less clumsy beginning to the shift in relationship between Ward Sister Mary Reynolds and student nurse Elizabeth Creacey. Unbeknown to the two, some shared physical attributes had already been commented upon by others. Both were tall, although Reynolds appeared shorter due to her leg problem. Each had dark hair, but Elizabeth's was longer while Mary favoured the shorter, fringed 'thirties' style. The younger woman was classically slim and fine-boned; the Ward Sister was heavier boned and more fully breasted. *'But,'* those critical 'others' had been heard to further comment, *'Mary Reynolds would probably look reasonably attractive wearing different clothes and the occasional smile.'*

In her newly additional role of student spokeswoman, Elizabeth now found herself being regularly invited to the Ward Sister's room to discuss whatever grievances she had been tasked by her peers to present. In the course of these visits, the line between 'official' and 'personal' was inevitably crossed.

On the third such visit to the Ward Sister's room, it was discovered that despite their age difference the pair had much in common. Whilst the Ward Sister was forty years old, her background resembled in part that of the younger woman. Both, it was revealed, had been supported by loving parents *through*, and had obviously benefited *from*, a good education. Both of them had enjoyed a semi-rural upbringing, and, contrasting the roles of surgeon and English teacher carried out by Elizabeth's parents, Mary's father had been a doctor of medicine at Saint Thomas's hospital and her mother had taught dressmaking.

On the fourth visit, Elizabeth was delightedly surprised by an invitation to dismiss formality during their private meetings. The invitation warmly accepted, from that moment on both naturally proceeded to address one another by their Christian names. On this memorable occasion Elizabeth reported no peer grievances but sought personal guidance on her approach to a particular 'study' problem. Mary Reynolds patiently answered questions, in addition to making several helpful suggestions. Over a shared tea-break, Elizabeth found out that Mary's parents, like her own, had been irrevocably lost to the war.

On the fifth visit, Elizabeth brought flowers for the Ward Sister's room and learned of the bicycle accident which had changed the young Mary's life. A fractured femur had not only left her with a shortened leg but had robbed her of confidence and shattered her social life. Only when Elizabeth had gently coaxed her, had Mary Reynolds continued her story. The older woman had blushed when quietly explaining that it had been at that low point in her life when she had first began to think about nursing as a career. How knowledge of her father's efforts to improve conditions at Saint Thomas's hospital, had made her think about how *she* could possibly make a difference to the lives of others. Thoughts which had ultimately placed her on the path to becoming a qualified nurse.

On the sixth visit, Elizabeth spoke about her own professional ambitions and even hesitantly mentioned her impossible dream of one day running a convalescent home for ex-servicemen and women. She was grateful of the more experienced woman's initial response, which was one of professional interest rather than derision.

Outside the Nurse's Gate on the last day of September, 'Alfie', the street vendor of fruit and flowers, was cheerfully and tunelessly performing his own version of Bing Crosby's *'Sunday, Monday or always'* as Elizabeth bought flowers to take to her seventh private meeting with Mary Reynolds. When she eventually entered the Ward Sister's room she immediately saw the words *Happy Birthday to My Wonderful Daughter* on the card which occupied pride of place on Mary's bedside table.

As a consequence of their earlier pact to respect each other's 'confidences', Mary Reynolds was more at ease now with the younger woman. Warmly thanking Elizabeth for the flowers, she quietly confirmed that today was indeed her birthday and smiled as she began relating the story behind the card.

"Dad bought it four years before he died. He liked the fact that it doesn't actually state any age. So he retrieved it after each birthday, hid it away, and then re-presented it each following year as if it were brand new. Blissfully unaware," said Mary, chuckling, "that mother and I knew exactly what he was doing." She paused, adding softly, "So now each year I bring it out... to remind me. Silly, I suppose...," she trailed off.

"It's not silly at all," responded Elizabeth, "and I think it's a lovely story."

"I think so too," agreed Mary, sighing, "He was a wonderful father."

Nostalgia briefly occupied the room as the women verbally compared memories of departed parents, each daughter amicably revealing character traits believed to have been inherited. Mary said she had been gifted with her mother's patience and her father's determination, whilst Elizabeth contributed the opinion she derived her mental strength from her father and the love of language from her mother. Wryly adding she also possessed the late woman's impulsiveness. "Which," she confessed with a grin, "has sometimes proved to be embarrassing." She then promptly proceeded to demonstrate her point by posing her question, "No admirers sending you cards, then, Mary?" she asked, keeping her tone light.

"No," the woman firmly replied, shrugging her shoulders as she added, "To tell you the truth, Elizabeth, I've never been completely comfortable with men. Especially since my accident. And the last time I actually trusted one, he plundered my savings and trampled all over my pride."

Elizabeth saw in her companion's eyes the decision to qualify her statement, and so finally heard Mary's version of the Saint Thomas's affair which the transfer nurse had gossiped about all those weeks ago. She heard of how an unscrupulous junior Doctor had lied his way into Mary's affections, and her savings. Discovered how Mary had finally learned the truth of his intentions when she'd overheard him discussing with another colleague, his plans for marriage with a completely different woman.

"One with even more money and not crippled," recited Mary, her tone bitter, "were the last words I heard him say before I was physically sick where I stood," she ended quietly.

Into the small silence following what she knew must have been a painful disclosure, Elizabeth reached out and touched the woman's hand before speaking. "Men can be so... so brutal, and thoughtless sometimes, but they're not all monsters, Mary. Perhaps in time... "

"I've never really," interjected Mary, "been able to speak to anyone about it. It was common knowledge at Saint Thomas's, of course, or at least a potted version of it was, so obtaining my transfer to here was easy enough without having to bear my soul any more than was necessary."

Elizabeth saw Mary rub her eyes and heard her sigh as she resumed, "But of course the environment remains the same, and I know they talk about me here. They don't talk *with* me, but they do talk *about* me." She paused again, her eyes seemingly on the birthday card as she continued, "I've found myself thinking about leaving, but cannot imagine where I would go."

Elizabeth then saw a wonderful smile suddenly transform the face before her as the woman added, "It's nice to have a friend to talk with properly. A friend one can trust."

"Yes," responded Elizabeth, thinking of Katherine and her lies, "Yes, it is."

"And you're right, of course, not all men are monsters," said Mary, still smiling, "Yours must have been a special man."

And so September closed with Elizabeth telling Mary Reynolds, her new friend, all about her time with Jack Matthews and about the letter he'd left behind. Returning to her own room later, Elizabeth carefully noted in her diary the birth-date of Mary Reynolds.

As fiercely as the winds of change currently blowing through many parts of the war-torn world, the Bart's hospital Harmsworth Ward buzzed with speculation throughout the month of October. Visitors to the Ward excitedly recounted London's cinema newsreel depictions of the entitled 'Asia Campaign', wherein Australian and American forces were being shown retaking occupied parts of the Solomon Islands, New Guinea, and the Dutch East Indies.

Not to be outdone in the heated media world, newspapers were stoking a different fire. They were reporting as fact; that locked into Hitler's ill-conceived 'second front' against the Soviet Union, and still reeling from their July defeat at 'The Battle of Kursk', under-supplied and overwrought German Generals were losing ground to the 'Red' army's winter offensive near Stalingrad. The speculative question on everyone's lips was *When would the Allied forces invade mainland Europe?* and 'Wager-Fever' was rife again on the Harmsworth Ward.

So on the 13th of the month, the same day the new government of Italy declared war on Germany, and perhaps inspired by such an event, Peter Corder opened up his own second front in his personal campaign to win over the affections of Elizabeth Creacey. Having observed the friendly chemistry between the Harmsworth Ward Sister and Elizabeth, he had decided to enlist the aid of Mary Reynolds.

His subsequent conversation with the Ward Sister served only to plunge him into despair. She advised him it was *too soon*, and that he must *give it time*. His question as to how *much* time was answered with a shrug of shoulders and an enigmatic smile. The emotional turmoil he felt inside himself being *outside* the bounds of his experience, and since there was nobody else he could ask for guidance, once more he withdrew. But he was determined to try again when he *somehow* considered the time to be right. So a disconsolate Peter Corder threw himself into his work with renewed vigour, expending his energies on patients. Using his feelings in the only way he knew, and needing no one else's guidance as to the timing of their application.

The frenetic activity of the Harmsworth Ward blurred October into November. Completely unaware of Peter Corder's personal therapy plan, Elizabeth Creacey was also immersing herself in work. Often snatching a short break before breaking shift-rota rules to appear again at a bedside, or generally assist wherever help was needed.

The hard-pressed Mary Reynolds had decided to allow her friend the freedom to bend the rules. Her own self-respect having been inadvertently restored by the young woman for whom her admiration was steadily growing, the fact of the matter was that she was only too glad to have Elizabeth *on* the Ward. She had observed new students loitering during shift-changes to seek out the advice of their spokeswoman, and had heard herself being defended yet again by Elizabeth as she'd rebuked a fellow student for claiming the Ward Sister was unapproachable.

"Ward Sister Reynolds is *not* unapproachable, but she does carry the weight of a responsibility which might convey that impression. One day you'll realize just how lucky you were to have such a Ward Sister. So approach her when you have questions, how else can you learn if you want to become a nurse? She might bite your head off but she'll be teaching you *something* while she does. So approach, ask, listen, and learn."

In addition to her work, Elizabeth also had her room-mate to look after. A different Katherine again, seemingly now ruled entirely by hormonal events. A chastened Katherine, who was afraid to even contemplate Tom Ball's reaction to the child she carried. A defiant Katherine, who had decided to brazen it out for as long as she could get away with concealing her pregnancy.

The Bart's golden rule on pregnancy was one Elizabeth fundamentally disagreed with, consequently she had made two important decisions. The first of which was that she wouldn't compromise Mary Reynolds by telling her about the second decision. Telling herself she owed it to the woman who had so thoughtfully created the sketched image of Jack, Elizabeth had decided to help her troubled room-mate.

Katherine's natural plumpness had helped in the beginning, but as the weeks became months it had always been a question of *when* someone would notice. It was the *how* which took them both by surprise, and, had it not been for Elizabeth, might also have taken the lives of Katherine and her unborn child.

One of the hospital corridors was abnormally busy that mid-November morning, particularly where it met the stairwell. Carefully negotiating a pathway to avoid collision, Elizabeth was pushing a patient-laden trolley whilst Katherine walked alongside holding aloft the patient's fluid-drip apparatus. The congestion impeding their progress was being caused by other trolley traffic, together with a steady stream of chattering people using the stairs to reach the corridor. An altogether noisy and suddenly impenetrable congestion. So much so that Elizabeth was made to veer close to the stair-rails and stop, forcing Katherine against the rails and pitching her slightly off-balance. With her free hand gripping the balustrade, Katherine used the trolley wheel as a step and managed to get a buttock on the balustrade to restore her balance.

The sudden shuddering jolt of an oncoming trolley against her stationary one, shot through Elizabeth's arms at the same instant her vision took in the picture of Katherine slowly toppling backwards. Without any pause for thought, Elizabeth launched herself at Katherine's airborne legs and felt her own stomach lurch at the stabbing thought that they would both crash to the stairs below. Blurred white flashed across her vision as something strong suddenly materialised around her waist, pulling her, and she felt her feet touch solid ground again. The blurred white then became recognizable as yet other white-coated arms which were even now hauling the hapless Katherine in to safety. Gasping for breath, Elizabeth saw an obviously unconscious Katherine lying on the corridor floor and wanted to call out. To stop people milling around the scene. To urgently warn about the baby. Then she saw Mary Reynolds kneeling beside Katherine and looking at the gold wedding band which had been dislodged by the fall and was glinting against Katherine's neck. Mary's expert hands were running over Katherine's body, pausing over the stomach, and Elizabeth knew that Katherine's nursing days were over.

The inevitable dismissal of Katherine followed some days after the incident which might have claimed her life. That she and her unborn child had survived, ironically served to diminish the pain of discovery and its consequences. The hospital authorities had said she must leave by the end of the month, and a subdued Katherine now faced the additional problem of finding a place to live.

For Elizabeth's part, the potential threat of damage to her relationship with Mary Reynolds had initially been her chief concern. But the Ward Sister had doubly surprised by saying she not only shared the Creacey viewpoint on Bart's pregnancy rule, but appreciated the reason why she had been kept in the dark about Katherine's condition.

To begin with, Elizabeth couldn't seem to bring herself to care any more about a problem which Katherine had irresponsibly brought upon herself. Only later, and she told herself it was perhaps because she'd played a part in saving the woman and her unborn child, did she experience a strong feeling of responsibility towards them both. She told herself it *was* both, reminding herself that her room-mate had gifted her the wonderful sketch of Jack, the only image of him she possessed. Quite firmly denying the small voice inside her which whispered *it was only the child she was concerned about*. The calendar they shared in their room finally stilled Elizabeth's inner voice and decided the matter of Katherine's accommodation problem. In addition to the cryptic markings Katherine had made upon it to chart the progress of her condition, the calendar showed that they were each destined to celebrate a birthday the following month. Katherine would be twenty-eight on the 4th of December and Elizabeth, she was now reminded, would be twenty-four on the 10th.

Elizabeth suddenly recalled Jack's light-hearted remark about *some mornings feeling like sixty-two*, and realized she'd forgotten all about her birthday. So much had happened to make age seem irrelevant, meaningless without the man whose other words *run the race* suddenly coursed through her mind and switched off her apathy. Impulsively, she presented her room-mate with an early birthday present.

"You can stay at Jack's apartment until you've had the baby," she announced to the clearly surprised and now relieved looking Katherine. "By which time," added Elizabeth, "you will have found a way to tell Tom Ball and persuade him to be the father of your child."

The sudden nagging doubt flowed through Elizabeth's mind as she watched her troubled room-mate avoid eye contact whilst taking in what had just been said to her. Elizabeth was unsure whether Katherine had understood the ultimatum behind the words, but was unwilling to express herself more clearly. Unsure also whether Katherine was aware that when she finally *did* tell Tom Ball, her problems would only then really begin. Glancing away from her room-mate, and already questioning her own impetuosity, Elizabeth's gaze registered the calendar and the bold pencil-scribbled date at the bottom of the December page. The scribbled *11th March 1944* denoted the calculated birth-date of Katherine's baby.

Thankful that their friendship had survived her aiding and abetting Katherine, the next day Elizabeth told Mary Reynolds of her plan. The Ward Sister listened closely, before making comments which only went some way towards removing the lingering reservations Elizabeth had retained overnight. Mary said that since Elizabeth had heard nothing further since she'd read Jack's letter, she should simply keep the key and look upon the apartment as her own. The Ward Sister had then smiled as she'd added the words, 'As your fiancé would have wished.'

Two days later, as November bowed out, and carrying between them sufficient rations to last Katherine a week, the two room-mates made their second journey together by underground train.

On this occasion there was no accompanying banter from a helpful sailor, and only stilted conversation between the fully laden pair before they eventually disembarked. Helpfully aided by a local air-raid warden, Elizabeth negotiated on foot his described route which finally brought them to the crescent housing the column-fronted buildings. Katherine called the location *Posh* in a tone of voice which made Elizabeth want to march her straight back to Bart's. It was with a mounting sense of trepidation she couldn't seem to overcome, that Elizabeth finally installed her ex-room-mate in the Knightsbridge apartment.

December howled into London on icily cold Gale-force winds that pinched at faces, penetrated clothing, and forced prostitutes off the streets. Outside temperatures had plummeted, in contrast to those of the multi-national patients now residing on the Bart's hospital Harmsworth Ward and currently engaged in heated debate. The bone of contention, contained within the pages of *The London Tribune*, had been thrown in their midst carrying the remarks of a writer bearing the name of George Orwell. '*It is difficult,*' began the passage which had already brought two patients to blows, '*to go anywhere in London without having the feeling that Britain is now occupied territory.*'

The newspaper was reporting on the growing influx of foreign nationals to the island of Great Britain. Thousands of Italian POW's had been spread around several locations, and, now that their own country had switched its allegiance, many more were now in evidence '*And,*' Orwell was provocatively suggesting, '*should be sent home.*' Headlines blazing, the newspaper further reported that Canadian, American, and Polish servicemen also now abounded in great numbers on London's streets. '*And,*' wondered The London Tribune in strident 'invasion-speculation-mode', '*when might they be shipped to somewhere they could do some good?*'

But it was neither of those vibrantly headlined nationalities who were currently raising temperatures elsewhere. It was a Scotsman and an Englishman who were trading blows on the Harmsworth Ward as Elizabeth Creacey, en-route to the evening lecture, came upon them. Peter Corder, obviously at a loss as to how to stop them, explained in his mild-mannered fashion that the Englishman had accused the Scotsman of being *a foreign occupier!*

Elizabeth snatched her weapon of choice from a bedside table, stepped up to the protagonists and delivered a hefty smack with the tray to the Englishman's pyjama-clad buttocks. The fighting abruptly stopped. Ignoring the outbreak of applause and cheers from her predominantly bed-ridden audience, she was giving the panting duo a piece of her mind as Mary Reynolds arrived on the scene. Both she and Corder amusedly watched as the men sheepishly stood together for their telling off before they shook hands as commanded.

Still dealing with her adrenalin-rush, silently wishing that *all* wars could be settled with a smacked bottom, Elizabeth handed the incident scene over to Mary and left smiling her grateful goodbye to the Ward Sister. Her gratitude stemmed from duty rosters having been arranged to free her for the forthcoming weekend. Once this next lecture had been attended she would be left to her own devices. She was anxious to visit the Knightsbridge apartment where Katherine had been for the past week. She duly endured the lecture on 'The Treatment of Bed-Sores', rushed back to the room which, thanks to Mary Reynolds, she now had to herself, and nibbled her canteen booty of stale biscuits as she hurriedly changed her clothes.

Walking to the station later, heedless of others rushing to unknown destinations and their own precious weekends, her mind was filled with positive thoughts. The friendship with Mary Reynolds was proving to be not only personally heart-warming, but professionally fruitful also. She was learning a great deal from the older and more experienced woman. She was also pleased with the progress of her studies, and felt confident she could do well in the forthcoming exams. Her steps quickened; she was looking forward to seeing the apartment again; already there in her mind, wondering if she could recapture its special atmosphere.

Only when she was seated alone once more on the train, in forced close proximity to couples seated around her, did her journey become one of painful introspection. She began to think of all the things she would have to deal with on her own if she ever permanently left the environment of the Harmsworth Ward. She recalled now Mary Reynolds also wondering what *she* might do were she to leave Bart's, and suddenly conjured a mental picture depicting both of them as two old spinsters sharing a bleak future. Now feeling depressed, cold, and lonely, Elizabeth disembarked at the Knightsbridge underground station and made her way to street-level. Stopping only to exchange some ration coupons for provisions, she once more successfully navigated her way on foot to the apartment.

Elizabeth entered the apartment to discover that Katherine had moved the lounge furniture around. The Katherine of old; complaining about having been stuck indoors because Elizabeth had taken the key. Grumbling about not having been able to celebrate her birthday; about not having any fun, and loudly bemoaning her physical condition.

Elizabeth was coldly furious. She commanded the woman's assistance and proceeded to reverse the unwanted furniture arrangement. To restore the lounge to how it had been when she and Jack had used it together; to how she was determined it would remain. In the process subjecting Katherine to a tongue-lashing Mary Reynolds would have been proud of. When everything had finally been returned to its original setting, the cause of the disruption sullenly retreated to the guest bedroom without uttering a word.

Suspending her thoughts on Katherine Swan, Elizabeth checked the master bedroom and was relieved to find it untouched since she herself had last used it. She stripped to her underwear, throwing her clothes on the bed, and went in search of cleaning materials. Finding what was needed in a kitchen closet, she gathered it together and returned to the lounge. Wherein, for the next two painstaking hours, she swept, dusted, wiped clean, and lovingly polished every suspect surface until she was satisfied Jack's mother would have approved. Momentarily halted by the thought of Jack's mother, she sat down on the *chaise-longue*. Her mind now suddenly occupied by the subject of mothers and their off-spring; wishing she'd actually known Jack's mother, wishing the woman and her son could be here now to survey her handiwork with shared pride. Instantly feeling guilty for not including her own mother in the imagined tableau, wishing she could hold her mother and tell her that her daughter understood now what pain was. She wondered what Katherine's mother had been like, wondered what she would have thought of her own wayward daughter, wondered if Katherine was beyond redemption. Sighing with regret, she rose from the *chaise-longue*.

Elizabeth went back into the kitchen and temporarily deposited her cleaning materials. She then re-visited the master bedroom, slowly donned Jack's dressing gown remembering the last occasion she'd worn it, before re-entering the kitchen determined not to cry. Having decided to award herself a break, she now busied herself making a cup of tea and a sandwich as she quietly hummed an Al Bowlly tune she and Jack had enjoyed listening to together. The tea and sandwich were impatiently devoured before she removed Jack's dressing gown, carefully hung it on the kitchen door-hook, and went straight back to work.

Much later, when muscles ached, when everything in the kitchen capable of doing so gleamed back at her sweat-filled eyes, she wearily re-housed her cleaning materials. Retrieving Jack's dressing gown she slipped it over her shoulders, immediately regaining the feeling of his closeness to her skin and pausing briefly to savour the sensation. Still refusing the threatening tears, she entered the bathroom to run herself a bath and her tired but still critical eyes immediately took in the evidence of Katherine's untidy usage of her surroundings. Without hesitation she took off the dressing gown once more, hooked it behind the door, and scurried back to the kitchen closet.

As her bathwater slowly rose in the tub, she used the time to repeat her cleaning endeavours. Her tiredness forgotten as she energetically restored the smaller area to its former, pre-Katherine, condition. That done, the cleaning materials were meticulously replaced in the kitchen closet.

Back in the now pristine bathroom, the bathtub was ready for occupation. With a heartfelt sigh of contentment she shed her underwear and slowly eased her aching body into the bathwater. She slowly lay back and closed her eyes; luxuriating in the enveloping warmth, aware of the sensual feeling engulfing her, and allowed her imagination to swirl with the water lapping at grateful limbs. She felt the unrestricted liquid fingers now reaching into all her secret parts; in her imagination becoming Jack's fingers once more caressing and exploring her naked body; reproducing those memorable sensations of relaxation, invigoration, and penetration...

The sudden sound snapped Elizabeth's eyes open, abruptly terminating her languorous reverie and reminding her she wasn't alone in the apartment. The sound was repeated, but identified now as something obviously being moved around in the guest bedroom and she realized she was listening to Katherine either displacing yet more furniture, or returning it to its rightful position. A jarring reminder of the woman's insensitivity.

She knew she would not now recapture the feeling to which she'd briefly abandoned herself. The arousing imagery conjured by her imagination had been replaced now by sharply re-focused thoughts brought on by the mood-altering disturbance. Painful thoughts of the injustice separating her from the woman in the guest room. Angry thoughts of how the older Katherine Swan had found her man, and married him, and had still not been satisfied. Angry *and* painful thoughts of both Katherine and herself. The one having gone on to find *another* man, whose name she couldn't even fully remember, and now carried his bastard child. Whilst Elizabeth Creacey was denied marriage with the man *she* had found, and would never carry his baby inside her. The bathwater's temperature had changed, its coldness emphasised by the hot tears now striking her bare skin, and she rose from the water unable to control her bitter tears. She forced herself through the motions of towelling dry her shivering body, and only stopped crying when Jack's dressing gown was once more wrapped around her. Instantly aware of the garment's comforting feel against her skin, she silently resolved it would not be parted from her again. She gathered up the discarded underwear, deciding it could be washed back at Bart's, and slowly made her way to the master bedroom trying not to think of the last time she had slept in its bed. She kept the dressing gown on as she aimlessly pottered about in the bedroom for a while, until gradually she felt calmer. She located her diary, and, oblivious to the time, sat down to faithfully record for Jack her thoughts of the day.

In the early hours of the morning, with her exhausted mind and body both now cleansed, She collapsed into bed and surrendered to mercifully dreamless sleep.

The following morning Katherine's meekly proffered apology ended the stony silence which had prevailed over breakfast, and the ensuing conversation centred mainly around how Katherine should tell Tom Ball about the forthcoming event. Later, under resented supervision, Katherine reluctantly began, and scrapped, several letters to Tom. Watching her, Elizabeth was reminded of the last time she had watched someone sitting where Katherine now sat. Remembering now when she'd watched Jack doing exactly the same thing. *'Who were you writing to, Jack?'* she wondered uselessly.

The letter writing was abandoned to failure and Katherine's problem remained unresolved as the afternoon light deepened and Elizabeth prepared to leave. It was only then, completely out of the blue, as Elizabeth actually stood in the street doorway, that the woman mentioned the word *adoption*. "Tom wouldn't," said a cool-sounding Katherine, "have to live with it then. He wouldn't have to be reminded every day that it's not his."

"Well, that's something else you can tell him in the letter which you *must* write," was all that Elizabeth could manage in terse response. Reminding the woman that sufficient provisions existed in the kitchen until her next visit, she forced a smile before turning away to begin her walk back to the underground station.

It was a troubled Elizabeth, struggling to reconcile mixed emotions, who travelled alone again back to Bart's with her conflicting thoughts moving faster than the train. She had wanted to provide a sanctuary, but was already regretting her decision to allow Katherine the use of the apartment. She couldn't believe the woman's words; didn't want to believe them; couldn't believe someone thoughtful enough to create the sketch of Jack, could already be thinking about giving up to adoption the baby she hadn't yet even brought into the world.

On the walk back to the hospital, she tried not to think of the fact that this fast-approaching Christmas would have been her first with Jack. Tried not to think of anniversaries, and failed.

Much later, back in the solace of her Bart's room, in the light of her propped-up torch, Elizabeth's diary entry that evening would record her thoughts as being far from festive.

Chapter Ten

Those who have some means think that the most important thing in the world is love. The poor know that it is money.
(Gerald Brenan)

Bart's Hospital

As the Christmas month inexorably rolled forward on the busy Harmsworth Ward, Elizabeth's December birthday slipped by unnoticed. Congratulations *did* come from another quarter, in the form of a letter informing her she had passed her written exam. A few days later, Mary Reynolds raised a quizzical eyebrow and told her to report to the Matron's office.

An appearance before the revered and feared Emily Chalfont, the woman currently presiding over Saint Bartholomew's nursing staff, was rare enough to encourage the wildest speculation but Elizabeth wasn't overly concerned. She quite calmly presumed the reason for the summons would be connected to her recent exam results.

Making sure her uniformed appearance was smartly correct, Elizabeth duly made her way through the bustling hospital corridors until she arrived at the one which housed the Matron's office. She was shown inside a spacious room, imposing in size, and her impulsive first thought was that it was wasted space which could have been turned into another Ward for patients. Underfoot was a highly polished floor, partly covered by a large and richly patterned carpet and several stylish looking chairs dotted about the room. Facing her from one end of the room, and obviously positioned to benefit from the light currently streaming in through a tall window, stood a huge ornate looking desk.

Elizabeth saw that two figures were seated on either side of the desk; the distinctly uniformed Matron and a young man smartly tailored in civilian suiting. Her second impulsive thought was that even when seated, the broad-shouldered and big-breasted Emily Chalfont was a formidable looking sight. She had never seen the slim and dapper looking man before. Surrounding her in silent witness, walled portraits of people she also didn't recognize benignly looked down upon her as she crossed to where the serious-faced Matron and the smiling stranger were even now rising from their seats to greet her.

"Well done, student nurse Creacey," opened the brisk-sounding Matron, "on your exam results."

"Thank you, Matron," replied Elizabeth, aware of the stranger's smile and feeling herself blush.

"Now then, Miss Creacey, this gentleman is Mister Jonathan Teale," introduced the Matron without further preamble, pausing only to allow the brief exchange of polite smiles and handshakes, "Mister Teale is a solicitor, and he has come here today to see *you*."

Elizabeth directed her puzzled look towards the smartly dressed man before her, quickly registering first impressions as she did so. He was slim, and tall, and as she studied him his dark-coloured eyes slowly blinked behind the glasses he wore; reminding her of an Owl.

"You need not be alarmed, young lady," resumed the Matron, "but it's probably best that I remain here while you hear what he has to say. Now, let's all sit down, shall we?"

With the solicitor flanking her, Elizabeth was led away from the desk by the Matron to an area of the room where three of the stylishly designed chairs she'd noted earlier were, she noticed now, strategically positioned. She was firmly steered to one of them by the Matron who promptly sat beside her, leaving the solicitor only one place to go. She knew then that this scenario had been pre-arranged, and her puzzlement was now mingling with anxiety. Feeling intimidated by the Matron's proximity, she was also acutely conscious of the fact that the man hadn't said a word since his muttered 'Pleased to meet you' which had accompanied his handshake. Her impulsive thought instantly escaped, *'Although he does have a nice face, which makes me think of an Owl, and father would certainly have approved of his suit... '*

Then the voice of Mister Jonathan Teale cut into her disjointed thoughts and she listened to his words with growing amazement. Mister Jonathan Teale was quietly and sincerely apologising for the delay in contacting her. Mister Jonathan Teale was calmly explaining that he appeared before her today on the instructions of his client, the late Mister Jack Matthews. Her brain almost *froze* at the mention of Jack's name, and then her disbelieving ears heard Mister Jonathan Teale say that the arrangements made on her behalf by his client were sufficient to substantially change the remainder of her life.

Her stunned disbelief now partnered by a light-headed feeling, Elizabeth was experiencing the sudden and shocking sensation of being physically split down the middle of her body. One half of her was seemingly back in the Knightsbridge apartment; reading Jack's letter and actually *hearing his voice* which was telling her that *others will contact you before long to explain the arrangements I've made...* whilst the other half of her was suddenly more aware of the vibrant colours in this imposing room and she was conscious of her wrist being held by the Matron.

A speechless Elizabeth stared at the solicitor; the man's lips were no longer moving but his mind-numbing words could still be heard inside her head. She saw his eyelids slowly close and open again over the dark eyes which regarded her with an expression she vaguely recognized as concern. The silence in the room was replaced by a roaring sound in her ears and one of the walled portraits looking down on her was shrinking. Shrinking to become Jack's sketch; spinning his familiar smile before her eyes...

Elizabeth Creacey passed out in the arms of the perceptively positioned Emily Chalfont.

Despite the ceaseless pace of routine activity throughout Bart's hospital during the last days of December 1943, human spirits and decorations were up all over the place on the Harmsworth Ward in the run-up to Christmas day. In the midst of it all, the gambling fraternity remained alert to opportunity. Following initial newspaper reports, the Harmsworth 'wager-kitty' had been steadily mounting along with the speculation as to whether a 'Brit' or a 'Yank' would be chosen to hold the newly designated title of 'Supreme Commander of Allied Forces'. The official announcement was expected before the 25th of the month and the Harmsworth 'odds' were favouring a British champion.

Elizabeth had chosen Christmas as the ideal time to make her own announcement, and, as she invited her to Christmas dinner at the Knightsbridge apartment, she pretended not to see the glistening eyes of Mary Reynolds. Expressive eyes that had reminded Elizabeth of her mother on the Shorncliffe station platform. Mary had readily agreed to come, and Peter Corder had accepted *his* invitation with a grinned enquiry.

"Am I being invited for my dazzling company, or because I've got a car?"

Peter Corder had laughed when she'd told him it was both, and the juggling of duty rosters had then proceeded apace.

On the 24th of the month the official announcement was broadcast to the general populace, which naturally included the clandestine gambling fraternity of the Harmsworth Ward. To the delight of some, the newly appointed Supreme Commander of Allied Forces was to be an American General named Dwight D. Eisenhower. As Elizabeth and her companions left the Ward that evening, the official announcement was still being discussed with voluble consternation. That Eisenhower had apparently gone from the rank of Colonel to that of four-star General in just two years was by itself remarkable, but what had astonished many commentators, in addition to the sore losers within the Harmsworth gambling fraternity, was the reported and now loudly paraphrased fact that *'Bleedin' Eisenhower has never actually won anything on a battlefield!'*

Overhearing the critique, Peter Corder made Elizabeth and Mary smile with his wryly voiced remark, "Harmsworth humour going down fighting."

Casting a surreptitiously 'sartorial eye' over the young doctor, Elizabeth registered his ensemble of light coloured slacks falling on highly polished brown loafers, topped by his white shirt under the brown jacket. All casually combining to make him appear what her mother would have called 'dashing'. She suppressed her chuckle at his tie, habitually askew and now crazily off-centre. It lent itself to his unpretentious manner, she fondly thought.

An out-of-uniform Mary Reynolds was a revelation, decided Elizabeth. Her friend had also opted to wear slacks, dark in colour, topped by a cream-coloured blouse and a red jacket which made Elizabeth envious. A complimentary remark from Peter brought a blush to Mary's face, and he followed it up by saying that the Creacey woman looked reasonably acceptable enough to join himself and Mary in the car.

"The obligatory gas-masks complete both your outfits perfectly," joked Peter.

Only then, behind Mary's familiar gait as she followed them outside, did Elizabeth notice Peter Corder's slight limp but she refrained from comment. Later, seated in the back of Peter's car with Mary, she reflected upon both her new knowledge and the fresh emotions caused by the act of travelling to Knightsbridge once more with Peter and for the first time with Mary. Her reverie was broken by the sound of them both comparing America's Eisenhower with Britain's General Montgomery. Peter was saying they'd got it right, but Mary was disagreeing.

"I didn't realize, Mary," interrupted a surprised Elizabeth, "that you had such an interest in our military leaders."

"A leader," responded Mary, "from whatever field, should lead by example. Would *you* want someone who'd never seen the inside of an operating theatre, stepping up to remove your ruptured appendix?"

A question which might have reduced the car's occupants to contemplative silence, had it not been for Peter Corder's choking laughter which almost drove them off the road.

Remedial male steering was immediately followed by mutual female agreement that their driver should be allowed uninterrupted concentration for the remainder of the journey.

With his passengers settled in the back and quietly chatting to one another, their driver was a contented man as he peered ahead through the windscreen seeking his memorised landmarks. He was carefully retracing the route he had used on the last occasion he had driven the woman who had subsequently dominated his thoughts and dreams. The difference on this occasion was the sudden change of fortune regarding his self-entitled 'Creacey Campaign'. Now he was travelling in hope, whilst sending repeat blessings to the generous parents who had provided him with his precious transport, and attempting to convince himself it didn't matter if his car was the only reason she had chosen to invite him this evening.

A brief silence reigned in the back of the car and Mary Reynolds was busy using it by attempting to solve a puzzle. Something was different about the young woman at her side and she couldn't decide what it was.

In the same silent interlude, Elizabeth was controlling herself with difficulty. She had wanted to confide in Mary before this, but had curbed her natural impulsiveness. Hoping now her friend would understand when the time came. Hoping now for many things.

The car was safely steered through the darkened London streets and finally brought the trio of differing mindsets to the Knightsbridge apartment. Which they entered to render its pregnant occupant speechless because, by deliberate design on Elizabeth's part, Katherine Swan had not been informed in advance of their coming. Hand-luggage was collectively abandoned in the hallway whilst the newcomers were treated to a quick tour of the apartment, and Elizabeth was relieved to see that Katherine had made no unsolicited alterations. This time, everything was as it should be. The tour having concluded with compliments carefully phrased by her new visitors, Elizabeth announced that their dinner party would be held in the kitchen. The hand-luggage containing their individual offerings for the planned festivities was then transferred from the hallway to the appointed venue.

In addition to Elizabeth's contribution, it was discovered that Peter and Mary had each brought a bottle of wine and a selection of rations. Mary explained her wine was a gift she'd been hoarding for months, and Peter said he'd chosen to go without meals throughout the last few days in order to appear benevolent this evening. To the sound of laughter, the rations were being unpacked as Mary became the first to enquire about Katherine's condition. Looking surprised to be asked, the now obviously pregnant woman started to complain about her physically restrictive condition and the mood in the kitchen seemed set to change for the worse until Peter popped the cork of a wine bottle and said, "Never mind, old girl, only nine weeks to go."

Ignoring her former room-mate's glare, Elizabeth brightly followed up Peter's encouraging remark, "Katherine missed her birthday celebration, so we can combine that with our Christmas dinner this evening, can't we?"

"Hear hear," responded Peter.

"Wonderful idea," agreed Mary.

A suitable atmosphere having been restored, Katherine then obligingly agreed to carry out Elizabeth's requests. Which amounted to preparing the table and humouring her hostess by setting an extra place for what she enigmatically entitled 'The Christmas Spirit'. So with a mollified Katherine occupied, not to mention mystified, Elizabeth and Mary set about deciding what might be concocted from the variety of offerings spread before them. They now had a total of six ounces of meat, a few potatoes, four parsnips, some Brussels sprouts, a small quantity of vegetable oil, two ounces of sugar and two ounces of tea.

"I don't believe," said Mary, "we've checked as to whether or not the gas is actually working."

"It was off today for three hours," responded a keen-eared Katherine in a tone obviously intended to convey the hardships she'd been forced to endure, "But it's back on now."

With the received confirmation that they *would* be able to cook a meal, and with their joint relief taking precedence, Elizabeth and Mary merely exchanged a knowing smile in response to Katherine's characteristic gripe.

The reasonably relaxed atmosphere prevailed as the women busily set about their tasks, watched by a wine-sipping and completely unhelpful Peter Corder. A short time later; with cooking well underway; with the table prepared; with the restless Peter having now moved to prowl the lounge; with a now redundant Katherine already moving to join him; the atmosphere changed again when the apartment's front doorbell sounded.

Realizing who it must be, Elizabeth moved into hallway with Mary on her heels to find Peter and Katherine now filling the doorway between lounge and hallway. Wondering what her final guest's reaction would be to such eagerness, Elizabeth opened the door, invited him in, and introduced him to his impromptu welcoming party now crowding behind her like sheep.

"This is Mister Jonathan Teale. He is a solicitor."

"A solicitor?" blurted Katherine, looking decidedly anxious.

In the few moments occupied by polite handshakes and spoken names, Peter Corder caught the look which the newcomer directed towards Elizabeth. *'I've got myself a rival,'* was his immediate thought as he strove to keep his smile in place and shake hands with the man. His disjointed thoughts raced to calculate this new factor in his 'Creacey Campaign' equation. *'This explains Elizabeth's extra place setting for the so-called Christmas spirit. Why would she want a solicitor here? And where the hell has she found the time to meet him?'*

What Peter saw before him was a studious looking man he judged to be a little over six feet in height, with a slender body encased in a well-tailored and expensive looking three-piece suit. He had a head of light brown hair, cut short, with Caesars curls falling on a broad forehead above bushy eyebrows. The word *sophisticated* floated through his mind. The man's face appeared round in shape with high cheekbones and he wore glasses, behind which the dark eyes looked large. The face also wore a benign looking smile, which made him appear friendly and relaxed, and even handsome. *'Sophisticated and handsome, definitely a rival if he chooses to be one,'* continued his thoughts as he kept the smile going to rob the question of offence.

"You were obviously intended to be a surprise, Mister Teale. A pleasant one, I trust?"

"Jonathan," said a smiling Mary, surprising both Peter and Elizabeth with the informality of her interjection, "Please excuse my colleague, he has probably left his manners in the car."

"Oh, that's quite all right, Miss Reynolds," began the smiling Jonathan, "Really I... "

"Do call me Mary."

"Yes of course, Mary," resumed Jonathan smoothly, "Really I..."

"It's my fault," interrupted Elizabeth, unable to contain herself, "I wanted everything to be a surprise. A *pleasant* surprise, thank you, Peter. Jonathan is here at my request to help me make an announcement."

"But not out here in the hallway, surely," said Peter mildly, allowing his smile to remain.

"No, Peter," responded Elizabeth, recovering some of her composure, "*Not* in the hallway. We will have our meal first, and then you can all hear what Jonathan and I have to say."

Elizabeth smiled and linked arms with Jonathan Teale as she proceeded to lead them all back into the kitchen. Where the solicitor was promptly relieved of his proffered offering of rations, comprising the luxury items of imported mince pies filled with raisins, four ounces of margarine, and yet another bottle of wine.

"Thank you so much, Jonathan," acknowledged a grateful Elizabeth, "Now why don't you and Peter sit down. Your timing is excellent, Jonathan, we're just about ready to serve."

Katherine promptly sat down at the table alongside the two men, and, with another knowing look exchanged between them, Elizabeth and Mary quickly served up onto plates the results of their labours before sitting down to join the others.

"We can now have a dessert later," said Elizabeth, "Thanks to Jonathan's mince pies."

Healthy appetites duly introduced themselves to the simple fare which was partaken of between bursts of conversation. Elizabeth sent a silent vote of thanks across the table to Jonathan, who was manfully doing all he could to contribute towards a relaxed atmosphere. In this valiant endeavour, she noted, the solicitor was being aided by Peter Corder. '*With an element of competitiveness,*' she amusedly realized.

So time passed at the table; with Mary Reynolds blushing and beaming at Jonathan Teale's harmless flattery; while Peter Corder made Elizabeth, and even Katherine, laugh at his irreverent humour. The mince pies came and went; the wine flowed; the laughter continued between questions which were answered easily or deftly diverted, until finally the moment arrived when Elizabeth began to explain why she had particularly wished for this evening to be spent in the present company.

He had of course only known her for a relatively short period of time, but listening to her now Jonathan Teale was struck once again by the maturity which belied Elizabeth Creacey's years. A maturity he'd first recognized when, as he was very much aware, she had been presented with a great deal to think about and to decide upon. Such was her quietly commanding presence this evening, he noted, that neither of the three whom he now also knew to be older than she, appeared to listen with anything other than respect. He silently perceived, however, that despite outward appearances the mood of the woman called Katherine was not entirely in harmony with her dinner companions. As he heard his client begin to explain why *he* had been included in this evening's grouping, he allowed the anticipated gasps of surprise to subside before he responded to Elizabeth's cue for him to speak.

"Yes, that is quite correct," he began formally to his raptly attentive audience, "Your colleague has inherited considerable wealth from her late *fiancé*. Whose estate has passed, by means of what we legal types entitle 'In Possession', to Elizabeth Creacey, the sole beneficiary."

Jonathan paused, using the pretext of allowing his statement to sink in, reminding himself that from this point on he must choose his words with great care. Knowing that he could *not* mention to the group, *which*, he regretted, *included Elizabeth*, the curious matter of the late *fiancé's* name. The letter from Rawlings had been abrasively clear on that point. Furthermore, the legal authority of the letter's author was absolute, because he had checked before unhappily conceding he must comply with the order.

"I'm so pleased for you, Elizabeth," began Mary, "that the mystery letter has resolved itself."

"I don't know," said Peter, guardedly, "what Mary's talking about, but I suppose this means," he continued flippantly, "you will be buying your own car and terminating my services."

"Quite the contrary," replied Elizabeth, her eyes sparkling and the words coming in a rush, "But it *does* mean that I'm leaving Bart's and I want you, *and you*, Mary, to come with me. I want you both to help me open a convalescent home for ex-servicemen and women."

Jonathan Teale had been carefully observing the differing reactions around the table as Elizabeth had began speaking. He had seen the resentment at her apparent exclusion from Elizabeth's plans, etched on the face of the pregnant woman, and he had seen the initially very visible dismay on the faces of Reynolds and Corder swiftly change to looks of astonishment as Elizabeth finished her statement of intent. In the palpable silence which followed, the Ward Sister's own "But how... " and Corder's "Just how... " were heard almost in unison.

"Perhaps," interjected Jonathan, directing his words to Elizabeth, "I should qualify matters at this point before you make any further comments." He kept his eyes on his new client as he waited for her reply, realizing with sudden alarm that he was becoming increasingly drawn to her sheer physicality. The lovely face was now displaying a mix of expressions; *'I can,'* he thought, *'almost see her innate common sense wrestling with her impatience.'* The sobering thought that immediately followed was that *'These are, in the given circumstances, not the kind of thoughts and feelings I should be having at all!'*

"Yes," replied Elizabeth, unwittingly disturbing the solicitor's unsettling reverie, "Yes, you're right. Katherine and I will make us all some tea while you do your qualifying."

As Katherine slowly rose to her feet, Jonathan wondered if he was alone in noticing that her sullen look conveyed both reluctance to leave the table and her frustration at being unable to manufacture a reason why she shouldn't. Plates were being gathered as he inwardly prepared himself, and he briefly wondered anew if he would ever again conduct such an important meeting in such an unconventional setting. Then his new client demonstrated her ability to read his mind.

"Jonathan, it's too noisy in here. Perhaps it would be best if you used the lounge."

Willingly led into the lounge and cordially seated by his target audience of Corder and Reynolds, Jonathan immediately started his qualifying exercise.

"Part of the estate inherited by Elizabeth," he began into receptive ears, "comprises a large house and grounds in the Carshalton district of the county of Surrey."

"I know that area," declared Peter.

"Do be quiet, Peter," said Mary.

Jonathan held up a hand to halt their interruption and resumed, "Elizabeth's late *fiancé* has expressed in his Will *the wish*, not a condition, that the house and grounds would be used to realize Elizabeth's dream of running a convalescent home for ex-servicemen and women." He paused, "My client intends to honour that wish, and fulfil her ambition."

Jonathan glanced at his wristwatch, mindful of the earlier briefing from his client as to the time she and her colleagues must return to the hospital, "Since Elizabeth is not properly qualified to apply for the necessary approval from the regulatory authorities, but you two *are*, I am instructed by her to formally invite you both to join her in the proposed venture." He saw their surprise before he added, "I am also authorised to advise you both that the remuneration would be far more attractive than that which could ever be offered by Bart's hospital."

The silence this time was filled by Elizabeth and Katherine arriving with cups of the preciously rationed tea. Peter Corder was staring at the carpet, seemingly lost in thought, whilst Mary Reynolds, noted Jonathan, had her gaze fixed on his client. Nothing was said as the cups were distributed, then Elizabeth and Katherine briefly exited before returning with kitchen chairs which they set down and sat upon to quietly sip at their tea.

Having deduced the reason for the silence, Elizabeth was now sensibly allowing her colleagues to think undisturbed. She was also trying hard not to think of the last time this lounge had been used for social intercourse of an entirely different nature. She forced her thoughts on to the unsatisfactory conversation she'd managed to have with Katherine as they'd prepared the tea, having been sulkily informed that Tom Ball had still not been written to.

Sitting across the lounge from Elizabeth Creacey, the thoughts of Peter Corder were a mixed bag of the practical and the illogical. The latter were currently holding sway. *'If I say No to this crazy scheme, she'll probably go ahead with it anyhow and somehow. Which of course means, 'Cautious Corder' old boy, that 'Sophisticated and Handsome' over there will have the field, and Elizabeth Creacey, all to himself.'* The practical element of his thinking gave voice to the question he posed Elizabeth. "So what about the contract for your student nurse scheme?"

"Jonathan says that's a technicality he can deal with," responded Elizabeth, calmly.

"In addition," came in Jonathan, "to the refunding of Elizabeth's sponsorship thus far, the authorities will recognize the fact that she will, after all, be continuing in nursing."

Irrationally annoyed at receiving the qualification from the prim-sounding voice of *his rival*, Peter Corder abandoned his normally polite manner and rudely ignored the man. He pointedly directed his next question to Elizabeth. "Why me?" he asked, genuinely puzzled.

"Because we student nurses talk to one another," riposted Elizabeth, pausing before resuming firmly, "Because it's common knowledge around the Wards that you're unhappy with the way you've been prevented from...," she hesitated slightly, selecting her next words with precision, "providing the kind of care, and after-care, which *you* believe to be more effective than that which is made available to patients now. Because *I* believe you're right. Because *I* believe you would have the opportunity to practice *your* kind of medicine in the kind of convalescent home *I* have in mind. Because I will need a doctor I can trust. Because Mary thinks you're a good doctor. And because you've been kind to me, and I like you."

As Peter Corder slumped back in his chair, eyes widened in surprise, Jonathan Teale stole another glance at his watch. He could see that the cocky young doctor was taken aback by the authority he'd heard in Elizabeth's articulate response, but nevertheless felt a timely intervention was called for. "The purpose of this meeting, doctor, is to inform you and your colleague of the objective, provide you both with certain assurances regarding the fundamental means of achieving it, and, ultimately, to find out if you and Miss Reynolds are willing to consider participation." He paused to smile, before adding, "Naturally, the hoped for ultimately positive commitment of you both is not expected this evening."

Jonathan looked away from Corder and directly addressed his client now, "Undoubtedly, after this evening, your colleagues will have more questions. Questions to which I'm confident answers can be supplied at a future meeting. Then again of course, and understandably, they will require time to consider their ultimate response."

"I can certainly think," responded Peter, clearly irritated, "of a question or three."

"My own research to date," responded Jonathan, "which may helpfully pre-empt some of your questions, has identified the various bureaucratic hurdles which must be cleared in order to run such an establishment as is proposed."

Jonathan paused, letting his eyes find Mary Reynolds before going on, "But it really all boils down to the main essentials of qualifications, money, and experience. In my own opinion, qualifications are number one. Money can't buy them, and for the field in which you and doctor Corder have chosen to excel, their very attainment bestows upon you both the knowledge gained from front-line experience. That same attainment which attests to your proven ability to be worthy of the licence to practice your skills. In addition, of course, to satisfying the regulators."

Jonathan let his smile move between Reynolds and Corder as he continued without pause, "Money is number two, with enough of it you can buy almost anything, even experience. A *great deal* of money will be required to bring this proposed project to successful fruition." He adopted a brisker tone to add, "So let me now assure you both, by sharing with you the fact that Elizabeth Creacey could now finance several such projects, if she chose to do so."

Jonathan saw the widened eyes seeking out his client as he continued hammering home his points, "Experience is number three on my list of essentials. Whilst it *can* be bought, personally acquired experience is beyond price. Between you both, Ward Sister Reynolds and Doctor Corder, is the experience which would be invaluable to my client."

As Elizabeth listened to Jonathan, she recalled now his embarrassed but honest explanation as to why it had taken him so long to reach her. He'd said he would quite understand if she chose to have her affairs dealt with by someone else, and she had decided in that instant to stick with this man. Having now heard the presentation to Mary and Peter, she knew she had made the right decision. She liked the fact that he was young, yet obviously *knew his stuff* as her father would have said. His face definitely made her think of a kindly-looking Owl, and his dark eyes continued to fascinate her with their way of slowly blinking whenever he spoke.

"You've obviously been very thorough in your research, Mister Teale," said Mary, quietly, "and have also been," she smiled as she paused, "very complimentary in your remarks. This has all been such a lot to take in," she glanced at Peter Corder as she added, "So much to consider, don't you think, Peter?"

Peter Corder's thoughts were all over the place as he responded, "Yes, there is, but," he grudgingly admitted, "you were right, Mister Teale, your presentation has rendered some of my questions unnecessary."

"I would be very pleased if you both just called me Jonathan," said the solicitor, glancing once more at his watch before adding, "Isn't it time you three were starting back?"

"Lord, yes," replied Elizabeth, "Thank you, Jonathan."

"So can I take it," asked Jonathan, regaining the attention of Reynolds and Corder, "that you leave here on a positive note, and that you are both willing to consider participation?"

A concerned sounding Elizabeth spoke up before her colleagues could respond. "Neither of them," she reminded Jonathan, "has had much of a chance to speak yet."

"We can talk in the car," said Mary, standing as she smiled at Elizabeth before turning to the solicitor, "Yes, Jonathan, you *can* take it that *I* am willing to consider participation."

"Splendid," responded Jonathan, "And you... Peter?"

"And I, Jonathan," retorted Peter, "have a head which hasn't stopped spinning since you two ambushed us." He made eye contact with Elizabeth,, "And as Mary says, we can talk in the car."

Jonathan had been carefully watching for his client's pre-arranged signal and, as she stood to join her colleagues whilst fingering an ear-lobe, he addressed himself to the still seated and silent figure of Katherine Swan.

"Miss Swan, as instructed by my client I have arranged home-help assistance for you in the form of a Mrs Bruce. Starting tomorrow, she will come here daily to clean, to do your laundry, and to top up your provisions. She will also be on hand to discuss any problems you may be experiencing in your current condition. Should there be any problem which requires some form of attention she herself cannot provide, she will contact *me* and I will endeavour to find a solution to whatever the problem may be."

What he didn't tell the woman was that Mrs Bruce would have her own key to the apartment. He watched now as the woman, decidedly unpleasant in his opinion, simply nodded her understanding as she stood up. The words *Thank you* were seemingly not in her vocabulary, concluded Jonathan as he too rose to make his departure. They moved *en-masse* into the hallway, and, as coats and gas-masks were gathered, he allowed himself to privately feel the glow of self-satisfaction. He was delighted that the evening had seemingly produced the outcome desired by his new client. He was delighted to have Elizabeth *as* a client, and relieved to have had the opportunity to make amends for Arthur Freemantle's historic misfiling.

Jonathan stood on the street alongside Reynolds and Corder and saw that Elizabeth had remained in the doorway and was talking to the woman, Swan. As he stood beside the two people he realized could become an integral part of his life if they committed to his client, a fresh thought occurred. "There is something else, which I didn't say inside. Another essential. An indefinable quality, so to speak, which in my opinion must be possessed by an individual setting out to achieve what others would find too daunting to even attempt. I firmly believe that *your* colleague, and *my* client, has that essential quality." And then the words *Merry Christmas, goodbye for now, thank you, Jonathan* were called to him by Elizabeth Creacey as he moved to his car, and those words were to echo in his mind throughout his lonely drive home.

A combination of eye-catching sights, discordant sounds, and turbulent thoughts, reduced Peter Corder and his passengers to silence on the early part of their journey back to East London. As Corder carefully negotiated his route through the dark, outside the car determined efforts to acknowledge the festive period were competing with more serious events. Consequently pulling the attention of his back-seat passengers from side to side of the steadily moving automobile.

When the back-seat passengers glanced through Elizabeth's window, they were looking at passing shop-fronts gaily bedecked with man-made decorations; the shuttered shop windows themselves back-dropping the bottle-waving 'die-hard' groups of Christmas revellers. Moments later, clashing starkly with the scenes already passed, a glance through Mary's window gave them a view of a huddled and sorry looking gathering of people on the pavement. The group were semi-clothed and standing outside what might have been the family home; the building now emanating flames and hotly demanding the attention of a now noisily approaching fire-tender.

Peter Corder safely manoeuvred his way through the incident area. As he did so he was silently and reluctantly revising his previously held opinion of the solicitor, Jonathan Teale. The man had won his grudging admiration. *'The man may very well be my rival,'* he thought now, *'but he certainly sounds like a professional. And if Mary Reynolds and I are going to commit ourselves to this dream of Elizabeth's, then we will need all the professionalism we can get.'* The solicitor's performance had been impressive, reflected Peter, which simply reinforced his earlier perception of the man as a serious rival.

Peter carefully drove on with the realization that even his initial feeling of unease at the idea of blindly following a woman younger than himself, and less experienced than himself, had been surprisingly assuaged by Jonathan Teale's final words on the street as they'd been preparing to leave. The final realization pierced his brain with searing clarity.

'Elizabeth Creacey was a woman worth following.'

Seated beside Elizabeth, and only partly registering the conflicting scenes they were passing, Mary Reynolds was wondering whether she'd read it somewhere, or whether it was some long ago forgotten proverb, or if the words in her head had come from the father she had adored. The mantra ran through her head again now, *'If you feel the need to radically change something, then why not start with yourself?'* Change was, she wryly reflected, very much a word on her mind these days.

Her own mother had often alluded to 'The Change' as being the reason for *her* mood-swings. *'And would probably,'* thought Mary, *'have perceptively diagnosed the same of her daughter today.'* Inside the darkened car she permitted the brief self-mocking smile to accompany *that* thought, *and* the one which followed, *'And what, pray, would mother have made of back-seat analysis?'*

She knew she'd been experiencing a change within herself for some time now. The feeling persisting that she'd not only lost money to a man who had used her, but had also lost something of her spirit, something which could never be replenished simply by working longer hours and counting the pennies. Too often recently she had felt strangely debilitated, as if she'd lost the will to live life as it *should* be lived; with purpose; with hope, and with a healthy self-esteem. Glancing to her side she saw that Elizabeth was staring out into the darkness with her own thoughts, and the unseen smile she felt emerging this time was one of warmth. *'And now this... girl? No,'* she told herself firmly, *'This very special young woman who has already rekindled the fires of friendship and trust, who has already inspired the process of restoring my self-respect, who has presented me with the opportunity to break away from an environment which has crippled my spirit even more than my body. A young woman, yes, but one with a mature head on her shoulders, and a young woman with the courage to strike out in this man's world. A young and inexperienced woman, yes, but a friend deserved of support... '* The voice of Peter Corder suddenly interrupted her thoughts.

"Do either of you realize how unnerving it is to have two women behind me in this car saying absolutely nothing at all?"

Elizabeth chuckled as she replied, "I thought you would appreciate the silence to concentrate on your driving," she paused before adding, " and of course your thoughts."

"Ah yes," said Peter, "My illustrious thoughts. Hello, what's this?"

Through the legally permitted thin beam of the Austin Seven's covered headlamps, could be seen a figure signalling with a torch. The figure was causing the torchlight to dance over some kind of obstruction in the middle of the road directly ahead of the car. Peter brought the car to a halt seconds before a uniformed policeman appeared beside his window. As he wound down the window he alerted his passengers with the words, "Identity cards at the ready, ladies."

Elizabeth and Mary were scrabbling in handbags as a new voice filled the car's interior.

"Well spotted, sir," said the policeman whilst quickly flashing his torchlight over two startled and still scrabbling passengers. "May not be any need for ID, ladies," said the policeman, "Which I presume is what you're looking for, but I *will* just glance at yours, sir, since you've gone to the trouble of producing it."

Peter's proffered document was accepted and quickly perused by torchlight as the policeman spoke again, "A doctor, well now, *there's* a thing. And from Bart's, I see. Well, you're almost home, so to speak. And would we be using our privileged ration supplement on essential war work, doctor?"

"I had to visit a pregnant woman with problems," replied Peter.

"Ah, I see, sir. And these two ladies will be your nurses, no doubt."

"Well they *are* nurses," responded Peter, "But technically, they belong to Bart's."

The torchlight once more briefly picked out the face of Mary Reynolds. "I *thought* I recognized you. Ward Sister Reynolds, isn't it?" identified the smiling policeman, "You very kindly helped me when I was visiting recently on the Harmsworth Ward."

As Peter retrieved his identity card and Elizabeth and Mary remained dumbstruck, the policeman spoke again, "So I won't be arresting you tonight, doctor. Not while you're carrying two angels."

"Most kind," drawled Peter, the beam from his car's headlamp's fingering the obstruction ahead, "You know," he continued, "that looks just like... "

"It's coal!" interjected Mary, the disbelief heard in her exclamation.

"That it is, Sister Reynolds," confirmed the policeman, "The rationed black gold we used to know as coal. And I'm stuck here for the rest of the night to prevent any nocturnal re-mining."

"How did it get here?" asked Elizabeth.

"Well now, my lovely angel," replied the policeman in a sonorous tone, "I would imagine it had the black market lorry variety of help, which, in its haste to flee the scene, neglected to properly secure its tailgate." He paused to chuckle at his own humour before once more addressing Corder, "Right sir, slow as you go and just follow my torchlight to get you started."

So once more Peter Corder slowly manoeuvred his way clear of an incident area, and no sooner had he done so before the voice of Elizabeth Creacey was in his ear.

"Well it *has* been an eventful evening," she began, "And *you*, doctor, were certainly cool under fire back there." The chuckle was heard in her pause, "That policeman mentioned black gold, which reminded me that before he stopped us, *you* were about to share your thoughts."

"His *illustrious* thoughts, he *actually* said," chimed in Mary, surprising *herself* as much as her now laughing companions.

Peter Corder saw the hospital gates a short distance ahead as he smiled at the banter. *'Imagine a world without humour,'* he thought, mentally shivering at the prospect as he responded to his back-seat tormentors. "Ah yes, as you rightly say, my illustrious thoughts."

He brought the car to a halt, adding to the queue of four vehicles waiting to be checked by the hospital's gatemen. "Well," he briskly resumed, "if the learned Mister Teale were to consider my own hospital contract as just another technicality he can deal with, and if the good Sister Reynolds intends to be on board and can learn to put up with me, then you can count me in on the great adventure."

Peter then felt a hand on his shoulder as Elizabeth's warm breath touched his neck and her voice became music in his ears.

"Thank you, Peter, you've made me so very happy."

The queue of vehicles was moving, but not as fast as Peter's heartbeat as he inched forward. His pleasurable glow was brief, dulled by the next words he heard.

"But the good Sister Reynolds," resumed Elizabeth, "as you rightly call her, *has not*," she pointedly emphasised, "actually said anything yet."

"The good Sister Reynolds," rejoined Mary, "wouldn't dream of leaving you to the mercy of the good doctor without my being present to supervise matters."

"Oh Mary, that's wonderful," exclaimed Elizabeth, "I feel so relieved, I think I'm going to cry. I don't know if I would even have tried without you," she confessed.

"Which of course," retorted Peter, "immediately leaves me striving to retain a modicum of pride and feeling quite superfluous."

"You are nothing of the sort, Peter Corder," Elizabeth firmly responded, "But would *you* have been happier without Mary?"

"Actually, No," replied Peter without hesitation, "It's the general consensus of my peers that she runs the best Ward in Bart's. We'd be lost without her on the Harmsworth." The reduced queue was moving again and he slowly eased his car forward.

Struggling to suppress her emotions upon hearing the remarks of her companions, Mary Reynolds decided it was time to introduce a sobering reminder. "There's a lot we still have to discuss. A lot to sort out," she ended firmly.

"Of course there is," agreed Peter, finally level with the gatehouse window and reaching through to once again proffer his identity card.

"One woman not enough for you, doctor Corder?" challenged the Gateman, cheerfully signalling that the passenger cards would not be required and waving Peter through.

Allowing the back-seat laughter to wash over him, Peter finally stopped the car in the reserved parking area, switched off its engine, and turned to face his passengers as he spoke,

"Of course there's a lot still to be discussed, but since our decision to go forward has taken us over the Rubicon, whatever else we need to talk about can wait until we've all had a good night's sleep. Hopefully," he added with a tired looking smile.

With Peter's closing summary receiving thoughtfully nodded assent from his audience, the trio exited the car. The words *Goodnight* and *Merry Christmas* sent Corder off towards the block housing the male quarters and propelled Elizabeth and Mary into their own cheerless block.

"Will you sleep at all tonight?" queried Mary, quietly, as they reached their shared corridor.

"I doubt it," replied Elizabeth.

"A cup of tea?"

"Oh, I would love that," responded Elizabeth.

"Let's go to my place," offered Mary, chuckling as she added, "I heard the dishy Clark Gable say that in a film once."

Elizabeth instantly felt the pang as her memory plunged her back in time to when Jack had lifted her off her feet and she'd told him *'Oh I saw Clark Gable do this in a film once'* and Jack had said...

"Here we are then," said Mary, opening the door to her room, "You sit yourself down and I'll make us a brew."

Inside the familiar and normally relaxing environment of her friend's room, Elizabeth inexplicably found herself reluctant to sit down. She was suddenly experiencing a disturbing physical sensation; a feeling of becoming two people in the same body. The one calm and mature; the other not yet fully formed. The older persona telling her the tension within her was a natural reaction to the strain of the evening; telling her she needn't be afraid; telling her there would be far more demanding challenges to be met on the journey ahead; telling her she was a perfectly capable woman who must set an example of strong leadership.

But the mirror in Mary's room was clearly reflecting one person only, and *she* had the face of a very young, and very vulnerable looking person who was maybe unsure of her future. Reactively turning away from her image, now feeling strangely self-conscious, she sat down on Mary's bed and forced her thoughts to take a different path. She was, she realistically realized, still struggling to come to terms with the magnitude of change impacting upon her *own* life, and, now seemingly destined to have a similar effect on the lives of Mary and Peter.

'So here we are then, Elizabeth Creacey,' she told herself firmly, *'and, in the circumstances, uncertainty and an overwrought imagination are only to be expected bedfellows and I must learn to live with them... '*

"...about *us*," sounded Mary's voice.

"I'm sorry, Mary, what did you say?" she asked, "I was daydreaming and didn't hear you."

"I said I can speak to Matron first about *us*," repeated Mary, pouring their tea as she added, "Which should make it less awkward for *you* when you see her yourself."

"Thank you," responded Elizabeth, smiling as she continued, "Though I rather think she'll be more upset at the prospect of losing *you*."

"Matron and I have clashed from time to time," revealed Mary, "and she didn't always win. So she'll probably be glad to see the back of me." She smiled as she added, "Peter will speak for himself, of course. He has a way with words, does our good doctor Corder."

Time then passed as they sipped tea and chatted about the evening's revelations.

"I'm concerned about Katherine," confessed a now more relaxed Elizabeth.

"Yes, I know you are," acknowledged Mary, "and probably with good reason."

Elizabeth then told Mary about Katherine's self-imposed dilemma, and of her having created the sketch of Jack, and of her own now mixed feelings towards the ex room-mate.

"When the time comes," said Mary, "we can arrange for her to have the baby here. As for the rest, well, we'll just have to wait and see, I suppose."

By this time both women were openly yawning, so Elizabeth bade her friend a warm *'Goodnight'* and made her way down the corridor to her own room. Where later, once she'd made a few notes in her diary, she went to bed still carrying the burden of thoughts concerning Katherine Swan and her unborn baby.

Mary Reynolds went to bed with the thought that Elizabeth seemed entirely oblivious of the fact that Peter Corder was in love with her. She lay in bed wondering what would happen when Elizabeth stopped grieving for the man she had lost; wishing she herself had actually met the man who had captured the heart of her friend, and had left three people on the life-altering threshold of *change*. She closed her eyes, her sigh a mixture of regret and contentment, and her last conscious thought was *'Change needn't necessarily be something to fear... '*

Peter Corder went to bed with the words of the cheerful Gateman in his head:

'One woman not enough for you, doctor Corder?'

His last conscious thoughts were once again a mixed bag: *'One particular woman would be enough... but will I ever have the chance to replace a man who is dead... but is still dramatically influencing Elizabeth's life?'* He was falling into the arms of Morpheus when the final thoughts played themselves in his mind; *'Maybe my parents were right... maybe I can't save them all...*

But by following Elizabeth Creacey... maybe I can save myself... '

Chapter Eleven

The heart has its reasons which reason knows nothing of.
(Pascal)

London, England, January through to April 1944

January opened 1944 with some of the newspapers boldly proclaiming it to be *'The Year of Decision'* for the commanders of the Allied forces. Whilst coincidentally, and possibly sympathetic to the plight of those hard-pressed leaders, Bing Crosby and The Andrews Sisters were teaming up in the music charts with *'Don't Fence Me In'*. Meanwhile, other newspapers were alarmingly reporting that the black market was now saturated with stolen ration books, bringing their illegal individual price down to the bargain-basement sum of £1.

Resisting at any price the dissuasive efforts of the hospital's hierarchy, Mary Reynolds and Peter Corder were scheduled to leave Bart's in April. Elizabeth's ties had been more easily severed, and, to Corder's chagrin, she had been spending as much free time as she could with Jonathan Teale. Time which had been spent in Jonathan's 'Middle Temple' office, slowly coming to terms with the legacy which Jack Matthews had bequeathed her.

An astonishing legacy: Comprising in part the Knightsbridge apartment, and, as the deeds held by Jonathan confirmed, 'Ridgeway House' and grounds in the Carshalton district of Surrey.

The so-called 'House', purportedly in good repair and standing in ten acres of partly wooded grounds, had been shown by the deeds to be a twenty-nine-roomed Edwardian mansion.

Scheduled to visit 'Ridgeway House' with Jonathan at the end of the month, since learning of its existence an incredulous Elizabeth had been fighting to control her impatience. Her incredulity hadn't just been confined to bricks and mortar however, because there had also been the matter of the money. *'Enough to last you several lifetimes,'* Jonathan had officially confirmed with a smile.

Determined to make up for the delayed start, and in an effort to satisfy Elizabeth's eagerness to learn more about the background of Jack Matthews, Jonathan Teale had pieced together a chronicle of events compiled from the comprehensive files and notes of his now retired mentor, Arthur Freemantle. *'A 'studied' compilation,'* regretted Jonathan, *'because he had to prevent his client from seeing the names on the Ridgeway House title deeds. Indeed he must be cautious as to how he presented any names at all!'*

So over a series of visits Elizabeth noted, and was appreciative of, the obvious care with which her solicitor had prepared the notes from which he recounted the information she so eagerly sought. She learned of the original family fortune amassed from an earlier generation's property and tea trading. A fortune which had eventually passed to Matthew S. Matthews, Jack's strangely named father. A strange name, hesitantly pronounced by Jonathan from his notes.

"Apparently not a man," said Jonathan, "with a head *for*, nor interest *in*, commercial life. From what I can gather, he was fuelled by different passions. More the artistic type, I'd say."

Elizabeth remembered Jack's poem and his few spoken words about the father kept alive for him by his mother's stories.

"The notes record his taking a painting holiday in France in 1911," said Jonathan, "where he apparently lodged with the *Cheval* family in *Bordeaux*. From what I've gathered, there appears to have been what the writers call a whirlwind romance before his marriage to *Chantal Cheval,* the family's only daughter."

Learning that Matthew S. Matthews, proudly determined to fight for his country, had brought his new wife and two year old son back to England in 1914, Elizabeth tried to imagine the anguish concealed by the dry notation of Matthew's death at *Passchendaele,* and tried not to think of Jack, *her* Jack, as a bereft and bewildered eight year old boy returning to France with his widowed mother.

On another informative session with Jonathan Teale, it was explained to Elizabeth that following the return to France of

159

Matthew's widow and her son, Jonathan's predecessor, Arthur Freemantle, had continued to handle Chantal's legal and financial interests in England. Which had evidently necessitated frequent liaison with Freemantle's French counterparts, in addition to bankers based in both France and England.

"From everything I've read about her," said Jonathan, "It's quite clear to me that the mother of Jack Matthews was a businesswoman ahead of her time. She shrewdly used her husband's inherited fortune to create yet more wealth by expanding a property portfolio, acquiring vineyards, and she had a factory making machine parts for the French military. Impressive enterprises. All successful. All driven," Jonathan dramatically qualified, "by a woman of power and influence by the time 1938 brought with it the early signs of what was to come."

Jonathan indicated his notes as he continued, "But she was also a woman with outspoken views on the new political order threatening her country's borders. A woman who apparently used her extensive contacts to warn and protect those families whose names were on a German Gestapo list. These notes allude to her as a woman who helped many of them get out of France. She was very probably a *marked* woman by that time," he solemnly ended.

Still constrained by the restrictions imposed upon him by the Rawlings' letter, a frustrated Jonathan's carefully edited and vocalised chronicle informed Elizabeth that Chantal and Jack had returned to England in 1938, bringing with them some of the proceeds from discreet sales made throughout the preceding period. The resourceful Chantal had then purchased the Knightsbridge apartment, where she and Jack had lived for a time.

"By the close of 1938," said Jonathan, "Chantal had apparently liquidated all of her French holdings. To the recorded dismay of her French bankers, I might add. *But*," he emphasised with a smile, "to the rivalling delight of your own new bankers, Elizabeth. Coutts of London will, I am sure, serve *you* as well as they did Chantal."

Elizabeth was intrigued by Jonathan's recital from Arthur Freemantle's notes concerning the early part of 1939. The notes seemingly referred to a meeting Freemantle had had with Chantal, wherein she had surprisingly informed her solicitor that she would once more be returning to France and wished to reorganize her affairs.

"My predecessor," said Jonathan, "records his frustration at Chantal's refusal to explain how she intended to get back to France at such a volatile period in her country's history."

Elizabeth listened closely as Jonathan told her that, so far as he could surmise, Chantal had left her son in sole residence at the Knightsbridge apartment in May of 1939. Some months later, as was now historically known, France had declared war on Germany.

"But as I've said," Elizabeth reminded him, "Jack *did* tell me that his mother was dead."

"I've found nothing to indicate what might have happened to her," replied Jonathan, "At her last meeting with Arthur Freemantle, she instructed him to transfer everything of value to her only son. From that point on, she seems to have simply dropped out of sight."

Each time Elizabeth had visited him to add to her knowledge of her late fiancé, Jonathan Teale had found himself wrestling with conflicting emotions. That he should be forced to withhold information from his client would have been conflicting enough by itself, but his inner torment was compounded by his growing awareness of his attraction to her. An attraction he dare not voice, for fear of irreparably damaging their professional relationship.

Completely oblivious to the effect she was having on the man, each time she returned from her sessions with Jonathan Teale, Elizabeth made careful entries in her diary of everything she had learned about Jack's background.

As 1944's January destructively made way for its February, many Londoners' were complaining about the lack of available underground shelters. They justifiably did so whilst bracing themselves for the continuance of renewed German bombing attacks which had started at the end of January. Consequently, ignoring the posters warning that 'Loose Lips Sink Ships, speculation was now rife around the pubs *and* around the question *When would the Allies invade fortress Europe?* However, upon receiving confirmation that conditional permission had been obtained for Katherine's baby to be born at Bart's hospital, Elizabeth Creacey's speculative question continued to be *When would Katherine Swan tell Tom Ball?*

As the music charts tunefully made room for Ella Fitzgerald and The Ink Spots singing *'I'm Making Believe'*, escorted by Jonathan Teale, Elizabeth made her first visit to the Surrey house and grounds she now of course realized had been Jack's intended destination on their last day together. A short walk away from the Carshalton district railway station, upon initial inspection the house seemed ideal for the proposed usage and Jonathan assured his excited client he would attend to the necessary details.

Having now completely severed her student ties to Bart's, and currently residing at the Knightsbridge apartment with an increasingly irascible Katherine, Elizabeth was still regularly visiting the Harmsworth Ward. The visits were used to update Mary and Peter on Jonathan's progress with the regulatory authorities, and to obtain the required signatures of her colleagues on the various forms periodically supplied by the solicitor. On these occasions Elizabeth found herself liaising with a quite different Mary Reynolds. An equally excited Mary, who said she was positively looking forward to the fresh challenge of a major change in her life.

Doctor Corder's reaction to her visits was an entirely different eye-opener. The 'Teale arranged' 'necessary business' petrol allowance and chauffeur-driven car now permanently at her disposal had produced a seemingly *piqued* Peter. Only Mary heard his later muttered words, "How can I compete with *that?*"

Elizabeth was quietly appalled at Katherine's determination to be rid of the child she carried. Not once had she heard the woman express any natural maternal thoughts. The more she thought about it, the less she liked Katherine now. She thought of what *she* would have given to carry Jack's child. Finally weary of her thoughts, driven by some inner-force reacting to Katherine's behaviour, she found herself impulsively telephoning Jonathan Teale to enquire about his knowledge of adoption procedures.

Immediately surprising her, Jonathan seemed to take the call's subject matter in his stride. Whilst even to her own ears she sounded almost incoherent, he made appropriate noises of understanding throughout her attempt to convey her reasoning of the situation and didn't interrupt her once. When she had finished, he then used carefully voiced legal jargon to explain the fact that the procedures surrounding adoption were both complicated *and* protracted.

"Unlikely therefore," he said, "to resolve Katherine's problem as quickly as she would like."

Feeling completely foolish now, Elizabeth opted for silence. Which was quickly filled.

"There would be," resumed Jonathan, "the additional problem of her requiring her husband's consent. As a legally married couple, the law would require his agreement to adoption. Which would," Jonathan dryly opined down the line, "tend to negate the exercise as far as Katherine's objectives are concerned."

Elizabeth thanked the solicitor, disconnected, and relayed the comments to Katherine who received them in abject silence and simply shook her head to the renewed suggestion that she should write to Tom Ball. Elizabeth gave up then, gratefully responding to the offer of tea from a seemingly remarkably calm Mrs Bruce. Seated in the kitchen, Elizabeth allowed herself to be diverted by the amiably sympathetic Housekeeper. They chatted about sorting out the newly purchased baby clothes and cot-bedding which had been completely ignored by Katherine, whilst choosing not to comment on the sound of the guest bedroom door slamming behind the troubled and pregnant woman.

Had it not been for the 'Teale arranged' presence of the stalwart Mrs Bruce over the seemingly interminable few days which followed, Elizabeth thought she might have strangled the monosyllabic Katherine several times out of sheer frustration before the woman was finally collected by Peter Corder and taken to Bart's hospital. When Mary Reynolds eventually telephoned the news of the safe birth of a boy child on the eleventh of March, the ensuing conversation revealed the event to be more of a pleasurable relief to Mary and Elizabeth than the boy's actual mother. Mary's caustic tone in Elizabeth's ear articulately confirmed that fact whilst also conveying the Ward Sister's disgust.

"Having carried her cross inside her for nine months, Katherine was obliged to briefly hold in her arms the manifestation of her waywardness. I have *never* seen a more reluctant mother."

As conditionally decreed by Bart's, two days later and escorted by Mary Reynolds, the subjects of debate were duly returned to the Knightsbridge apartment. Whereupon entering the lounge, Katherine Swan immediately rejected the infant. Displaying no emotion whatsoever, the woman unceremoniously placed her new-born child in the arms of Mrs Bruce and walked away into the guest bedroom without uttering a word. Profoundly angered by Katherine's action, Elizabeth was then astonished to hear Mary and Mrs Bruce confess that they had anticipated problems of this nature.

"Asking her to breast-feed would be a fruitless exercise," declared Mary, indicating the bag she carried as she continued, "So I came prepared."

Mary's bag was opened to reveal several tins of dried milk and two feeding bottles complete with teats as Mrs Bruce spoke up firmly. "And *I've* moved the cot into the master bedroom. This baby should not be left through the night with that tortured soul of a mother."

Relieved beyond measure by the foresight of Mary and the Housekeeper, Elizabeth took the baby from Mrs Bruce and held him in her arms. Immediately captivated by the tiny face, she smiled down at the warmly bundled and still sleeping infant and didn't see the look which passed between her on-looking companions.

"I'm going to look in on Katherine, but I must be going soon," announced Mary, "I've left a hospital driver outside and he's probably wondering what's keeping me." She smiled as she began moving towards the guest bedroom, "I'll be leaving the little one, and *you*, Elizabeth, in the capable hands of Mrs Bruce."

"*I'll* be sleeping in the lounge for a few nights," declared the determined sounding Housekeeper to a surprised looking Elizabeth, "Just to help you with the feeding routine, and such like," she ended, her tone conveying it would be pointless contesting her intention.

Mary returned saying that Katherine was okay and would probably sleep for hours, and then she bade her reciprocated farewells.

Accompanied by Mrs Bruce, Elizabeth carried the baby into the master bedroom. The cot stood alongside the bed, and, realized Elizabeth, had been positioned so that when *she* was lying in bed she would have an unobstructed view of the cot's intended occupant.

"You can just lie him down on top of your bed, if you like," said Mrs Bruce, "He'll be quite safe, and I've no doubt he'll be waking any time now. And he'll be ready for a feed when he does, I shouldn't wonder, so I'll just go and see to that now, love."

Katherine surfaced late in the evening, made straight for the kitchen, mumbled her thanks for the meal prepared and served by Mrs Bruce, and stumbled back to her bedroom without saying a word about the baby. Mrs Bruce sent a silent prayer to the poor woman's maker, before returning to two other souls she considered were more worthy of her assistance.

And so began Elizabeth's first evening and night spent looking after a baby, and at some point she readily acknowledged to herself that she would never have managed it all without the unflagging support of the indomitable Mrs Bruce.

For Elizabeth, it was a return to the shift-rota system over the next few busy days and nights at the Knightsbridge apartment. The difference this time was the combination of exhaustion *and* exhilaration as she and Mrs Bruce took turns to sleep in between tending to the needs of the still un-named baby. She rapidly discovered that her own childhood memory of washing and dressing already clean and silently compliant dolls, was entirely at odds with the real thing. Reality was the messy, crying, wriggling, legs-scissoring small individual timing to perfection his vertical spurts of hot urine to begin the instant after he'd been washed and powdered and laid on a dry towelling napkin.

Intermittent parts of the fast-moving days were also emotionally disturbing. Whenever the baby's mother emerged from her room to eat and drink, she continued to reject efforts to re-unite her with the child, and it was worriedly observed that the woman's behaviour was exacting a terrible toll on her physical appearance. Still refusing to write to Tom Ball, a hollow-eyed and for the most part uncommunicative Katherine sometimes appeared in the lounge. Wherein she would just sit for a while watching, with a sullen-faced expression, Elizabeth's every move with the baby. But she refused to even hold him.

Time moved on, and the daily and nightly routine was now being satisfactorily managed. Mrs Bruce's offer to stay at the apartment full time once Katherine eventually moved out, had been gladly accepted. And Elizabeth was finally finding time to think about herself. It was as she looked at the infant, again asleep on top of the bed in which she and Jack had made love, that her thoughts moved towards the decision.

It was now abundantly clear to her that the child faced a bleak and uncertain future with Katherine. A Katherine who, in her present state, if forced to keep him, could abandon the mite again. Could simply leave him somewhere... to be found... she abruptly closed down that thought channel. Unable to even *think* about any harm coming to the tiny figure on the bed. Over these past memorable days of inescapable bonding with the child, she had already begun to think of him at times as her own... and Jack's. Elizabeth carefully sat down on the bed beside the sleeping infant and soberly considered her thoughts and feelings. She suddenly felt sure that she would never marry, that she would never stop being faithful to the memory of Jack, and was inwardly at peace with the feeling.

'How perfect it would be,' she thought, 'The gift of a child. A baby I have nursed, and fed, and cared for since he came into the world.' She remembered now Jonathan Teale's words; 'Enough money to last you several lifetimes.'

'I won't have several lifetimes,' she told herself now, 'I will have one life, like everyone else. And like everyone else I don't know how long that life will be. So when the time comes, why not pass on the legacy to someone I can love now without dishonouring Jack's memory? As Chantal had passed it on, to her own son, to Jack.' She looked at the sleeping boy on the bed. The boy who could become *her* son, and finally made her decision. She went in search of Mrs Bruce.

Found in the kitchen, the woman responded to the news by saying her prayers had been answered. Resolutely they then went together to the guest bedroom, where the reluctant mother was quietly informed that Elizabeth would somehow find a way to adopt the baby boy. Unwilling then to prolong the conversation, immediately feeling unable to remain in the same room as Katherine, Elizabeth returned to her own bedroom and lay down beside the still-sleeping child.

The next morning Katherine was gone. The note found by Mrs Bruce simply told them that she would be staying with Tom Ball's brother, and gave the address. The note made no mention of the child, said nothing of Elizabeth's declared intent, and the words *Thank you for all you've done* were also noticeably absent.

When later Elizabeth telephoned Jonathan Teale to update him, and to explain what she had done and *why*, he sounded sympathetic but immediately expressed his concerns over the legal ramifications of her proposed course of action. As she listened to him, she found herself thinking of Jack's mother; of Chantal's recorded determination in the face of adversity. Using a tone of voice which she knew was surprising the solicitor, she told him it was *his* job to deal with legal ramifications. She sustained the firmness when telling him she was keeping the boy.

Several hours later Jonathan rang back to say that, as he had predicted, adoption in these circumstances was a legal minefield. She could hear by his tone that if there had been some way of making it happen, he would have found it. She told him she'd get back to him when she'd had more time to think about it.

Of their own volition it seemed, her thoughts turned again to Jack's mother. She tried to imagine what Chantal might have done in the given circumstances. *'She would have used her contacts, that's what she would have done.'* Ensuring the baby was happily occupied by the willing Mrs Bruce, she found her handbag, retrieved the till-now-forgotten card and dialled the number which connected her to a politely official sounding switchboard operator. She gave her name, and, when she asked for him, was immediately put through to Major Simon Rawlings.

Rawlings expressed his delight at hearing from her, and, without further preamble asked if there was anything he could do for her. When she began to tell him, he stopped her to ask if she was calling from the Knightsbridge apartment. Surprised, she confirmed that she was and he said he would come to her within the hour.

Rawlings arrived at the apartment's front door forty minutes later; a chubby man with a face which still looked tough even though it wore a smile. His pleasant sounding greeting was delivered in the hard 'no nonsense' Londoner's voice she had come to recognize on the Harmsworth Ward. Standing before her, radiating energy without even moving, was an image she hadn't expected at all. He wasn't wearing the army uniform she remembered from their last meeting, and his civilian clothing made him look shorter than she'd remembered him as being.

Ushered inside, when he shook her hand she felt the strength in his thick fingers. He patiently stood in the hallway as she openly examined him, watching her in turn through sandy-coloured eyes set in the weathered-cheeked face which had, she professionally recognized, suffered a broken nose in its past. Something about the man's bearing, something the civilian clothes couldn't totally conceal, brought to the surface of her mind memories of Jack. Her visitor was *a man of action,* she sensed, and that instantly linked perception might have prompted questions had it not been for the appearance of the inquisitive Mrs Bruce carrying with her the root cause of the current situation.

Introduced to Mrs Bruce and an un-named baby, Rawlings politely declined the woman's offer of tea and was briskly led away by Elizabeth to be seated in the lounge. Reminding herself that Jack had said this man could be relied upon *for anything,* and apologising for her haste to explain, she quickly outlined the problem. Whereupon he made her go through the whole story of Katherine Swan and Tom Ball. Insisting upon a detailed account, and using what she deduced was a form of shorthand, he rapidly scribbled into a pocketbook as she spoke of when and how the couple had met, her personal recollection of anything which Katherine had divulged about their relationship, the name of Tom's regiment, Katherine's fateful dalliance with someone called Larry, and her own conversations with Jonathan Teale about the proposed adoption. When she'd finished, Rawlings promptly asked her more questions. Questions which, she thought at the time, were more or less forcing her to repeat the entire saga again and merely soliciting information she'd already given.

But a little later, when she'd left him in the lounge while she responded to a call for help from Mrs Bruce, she realized his last set of questions had focused on Katherine's behaviour both on and off the Harmsworth Ward. He had persistently probed for Katherine Swan's reactions to just about anything which could be remembered from the time she had first met the woman.

She returned to the lounge to find Rawlings standing there, hands in pockets, head bowed, and she almost fainted. When he came to her quickly, concern on his face, she recovered enough to apologise whilst attempting a brief and halting explanation of the memory of Jack standing in this room, *hands in pockets, head bowed in thought...*

Rawlings brought the present situation back into focus by saying he was returning to his office, and that she would hear from him shortly.

One hour later Rawlings rang her to ask if she knew the name of the doctor who had delivered the baby, and she told him about Peter Corder. When she questioned his obviously pleased response, he explained that he'd already spoken to Jonathan Teale and now knew of the planned convalescent home and Corder's connection to it. He told her not be concerned about his interest in the doctor, and disconnected.

In between attending to the baby, her afternoon was dominated by the organizational requirements involved with moving into the apartment the widowed woman increasingly being thought of as a second mother. The sprightly white-haired and rosy-cheeked Mrs Bruce had arranged for her brother, a grocery shop and bread van owner she currently lived with, to deliver her clothes and sundry items she wanted to have around her in her new abode. Duly delivered, the two women cheerfully set about turning the guest bedroom into what Mrs Bruce tearfully called a 'home from home.'

Evening fell upon the Knightsbridge apartment with its usual stealth. A busy and contented Mrs Bruce had fed and changed the baby. She was laying him in his cot with a whispered *'Fingers crossed for a good night's sleep'* when the doorbell rang.

Opening the door, Elizabeth was surprised by the re-appearance of Rawlings, this time heavily laden, and she was amazed to see that he was accompanied by a decidedly unhappy looking Jonathan Teale. Her visitors were shown into the kitchen, where it was revealed that the Rawlings burden was a large box of rations. Which, as was revealed by a delighted and already unpacking Housekeeper, were rations specifically selected for two adults and one child. She stood in the kitchen at a loss for words, doubly thrown by the generously thoughtful and precious gift, and the unexpected presence of a clearly bemused solicitor. Before she could gather her wits enough to dispel the suddenly awkward atmosphere, the rations had been quickly stored by the efficient Mrs Bruce and the perceptive woman was saying she would 'leave them to their business now.' The Creacey tongue was belatedly found when Mrs Bruce left.

"Privileges of rank," Rawlings said simply to her finally uttered thanks.

She wasn't given time to query the remark, or even properly acknowledge Jonathan, because Jack's friend was obviously impatient to get to the point of his second visit of the day.

"Congratulations are in order, Miss Creacey," he briskly began, "You've just given birth to a baby boy," he announced, "Provided of course you agree," he added with a wolfish grin.

She somehow managed to sit down rather than collapse, whilst absently noting that Jonathan's shock appeared to match her own as the two men sat down at the kitchen table.

Both she and the solicitor then proceeded to listen as Rawlings faced them across the table and followed up on his verbal bombshell.

"Rather than involving more people in the complex matter of adoption," he began again, "and given our specific problem in *this* instance, it will be simpler to arrange the necessary documentation to show *you*, Elizabeth Creacey, as the natural mother of the child."

She sat, knowing she did so open-mouthed, and she noted now that Jonathan's face appeared to wear an even more thoughtful expression than the one she'd grown accustomed to. She wondered why her solicitor hadn't said a word since he'd arrived and was even now avoiding eye contact.

"Despite our respective roles in this affair," resumed Rawlings, offering a smile to his audience, "and our mutual interest in confidentiality with regard to the present circumstances, I am not fully at liberty to explain how I can arrange such a thing." He paused, glancing at Jonathan before continuing, "I *can* go so far as to say that the government work I do gives me the unchallengeable authority to produce the perfectly legal documents which will be required, and that my office will properly liaise with all the relevant official channels."

She realized she'd been holding her breath, and exhaled now with the question, "What about Katherine?"

"I have concluded," responded Rawlings, "from your earlier remarks, that she is unlikely to lay claim to the child at a later date." He paused, and his voice sounded even harder when he resumed, "But even if she did, she would find it impossible to prove her case."

Startling Elizabeth, Jonathan Teale suddenly interjected at that point.

"Katherine Swan knows about Elizabeth's legacy. She is therefore aware that one day the boy will become a wealthy man. Which might very well," he argued, "tempt such a woman into making a claim at a later date."

Elizabeth then realized that Rawlings was looking directly into *her* eyes as he responded to the solicitor, "Not a scrap of paper will exist to show the child was born to her. The people who attended the delivery have already signed the papers which will show the child was born to *you*."

She saw the intensity in the sandy-coloured eyes soften with his smile as he quietly said, "All *you* have to do is name the child and *my* people will do the rest."

Jonathan Teale was completely still where he sat. Unmoving but far from unmoved. Angered by his impotence in this affair. An impotence rendered by this man Rawlings, who, on their way here together, had refused to remove the restraints which had been placed upon him. He realized only too well now how badly

Elizabeth wanted this child to become her own, and he might in time come to understand why she wanted it so, but never in his wildest imaginings could he have envisaged a scenario such as the one Rawlings could seemingly turn into legally backed reality. Was there anything these bloody cloak and dagger people couldn't do? And why wasn't this infuriating man telling his client everything now?

Elizabeth looked across the table without speaking. Acutely conscious that she'd been listening to the same quiet authority and confidence in the voice of Rawlings, as she had once heard in Jack's voice. She remembered again the letter saying that this man could be relied upon for anything, and without further hesitation or discussion she told him to go ahead with his plan.

"What Christian name do you wish the boy to have?" responded Rawlings.

She thought of Chantal's love for the husband she had kept alive in her own son's affections; thought of the father Jack had never really known.

"I would like," she told Rawlings, "the child to be named Matthew."

Arrangements had been made with the unflappable Mrs Bruce, who would remain at the Knightsbridge apartment. In addition to maintaining the property, and sustaining a presence, she would deal with the forwarding of mail when necessary.

So four weeks after her momentous meeting with Rawlings, and as April rushed to clear its last days on the calendar, Elizabeth Creacey left behind the London apartment and journeyed with her infant son to the Surrey mansion entitled 'Ridgeway House'. There she met up with Mary Reynolds and Peter Corder, who made a tremendous fuss of little Matthew who gurgled happily at his new admirers. Watching them, Elizabeth formed the opinion that her baby son had just now acquired his first Aunt and Uncle.

Her diary entry that evening reflected her contentment. Tinged with sadness.

Chapter Twelve

In plucking the fruit of memory, one runs the risk of spoiling the bloom.
(Joseph Conrad)

Redhill district of Surrey, England, Home of Matthew and Alicia Sands, Monday evening, 13th January 1992

At ground level around the cluster of detached 'trophy' homes standing in the leafy cul-de-sac, the promise of overnight frost was already in the air being used now by 'gloved-up' and warmly wrapped dog walkers. High above all this a jet plane lazily moved at deceptive speed, its navigation lights twinkling in sorry competition with the myriad of stars scattered across the night sky and glittering like diamonds on a bed of black velvet. Evidently negating the need for their detached garages, the 'state of the architectural art' houses sported individually crafted driveways; perhaps designed to convey the impression that money was no object whilst showcasing the gleaming four-wheeled chariots of capitalism. The first fingers of moonlight were even now reaching down to stroke the silent Jaguars and other motorised beasts which waited for daylight, and owners who would be transported once more to various points of the commercial compass following their nightly dosage of suburban slumber.

One of those chariot owners was currently, impatiently, pacing the lounge floor of his luxury home as he caught the tail-end of a radio news broadcast... *so Saint Bartholomew's hospital, which has seen off numerous threats since its foundation in eleven twenty-three, such as the turmoil during the dissolution of the monasteries and the great fire of London in sixteen sixty-six, now awaits publication of the Tomlinson report on the future of the London health service. Already leaked passages of the report, question whether the hospital should remain open...* His impatience suddenly demanding silence, Matthew Sands switched off the radio.

He had toothache. The faint nagging which had started earlier in the day, reaching the incessant stabbing stage by late afternoon, had finally forced the surrender to his well-meaning secretary. As he'd left the office, she had been cheerfully booking his appointment with the dreaded chair. So his relief, or his torture, would come tomorrow.

An early evening meal had virtually survived intact his half-hearted picking and now, with nerve-ends hammering for the white-coated attention they craved, his thoughts roamed impatiently as he waited for Andrew Teale. The meeting had been set for eight-pm and he wondered yet again why Andrew needed to see him. Nor could he imagine why the solicitor had insisted on an evening meeting here. They'd necessarily spoken on the phone several times since the death of Andrew's father, and had of course met at Jonathan's funeral, but the urgent request to see him at home was a new twist in their relationship.

As a solution to the problem he'd faced upon the death of Jonathan, replacing the father with the son had worked seamlessly. Andrew Teale had effortlessly picked up the reins controlling the legal affairs of Compass Designs, and had already brought himself up to speed with the currently tricky French scenario. Andrew was also privy to the problems presented by an unknown Mole in the company, so in turn *he* felt he knew his man and had come to respect his judgement. *'So what the hell was tonight all about?'*

His impatience becoming annoyance, Matthew drifted to the drinks cabinet and poured himself a brandy from the decanter; *'A wedding present from Jonathan,'* he recalled now, his restless thoughts suddenly focusing on the man who up until his death had been a part of Matthew's life for as long as he could remember. His mother had told him she'd met Jonathan during the war, and he now wryly recalled himself as a boy growing up whilst calling Jonathan Teale *'Uncle.'* Sipping the brandy, still trying to deflect the pain in his mouth, he allowed his thoughts to open out to the past. And his mother. *'Toothache,'* he reflected, *'wouldn't even have dented that woman's smile.'*

He moved to where he could see out into Alicia's garden, and the memory tapes instantly spooled backwards to let him watch and listen to the scenes from his past...

The first and only time he'd seen his mother depressed had been when his Aunt Mary had died. He had just turned eighteen, but still remembered crying along with his mother. Aunt Mary had been something special. Even Peter Corder had cried for Mary, and up to then he'd always been the type to shrug off practically anything with a joke. The same Peter Corder who had encouraged a young Matthew's early sketches and had even, unforgettably, adopted his very first innovative space-storage plan for the Surrey convalescent home. The same Peter Corder who, more than anyone, had helped him get through the aftermath of his mother's death when he'd just reached the magic age of twenty-one and had joined Compass Designs.

A very different 'Compass' in those days. Whose founder, Stanley Crane, had engaged him on the strength of his sketching skills to make up a team of seven in his company which was specialising in the design and sale of kitchens. With all the vigour of untried youth, he had enthusiastically emerged himself in both activities. Then had come the visit to the home of a prospective client, the wife of a dairy farmer, who had wanted her kitchen completely redesigned. As the dairy farming husband had stood in the kitchen observing the space being transformed on Matthew's sketch pad, he'd wryly remarked that if he could as easily do the same to his cattle-feed processing system, he'd double his production.

He had asked to take a look while the farmer's wife studied the sketches he'd made of the proposed new kitchen design. The farmer had humoured him, whilst commenting, "It will take more than a sketch pad to put my feeding sheds to rights, and probably more money than I can afford."

He had firstly sketched what he'd seen, before going back to the car for the camera he always travelled with. When he'd taken the shots he wanted, he'd told the farmer he would give it some thought, free of charge. He'd said nothing to Stanley Crane, and had used a week's spare time meticulously sketching till he'd been completely satisfied. Then he'd spoken to some people unconnected to 'Compass'.

When he had gone back to the farmer and had shown him the results, the man had shaken his head in disbelief at the way Matthew had cleverly redesigned the positioning of the existing machinery parts. Thus creating space which he had also re-planned functionally. Alongside his plans of the newly structured feed-process system, he'd presented production ratio figures which had shown throughput could be increased by thirty-five percent over the existing system.

"How did you arrive at these figures?" the farmer had asked incredulously.

"I took my pictures," Matthew had replied, "of your existing system to the National Farmers' Union. From their records of your dairy stock, they calculated your likely throughput using your current system. Then I showed them my redesigned system which, by the way, they confirmed would work. Their revised figures are what you see now."

The farmer had shaken his head again before saying, "I could possibly memorise these sketches of yours. Enough to make a difference, maybe. What makes you believe I won't cheat you? Say No to you now, and copy out what I can remember when you've gone?"

"You won't do that," Matthew had confidently replied.

"But what makes you so sure?" the farmer had pressed.

Matthew had grinned whilst responding, "Because then your wife wouldn't get the kitchen I've shown her she can have. Do you really think you could handle that?"

The farmer had roared with laughter. "No, I certainly could not. Any more than I'd cheat you, youngster. We've got a deal, provided of course I can afford it. What will it cost?"

"I haven't shown it to my firm, yet," he'd confessed.

"When you do," the farmer had said, "come back to me and we'll take it from there."

Then he had told Stanley Crane. Who had taken a deep fiscal breath and had memorably made the decision to back a young horse. They had managed to take only a small profit from that chance beginning, and a youngster's ingenuity...

Matthew sipped at his brandy, the action bringing the memory tape to a halt and his thoughts back into the present. Not that he would ever forget his dairy farmer encounter. From that chance beginning the company had expanded into the agricultural space-design market. Along the way, adding their own space to house the new fabrication workshops. Factory and office space designs had naturally followed, and Compass Designs had quickly established the reputation for excellence which had attracted the talented designers and computer graphics specialists, along with the skilled engineers and carpenters, the innovative marketing team, and a sales force which had more than doubled turnover under their dynamic Sales Director. He smiled now at the fact that two *Queen's Award for Industry* plaques now occupied pride of place on the walls of Stanley Crane's boardroom.

He pulled his gaze away from Alicia's garden and made an effort to rein in his thoughts. The passing years had claimed so many people; changed so many things. Stanley Crane was now Chairman of a 'forty-strong' company that Matthew, as its Managing Director, was poised to take into a European merger. Providing of course they could overcome the objections of some of the French company's management. Not to mention plugging the leak within his own boardroom. He consulted his wristwatch; *Seven fifty-five;* and considered the decanter again. *'Preferable to the dentist,'* he decided silently. The doorbell pre-empted his pouring and he moved in response.

Leading his guest back into the lounge, he indicated the wooden box Andrew was carrying,

"What have you got there, duelling pistols?"

Andrew Teale's response was a nervous sounding laugh and a question, "No Alicia?"

"She's at her gardening club meeting. Comparing green fingers, or whatever it is that they do," he paused to wave Andrew into a chair, "Drink?"

"Something soft will do, thanks."

"Anyhow," resumed Matthew, watching the wooden box being carefully positioned at the solicitor's feet, "You said on the phone last night that you wanted a *private* chat."

"Yes, yes I did," agreed Andrew, accepting his drink with a tight smile and waiting till Matthew was settled in his chair before adding, "You look a bit frazzled."

"Bloody toothache," explained Matthew, grimacing, abruptly adding, "Is this anything to do with the merger?"

"No... No it's personal," replied Andrew, "To you, I mean," he added quickly, then, seeing his host's brow furrow, he set his drink down and picked up the wooden box as he continued, "There are however," he paused to select his words with care, "*elements* of the personal which *could* be brought to bear on the merger. Should you choose to do so," he ended quietly.

"What do you mean by personal?" challenged Matthew.

"Let me try to explain," responded Andrew, clutching the box as he gathered his thoughts.

He began with his account of the clearing out of Jonathan's office, and his subsequent discovery of the wooden box. Explained how he'd taken the box home in the natural belief it had held something his father had been dealing with which might have required further attention. Explained how Jenny, whom Matthew fortunately knew to be discreet, had read and had organized the revealed contents of the box.

He ended by stressing the importance of the material being read in the order which Jenny had marked out, telling Matthew it would hopefully help him to understand the motivations which had led to the decisions made by the various people concerned.

"What the hell have you got in there?" asked a clearly agitated Matthew.

"A variety of written material," responded Andrew, resorting to the stiffly formal language he was comfortable with during *un*comfortable scenarios, "All of which relates to the past. Letters and diary journals, mainly. The journals contain extremely detailed entries, which are vividly informative of the periods during which they were written."

Andrew paused, took a deep breath, and added quietly, "The diaries evidently belonged to your late mother." Instantly seeing his client's body language signalling its surprise, Andrew continued quickly before Matthew could speak, "My father obviously made a decision many years ago to withhold this material from you. But when you've read it all, you may understand why." He held up a hand to stop his client's clearly intended outburst, "I'm almost finished Matthew, bear with me, please. *I've* read the material as your solicitor, and, from a commercial as well as a personal standpoint, and given the changed times and circumstances, I've been able to reach a different decision to the one my father made so long ago." He paused to ensure he had eye contact, "It wasn't an easy decision to make, Matthew, there is information in this box which you are obviously unaware of. Information which you will undoubtedly find distressing."

He leant forward and passed the wooden box to a now bewildered looking client, "Jenny and I will of course respect the confidence which the personal element demands, but should your own interpretation of the commercial significance agree with *mine*, then you will presumably need to discuss that with me later." Once more pre-empting any response, he rose from his chair whilst concluding firmly, "Now I think I should leave you to read in private. Don't get up, I'll see myself out." Leaving the room, he was aware of the bitter irony. He was leaving behind a man holding a box containing more pain than the toothache he'd had before *he* had arrived.

Left alone, his thoughts leapfrogging one another in their haste for supremacy, a bemused Matthew Sands opened the wooden box on his lap and extracted the listed sheet which came firstly to hand. The list bore a preface in Jenny Murray's immediately recognizable scrawl, which was *strongly* advising him to start his reading with the numbered diaries of Elizabeth Creacey, which he also recognized as his late mother's maiden name. He was to read the diaries up to Jenny's marker, then the numbered letters except the one marked *Returned Unread* , before returning to complete the diaries. He was *then* to read the letter marked *Returned Unread* before finally looking at the typed reports from *Ramsay & Shields,* a firm of private investigators.

Whilst holding Jenny Murray's instructions in one hand, and clutching the wooden box with his other hand, Matthew sat quite still as Andrew Teale's words churned around inside his toothache-ravaged head. Still trying to understand why the solicitor had presented those words in such a melodramatic manner, yet disturbingly aware that Andrew must have had a sound reason to behave as he *had* done. His tongue worried the offending tooth, and, surprised by its weight, he carefully laid the box on the floor alongside Jenny's listed commands before rising to pour himself another brandy.

'Only one way to find out what it's all about,' he told himself, and as he settled back down in his chair again he heard Alicia's key turn in the door. 'Why did he now always feel apprehensive whenever he heard that sound?' he wondered uselessly.

Alicia joined him in the lounge, seemingly in good spirits, brightly chattering as she mixed herself a drink. Smiling as she sat down opposite him, telling him about the latest exciting catalogue 'find' her club had been responsible for. Or some such thing; he rarely listened properly to her anymore and he watched her now with most of his mind still on Andrew's visit. She'd been twenty-nine when they'd married and the ten year age difference hadn't mattered to either of them, then. He wondered what she thought of it now. At thirty-seven she was still a strikingly attractive woman. Her dark hair was currently cut short, which made her face look fuller, and the cream-coloured sweater she was wearing over fawn slacks also had the effect of making her figure appear heavier than he knew it to be. He could still remember how she used to laugh and say she was built for speed...

"...have things to do," ended Alicia.

"I'm sorry," recovered Matthew, "What was that again?"

"I said, I can see you have things to do," she briskly repeated.

He hated these moments; seeing them now as tests she would occasionally subject him to. 'Does she or doesn't she mean if I had nothing to do, would I like to take her to bed? Answer required immediately, or forfeit the prize.'

Alicia stood suddenly, and Matthew knew he had failed the test. If indeed there had been one to pass. He wondered then, irrationally, he knew, why one of them always seemed to be leaving the other behind in a room. He also wondered, impatiently, what the hell it was, exactly, that Andrew Teale had brought to him in a wooden box.

"I'll go up, then," said Alicia, leaning down to kiss his forehead.

Refusing to allow what he realized was his probably unreasonable anger to surface with a remark about patting the dog, refusing the worm, he said goodnight to his wife and had opened the diary before she'd even left the room.

His guilty thoughts now nagging him along with his troublesome tooth, Matthew Sands began reading the first diary of Elizabeth Creacey.

Chapter Thirteen

Surprises are foolish things. The pleasure is not enhanced, and the inconvenience is often considerable.
(Jane Austen)

London, and Carshalton district of Surrey, England, Closing days of May... through to December 1944

For *'Creacey's Cavaliers'*, as Peter Corder had wryly entitled them, the month of May passed in a blur of blue skies; bonding encounters; bureaucratic battles, and surprises.

In London, on the 30th of May, one of those so-called Cavaliers took a phone call in his office and was astonished to hear the voice of his caller inviting him to lunch. Rampant curiosity vying with mild trepidation, Jonathan Teale accepted the invitation from Simon Rawlings.

They met on the neutral and expensively exclusive ground of Piccadilly's *'Gentlemen Only'* Marlborough Club, and the solicitor was suitably awed by the lushly furnished and carpeted retreat offering privacy and a food menu displaying discreetly acquired black market luxuries. The meal enjoyably consumed, upon reaching the 'post-fare' drinks stage Jonathan Teale found himself hanging on to every word emanating from the mouth of a proverbial gift horse.

Yet another Rawlings 'paperwork miracle' had seemingly been performed and this one had apparently produced the special licence being granted to Elizabeth Creacey's proposed convalescent home. *'A licence,'* it was quietly explained, *'which would enable Jonathan's client to cut through the red tape of local bureaucracy.'* Additionally, and coincidentally, Jonathan was confidentially informed (*or expected to believe,* he thought) the licence would be hand-delivered by *'A small team of fully equipped and skilled men*' her benefactor intended covertly 'diverting' from some un-named project to that of Jonathan's client.

"She'll have to house them and feed them, of course," Rawlings briskly qualified.

Jonathan's thoughts raced; *'Elizabeth had been vague about what she would need to carry out the predominantly internal work which was required.'*

"No problem," he told Rawlings, fervently hoping his client would share that judgement. "How many men make up a small team?" he asked fearfully.

"This particular team comprises four men," replied Rawlings, "and she can have them for four weeks. They will be led by a man named Carter, and they will arrive in Carshalton tomorrow. So please alert Miss Creacey."

Jonathan's thoughts merrily cantered on; *'Telephone lines have been disconnected in so many areas throughout the country, including parts of Surrey. I may not be able to reach her by phone so this is an excellent reason to see her again. She should be delighted by this news. So I could drive down this afternoon and...'* The voice of his host penetrated his speculation and anticipation, and he listened anew.

"Carter," resumed Rawlings, calmly, "will be able to get hold of some of the materials she will doubtless need. Which, as I'm sure you know, is no small feat these days."

Jonathan's thoughts now moved at the gallop; *'I am indeed only too aware of the difficulties facing countless numbers of people attempting to repair their bomb-damaged homes. Local authorities are doing their best to supply materials in the face of shortages, but even they couldn't conjure up 'special licences' and present them along with 'ready-made and equipped' teams of skilled men...'* His thoughts were exhausted, leaving him free to express the candour, "Why are you doing all this? And why are you not telling my client yourself?"

"I made a promise to Miss Creacey's late *fiancé,*" began Rawlings, pausing to shake his head before adding, "Which is all the answer you'll get to your first question."

Before he could react, Jonathan was suddenly aware of the transformation across the lunch table and across the face of Rawlings. The man was actually smiling!

"As for your second question," resumed Rawlings, "Call it recompense. This time instead of withholding information from her, you can be the bearer of glad tidings."

Jonathan's thoughts were already in free-fall when his host playfully added, "And besides, at our last meeting, I noticed how you looked at her, Mister Teale."

Whilst Jonathan Teale was embarrassedly but happily concluding his productive London lunch meeting with Simon Rawlings, in the sun-kissed grounds of 'Ridgeway House' the other three so-called Cavaliers were currently also being embarrassed. However *they* could find nothing to be happy about in the words they were hearing from one of the two local government officials they now faced.

"We can't even replace the glass in our *own* broken windows. *You've* only been here for five bloody minutes and you expect... "

"That will do, Shaw," interjected the other official before turning to Elizabeth, "Miss Creacey, I apologise for my colleague's language, and his manner."

The two officials represented Carshalton's town council and the apologist was the senior of the pair. He was a well-dressed, rotund and florid-faced man who'd earlier introduced himself as Arthur Arkwright and Elizabeth had calculated he was in his mid-fifties. She liked the sound of his wonderfully deep voice, and heard genuine regret as he continued speaking now.

"Your situation is currently impossible to resolve, Miss Creacey. We may be able to supply *some* of your needs, but the manpower and amount of equipment you require is simply not in my power to provide, *and*, for the most part, not even available locally."

Arkwright's face signalled his rising blood pressure as he warmed to his theme, "What you are proposing to do here is laudable, Miss Creacey, I'm not denying that fact, and I would really like to help you. But even if I knew *where* to get the beds, and everything else on your list, the council cannot afford to buy them. And besides, we neither of us have the transport to collect your requirements, and even if we *had* the transport, we don't have the fuel, *and*, in any event, *even if we had both* and could find volunteer drivers, they would probably get lost trying to circumnavigate the no-go areas." A now breathless Arthur Arkwright stopped to produce a handkerchief from a voluminous looking pocket and began mopping his brow.

Flanked by a stern-faced Mary Reynolds and a worried looking Peter Corder, Elizabeth was being confronted by the overweight figure of Arthur Arkwright for the first time and she instinctively liked the man. She admitted to herself that the same could not be said of his odious companion, the heavy-set and sour-faced Harold Shaw, a man she estimated to be in his thirties and who, over the past weeks, had been persistently unpleasant to her. She could now only nod to Arkwright her acknowledgement of the difficulties being presented. She already shared the town's 'Grapevine-fed' common knowledge of the civilian 'no-go' areas. *Areas,* said the 'Grapevine', *imposed and policed by the military as a consequence of the massive troop movements taking place countrywide.* Since it was also commonly assumed that, as with Carshalton, other places would have had their public telephones disconnected and seen their post-boxes sealed to prevent communication, the ever busy 'Grapevine' was collapsing under the growing weight of opinion that *The big push was underway at last!*

Elizabeth smiled sweetly at the perspiring official as she spoke, "It's so kind of you to express the wish that you could help us, Mister Arkwright. Naturally we understand the pressures *you*," she paused to include 'sour-face' in her smile, "and your colleague must be facing and the last thing *we* want to do is add to those pressures. On the contrary, as I explained to Mister Shaw on his very first visit, we can pay for our needs, and, as I also told him, should there be any way in which *we* might help *you* to... "

"Nobody asked for your help," came the snarled interruption, "We... "

"Really, Shaw!" interjected Arkwright, "that is quite... "

"I *do realize*, Mister Shaw," interrupted Elizabeth, firmly, retaining her smile with difficulty, "that no-one has actually *asked* for our help. Nevertheless the offer still stands. We should, I believe, help one another whenever we can during these troubled times."

"Quite so, Miss Creacey," responded Arkwright before rounding on his council colleague, "I'm bound to say, Shaw, that you owe Miss Creacey an apology, and myself an explanation."

Completely ignoring Arkwright's appeal to manners and explanations, the burly Shaw responded by directing a frighteningly malevolent glare at Elizabeth. He then abruptly turned on his heel and stormed off in the direction of the automobile which had earlier brought the two men on their official business.

In the ensuing brief silence Shaw had disturbingly left behind him, the sweet sound of birdsong filling the air suddenly seemed incongruous. The remaining group wordlessly watched the man climb into the waiting car and clearly saw and heard the door being violently closed behind him.

"There goes a troubled man," Peter Corder said, quietly.

"You mean, there goes trouble," said Mary Reynolds.

"He's not going anywhere, actually," announced Arthur Arkwright, "Not without me. Fact of the matter is, the man can't drive."

Peter Corder led the quietly responsive chuckles which instantly relieved some of the tension within the quartet. "If he likes throwing his weight around, why isn't he putting his aggression to good use in the armed forces?" queried Peter.

"Ah, sore point that," responded Arkwright, "His father has a bit of clout in high places. So, *Hey Presto,* the son is medically unfit for service."

"Which explains a lot," acknowledged Peter.

"Oh stop being so Freudian, Peter," remonstrated Mary, "A bully is a bully."

"This is so embarrassing," resumed Arkwright, "He led me to believe you were more or less demanding we not only supply your needs, but pay for them as well. And as you've observed, he's obviously a bit of a hothead."

"It is *your* hot head I'm more concerned about, Mister Arkwright," declared Elizabeth, surprising only two of the assembly before continuing with a smile, "Have you had your blood pressure checked recently?"

Clearly taken aback by the question, the man could only manage in reply, "Well, No. Never really thought about it."

"It's time you did," announced Mary Reynolds in complete awareness, "You can be our very first patient, Mister Arkwright," she told him, stepping forward to link arms with the surprised man, "And don't you worry," she added cheerfully, "I haven't killed anyone for weeks now."

"You lie, Reynolds," cried Peter Corder, "I haven't seen the gardener for two days."

"Ignore them, Mister Arkwright," advised Elizabeth with a smile, "We haven't even *got* a gardener to lose, and checking you blood pressure will only take a few minutes while you say hello to Matthew."

"Thank you... Miss Creacey," replied Arkwright, allowing himself to be steered towards the house as he returned Elizabeth's smile with the question, "Matthew?"

"My baby son," she qualified, pausing to meet his gaze as she added, "And if we are going to be friends, you must call me Elizabeth."

They had reached the front door of the house and Mary Reynolds, in the act of leading Arkwright inside, was stopped in her tracks by her colleague's forwardness. Beside her, Peter Corder's eyebrows reached for the sky, whilst the council official was observing Elizabeth with a bemused expression on his reddened face.

"I would imagine," continued Elizabeth into the awkward silence, "that this community will have its share of those servicemen and women coming home with a need of the services we will be providing here. So we will find ourselves working together, you and I, and that will be much easier if we can be friends," she ended, smiling serenely and leading the quartet inside.

Ahead of them stretched a long corridor, off which several doors could be seen. On either side of the hallway where they now stood, a grand staircase horse-shoed its way to the upper landing and Arkwright waved a hand around to encompass their surroundings as his enigmatic words commanded the attention of his audience.

"Must be something about this place which invites familiarity."

As Elizabeth and her colleagues were each puzzling over Arkwright's words, the man proceeded to add to their confusion.

"Now, as I recall, on the upper floor you've got two bathrooms and two toilets, and eight or ten bedrooms. And on the ground floor here, you've got a large kitchen, two bathrooms, two toilets, a lounge, a library room, another eight or ten bedrooms if you count the old servant's quarters, and two other rooms, I believe."

Arkwright smiled at his thoughtfully silent audience before continuing, "This house was scheduled for requisition by the army in early '39 and I was sent out here with one of their top brass to corroborate an inventory." He paused to scratch his chin, "Hence my little knowledge being presented like a shopping list."

"Risking the obvious observation," said Peter, "The top brass hat changed his mind."

"Had it changed for him, more like," replied Arkwright with a chuckle, "I remember a pretty forceful visit from a chap named Rawlings and *Hey Presto* the top brass man disappeared and a new owner arrived on the scene. A woman."

Arkwright used the pause to find Elizabeth's eyes with his own as he continued, "Which brings me back to familiarity linked to *this* place. The first woman," he paused, his eyes twinkling at Elizabeth, "and the only one up until now to be so direct with me, was a French woman who stood in this very hallway insisting I use her Christian name of Chantal."

Seemingly oblivious to the mix of facial expressions around him, Arkwright added, "Lovely woman she was too."

Quite aware of the perplexed looks emanating from Mary and Peter, Elizabeth stared at the council official as her thoughts demanded to be put into words. "You knew Chantal?"

"Heavens, No," replied Arkwright, shaking his head, "Can't say I *knew* her, but when she bought this place I met her here. Can't recall why, now," he confessed, scratching his chin again, "May have had something to do with the history of the place," he ended.

"I can hear Matthew, Elizabeth," said Mary Reynolds, "and if we're going to check your blood pressure, Mister Arkwright, we should be getting on with it," she ended firmly.

"Right you are," acquiesced Arkwright, grinning as he added, "Mustn't be *too* long, though, because you *do* know you've got the wrong man here. Shaw's blood pressure is probably going through the roof of the car as we speak."

Curbing her impatience to question the man further, Elizabeth smiled at him as she spoke. "You're probably right, Mister Arkwright, but it really won't take long. You go with Mary and Doctor Corder and I'll bring Matthew along to see you in a moment or two."

"Oh look here," said Arkwright, smiling broadly now, "You're quite right about dispensing with formality. So *I* will happily agree to address you as Elizabeth if *you'll* likewise agree to call me Arthur. How about that?"

"Very well, Arthur," acknowledged Elizabeth with a warm smile, "Now off you go before Mary breaks your arm."

Elizabeth watched the man being led away. He would, she knew, be taken to what had been designated as a future treatment room. Still preoccupied by the unanswered questions in her head, she hurried off to where she had earlier left Matthew sleeping peacefully in his cot.

A little while later, with Matthew's napkin changed, having made the decision to feed him once Arthur Arkwright had gone, with a head still bursting with questions and arm muscles protesting at Matthew's weight, Elizabeth rejoined the council official and her colleagues in attendance. As she entered the treatment room, the patently unfit Arkwright was rolling down his shirtsleeve and Mary was carefully replacing the Sphygmomanometer she had used to record the blood pressure readings.

"He's one hundred and eighty-nine over eighty-seven," announced Mary, "and I've told him I won't need to kill him, because he's doing a fine job of it all by himself."

"Lovely bedside manner you have there, Reynolds," chided Peter.

"He smokes too much," declared Mary, ignoring Peter and adding, "Likes his fatty foods, and doesn't get enough exercise."

"But the wicked witch is right, Mister Arkwright," said Peter, "So listen, and live longer."

"Well," responded Arkwright, busy struggling to re-cloak his corpulent frame with his jacket, "At least I know where to come when I need cheering up."

The man's dry humour once again elicited an instant response, this time in the form of laughter surprisingly led by Mary Reynolds. Arkwright then jovially advanced a podgy finger for Matthew to clasp in his tiny hand.

"A fine looking baby you have here, Elizabeth," complimented Arkwright with a smile.

"Yes, he is," she replied, striving to retain an air of normality, silently wishing she could just detain this man for questioning. Then Peter's voice, signalling surprise, was saying, "Hello, look who's here."

Through the open doorway of the treatment room, Elizabeth could see the figure of Jonathan Teale approaching along the corridor. The solicitor had seen her, and was coming towards her with a purposeful stride and a beaming countenance.

"Wonderful news, Elizabeth," called Jonathan whilst still on his approach.

Elizabeth saw the solicitor break stride and lose his smile when Arkwright made himself visible in the treatment room's doorway.

"Oh, I'm sorry," said Jonathan, "I didn't realize... "

"Quite all right, young man," said Arkwright, "I'm just leaving. I've taken up far too much of Miss Creacey's time already."

As Elizabeth saw Jonathan come to an awkward halt outside the doorway, Arkwright turned to Mary Reynolds and was smiling as he addressed her.

"Thank you, Nurse, for the treatment, and the good advice. I will endeavour to obey."

"Arthur," said Elizabeth, managing to smile whilst silently cursing Jonathan's timing, "This is Jonathan Teale, my solicitor. Jonathan, this is Arthur Arkwright. He represents our local council."

The two men exchanged handshakes and polite nods of the head, whilst Elizabeth told herself there was no way now that she could invite Arkwright back without being overheard or misunderstood. If she was going to find out what else he might remember about Chantal, she would have to engineer another meeting for another time.

"Well, goodbye then, Elizabeth, " said Arthur Arkwright, "For now, at any rate. If I find that there *is* some way I can help, I'll be in touch."

"Goodbye, Arthur," said Elizabeth, "You will be welcome here anytime."

Then Arkwright was gone and Jonathan Teale was rapidly gaining her full attention as the import of his news got through to her.

"Our Mister Shaw won't be too happy about a special licence," pronounced Peter.

As Elizabeth led the way into the kitchen with her declared intent to prepare Matthew's feed, Peter Corder's solemnly delivered conclusion to Jonathan Teale's news refused to clear itself from her crowded thoughts.

Chapter Fourteen

Who is the happy warrior? Who is he whom every man
in arms should wish to be?
(Wordsworth)

Saturday 31ˢᵗ May 1944

The last day of May was only four hours old in the County of
Surrey when the camouflaged army truck slowly coasted to a halt
on the darkened driveway of Carshalton's 'Ridgeway House'.

Early risers within the feathered fraternity chattered their
individual versions of 'salute the morning', whilst down-wind of
the now stationary vehicle a prowling dog-fox warily flattened
himself to the ground as he saw four shapes with the scent of
man detach themselves from the thing which now stood between
him and his den. The shapes moved towards some trees before
stopping and the animal saw the steam as its nostrils registered
another familiar scent. The four shapes then moved back to meld
with the thing which had brought them here, and only then did
the fox rise to pad silently in search of a safer way home.

Already closing their eyes in anticipation of two hours sleep,
the two Frenchmen, *Laporte* and *Chevalier,* were in the back of
the truck wordlessly wriggling into their sleeping bags. *Laporte,* a
leanly tall and darkly handsome man in his thirties, was a skilled
Carpenter by trade. *'A man with the hands of an angel and the
eyes of the devil'* was how, in pre-war days, he had been described
by those *Parisienne* mothers who had foolishly allowed their
daughters to accompany them when browsing to buy a *Laporte*
creation to grace their homes. Those same angelic hands which
had deftly disrobed *Parisienne* daughters as skilfully as they'd
brought inanimate wood to life in the form of elegant furniture,
had spent the past five years fashioning quite different creations.

Laporte's explosive devices had been used to devastating effect against his country's invaders.

Chevalier, Jewish by birth and Structural Engineer by profession, had reached his ripe old age of forty-two summers only because some years before he'd set eyes on the truck within which he now lay, thanks to a woman named Chantal he had narrowly evaded another kind of truck on its way to Auschwitz.

Both Frenchmen lay now in British army uniforms, in the back of a British truck on English soil, because two weeks ago they had been chosen from the several who had stepped forward in a *Bordeaux* farmhouse cellar in response to a call for volunteers.

The Welshman and the Englishman were slouched in the front cabin of the truck; both wearing British battledress proclaiming them to be serving with the Royal Corps of Signals. Sergeant's stripes authoritatively adorned the tunic sleeves of the powerfully built Welshman named Glyn Parish, whilst on each shoulder of the Englishman's slim frame was a dullish-bronze crown denoting the rank of Major. The Englishman named Carter had lost the toss to decide who would grab an hour's sleep first, so he was currently awake.

Even seated and asleep, the Welshman looked ferocious. Still remembered by his former regiment of Fusiliers as *'Parish the Power',* the British Military Police report of a 1942 incident in the bar of a famous London hotel, had been responsible for bringing him to the attention of *Special Operations Executive* and Simon Rawlings. The MP's report had dryly stated that the Welshman had single-handedly taken on a group of rowdy American soldiers (reportedly eight) who had been behaving abusively to elderly bar staff and female guests of the hotel. *'Some of the Yanks just bounced off him and he swatted the others like flies'* had been the statement of one awestruck witness. Striking a deal which had salvaged wounded American pride, Rawlings had arranged for all mention of the incident to be expunged from the records and had spirited the Welsh warrior away to where his talents could be put to more advantageous use.

The twenty-eight year old 'Parish the Power' had been a builder in peace-time, but for the past two years had been Carter's 'right hand man' in war-torn France. It had been there that the

Welshman's other skill, that of 'Scrounger', had come to the fore. Time and again, when others had gone before and failed, Glyn Parish had demonstrated his ability to sniff out and 'liberate' urgently needed material. Consistently emerging triumphantly laden from places nobody else would even have thought of or would even have dared to look.

Beside the sleeping warrior in the front cabin of the truck, was the twenty-nine year old *Protégé* of the late Jack Matthews; the man to whom both he and *Laporte* owed their lives. Carter had been a musician in his previously peaceful life, but it had been his talent for languages which had drawn him into the war-time net cast by Simon Rawlings. It had been Carter's subsequently discovered man-management skills, surprisingly coupled with sheer ruthlessness, which had attracted the patronage of Jack Matthews.

One side of Carter's face bore the scars to remind him daily of how close he'd come to losing the life which Jack Matthews had saved, and he subconsciously scratched there as he idly wondered what kind of woman Elizabeth Creacey would turn out to be. Abandoning what he realized was needless speculation, and to keep himself awake, he began roughly paraphrasing in his mind the specific briefing he'd been given by Rawlings for this operation.

'A clandestine operation in his own country was, he knew, breaking all the rules. So he was illegally kicking off an operation already riddled with aspects which were, to put it politely, frustratingly devoid of explanation. He and his team had four weeks before being parachuted back into France. Whilst they were here, and to the best of their abilities, they were to use their considerable skills to provide Miss Elizabeth Creacey with whatever she required. Before leaving France they'd been told of Elizabeth Creacey's relationship to Jack Matthews, but, had it not been for Chevalier's emotional disclosure, they might never have known of the connection between Jack and Chantal. That piece of news had been a stunner. Chantal had been one of their best, and, in retrospect, Jack had obviously been a chip off the same incredible block.'

Carter sighed with his afterthought; *'And as if all that hadn't been enough to chew on, before driving down here Rawlings had taken them aside, given them that glacial look of his, and ordered that Elizabeth Creacey was not, under any circumstances, to be informed of the role which Jack Matthews and his mother had performed within SOE. Neither were they to reveal the fact of their own membership of the organization.'*

The Englishman consciously deflected his restless fingers away from his scarred face, allowing them instead to find his tunic pocket which held the envelope containing the special licence for Elizabeth Creacey. *'Albeit a devious bastard by necessity, Rawlings had surpassed himself this time'* thought the weary Carter.

Unable to completely fathom the reasons behind the restrictions imposed upon him by Rawlings; Carter quietly emitted another sigh of frustration into the darkened cabin beside the slumbering Welshman, knowing he probably wouldn't be able to sleep when Parish woke up. He settled back in his seat to wait for daylight, suddenly impatient for his first sighting of the woman who had caused a man like Simon Rawlings to initiate such an extraordinary operation.

The dormant artistic part of the man named Carter silently admitted to himself in the dark, that he was also anxious to finally see the woman who had captured the heart and mind of a man such as Jack Matthews.

Despite the way he felt, he couldn't very well complain about it. After all, *he had* elected to fill the first slot in their organized domestic rota. So, at 6am. on the last day of May, accompanied by his unholy trinity of melancholia, misgivings, and knee-ache, Peter Corder yawned as he blearily confronted his image in the bathroom mirror. Routinely preparing to shave, he was again reminded that the past weeks had seemingly dissolved as rapidly as had his soap ration.

The morning discomfort of his aching knee was nothing new, and by itself was insufficient to cause his current state of mind, and he wearily reflected now on the thoughts which last night had robbed him of untroubled sleep, inducing under the skin of his normally cheerful persona the debilitating feelings of melancholy and misgivings.

The melancholy, he knew, stemmed from the realization that whilst Elizabeth Creacey seemed perfectly content to include him in her ambitious plans for the future, that inclusion was firmly embedded in professional practicality. Yesterday she had quietly announced her intention to name this place the Chantal Cheval convalescent home, and to make it the first of several such homes in England. The route to her arrival at the name Chantal Cheval, had finally been explained to him. Describing the role she hoped he would play in her plans, she had in effect been offering him the kind of professional future his wildest dreams could never have conjured. So she had certainly been outlining a relationship between them; it just hadn't been the kind he'd romantically entertained when he'd agreed to follow her to here.

'Sure, she likes me,' ran his thoughts, *'But will she ever share a bathroom with me?'*

His misgivings were, he considered, a natural but no less unsettling extension of his melancholy. In coming here he had allowed his head to follow his heart, and was now trying to belatedly rationalise his decision to do so alongside his current feelings. Because the Elizabeth Creacey he now found himself with, was different from the one he'd known at Bart's. It was as if her change of fortune had unlocked hitherto hidden depths of character, revealing a woman he felt even more drawn towards, bringing her tantalisingly closer in some respects whilst somehow distancing her in ways he was still struggling to comprehend.

A now sluiced and clean-shaven Peter Corder vacated the bathroom with clear-headed conclusions. The additional factor of the child had, he knew, made him realize there was little space in Elizabeth Creacey's life for the kind of personal relationship which he had hoped to engender. He would, therefore, take full advantage of a golden opportunity to participate in a venture which promised to make a positive difference to the quality of care offered to those returning from far-flung battlefields. There had been no 'hands to hold' of late, but that would change soon enough. Time and circumstance could change many things. They might even change again, the relationship between himself and Elizabeth Creacey.

As imaginatively entitled by Peter Corder in the wake of his cosmetic restructuring endeavours, the *'creatively transformed three-bed-roomed cottage'* situated at the rear of the main house and separated from it by an untidy rectangle of over-grown lawn, currently housed baby Matthew in addition to Elizabeth Creacey and two of her so-called Cavaliers.

It was here, at 6-15am. on the last day of May, fresh from his napkin change, that Matthew lay on his cot gurgling in anticipation as Elizabeth warmed his morning feed on the small gas stove she shared with Mary Reynolds. The main body of the L-shaped room occupied by mother and child, was taken up by Elizabeth's single divan bed which stood along one wall within sight and easy reach of the child's cot which resided along the opposite wall. A presently closed doorway between bed-head and cot accessed the lounge; one of the five doors leading off the lounge area. The other four comprised; the front door of the annexed cottage; one to the only bathroom; one to the kitchen; and one to Peter Corder's bedroom.

A few paces away from the end of Elizabeth's bed, a window offered a view of woodland shrouded now in morning mist. Beneath the window stood a table upon which rested a telephone, a reading lamp, some scattered sheets of paper depicting numerous lists and scribbled notes, the framed head and shoulders sketch of Jack Matthews, and Elizabeth's current diary journal. To the left of the window, tucked into the tail of the L-shape and hidden from the sleeping area, a small sink stood beside the equally proportioned stove which an already dressed Elizabeth was using. To the left of where she stood was the toilet cubicle she also shared with Mary. The two-door cubicle accessed the tiny space which, courtesy of Peter's inventiveness, was being used by Mary as a bedroom. Presumed to have been a storeroom in its former life, it boasted its own small window granting a partial view of the driveway to the main house.

It was from the adjoining cubicle door that Elizabeth's friend now emerged still clad in pyjamas and bearing news.

"There are four soldiers having a brew-up beside their truck in the driveway."

"Matthew still has to be fed," responded Elizabeth, calmly adding, "So the British army will just have to wait."

"You're already dressed, I see. Did you beat Peter to the bathroom?"

"I just couldn't sleep," explained Elizabeth, "So I got up to update my diary. It was cold, so I had a quick wash here at the sink and then got dressed."

"Have you had anything to eat?"

"Attending to His Lordship first."

"I could do that, if you like," offered Mary, smothering a yawn, "If you want to welcome our visiting party before they break down the door in search of food."

"I would imagine they've brought their own rations."

"Yes, Elizabeth," said Mary, smiling to soften the reproach, "And we can probably both imagine how much they might enjoy something cooked in a proper kitchen."

Mary paused, her quick appraising look a mixture of envy and concern. Her friend, she enviously observed, still somehow managed to look good in a shapeless woollen sweater and baggy trousers which fell to flat canvas shoes on her feet. Devoid of make-up, and with her long dark hair pulled back and held by a snood, she looked even younger than usual.

'Vulnerable looking', thought Mary. Her concern for Elizabeth, who was now testing Matthew's bottle-feed on her arm, wasn't just in regard to the woman's seeming indifference to any suggestion that she might find love again with another man. It was also the thought that Elizabeth's new-found wealth, coupled with her single-minded focus on professional objectives, would, even if one came along, make it very difficult for her to recognize the genuine man from the fortune hunter. Pushing aside her concern, she voiced an afterthought.

"And they certainly won't have a bathroom on their truck."

"You're right, of course," responded Elizabeth, "As usual," she added, sticking her tongue out at Mary as she passed her the bottle-feed in acquiescence, "Okay, you do Matthew, please, and I'll go out to them. And to salve the Reynolds conscience, I'll even offer them breakfast."

"If I know His Lordship," said Mary, moving towards Matthew's cot whilst smiling to herself at Elizabeth's naturally assumed air of authority, "he'll have finished this before you can even get out the door." She giggled suddenly before adding, "So *I* should be able to use the bathroom before *you* return with our very own private army."

Stifling an involuntary yawn, Elizabeth didn't respond to Mary's humour. Suddenly feeling peeved at being deprived of the pleasure she derived from personally feeding Matthew, she made her way through the connecting door to the lounge area and from there exited the cottage. Outside, she was momentarily stopped in her tracks by the crisply cold air penetrating her clothing to reach tired limbs and muscles. The tiredness reminding her that yet another night had passed with her never having been completely relaxed; her mind and body were always alert now to the slightest movement in the cot beside her bed. Throughout all her Surrey nights thus far, since leaving Knightsbridge and the supportive Mrs Bruce, a part of her never slept. She stood still now, unable to stop the smile forming, feeling utterly exhausted and simultaneously refreshed by the cold air kissing her face, perfectly aware of the fact that she was secretly revelling in the new-found role of motherhood and all its aspects; including the sacrificial ones.

She began moving, savouring the morning freshness, her eyes watering, feeling the skin tighten on her face, feeling good to be alive. Awakened by the cold, her sharpening senses were now taking in her immediate environment, *and* the suddenly remembered fact that she had forgotten to check her appearance in a mirror before leaving. Silently rejecting the idea of going back to check, telling herself there was absolutely no reason why she should pander to vanity at *this* hour, she continued walking to her intended rendezvous point.

The ground level mist which had earlier surrounded the cottage was slowly disappearing and she could see now the grass glistening with dew on a more direct route to the front of the house. Opting to keep her footwear dry, she decided to use the path which she knew wound its way round a small copse before linking up with the area of driveway where the soldiers had been spotted by Mary.

Negotiating the path, a part of her mind was on Simon Rawlings and this latest entirely unexpected and extraordinary development brought about by the man. Yesterday's attempt to reach him by phone had failed, and she made a mental note to try again today. But most of her mind was still largely preoccupied with thoughts of Matthew. Feeding him herself had become an important part of her daily routine, and already she felt emotionally dislocated by being forced to miss out on even one of what had become valued bonding sessions between them.

'Am I over-reacting?' she silently wondered. 'Something else I can discuss with Jack', responded the voice in her head.

She was perfectly aware of the fact that her diary had become almost a daily crutch, but, employing the ever present voice of reason, she'd also privately concluded that it was a useful tool. By conversing with Jack through her diary, she had on occasions found herself re-thinking her way through problems from a different and often more positive perspective.

The sudden sighting of the four soldiers jolted her out of the reverie, and she saw one of them detach himself from the quartet and come towards her. A few paces still separated them when she heard his voice calling its introductory greeting.

"Good morning. My men and I are here to see Miss Elizabeth Creacey."

The tone of vocal delivery surprised her. Sounding completely at odds with the present setting, *and* his appearance, the softly delivered and casually drawled words had sounded warm and relaxed. 'As if he was attending a social function' thought Elizabeth. Her tired eyes registered the reddened skin around the scars on one side of his face; the decidedly unmilitary looking long hair, and the shoulder crowns and insignia proclaiming the man's rank of Major in The Royal Corps of Signals. A memory of Jack *thought-flashed* and was gone as the man, who wasn't as tall as Jack had been, stopped directly in front of her. She saw quizzical blue eyes regarding her from the damaged face which smiled as he extended a hand towards her.

"My name is Carter. Hope we didn't wake you."

Two sensations instantly struck Elizabeth, rendering her momentarily speechless. The first was the toughened skin of the hand now clasping her own in a handshake. The second was the unmistakable smell of mothballs emanating from his remarkably new looking uniform. Memories of Jack now flooded her mind; *The smell of his uniform when they'd danced together. The feel of his hands on her skin... not the hands of a paper shuffler...*

"Are you okay...? Miss...?"

"Yes," replied Elizabeth, thankfully finding her voice, "Yes I'm fine, thank you. I'm sorry, for a moment you reminded me of someone." She paused, summoning up a smile as she resumed, "And No, you didn't wake me and you've found the person you came here to see. My name is Elizabeth Creacey."

She saw the blue eyes widen with unconcealed surprise as he responded.

"Rawlings said you were a Nurse, but he forgot to mention you're a... "

She now saw the embarrassment on his face as he broke off abruptly before visibly recovering himself to continue.

"Let me introduce you to my men, Miss Creacey."

She moved alongside him, wondering what he'd stopped himself from saying, wondering what Simon Rawlings had forgotten to mention. The words were out before she could stop them. "Rawlings forgot to mention I'm a... what, Major Carter?" She heard his softly mouthed *'Me and my big mouth'* at the same time as she became aware of the other three soldiers coming towards them. All three were bareheaded, she noticed. Carter's *sotto voce* words had obviously travelled to keen ears, she realized, because the powerful looking one of the fast approaching trio was grinning as his deep melodious voice reached out to her.

"Put his foot in it already, has he, Miss?"

Elizabeth thought the combination of barrel chest, a seeming absence of neck, and close-cropped hair on his solid looking skull made the speaker look quite ferocious. But his grin was infectious and she felt herself return it as she replied, "It would seem so."

"Miss Creacey," began Carter, his theatrical sigh signalling mock formality, "This charming Welsh Gorilla in uniform is Sergeant Parish."

"Miss Creacey, is it?" said the Sergeant whilst proffering a massive hand to Elizabeth, "Pleased to meet you, Miss, and Rawlings probably forgot to mention that you're beautiful," he smilingly ended.

She felt the blush suffuse her face and was still wondering how to respond when, with an unmistakeable French accent, the older looking of the other two soldiers spoke.

"We are teaching the Welshman the charm, *Mademoiselle*, but alas his technique is, how do you say...? Desiring?"

"*Wanting,* Maurice," corrected Carter, "The word you seek is, *Wanting.*" He turned to Elizabeth, continuing his introductions with a wry looking smile, "Miss Creacey, this ageing charm instructor is Sergeant *Chevalier*, and the ugly quiet one beside him is Sergeant *Laporte.*"

Elizabeth smiled and shook hands with *Chevalier*. Of medium height, the podgy middle-aged looking individual sported an obviously swollen nose set in a chubby-cheeked face. A face nevertheless wearing an amiable smile as he bobbed his uncovered head of thinning hair and acknowledged her with politely spoken French.

"*Enchanté, Mademoiselle*"

Refraining from commenting upon Carter's clearly misleading description of the next soldier, she made to shake hands with *Laporte* and almost gasped with the memory of Jack as her hand was raised to brush the man's lips. His breath was warm on her skin as he delivered his words, and once again she heard the captivating French accent stroking the English language.

"Rawlings could not have described such beauty as yours, *Mademoiselle.*"

"So you can see now, Miss," growled the Welshman, "who the charmer really is. Give the lady her hand back, lover boy."

Elizabeth's hand was promptly released by a mock-pouting *Laporte* , who winked an eye at her as he did so.

"As you have now observed, Miss Creacey," drawled Carter, "we are not, perhaps, what you might have been told to expect." He paused, a smile forming on the scarred face, "But don't be disheartened, Miss Creacey, or allow yourself to be misled by appearances. What stands before you, does so willingly. Every

'Man-Jack' of us volunteered to help you, and that's exactly what we'll do."

Elizabeth now saw that following Carter's declaration of intent, there was a perceptible stillness in the men she faced. She could feel their collective gaze on her as she considered her response, whilst the unspoken questions crowded her mind. *'Had he deliberately used the phrase 'Every Man-Jack'? Why have they volunteered to be here? Why are they all wearing brand new uniforms? And why are three of them bearing the rank of Sergeant?* Suddenly remembering her manners, she decided to shelve her questions.

"Well whatever your reasons," she carefully opened, "for *choosing* to be here, I thank you all for coming. I can certainly use some help." She paused to look directly at Carter before continuing, "I've been unable to make contact with Major Rawlings, but he did pass the message that you could obtain some of what we need here." She stopped, aware of Carter's disconcerting blue-eyed stare, suddenly wishing she'd dressed differently, and she shifted her gaze to the Welshman as she resumed, "Although I cannot imagine how you would propose to do what everyone is telling me can't be done."

"Where there's a Welshman, there's a way," said the grinning Sergeant Parish.

Elizabeth returned his infectious grin with one of her own as she resumed, "Anyway, I imagine you four could use a cooked breakfast this morning."

"*Sacre Bleu,* we are in heaven," cried *Chevalier* as he raised his arms skywards.

"She certainly looks like an angel to *me*, Boyo," said a still grinning Parish.

Elizabeth laughed, already warming to the Welshman, stepping forward and linking arms with the clearly surprised but delighted looking man as she spoke, "And since you wonderful men have come here to help me, I insist that you address me as Elizabeth."

"No sooner insisted upon than done, Elizabeth," responded the still grinning Welshman.

"You cannot," said Carter, his tone conveying mock-horror, "let this lot loose on your breakfast rations. We've brought our own in the truck, so we can pool resources."

"Pool resources, is it?" said the Welshman, gently squeezing Elizabeth's arm as he added, "That's why he's the officer, Elizabeth, he's full of excellent ideas. He just needs us to implement them, and in this case I think one of our French brethren will oblige. Isn't that right, *Laporte?*"

"*Certainement,*" responded *Laporte,* seemingly unoffended and smiling as he added, "Anything to prevent a Welsh Gorilla from selecting my breakfast rations."

Parish merely grinned in response, and Elizabeth laughed before pausing the Frenchman mid-stride on his way back to the truck. "This path will lead you," she advised, pointing, "to the cottage we're going to."

"*Merci, Mademoiselle.*"

The path was wide enough for two, so Elizabeth, still linked to Parish, began leading the way back to the cottage followed by Carter and *Chevalier.* She could hear them behind her, conversing quietly in French. She decided on a casually voiced approach.

"You do seem to be a rather unconventional quartet. For soldiers, I mean," she hastily added.

"Elizabeth, Girl," replied the Welshman, his grin reappearing, "You are diplomacy personified. You've just very politely described what most English folk would call a pretty rum bunch."

Emboldened by his jocular response, Elizabeth extended her enquiries, "Why are three of you Sergeants? *I* thought trained Sergeants were desperately needed everywhere, to bring on and look after less experienced men. I've even heard Officers say they wouldn't survive for very long without their Sergeants." She was watching him closely, but before the suddenly serious looking Welshman could respond, it was Carter's lazy drawl which floated over her shoulder.

"It takes three of them to look after *me*, Elizabeth. Equal rank keeps them compliant."

"Mix up in the stores, more like," said the Welshman beside her, "I should have been a General, really," he ended, gently nudging her with an elbow.

Recognizing the playful badinage as outright evasion, Elizabeth decided not to question them further. *'Don't look a gift horse in the mouth,'* she told herself, *'If I can't get a straight answer to a straight question now, then I'll just have to bend my questions later.'*

They duly arrived at the cottage and she led them into the lounge to find Peter Corder trying to wrest his finger from the grasp of baby Matthew who was being held in Mary's arms. Introductions noisily proceeded, during which Elizabeth explained about *Laporte* and the forthcoming additional rations.

"I could use some fresh air," said a tired sounding Mary, passing Matthew to Elizabeth as she announced her intention. "I'll go and help him."

As Mary left to find the ration-deployed Frenchman, the huge hands of the Welshman gently plucked Matthew from Elizabeth's grasp and there was laughter as the baby's tiny fingers immediately gripped the man's mouth and pulled down his lower lip. Seizing the opportunity, a now concerned Elizabeth hand-signalled Peter to follow her into the kitchen.

"We'll have to eat in shifts," she told Peter, "We can't fit everyone in here at one sitting."

"Our usual sitting of three," said Peter, shrugging, "followed by one of four should do it."

"Stick to your usual arrangement, please," said the drawling voice of Carter who suddenly appeared in the kitchen doorway, "*Laporte* will bring our mess-tins, and we can eat outside, so don't worry about us. We didn't come here to add to your problems," he ended with a smile.

Carter then asked if he and *Chevalier* could have a look inside the main house while breakfast was being prepared, and, with an assenting nod from Elizabeth, Peter Corder obligingly led them off. The Welshman appeared in the kitchen with an infant who was clearly absorbed with his huge handler, and the man willingly agreed to remain in charge of baby Matthew whilst breakfast was prepared. Watching her son being handled by the powerful Welshman, Elizabeth's concern rapidly evaporated. She was relieved and amazed to see how incredibly gentle the man was as he allowed the baby to poke and prod him. The more ferocious he pretended to look, the more Matthew happily giggled and gurgled.

Mary's unexpectedly shouted "We're back" preceded her appearance at the kitchen doorway. She held a small ration pack underarm whilst behind her the smiling *Laporte* carried an evidently well-laden kitbag. Elizabeth immediately noticed the difference in Mary. Her friend's face was flushed and all signs of tiredness had disappeared from eyes which now positively sparkled as she excitedly made her announcement.

"Gerrard has brought us lots of goodies."

"Gerrard, is it?" chortled the Welshman, "Well let's be having them goodies, lover boy, and we can sort out our Nosh."

Elizabeth saw Mary's face colour quickly at the Welshman's words 'lover boy'. Then as her friend made room to allow *Laporte's* entry to the kitchen, she saw the Frenchman place a hand on Mary's arm as he eased past her. She saw the woman's instant reaction to the touch, an unmistakable reaction, one which now plunged her back in time... to when she herself had reacted in just such a manner to Jack's touch...

"Ignore the Welshman, *Mademoiselle*," said *Laporte* , interrupting Elizabeth's memory and smiling at Mary as he passed her, "He is unable to understand why a man would take pleasure from the simple matter of a woman's company."

Mary's face was bright red now, saw Elizabeth, but the visitors gallantly effected not to notice. They recommenced their jocular *repartee* whilst under the watchful gaze of baby Matthew the kitbag's contents were emptied out onto the kitchen table. Parish and *Laporte* then retreated to the lounge, where they could be heard good-naturedly entertaining their infant audience.

Mary wordlessly helped Elizabeth collect up the chosen menu items before joining her at the stove, and the release of emotion was immediately evident in the words used by the normally level-headed woman who sounded almost breathless as she spoke.

"That man's voice makes me go weak at the knees," she confided, "And I swear he can read my mind. God, he's such a handsome devil," she ended, visibly shuddering.

Elizabeth stared at her friend in astonishment, momentarily stunned before she managed to get the words out, "Mary, for heaven's *sake!* You've only been with the man for the time it took to collect some rations from a truck in our own driveway."

"I know," responded the bewildered looking woman, "It's unbelievable, I know that, Elizabeth, but he said so much to me in such a short time, it's like he's known me all my life, and my head is spinning with it all, and I... "

Elizabeth continued staring as her friend abruptly stopped speaking. Mary turned her face away in obvious embarrassment, busying herself at the stove, and then she suddenly spoke again and her intensely fierce tone of voice delivered another shock.

"If I could only make love once more, ever again in my life," said Mary Reynolds, "then I would want it to be with a man like that."

Overwhelming Elizabeth's barely concealed surprise at this disclosure, was her own sudden feeling of seeming emotional numbness coupled to her current thoughts. *'Laporte is certainly handsome, but is that enough to evoke the kind of reaction which Mary is displaying? Peter Corder is also handsome, but that hasn't made any difference to Mary's attempts to push me in his direction. Men simply don't matter to me in that way anymore.'*

She shook her head, rejecting the scornful reminder that she was only twenty-four and had her whole life ahead of her, refusing the idea of once again experiencing *the thunderbolt,* trying to focus on the practical reality of opening a tin of army rations, trying not to wonder if she would ever again experience what Mary was obviously feeling now. A new thought pierced her mind; *'Perhaps a vital nerve, somewhere deep inside, is severed when you lose someone you have loved,'* and she was about to finally respond to Mary but her friend wasn't finished.

"He was a cabinet maker before the war," said Mary, sounding calmer as she continued, "And a very successful one, I gather. He designed furniture which apparently sold for a lot of money, so I'll bet he could work wonders in the main house if they really *can* get hold of the materials we need here, Elizabeth."

Elizabeth was once more subjected to a sense of *Déjà Vu,* remembering when Katherine had elicited so much information about Tom Ball in such a short time *on the dance floor...*

"Gerrard also told me," whispered Mary, "that Major Carter was a close friend of your Jack."

And in that heart stopping instant the capacity to breathe seemed to be denied to Elizabeth. But breathe she did, and somehow despite feeling intermittently remote from the proceedings, she managed to produce a breakfast with the aid of an uncharacteristically disorganised companion. *'What a pair we make,'* she thought at one point.

They were busy serving up into the assembled mess-tins when Carter soundlessly entered the kitchen. *'He moves like a cat,'* thought Elizabeth, suddenly irritated by *that* notion along with the realization that she couldn't question him about Jack in front of the others. Then her friend promptly surprised her yet again.

"*You* can eat in here, Major," said Mary, studiously avoiding eye contact with Elizabeth as she added, "I've commandeered one of your mess-tins as I would like to eat outside."

"Stay away," said Carter, startling Elizabeth and causing Mary to freeze, "from the Welshman. He might just eat you if you haven't put enough in his mess-tin," he qualified with a grin before raising his voice to call, "Come and get it, you lot."

The Welshman came first, exchanging a protesting baby Matthew for the generously filled mess-tin proffered by Elizabeth. *Chevalier* took his meal from Carter, and Mary, blushing again now, left clutching two mess-tins. As her friend departed, Elizabeth pretended not to see the look which passed between the Welsh Sergeant and his officer before the Welshman and *Chevalier* made their own way outside. Holding Matthew, she wordlessly seated herself at the kitchen table beside Peter Corder and Carter with the disturbing thought that; *'Laporte had known that Mary would bring him his food.'*

"Elizabeth, I can assure you he's not an attack dog," said Carter, looking directly down at his food as he calmly added, "But if you want me to, right now, I'll put a muzzle on *Laporte*."

Shaken by the fact that he had accurately divined her channel of thought, yet perversely determined to match Carter's calmness, Elizabeth manufactured a cool smile to accompany her quietly voiced response. "Major, that would only serve to further embarrass Mary. And besides, if you did that, how would the poor man eat his food?"

Head bowed over his breakfast plate, Peter Corder coughed and waved a hand at them as he choked back his laughter. Carter merely smiled before turning his full attention to his food. Pleased with the effect of her words, but quietly determined not to show it, Elizabeth now concentrated on forking some egg with her free hand whilst using her other hand to steady Matthew on her lap. It seemed to her like only a few forkfuls later that the portly figure of *Chevalier* re-entered the kitchen carrying his empty mess-tin.

"*Mademoiselle* Creacey, that was most enjoyable."

"I'm glad you thought so, and please call me Elizabeth," she replied, laying down her fork.

"*Pardonner mois, Mademoiselle,* I am interrupting your meal."

"I'm not really hungry, Sergeant. Too much excitement this morning."

She watched as the Frenchman visibly squared his shoulders as he addressed her once more in his lyrical mix of languages.

"*Mademoiselle* Elizabeth, when the good Doctor was showing me around your splendid building, I saw your rough sketches for the design layout of a name which I understand is intended to grace the signboard of your convalescent home, *Oui?*"

"Oh *those,*" she acknowledged, smiling as she dismissively added, "I'm a poor artist, Sergeant."

Suddenly curious about the man's evident demeanour and apparent interest in her sketches, the words were out before she could stop them, "Are *you* an artist, Sergeant?"

Carter's quiet interjection was made before the Frenchman could respond, "No, he's not that kind of artist. He's a skilled Engineer by design and application, and an aspiring sign-writer since he saw the charcoal-scrawled name on a piece of wood in your building over there. It got his attention because a few years ago Chantal Cheval saved his life."

Conscious of Peter Corder's increased interest in the conversation, Elizabeth's thoughts raced as her dumbfounded gaze moved from Carter's watchful blue eyes in the damaged face *'which had known Jack?',* to the swollen-nosed face of the man *'who had known Jack's mother?'* Then she saw the Frenchman discard his mess-tin and bring his overweight frame almost stiffly to attention as he executed a polite bow of his head and spoke again.

"If you would permit, *Mademoiselle,* upon our return here with your requirements, *Laporte* and I would be honoured to create for you the signboard *which*," he emphasised with a shy looking smile and a *Gallic* shrug of his shoulders, "could then display the name you have chosen for your new convalescent home, *Oui?*"

For a second, Matthew's gurgling was the only sound in the kitchen as the questions in Elizabeth's mind jostled for priority and release. She kept her eyes on the Frenchman as she spoke. "Sergeant *Chevalier,* your gracious offer is gratefully accepted, *and*, if I'm not mistaken, that's a nasty insect bite which your nose is reacting to. I'll give you something for it later." She forced herself to allow the pause before adding, "Sergeant, how *well* did you know Chantal?"

"Alas, *Mademoiselle,* we never met," replied the Frenchman.

She smothered the gasp of realization, recalling now Jonathan Teale's summary on the people Chantal Cheval had helped to escape the Germans. Now inwardly questioning the coincidence of *Chevalier's* inclusion in this group of men sent to her by Rawlings, she swung her gaze back to the table and the blue eyes of another thought-provoking individual. She was still forming the words in her head when the Welshman lumbered into the kitchen carrying three sets of mess-tins.

"Went down a treat, did that," said Parish, "Can't beat a woman's touch on the old Nosh."

She saw Carter's blue eyes narrow in the damaged face as they glanced at the Welshman's face before focusing back on *her*, and his relaxed sounding drawl *'was not unpleasant to the ear'*, she found herself thinking.

"You probably have a dozen or so questions for *me*, and I've got a special licence for *you* in my pocket. So, since you don't seem destined to finish that breakfast, why don't we take a walk around inside," he paused, smiling as he resumed, "The Chantal Cheval convalescent home for ex-servicemen and women. You can tell me how you visualise the interior should be, and I can tell you if we can turn that vision into reality. You can also ask your questions, and I can explain what this licence is going to mean to you."

"I'd best come with you, don't you think?" the Welshman casually suggested.

Elizabeth saw pain in the blue eyes as the Major scratched the damaged side of his face, but the lazy smile remained in place as he spoke again.

"Sergeant Parish has a special talent which will benefit your intentions here, so he needs to see the layout for himself."

"I will attend to the little one, *Mademoiselle*," declared *Chevalier*.

"Just great," snorted Corder, "That leaves *mois* with the dishes."

"Should be a doddle, Doc' ", said the grinning Welshman, "You're familiar with scrubbing up."

An un-protesting baby Matthew was transferred to the enveloping arms of a Frenchman and a mildly protesting Peter Corder began clearing kitchen table debris as Elizabeth, still almost bursting with unanswered questions, was led from the kitchen by Carter and Parish. Outside the cottage, Birdsong filled her ears and the air was no longer cool on her skin. *'No sign of Mary or the handsome devil'* noted Elizabeth, but in keeping with the others she refrained from comment. The sun's rays were already making themselves felt as the ground between cottage and main house was traversed by the trio.

"It's going to be a hot one," voiced Carter.

"Well at least we don't have to dodge about in it," Parish enigmatically responded.

Elizabeth allowed herself the exasperated sigh; *'Even a banal remark about the weather is coupled with an obscure response'* she thought, wondering suddenly what her father would have made of these men. As they reached the main house she was also wondering where Mary and the other one had got to, fervently hoping the pair wouldn't be found making love inside the building now being entered by herself and two of the most unusual soldiers she'd ever encountered.

Once inside the hallway, before she could even speak, Carter handed her an envelope. He then almost stopped her thought processes completely as he began explaining the powers granted to her by the special licence. A licence which incorporated the provision for special food rations and medical equipment; which allowed her the extra petrol ration and authority to travel (when required) by 'a goods-carrying vehicle'. A licence which, she was assured, now enabled her to do many things without subjecting herself to local council restrictions. Even as her mind reeled, a part of it wondered how the sour-faced Harold Shaw would react to her newly acquired powers.

As she stood before him trying to take it all in, Carter just kept on talking. He even began pre-empting some of her previously unanswered questions, and immediately creating others as he did so. He informed her that Sergeant's *Chevalier* and Parish would be advising on any structural alterations she might have in mind. Whilst *Laporte* , it was explained, could perform miracles with wood and manufacture all kinds of things provided he had the materials. Which was, she learned, where the previously mentioned 'special talent' of the Welshman came into play. In almost laconic fashion she was told that, aided by Carter, Sergeant Parish would be sourcing and 'liberating' *Laporte's* materials.

"Whatever your requirements," drawled Carter, "no matter how large or small, tell us what they are. We probably won't get them all, but then again we may get lucky."

For a brief moment Elizabeth experienced the giddy sensation of her mind spinning out of control. A part of her bombarded brain linking what was being said to her, with surreal scenes from a half-remembered Hollywood film; her special licence held in the hands of a mysterious and handsome hero pitting himself against impossible odds to rescue a damsel in distress. Another part of her spinning head was hearing Arthur Arkwright vocally listing the logistical equivalent of a wartime materials nightmare.

Elizabeth pulled her mental focus back to where it needed to be; to the reality of her current situation. But it was still a conflictingly unreal kind of reality, she thought, which made up the scene before her now in the shape of two uniformed and casually postured men giving every appearance of waiting for a normal everyday shopping list.

Struggling for self-control, attempting to suppress her natural impulsiveness, keeping her mouth firmly closed, she tried telling herself that whatever their personal reasons were for being here, these well-intentioned men had come to her through Simon Rawlings. She reminded herself that not only had Jack told her in his letter that Rawlings could be relied upon, but that the man had already proved himself by his actions which had unarguably gifted her a son. Nevertheless she now found herself trembling with pent-up frustration, and the words were spilling out in a rush before she could stop them.

"*Why* is Rawlings doing this? *Why* have I been granted this special licence? *Why* has he made it possible for you and your men to be here? Don't forget I've nursed soldiers, and you and your men are clearly *not* what anyone would call ordinary soldiers. *Why*, as you've already pointed out, have you and your men with so-called special talents *volunteered* to be here? Your Sergeant *Chevalier's* life was saved, you tell me, by Chantal Cheval. Tell me, Major Carter, am I expected to believe that's a coincidence? And speaking of coincidence, you can also tell me, just how close a friend *were* you to Jack Matthews?"

Into the silence following her barrage of questions, came the Welshman's melodious sounding verbal appendage. "You're on the rack now, Boyo."

Still trembling, she watched the blue eyes in Carter's calm looking face regarding her steadily as he responded to her outburst.

"I don't exactly know why Rawlings is doing this. You would have to ask him that yourself. I somehow don't doubt he would tell you, since he seems to hold you in high regard. But since you're obviously still in the dark, he must also have his reasons for keeping you there."

"Is *that all* you can think of to say to me?" she responded angrily.

"I *do know*," responded Carter, still steadily meeting her eyes with his own, "that Rawlings is an honourable man, but... "

As he hesitated, Elizabeth saw his flicked glance to the Welshman before he resumed, "...he also has a bigger picture to consider. So I imagine he's waiting for the right moment to bring you into the light."

She saw something indefinable in the blue eyes a second before he raised a hand to his damaged face and began scratching. A heavy sigh prefaced his next words.

"Whatever his reasons, I'm very glad he has arranged for us to be here. Because it gives me and *Laporte* something of a chance to repay our debt."

She now heard the man's deep intake of breath and she saw the blue eyes harden as he immediately continued, "You *should* know that Rawlings had his pick of volunteers to come here. A lot of people also saw helping *you* as their way of repaying a personal debt to Jack Matthews. So... "

"Steady, Boyo," interjected the Welshman, placing a huge hand on Carter's shoulder.

Elizabeth clearly saw the conflict registering itself in the blue eyes as Carter visibly gathered himself to speak again.

"Sergeant Parish is subtly reminding me I could be court-martialled for telling you too much." He shrugged his shoulders, "As I was about to add, so when Rawlings told me what you planned to do with this place, I selected a team which I figured could actually achieve something."

Elizabeth suddenly heard what sounded like a growl coming from the Welshman, who was now looking at her with a worried expression on his face as he spoke.

"God help us, Elizabeth, I know that tone of voice. He'll get us all shot."

"Unpleasant repercussions, my Welsh beauty," drawled Carter, "resulting from any indiscretion on *my* part will only occur, I reckon, if Miss Elizabeth Creacey isn't allowed to hear some answers to *some* of her questions."

Elizabeth saw Carter's lazy smile flicker and die before he continued in a tone of voice which was filled with clearly heard emotion.

"Just how close a friend? was I believe, your question, Elizabeth. The answer is that I'd like to believe that Jack saw me as a friend he could trust with his life. As *I* trusted *him* with mine. And in the world within which we worked together, that kind of trust isn't bestowed to just anyone and everyone. So I'd say that in the scheme of things, we used to be close friends."

"I didn't mean to...," she began, but Carter was over-riding her attempt.

"As to why you've now got *us* on your doorstep... "

"I can feel the rope on my neck," interjected the Welshman.

"All four of us," resumed Carter, "were privileged to serve with Jack Matthews; and *Laporte* and I owe our lives to the man. My friend here currently strangling me in his Welsh mind also reckons he wouldn't be walking around, had it not been for Jack. *Chevalier* is genuinely here for his skills, but this is also *his* chance to repay his own debt to Jack's mother. And I would really prefer everything I've just said to be considered as being for your ears only."

"This is all so... so extraordinary," managed Elizabeth.

Carter nodded his head as he responded, "We live in extraordinary times, do we not? I understand what you meant earlier, when you compared us to soldiers you've nursed. But we're still just ordinary men in uniform," he paused, the lazy smile reappearing as he added, "We're just frequently called upon to do extraordinary things."

"So then, Elizabeth Creacey," voiced the still worried looking Welshman, "Do you now run to Rawlings and reveal this order-breaking Boyo's indiscretion, or do you have what it takes to keep your powder dry until Rawlings decides the time is right for him to come to *you*?"

"She's the *fiancée* of Jack Matthews," drawled Carter, "I reckon she has what it takes."

Elizabeth aimed her words at the stony-faced Welshman, "I'll keep my powder dry, Sergeant, I would never do anything to harm Jack's comrades." she faltered, lowering her head, suddenly unable to stop the sob escaping, "That's not quite right anymore, is it, silly of me... "

"It's perfectly right," came Carter's firm response.

She flinched as her shoulder was suddenly gripped by a massive hand and she looked up into the smiling face of the Welshman as his melodious voice sounded again.

"You're *all* right with *me*, Girl. We're *all* comrades here. In flesh and blood, *and* in spirit."

Deeply moved by the Welshman's words, she felt the huge hand move from her shoulder and gently cup her chin as he continued speaking.

"Now why don't we get this show on the road, what do you say?"

"We can start upstairs," she replied, "and work our way down."

"Excellent idea," responded Parish, grinning fiercely as he added, "You could be officer material, Girl, or even Welsh, perhaps."

Even as she smiled and heard the Major's own mock-groan of response, she was wondering if she would ever know how Jack had saved the lives of *Laporte* and Carter. Forcing herself to refocus, she led them upstairs. She then spent the following hour walking them through the building and painstakingly outlining, room by room, what would be needed to bring about her vision of the convalescent home. Right from the start she saw the transformation in both men. Gone was the extraneous banter. Replaced now by serious looking individuals seemingly intent upon absorbing everything she mentioned and making detailed entries in a notebook which was frequently passed between them. Occasionally the Welshman would wander off on his own, and Carter used one of those occasions to further surprise her.

"We'll be pulling out within the hour. We've got a lot of driving to do. We'll probably be gone several days, but hopefully we'll be coming back with enough to make a difference here."

Unable to imagine what they could possibly bring back in a truck that would make any significant kind of difference, and now reluctant to question him, she merely smiled and didn't comment on his prediction. "You're not going anywhere," she replied instead, amused at the surprise on his face, "until I've prepared a compound for your face. It will stop you scratching, ease the pain, and allow the skin to heal more effectively. I'm not even going to ask you what happened. I also promised Sergeant *Chevalier* something for his nose. So you can have some more tea while I prepare things, it won't take me very long."

"Definitely officer material," pronounced the re-appearing and keen-eared Welshman, "You tell him, Girl, and tea sounds just the ticket."

"Thank you, Elizabeth," said Carter, smiling, "That all sounds good."

No further words were exchanged as the two men followed her out of the building, and, sensing their need for quiet thought, Elizabeth silently marvelled at how differently she felt about them. She found herself recalling Jack's poem, with its line about *companionable silence.* They re-entered the cottage to find *Laporte* deep in conversational French with *Chevalier.* There was no sign of baby Matthew or Peter Corder, but a smiling perfectly relaxed looking Mary Reynolds emerged from the kitchen bearing steaming mugs of tea as she informatively announced, "Matthew is asleep, Peter has gone for a walk, and you're just in time for tea."

"I'm always in time for tea," said the Welshman, "It's a natural gift I have."

As Mary distributed her offerings to the Frenchmen, Elizabeth quickly explained to the woman her urgent requirements for *Chevalier* and Carter.

"We can do it together," said Mary, "I'll just make two more... "

"We can handle the tea," interjected Carter, "Don't let that hold you up."

Aware of Carter's impatience to be on the move, Elizabeth whisked Mary out of the cottage for the return to the main house with its improvised treatment room. Imagining her friend would eventually tell her everything later, Elizabeth refrained from asking about *Laporte* so the journey was made in silence. Inside the treatment room they swiftly prepared the Petroleum Jelly compound which would be applied to Carter's damaged face. Next, and more slowly, they made up the filling for the 'Reckitts' blue bag of dry linen destined for application to *Chevalier's* nose. They were back at the cottage inside thirty minutes but it was fast approaching mid-day and the sun was already blazing down on the four soldiers who stood outside waiting for them.

"The good looking Doctor Corder is inside doing the babysitting," said a grinning Welshman.

Elizabeth approached *Chevalier* first, showing him the carefully shaped 'Reckitts' bag.

"You must," she told him, "moisten this under cold water from your canteen before applying it over your nose, like so," she demonstrated now with her water canteen, "Apply it three or four times a day, and keep it in place for ten minutes each time. The swelling should reduce in a couple of days."

"*Merci, Mademoiselle.*"

As she then moved towards the Major and the Welshman, she saw *Laporte* kissing Mary's hand. The Welshman's knowing wink made Elizabeth smile, but she didn't comment.

She handed Carter the small jar of prepared compound. "Rub a little in twice daily," she succinctly advised, suddenly at a loss for words as the blue eyes twinkled in the damaged face.

"I'll have Sergeant Parish do it for me, he has a delicate touch."

"I could always delicately shove it down his throat," said the Welshman, grinning at Elizabeth.

Suddenly the uniformed quartet were purposefully striding away from the cottage, back along the path which would take them to the driveway and the waiting truck. Elizabeth watched them disappear on the path and stood where she was until she heard the truck's engine noisily start up. She remained where she was, visualising the vehicle negotiating the driveway until, inevitably, the engine sound gradually faded away. The figure beside her stirred.

"Not quite what we expected," said Mary Reynolds, quietly.

"Not what we expected at all," agreed Elizabeth, conscious of the understatement.

That evening, with Matthew peacefully asleep, Elizabeth said 'Goodnight' to a still unforthcoming and subdued Mary Reynolds and a contrastingly buoyant Peter Corder. As her bedside radio quietly informed her it had been the hottest day of the year thus far, before going on to play Jo Stafford's current chart success *'It Could Happen To You'*, Elizabeth commenced a new diary journal. She wrote long into the night, faithfully recording the events of a memorable day and conveying to Jack her indelible impressions of his former comrades.

Chapter Fifteen

But true love is a durable fire,
In the mind ever burning,
Never sick, never old, never dead,
From itself never turning.
(Walter Raleigh)

Carshalton, Surrey, June 1944

What were destined to become the historically eventful opening days of June were currently proving to be decisive ones for Allied Forces Commanders, and fruitful ones for the ever alert guardians of Carshalton's village 'Grapevine'.

In Italy; on June 4th 1944 and having started in September 1943, the race to liberate Rome was finally over and the initial radio broadcasts heard in Carshalton reported that troops from America's fifth army had reached the finishing tape first. Some of those in the Carshalton village, with or without a radio, were unable to accept this news as fact. *'How could American tanks be faster than British ones?'* they argued through the bristling 'Grapevine'. *'Look how long,'* they righteously pointed out, *'it had taken them to actually turn up for the bloody war!'*

Thankfully for those of a neutral inclination, and for the sake of *'Peace in our pub'* (as one village 'wag' was heard to comment) nobody was going to contradict Winston Churchill when he announced to England's Parliament on June 5th that Allied Forces led by General Alexander had captured Rome and the hearts of the Italian people.

Hot on the heels of *that*, on June 6th, defying uncertain weather and improbable logistics, Allied Forces in unprecedented numbers finally invaded mainland France. Having wrong-footed the enemy to land on a less fortified stretch of Normandy beach, the much awaited *'Big Push'* was irrevocably underway.

Something more local was also very much underway and as the first official 'D-day' announcement reached Carshalton on June 6th, four heavily laden British army trucks rolled to a halt on the driveway fronting Carshalton's 'Ridgeway House'. However, unlike their more successful allied counterparts, this smaller convoy had not reached its destination unobserved. That evening in *The Strife and Strumpet* pub, the village grapevine's main watering source, speculation was rife.

"We're being invaded by what sounds like Italians," was Peter Corder's incredulous sounding report which brought Elizabeth Creacey and Mary Reynolds rushing to the front entrance of the main house to be met by a grinning Sergeant Parish.

"Don't panic, Ladies, we come in peace," declared the Welshman, waving a huge hand towards the scenes of bustling activity behind him on the driveway as he added, "We borrowed some helping hands."

In addition to the recognized figures of Carter and the two Frenchmen, Elizabeth counted six men in 'Spruce-green' uniforms busily engaged in unloading four stationary vehicles. Her questions immediately demanded a voice. "Who *are* those men? Where *do* they come from?"

"They're Italian POW's," replied Parish, his grin disappearing as his voice became serious, "Believe it or not, even though Italy surrendered in September last year, I'm told we now have over one hundred thousand of them spread around the British Isles. And they're still coming by all accounts, so it's a slave labour force our government is loathe to part with. This job-lot are what's officially known as 'co-operative workers', which means they don't have to walk about with a target pinned on their backs."

Suddenly reminding Elizabeth of the London 'Cockney' stall-vendors she'd seen, the Welshman's returning grin was twinned with a finger tapping the side of his nose as he added, "We borrowed them from one of the camps which provided some of your booty. They'll cost you nine shillings per-man per-week, and we have to return them inside two weeks."

"You speak of them as if they were commodities," said Mary, her disapproval clearly heard.

"Save your reproach, Nurse Reynolds," retorted Parish, dismissively, "Not *too* long ago, some of *them* would have done for some of *ours*."

"Where will they sleep?" rejoined Mary, seemingly ignoring the Welshman's defence.

"Under canvas. We brought tents," replied Parish, his grin fiercer as he added, "We *do* look after our slaves, Nurse Reynolds."

"I never expected you to return with four truck-loads," confessed Elizabeth, "So much...," she trailed off, suddenly at a loss for words.

Beginning to steer them towards the vehicles, Parish smiled as he replied, "The bulk of your list comes to you courtesy of Uncle Sam," he revealed, adding, "God bless Yanks, what *they* casually call surplus would equip Montgomery for a major campaign."

Drawing closer now to the scenes of activity, Elizabeth saw bed-frames and mattresses being unloaded under the supervision of *Chevalier*, whilst from another truck *Laporte* was directing the placement of timber planks and other shaped pieces of wood she couldn't identify. Variably sized boxes had already been stacked alongside the trucks and she saw that these containers, some wooden, some cardboard, bore unmistakable *USA Military* markings in addition to neatly printed labels. Her astonishment grew as she read the labels bearing titles which included *Kitchen Equipment; Rations; Bedding-Linen; Toiletries;* and *Medical Equipment.*

She suddenly spotted Carter and was disconcertingly aware of the quick *tug* in her stomach, followed by her amazement as she realized he was supervising the unloading of panes of glass. Knowing that glass was deemed to be impossible to obtain by *anyone* these days, questions once again filled her mind. Even from a few paces away she could see the improvement to Carter's face, and automatically made a mental note to check if he needed more of the compound.

"How on *earth* did you manage to get hold of glass?" she asked Parish, "And why *so much*?"

"Ah, well now, Elizabeth," replied the Welshman, "Modesty, and a morbid fear of imprisonment, forbids my disclosure. But *your* Boyo, Doctor Corder, apparently mentioned to *my* gallant leader that providing glass for some of your local neighbours would do a power of good for your public relations."

Elizabeth's thoughts on a suitable response were interrupted...

"Major Carter seems to talk their language," observed Mary.

"Curses fluently in *many* tongues, does our talented Major," Parish glibly responded.

Accompanied by one of the Italians, Carter suddenly began approaching them and Elizabeth immediately found herself wishing she'd worn something else instead of the shapeless sweater and badly creased slacks. She also resisted the urge to touch her hair, which she'd allowed to fall free today. The man beside Carter, wiping his hands on uniform trousers as he walked, was small and swarthy looking and his bearded face was expressionless as he was brought to a casual halt in front of her. There was no lazy smile of acknowledgement on the British Major's face, she noted.

"Okay Glyn," said Carter briskly to the Welshman, "Better start getting this stuff inside and out of sight."

The Welshman moved off without demur and Elizabeth realized that she now knew the Christian names of all her benefactors except one; the man with strained looking blue eyes in the improved face finally addressing her.

"*Le present Gianfranco,*" said Carter, shaking his head and starting again, "This is Gianfranco," he repeated, indicating the swarthy man. "He's the only one with any English, so if I'm not around and you need to speak to any of them, you can communicate through Gianfranco."

Elizabeth saw a shy looking smile emerge from the bearded face as the man extended his hand to her. As she shook his hand, the man's high-pitched voice conveyed his nervousness.

"*Buonasera, Signora, piacere.*"

"That's Good afternoon, he's pleased to meet you," translated an impatient sounding Carter.

"*Buonasera, Gianfranco,*" responded Elizabeth, smiling warmly into brown eyes which brightened in the bearded face.

If Carter was surprised by her use of the man's language, he gave no sign of it and immediately followed up with tersely spoken words of his own.

"Okay, there's a lot to be done before nightfall, so if you'll excuse me."

Thrown by Carter's abruptness, and given no time to respond, Elizabeth could only watch him leading the Italian POW away.

"Bit grumpy, wouldn't you say?" commented Mary at her side.

Understanding belatedly dawning upon her, Elizabeth voiced the realization. "God knows how many miles they've travelled to obtain what we can see before us. They're probably half-dead on their feet. Don't forget how crotchety *you* can be if you don't get your seven hours."

"True enough, I should have thought of that," admitted Mary, "And we won't even mention your own reaction to sleep deprivation."

Responsively chuckling to conceal her fresh concern for Carter and his men, and very much aware that Mary had made no attempt to communicate with *Laporte*, Elizabeth linked arms with her friend for their return to the cottage.

"He didn't even give us a chance to thank him," she quietly remarked to Mary, "And just *how* do we thank him anyway, I can hardly *believe* what they've managed to bring."

"Nor can I," acknowledged a solemn sounding Mary, brightening as she suddenly enthused, "*I* know, when they've finished whatever they're going to do here, we could give them a party before they leave."

"That's a wonderful idea," responded Elizabeth, immediately wishing she'd thought of it first.

"Right now, though, I expect they would welcome a cup of tea," said the pragmatic Mary.

The manifestation of Mary's pragmatism was well received. As the abundance of material was deployed to Carter's order throughout the afternoon, she and Elizabeth ferried countless cups of tea to the seemingly tireless Major and his multi-national workforce. Observing how cheerfully the Italians were responding to Carter and his group, Elizabeth made a mental note to contact Jonathan Teale about the money she was now apparently obligated to provide.

Later, as the day was beginning to surrender its last natural light, inside the cottage a compliant Peter Corder was being held prisoner on the lounge couch by a playful baby Matthew. The smell of cooking and the sound of music coming to them through an open window, prompted Elizabeth and Mary to don jackets, grab a torch, and allow their senses to lead them to the rectangle of lawn behind the main house.

On the previously empty lawn they found five erected tents and could hear Bing Crosby melodiously *'Swinging On A Star'* from inside one of them. Quietly chattering Italians were dowsing lamps and putting away the portable gas stoves which had obviously produced their meal, and fireflies glowed and darted around the head of Gianfranco as he waved to them in greeting. Off to one side of the POW's, Carter and Parish were bent over a small fold-up table, using torchlight to peer at what Elizabeth firstly mistook for a map. Until drawing alongside them she saw that it was a professionally drawn sketch of the main house interior.

Acknowledging their presence with a tired looking smile, Carter quickly began explaining his action plan for the following day. As he did so, Bing Crosby was briefly louder as *Laporte* and *Chevalier* emerged together from their obviously shared tent and came to join them.

"I *had* thought," began a surprised sounding Mary, "that you and your men would be sleeping inside the main house, Major."

"Two of these tents are ours," replied Carter, "Leaves the work area clear," he succinctly qualified, "and enables us to keep an eye on... our co-workers."

"Co-workers, is it? Now *that*," emphasised the Welshman who was looking directly at Mary, "I have to admit, does sound better than *commodities*. Which is why, Nurse Reynolds, he's the officer and I'm just the lowly Sergeant."

Instantly reminding Elizabeth of days gone by, the voice of Mary Reynolds whip-lashed through the night air.

"I *do think* we can draw a line under that now, Sergeant Parish."

"Yes Ma'am," Parish meekly concurred.

The awkward silence was filled by *Chevalier* addressing his fellow countryman.

"*Mon dieu, Gerrard,* observe the Celtic warrior still working his charm."

"He needs to *keep* working it, *Mon Ami,*" replied *Laporte,* smiling as he looked towards Mary whilst adding, "The gentle sex requires *much* work. You are well, *Cherie?*"

"Well enough to hit *you* over the head with this torch," responded Mary.

The resultant all-round laughter drowned out Bing Crosby's voice but even as she joined in, Elizabeth was watching *Laporte's* satisfied expression. She instantly realized the handsome Frenchman had deliberately invited the response he'd received in order to defuse the tension which he'd rightly perceived to be present within the group. Realizing also now that Mary had clearly recovered from her infatuation with the French *devil,* Elizabeth saw that an equally perceptive Carter was smiling as he carefully folded and pocketed the prepared drawing of the proposed home's interior. Suddenly aware of her heart beating and irrationally wondering if the pounding in her ears could be heard, she quietly addressed the young officer.

"The compound has been successful, I see."

"Wonderful," he acknowledged, looking obviously embarrassed, "Sorry, I've been remiss. I should have thanked you earlier."

"You've had enough to think about."

She was about to say more but was rendered speechless when he suddenly closed the distance between them to put his hands on her shoulders as he spoke.

"Nevertheless, thank you," he said softly, "It *has* made such a difference."

"Which is...," she began hesitantly, aware of his grip still firmly in place on her shoulders, knowing that Mary and the others could hear every word, finally managing to smile into the blue eyes as she continued, "what you and your men are clearly intent upon making here."

"That's the plan," he replied, returning her smile as he released his grip and stepped back.

Still hearing the heartbeat in her ears, and glad of the poor light concealing the heat she could feel on her face, Elizabeth inwardly fought to dismiss from her mind the thought that *'His touch had felt so... '*

"We both wanted," began Mary suddenly, "to thank you all, didn't we, Elizabeth?"

Instinctively aware that Mary had somehow realized her predicament, Elizabeth rallied her senses, hoping her inner turmoil wasn't transmitting itself to *everyone* present. "Yes, we did. How you managed to obtain so much, *and* the glass, I don't know, *but*," she emphasised whilst spreading her smile between the four men, "however you did it, it's really incredible, it's truly appreciated, and we thank you all."

"Well now, Elizabeth," said the Welshman, his ferocious looking face appearing even more frightening in the half-light, "That's very gracious of you, I'm bound to say, but I should just point out to you that these three had nothing to do with it. It's this humble Welshman you should be thanking," he ended to more laughter from the assembly.

"Are these men to be confined here?" asked Elizabeth when the laughter subsided, indicating the Italians who were disappearing into their tents.

"Not really," replied Carter, "If somebody drives them into the village, they're allowed to use the shops and spend the money you'll be paying them."

"But not the pub," qualified the grinning Welshman.

"No, not the pub," acknowledged a tired sounding Carter, "But they won't have much time for shopping. We have a pretty full programme to get through here, and time is against us."

As Carter spoke those last words, Elizabeth told herself she was imagining the meaningful look being directed her way. She opened her mouth to speak but was thwarted.

"You will, I hope, be allocating some of that time to rest, Major," said Mary.

"Even a boastful Welsh Gorilla must rest, *Mademoiselle*," said *Laporte*.

"Watch it, lover boy," growled Parish.

Deciding another diversion was required, Elizabeth quickly addressed *Chevalier*, "You are pleased, I trust, to have your nose back, Sergeant?"

"*Oui, Mademoiselle* Elizabeth," responded the Frenchman, smiling as he stroked his nose and added, "I will be designing for you the most wonderful sign for your new convalescent home."

"Time we called it a night," announced Carter, curtly adding, "Early start tomorrow."

Back in the cottage, Peter Corder was relieved of babysitting duties and retired to his room, Mary Reynolds yawned her *Goodnight,* Matthew was laid in his cot, and a perversely *unsettled* Elizabeth Creacey settled down to begin her diary entries.

Carter's quickly and firmly established routine dictated the manner in which the following days proceeded. He and his work-force started early each morning, and only a lunch break briefly intervened before they recommenced their labour programme. Often continuing well into the night, it was a mentally and physically brutal schedule.

Elizabeth and Mary were frequently consulted, and their excitement grew as they witnessed the daily transformation. They watched in awe as, to enlarge certain areas, '*Parish the Power*' demolished walls with ease. They looked on in amazement as *Chevalier* cleverly re-fashioned new walls using a combination of bricks and timber. They gazed with puzzled eyes as Gianfranco and two of his compatriots weaved intricate pathways with trailing wires which would carry electric power, and marvelled at the amount of debris being ferried away daily to some unknown destination. And all the while, slowly but surely, something close to Elizabeth's initial vision began appearing before her eyes.

The days blurred into two weeks, and *Laporte's* promised miracles with wood had been duly performed. Producing professionally crafted examples such as storage units; drawer cabinets; and wardrobes not just occupying their allotted space but *dressing* rooms now containing assembled beds covered with clean linen. Rooms which also boasted 'French-made' tables matching the comfortable chairs '*Which the Yank's Officer's Mess would never miss*', a grinning Welshman had assured them.

Then had come the unforgettable day when *Chevalier* had led Elizabeth to the front of the main house and she had seen the new signboard for the first time. *Laporte's* now recognizable craftsmanship was evident in the strikingly carved post supporting the polished wood frame upon which had been elegantly sign-painted the legend: *'The Chantal Cheval Convalescent Home for Ex-Servicemen and Women' Founded by Elizabeth Creacey, 1944.*

Carter's closing words to her that day, could never have prepared her for what was to come:

"Tomorrow, Elizabeth, we take you into the village to play Lady Bountiful."

The following morning, Elizabeth wasn't really surprised when she was told that no Italians would be sharing her truck-ride to the Carshalton village. Their leader stood before her now, smiling politely, and she was reminded that throughout their enforced albeit paid tenure, Gianfranco and his countrymen had consistently displayed obvious signs of pride in their variably performed tasks. More of the same had seemingly ruled out any visit to the village.

"*Ultimi ritochi,*" said Gianfranco, proudly marching his acquiescent band to the main house.

"Finishing touches," translated Carter by way of explanation.

"Women's work," growled the Welshman whose seeming dislike of all things Italian had not abated in any discernible way.

Consequently leaving behind two disgruntled Frenchmen supervising six apparently happy Italians, and with Mary and Peter remaining to share babysitting duties, Elizabeth's transport set off for the journey into Carshalton village. Positioned between Carter and Parish, in the front cabin of a truck generously laden with the Welshman's 'sourced and liberated' largesse, she secretly admitted to herself that she was looking forward to her anointed role of 'Lady Bountiful'.

She didn't question the fact that the Officer was behind the steering wheel, having already observed over the past weeks that these men paid scant attention to conventional military protocol. With surprising difficulty she also elected to ignore what she imagined to be the admiring glances she was receiving from her blue-eyed and silent driver. She was trying not to wonder if he too was having trouble with his thoughts.

She was therefore glad of the Welshman's presence. Cheerfully dispelling what might otherwise have been an awkward atmosphere, for the duration of the journey he regaled her with colourful stories and descriptions of a place she mistakenly took to be the biblical Nazareth. Upon realizing her mistake, he laughed and corrected her with the given name of Narberth, the village he'd left behind in his native country.

"If you ever get to Narberth, Elizabeth, just ask for me. Anyone will know where to find me. I'll show you around just one example of the wonderful world of Wales."

Upon reaching their destination and voicing the need for discretion, Carter drove around to the rear of the Council buildings. Whereupon their collective curiosity was aroused as the truck was brought to a halt beside an incongruously placed piano; standing as it did, exposed to the elements in the otherwise deserted looking area. Surprising Elizabeth, Carter was out of the truck and standing beside the instrument even as Parish was still in the act of helping her to the ground.

The sudden sound of the musical notes resonating around the patch of ground bordered by what appeared to be lock-up sheds, caused her to catch her breath and grip the arm of the now grinning Welshman.

"I know, Elizabeth," he said, gently patting her hand, "Took *me* by surprise when I first heard him play about a year ago. Fair-do's, the man's gifted."

Enthralled, Elizabeth watched and listened. She saw that Carter's eyes were actually closed as his fingers travelled up and down the keyboard with dazzling speed, performing a piece of classical music she recognized but maddeningly couldn't name. Then she saw his head lift, and the blue eyes open, and the lazy smile was directed towards her as she heard the unforgettable melody of *As Time Goes By* soaring into the air all around her and floating her mind back to the Hammersmith dance hall and her very first dance with Jack...

The spell was broken when Carter abruptly stopped playing, and she watched him close down the lid of the piano. She could still hear the music in her head as he came towards them, and even the Welshman's voice was different when he spoke.

"You haven't lost the magic touch, Boyo."

Carter merely smiled but Elizabeth could see the transformation in the man; the blue eyes radiated a sparkle she hadn't seen before and he suddenly looked even younger.

"Okay, Glyn," he drawled, "You stay here with the gear, and *we'll* go and find Arkwright."

Still speechless, Elizabeth was courteously escorted away from the scene of her impromptu concert entertainment by its performer.

Inside the Council building, the amiable Arthur Arkwright was quickly found to be free and was easily persuaded to accompany them in order to cast an appraising eye over Elizabeth's announced offerings. Outside, behind the Council building, the mystery of the piano was simply solved by Arkwright's *'Being collected'*, seconds before he was effortlessly pulled up into the rear of the army truck by the Welshman.

"*Oh my Sainted Aunt,*" was Arkwright's initially voiced reaction, followed by disjointedly expressed opinions such as "*Enough glass here to warm more than a few homes and hearts,*" as well as, "*Oh my Giddy Aunt, not just your garden variety rations but luxury items too,'* along with various other exclamatory mutterings dedicated to several more colourfully described Aunts.

To then save Elizabeth from the intermittent but increasingly robust bear-hugs, and to stop his own hand being repeatedly shaken, Carter diplomatically suggested that his Sergeant should transfer the gifts to a place of safety. Arkwright sobered up and indicated which of the lock-up sheds near to where they were parked would meet the required criteria. Parish drove the truck nearer to the appointed shed, and a perspiring Arkwright helped the two men and an insistent Elizabeth to effect the transfer of goods.

Parish had climbed into the back of the truck and was quietly tidying its interior when the burly figure of Harold Shaw suddenly materialised on the scene outside, roughly shouldered Carter aside and confronted Arkwright who still hadn't closed the storage unit's door.

"What the hell's going on? What's Miss high and mighty doing here?"

"Really, Shaw," spluttered Arkwright, "Elizabeth, I do... "

Arkwright abruptly closed his mouth, alarmed by Shaw's look of rage as it took in the newly-housed glass and the rations.

"Is *this* what her special licence is all about?" spat out Shaw, "Smuggling illegal black market goods and bribing gullible Councillors?"

"Now wait just a minute...," began Carter.

"No *you wait*, soldier boy," snarled Shaw, already jabbing an accusatory finger as he advanced on Elizabeth, "This snotty bitch is going to lose more than her bloody special licence before *I'm* through with her."

Frozen with shock, a white-faced Elizabeth was rooted where she stood. She was dimly aware of Carter starting to move but so close was Shaw now, the man's spittle was striking her face. But the aggressively outstretched finger never reached her chest. Without any sound whatsoever the Welshman was suddenly beside her and gripping Shaw's finger in one of his huge hands. She heard the unmistakable *Crack* of breaking bone followed by Shaw's scream of pain, and then the Welshman's powerful fist connected with Shaw's jaw and the scream died as the man crumpled to the ground. Ignoring the downed man, the Welshman turned to face her.

"You okay, Girl? Hang on to me for a bit, can't have you swooning at my feet now, can we?"

She smiled into the face that still looked ferocious even as it expressed concern. "I will just hang on for a moment," she shakily responded, "He really frightened me."

Carter suddenly gripped her arm as he calmly spoke to the Welshman, "Okay, she can hold on to *me*. Get *him* out of sight, Glyn, while we evaluate."

Elizabeth watched, transfixed, as Shaw's body was promptly lifted by the scruff of its neck as if it was weightless, casually draped over a Welsh shoulder, and unceremoniously dumped out of sight inside the storage unit. Carter's voice by her side was now addressing the still shaken Arthur Arkwright.

"Who the hell *is* he?"

She saw Arkwright produce a white handkerchief from a trouser pocket, and the perspiring face was wiped as he explained in a few brief sentences the identity and character defects of the man now occupying floor space in the storage unit. A thoughtful looking Carter seemed unaware, she realized, that he was stroking her arm as he mulled over the supplied information. In a despairing tone of voice, Arkwright then introduced the spectre in the wings of a father influential enough to have engineered Shaw's avoidance of military service.

"He'll come to, shortly," advised Parish, also looking thoughtful now as he turned to Arkwright and questioningly added, "Is he married?"

"No bugger would have him," retorted Arkwright, instantly signing his apology to Elizabeth.

The Welshman was grinning as he spoke to Carter, "I *could* just pop our sick comrade in the back of the truck."

"You could be wrong, Councillor Arkwright," drawled Carter in complete understanding of his Sergeant's train of thought, "about no bugger wanting him. What do you reckon, Glyn, would King and country have him?"

"All *you* have to do is make the phone call, Boyo," said Parish, "Big strapping lad like him, even with nine fingers they'd soon find a spot for him." The grin became fierce as he added, "We can even deliver him personally when we return the *Eyeties*."

"No one would mourn his absence, but it could never happen gentlemen," said a forlorn sounding Arkwright, "I *told* you, his father is influential in high places."

"There's always someone *more* influential," responded Carter, calmly adding, "I think our hero is recovering, Glyn."

The Welshman strolled to the storage unit and promptly repeated his effortless lift of a now loudly groaning Harold Shaw, and hoisted him into the rear of the truck. "I'll just pop in beside him," said Parish, "A lullaby should quieten him down."

Elizabeth watched the powerful Welshman smoothly hoist himself over the truck's tailgate and disappear inside the vehicle. The groaning sounds from within abruptly ceased.

With a perspiring face which clearly couldn't believe what its eyes were witnessing, Arkwright was busy with his handkerchief again when Carter spoke to him once more.

"We'll be on our way now, Councillor. All a bit unorthodox, I know, but you'll receive in time an official notification verifying your ex-colleague's entry to His Majesty's armed forces. So you needn't worry about...," he paused, smiling as he resumed, "questions in the house."

"Oh very funny, I'm sure," responded the clearly agitated Arkwright.

Despite her own still lingering shock, and briefly wondering if Carter's arm stroking had somehow transmitted his calmness, Elizabeth smiled as she quietly contributed, "If she could see you now, Arthur Arkwright, then Mary would be concerned about your blood pressure."

"You do seem remarkably sanguine, Elizabeth, I must say," responded Arkwright, mopping again at his brow, "You presumably must have confidence in these fellows."

"Complete confidence, Arthur," she assured him.

Arkwright pocketed his handkerchief and turned away from them to close and lock the storage unit door. He turned back to them and stepped forward to shake Carter's hand, and his voice sounded stronger. "As *I have* in Elizabeth Creacey, Major, so *Bon voyage* to you."

They watched the departing back of Arthur Arkwright for a moment and then Carter smiled and bowed slightly at the waist as he waved a hand to indicate the truck's cabin.

"Shall we?"

"Not until," she smiled into the puzzled looking blue eyes, "I know your first name."

She saw the puzzlement vanish from the now amused looking blue eyes.

"My name is Alan...," he paused, smiling as he added, "*Piacere*."

"*Piacere* to you too," she replied impishly, stepping around him to climb unaided up into the front cabin of the truck. She was no sooner seated when he appeared beside her, and then her hands shook as a fresh wave of post-drama nausea suddenly washed over her body. She was aware of Carter's hands, completely steady hands, one on her shoulder, one enveloping her own trembling hands and warm against her skin. She stared into the blue eyes as he smiled.

"You'll be fine," he said quietly, "It's a natural reaction, and it will pass."

She saw the smile broaden on his face, and his voice was calm as he continued, "Happens to all of us, so don't be embarrassed. A quite fearless French friend of mine always gets the shakes after a bit of violent action."

She saw the blue eyes twinkle as he paused before resuming, "He says it always reminds him of how he feels when he's made love to his wife."

Elizabeth felt the shaky beginnings of her own smile, and couldn't stop the words any more than she could the blush which came with some of them, "Happens to all of us, you say, but I haven't seen you or the Welshman shaking. Besides, Major Carter, I've experienced lovemaking and this is an entirely different feeling."

She felt herself blushing into the silence following her disclosure and rushed her attempt to cover the embarrassment, "And your fearless French friend is probably a figment of your imagination. Does he even have a name?"

Carter released the steadying grip on her shoulder, and the enveloping warmth of his other hand covering her own was removed as he turned his attention to starting the truck. Then above the roar of the engine coming to life, she heard his shouted response, "Jack used to refer to him as the dependable *Dubois,* but I just call him *Claude.*"

She could feel the strength flowing back through her limbs as she once more impulsively gave voice to her thoughts, "Was it in France that Jack saved your life?" she asked, watching him carefully. The blue eyes rested on her briefly before he looked straight ahead with his reply.

"Yes, it was, but I'd rather you kept that fact to yourself."

The truck was negotiating a steeply rising road taking them away from the village centre, and in contemplative silence Elizabeth glanced out at the passing scenes. Two women leaning against a sand-bagged shop-front waved at the truck, and her responsive wave abruptly plunged her back in time... *To Knightsbridge, when she'd gaily waved to other women on what had been destined to be her last day with Jack...* Her reverie was disrupted as the truck crested the hill and her driver spoke once more.

"This new passenger of ours alters my plans," he informed her, "I *had* intended leaving tomorrow, but now I'll need to use your telephone when we get back. And then me and mine will be leaving you and yours after lunch."

Elizabeth's memory of unwanted departure news being delivered to her was instantly reprised, chased now by freshly disconcerting thoughts; *'Would this also be the last time she would see the man seated beside her now? And should she care?'* Her response was out before she could stop it, "But I haven't even had the chance to thank you properly." She paused, feeling the heat on her face as she resumed, "I mean, Mary and I had planned a thank-you party."

"No time for that now, I'm afraid," he replied, "It will take us long enough to return three trucks and six Italians, and now we have what's no doubt a reluctant conscript to offload."

She made no attempt to conceal her disappointment and he was quick to respond.

"Sorry about the party, Elizabeth," he paused, smiling ruefully as he added, "I can't even *vaguely* remember when I last attended a party."

"Where do you go from here?" she asked, uncontrollably thinking of Jack as she spoke. She saw him hesitate, but he answered her steadily.

"France, but that's something *else* you don't know, Elizabeth, and something else I'm afraid I can't elaborate on."

Painfully recalling her memory of believing Scotland to be safe for Jack, she refused the urge to question Carter's safety in a place like France. Nobody was safe in France. They travelled in silence for a while before his voice penetrated her confused thoughts.

"Before we leave, can you let me have something to keep Shaw sedated for his trip?"

"Yes I can," she replied without any hesitation, realizing as she spoke that she felt completely indifferent as to the belligerent Shaw's fate.

Each of them of course unaware of the other's thoughts, the journey continued in silence. Alan Carter was once again reminding himself that the very desirable young woman beside him was strictly off-limits. He was wishing she wasn't.

Whilst Elizabeth Creacey, having wound down her window for some mind-clearing air, was wrestling with memories and listening to a forlorn sounding inner-voice expressing the hope that when they reached their destination, the telephone would be disconnected. All too soon the truck was accessing the driveway and approaching the new sign fronting the main house. Sighting it granted some relief to Elizabeth's troubled conscience and she spoke quickly as the truck came to a halt.

"Peter will show you where the phone is in the cottage. I'll get what you need for Shaw." She paused thoughtfully as he eyed her, "We should also splint his finger before you sedate him. Then he'll be less troublesome to you *and*," she grinned into the watchful blue eyes, "he'll be fit for duty all the quicker."

"My but you're a hard one, Elizabeth," said the Welshman outside her opened window, grinning as he continued up at her surprised face, "But you'll do for *me*, right enough. Our Boyo's behaving himself as we speak, but don't be long. I'll babysit him till you get back."

For Elizabeth the next two hours were regrettably consumed by medical and military efficiency. Upon hearing recent history, Mary Reynolds briskly prepared a concoction for its instigator whilst Elizabeth gathered her own requirements. With *Chevalier* and *Laporte* also appraised of the situation, as Elizabeth began her return to the truck she saw that French and Italian teamwork had already began dismantling the makeshift camp behind the main house.

His compliant behaviour attributable to the close proximity of a ferocious looking Welshman, the profoundly shocked Harold Shaw was having his finger splint applied when Elizabeth overheard Carter tell Parish that contact had been successful. Without being told, she knew that Carter had spoken to Simon Rawlings. She then saw the Officer whisper to his Sergeant and heard the Welshman's incredulous sounding 'Horse guards?', but she was too busy to think about it.

Accompanied by Mary, she later bade an emotional farewell to the two Frenchmen and if *Laporte* was disappointed by the seeming nonchalance of her friend, he didn't show it. On behalf of *his* fellow countrymen, Gianfranco took receipt of their financial dues and his eyes widened as he realized the amount of bonus she had added.

"*Grazie, Signorina,*" he acknowledged, hesitating as he displayed a sad looking smile and waved a hand to indicate the home he and his men had proudly laboured over. His high-pitched voice quivered in two languages as he resumed, "This crazy war, *Signorina,* it is sometimes the *Divina Commedia.*" He paused, and the sad smile became a happy beam which lit up the swarthy face with his next words, "*Questo e mio Paradiso.*"

Needing the translation, Elizabeth silently appealed to the watching Carter. Who promptly responded with a sad looking smile of his own as he obliged.

"A man called *Dante* once wrote a poem, over... maybe six hundred years ago, and he entitled it *Divina Commedia.*" He paused, "Divine Comedy," he translated, his tone bitter.

Aware of how different he sounded, Elizabeth stared into the blue eyes as he continued, "He split the poem into three sections; *The Inferno; The Purgatorio;* and *The Paradiso,* which translates as Hell, Purgatory, and Heaven. Gianfranco is saying that war can sometimes be divine comedy because working on your convalescent home has been his short time in heaven."

Instinctively sensing that Carter was using the translation to convey to her his *own* message, but nevertheless wondering if she was just imagining it, Elizabeth couldn't trust herself to find the right words. So she simply smiled her thanks to the Italian POW, who returned the smile with one of his own as he saluted her before turning away towards the waiting trucks. She smiled as the Welshman then stepped forward. Her shoulders were gripped by the huge hands and his grin was fierce as he spoke.

"Keep the home fires burning, Elizabeth, Girl."

"I hope you see Narberth again soon, Glyn," she replied quietly before kissing his cheek.

As the powerful Welshman released his gentle grip and turned away from her, she could still feel his hands on her shoulders. It occurred to her that he had controlled that power earlier also, and that Harold Shaw had been fortunate to escape with his jaw intact.

The afternoon sun was now hot on her skin but she nevertheless felt strangely chilled.

The realization strong now, that the time had come to render what she knew would be an inadequate goodbye to the remaining man who had done so much for her. A man who had reawakened within her, feelings which had, for a time, unsettled her. A man who, along with herself, would never have been in this place at all, had not *his* life been saved by the man who had made it possible for *her* to be here. Yet another man, like Jack in so many ways, who remained a stranger to her. She stood now wondering if she was looking into the blue eyes for the last time. "We owe you a party," she said, forcing the smile, "Come back after the war, and play the piano for us as beautifully as you did this morning."

"I'll do that," he replied, returning her smile, "It has been a pleasure knowing you, Elizabeth."

The words were out before she could stop them, "But you *don't* know me."

Alan Carter paused as his choice of words was carefully sought. Still in his mind's eye, beside the telephone he'd used to call Rawlings, had been the sketched image of the unforgettable face of Jack Matthews. He looked now into the watchful eyes of Elizabeth Creacey and imagined he saw what might have been.

"I know enough to say that Jack would be very proud of you. Goodbye, Elizabeth."

The kiss on her cheek was delivered so fast she had barely registered it before she was watching him stride away towards the trucks. He didn't look back, and his parting words were still in her ears long after she saw the last of the vehicles disappear from view.

Later that evening, long after everyone else was asleep, commanded by feelings demanding release, Elizabeth finally opened her diary journal and attempted to record the recent events which had thrown her thoughts into such disarray.

Later still, when she had poured her thoughts and feelings out onto the pages, with peace of mind restored through her silent communion with the man who still lived in her heart, she raised to her lips the framed sketch of Jack and kissed him Goodnight.

Chapter Sixteen

Whosoever, in writing a modern history, shall follow truth too near the heels, it may happily strike out his teeth.
(Walter Raleigh)

Remainder June... through to December 1944

For 'Creacey's Cavaliers', time and events inexorably rolled forward in the months immediately following the departure of Carter and his men. Time itself, in its normally measured sense, almost became meaningless as both European and local events catapulted days into weeks which blurred into months. Consequently, Elizabeth's diary journals steadily grew in number and her cathartic entries encapsulated a memorable series of triumphs and disasters.

In June she wrote of the shock waves felt throughout the village 'grapevine' at the news of a 'flying bomb' which had landed in London's 'Horse guard's Parade'. Damaging the Guard's Chapel of Wellington Barracks (a stone's throw from Buckingham Palace) the bomb had killed and injured many servicemen and civilians. Elizabeth's diary entry recalled her memory of the Welshman's incredulous *Horse guard's?* response to Alan Carter's whisper.

She wrote despairingly of the frustration caused by bureaucratic delays in processing the necessary documentation required before she could officially open the convalescent home; but scribed with optimism the progress of ongoing recruitment interviews to find the staff needed for kitchen and care duties. The creation of a special June entry had been caused by the wartime vagaries of the postal service, belatedly bringing the letter forwarded from Knightsbridge by the reliable Mrs Bruce. The writing on the envelope had been unfamiliar to Elizabeth, but when opened had revealed the letter, written in April, to have come from Katherine Swan. Imagining some kind of threat to the life she'd started with her son, Elizabeth's diary entry reflected the panic she'd felt at the time.

Instead she had read the few lines informing her that Tom Ball had managed to wrangle two days leave during April and they'd had a *marvellous* time. Katherine had also disclosed that she was pregnant, and wasn't *that* marvellous. Her recognizable scrawl had gone on to say that Tom had told her the war would soon be over, *and wouldn't that be marvellous!*

The letter had ended abruptly; briefly expressing the hope that Elizabeth was well and advising she would write again soon. Having counted the number of times Katherine had scrawled *marvellous,* Elizabeth had concluded that it must have been the fashionable word in London at the time of writing. However, as her diary entry emphasised, Katherine had not enquired about the child she had abandoned to Elizabeth's care.

Elizabeth's diary entry would also show that she had immediately written back to Katherine, thanking her for the letter and congratulating her on her pregnancy. In a few carefully worded lines the diary entry also recorded her decision to abide by the advice she had been given by Simon Rawlings. So in her reply to Katherine, she had made no mention of the fact that she was now, in the eyes of the law, the natural birth-mother of Matthew Creacey.

Even in the little time the month had left to run, periodic diary entries conveyed the village grapevine's horror of Hitler's flying bombs continuing to wreak their carnage as the June of stalwart Londoners' shuddered to a close.

The diary journal described her July delight when Arthur Arkwright had arrived with a group of local women wishing to personally thank her for the gifts of glass for their broken windows and the extra rations for their sparsely filled kitchen cupboards. At a stroke, recorded the diary, she had found her willing team for the convalescent home's future domestic demands. A further entry noted her ambivalence towards Arkwright's news that he'd received the official notification of Harold Shaw's conscription and overseas posting to The Pioneer Corps.

Along with the announcement that he was setting up his own office in Carshalton, Jonathan Teale received several 'mentions in despatches' for his invaluable help with financial forecasts for the convalescent home. A few lines were given over to his invitation to a London theatre outing which Elizabeth had diplomatically declined.

Elizabeth's astonishment leapt from the diary entry recording the visitation from Ministry of Defence officials appearing to inform her that, upon the recommendation of Simon Rawlings, they would be contracting with *The Chantal Cheval Convalescent Home*.

Duly transcribed in the diary was her telephoned attempt to reach Rawlings. Told that he was unavailable, her entry conveyed regret that the heartfelt message of thanks left with the remembered and still politely official sounding operator, would probably have been diluted by the ultimately filtered transmission.

The month of July was closed with the simple entry denoting that the first anniversary of Jack's death had come to pass very quickly. An August entry amusedly told of the village grapevine's belatedly newsworthy excitement. Upon learning that during the previous month a group of German Generals had failed in their attempt to assassinate Hitler, this news had allegedly prompted another village 'wag' to suggest Carshalton could have succeeded by sending in their very own *Delicate Doris*, a woman memorably identified in Elizabeth's diary as the solidly muscled 16 stone barmaid and cook for *The Strife and Strumpet* pub.

Fresher news 'off the vine' of the French Resistance movement openly rising against the Germans on August 19th, occasioned Elizabeth's recorded feelings of trepidation. Days later, having read the triumphal newspaper reports of August 25th telling of General Jacques Leclerc receiving the unconditional surrender of the Germans, she had boldly written in her diary the words *Paris is Liberated!* But her footnote had expressed concern for the whereabouts and well-being of Alan Carter and his men.

In the face of a government-imposed total news 'blackout', September entries praised the village grapevine's successful efforts which brought news of Hitler's so-called V2 rockets being launched from Holland to strike northern parts of beleaguered London.

Elizabeth's notations were considerably more light-hearted when charting the ongoing progress of baby Matthew, and a November entry recording 'Armistice Day' told of her joy at the reported appearance by Britain's Prime Minister Churchill on the *Champs Elysees* of a now liberated Paris.

Elizabeth closed an early December page with the remark that her colleagues had 'raised a glass with her' to toast her 25th birthday. A following entry recorded their very first Christmas celebration at the now ready, albeit unopened convalescent home. Those local women agreeably designated to be the home's future domestic squad had attended this special occasion, along with the jovial Arthur Arkwright; reportedly delighting Mary with his weight loss and baby Matthew with the presented cuddly toy. The diary entry strove to explain Elizabeth's retrospective sense of unreality felt whilst listening to Arkwright regaling everyone with his witty recounting of their historical storage unit adventures.

Christened this time with reports that countrywide increases in ration-book theft were nevertheless being overtaken by clothing coupons as a black market 'top seller', a new diary journal was commenced. This one closed down December with an entry expressing the writer's 'almost disbelief' that the eventful year of 1944 had finally come to an end.

January... through to... March 1945

The entire country was now in the vice-like grip of a winter more bitter than some people could remember having experienced for five decades. Despite this, some hardy varieties of plant life managed to spread their roots. So, nurtured by the determined faithful and cross-pollinated by intrepid commercial foot-soldiers, informational fruit continued to fall from the Carshalton village grapevine.

Thus, whilst frustrated newspaper editors remained forbidden to print about the daily deaths and destruction caused by the lethal V2 rockets, January's 'word of mouth' hushed transmissions told Carshalton inhabitants of the still widespread attacks over London and parts of Essex. It was by this means that Peter Corder learned that the fellow Doctor who had stood beside him at Bart's telling him *'You can't save them all'* had been one of the five killed when a V2 rocket had struck London's Royal Hospital.

Elizabeth's own return to London, an event destined to produce its own dramatic consequences, was occasioned by the surprise invitation from Thora Silverthorne. A revered figure within the nursing profession, Thora was widely recognized as the woman largely responsible for the formation of the 'Association of Nurses' (the first Trade Union for Nurses).

"You *do* know, I suppose," said Mary, "that she's an active member of the Communist party."

"I know she saved countless lives by her actions in the Spanish civil war," replied Elizabeth.

The invitation had requested Elizabeth to be at London's Ritz Hotel at the appointed date and time and she was still standing at the reception desk, gazing around in wide-eyed wonder, when the woman introducing herself as Thora Silverthorne's assistant came to collect her.

"How the other half live, eh?" said the woman without preamble, "Opens your eyes as well as your mouth when you first see this place," she cheerfully added. "My boss has been attending a meeting here, so this was a convenient venue for her to see you," she qualified, leading her audience at a brisk pace to the door of a ground-level room. Standing beside the assistant at the door, something must have shown itself on Elizabeth's face because the woman patted her arm before quietly saying, "In you go, love, she won't bite you."

Inside the opulently furnished room, seated at a table surrounded by displaced and empty chairs, was the attractive looking woman whom Elizabeth knew to be the thirty-five years old Thora Silverthorne. The woman rose to her feet, smiling as she extended a hand in greeting.

"Well we both know who we are," opened Thora, "so we can dispense with that bit. Come and sit beside me, my dear."

Elizabeth complied, already warming to the woman, wondering why *she* was here.

"Thank you for coming to see me, my dear," said Thora, smiling as she went on, "When I learned of the pipeline existence of a convalescent home for ex-servicemen and women, I applauded. When I was told the age of its founder, I must confess to you that I gasped."

"I have qualified and experienced people alongside me," Elizabeth pointed out, but her hostess was waving away the interjection as if it was superfluous to current requirements.

"But when they *finally* told me," said Thora, her smile even wider now, "the Frenchwoman's name which had been given to the proposed establishment, I insisted upon being given the opportunity to meet the name behind the name."

"You are familiar with the name, Chantal Cheval?" queried an astonished Elizabeth.

"Relatives of mine would not be alive today, but for Chantal Cheval," said Thora, "She helped them escape the Germans. But you must *know* her, to be using her name. Is she in England now?"

Struggling to retain her composure, inwardly reeling from the woman's disclosure, Elizabeth quietly explained the little she knew about Chantal, and of how she had come to know even a little.

"My dear child, I am so very sorry to hear about the loss of your *fiancé*. And devastated to learn about Chantal. Your choice of name for the convalescent home, is of course now understood."

Watching her as the woman paused, Elizabeth knew that she was being scrutinised.

"May I call you Elizabeth?" asked Thora.

"Please do," replied Elizabeth, failing to mask her surprise.

"I met Chantal once, Elizabeth, some time ago now, but I still remember her. I feel sure she would have been proud to know you as her daughter-in-law." She paused, frowning, "My assistant gave me only *some* background information, so of course I don't know *everything*. But we were both surprised, my assistant and I, by the pipeline reference. Is there any particular reason why your convalescent home is still not open for business, Elizabeth?"

Elizabeth took a deep breath, then began explaining about the bureaucratic hurdles she had been attempting to clear.

"Can you give me the names of these bureaucrats, Elizabeth?"

Elizabeth effortlessly reeled off the names of those who had been obstructive.

"I know them all," said Thora, "and *they* in turn know *me*. My assistant will look after you while I make some telephone calls. You should have time to sample tea at the Ritz, my dear."

On their second coming together the assistant introduced herself as Gladys, and she cheerfully steered Elizabeth through the social etiquette of 'tea at the Ritz' whilst furnishing a further surprise.

"Well you can now consider your bureaucratic hurdles to be things of the past, Elizabeth," said Gladys, daintily dealing with an escaping biscuit crumb as she added, "If you've ever had any dealings with Welsh people, then you'll know that they don't suffer fools gladly and they don't hesitate to speak their mind. Apart from her political clout, my boss is the daughter of a Welsh miner. So when *she* picks up the phone to sort out a problem, believe me, it gets sorted."

Elizabeth decided not to mention her own experience of things Welsh and one hour later found herself back with Thora Silverthorne.

"I won't bore you with their excuses, Elizabeth. Your officially required documentation will be couriered to Carshalton tomorrow," declared the steely-voiced Welshwoman.

"I don't know how I can ever repay you for this," responded Elizabeth, trying to keep her elation from turning to tears but realizing that she was failing.

"The work you will be doing is all the repayment I need, Elizabeth. I shall be expecting great things of you, and I don't believe you will disappoint. Dry your eyes, my dear, Chantal's name will never be forgotten, thanks to you."

A Chauffeur-driven Elizabeth travelled home deep in thought; *'She was leaving behind a London crippled by 'Union-called' strikes on the city's docks; its transport network; and its factories. The irony not lost to her that another form of union, bonding Thora*

Silverthorne to Jack's mother, was now enabling her to finally open the convalescent home.'

Later that evening, her diary entry spoke of Mary's then music charts favourite having been apt for the new circumstances and that she had happily found herself humming along with her friend, the Harry James rendition of *'I'm Beginning To See The Light'*.

At the end of January, courtesy of officially approved documentation and a galvanised MOD, the first patients were admitted to the convalescent home.

Meanwhile the village grapevine belatedly and cautiously reported that Hitler's flying bombs had apparently ceased flying. However the vine itself shuddered when *Delicate Doris* successfully applied for the job of Head Cook at the convalescent home, and, in retaliatory mode, *The Strife and Strumpet* regulars threatened to stop grapevine news getting through to Elizabeth and her growing band of Cavaliers.

The February opening of Jonathan Teale's Carshalton office was overshadowed by more potent events elsewhere. On the 13th, Britain's RAF launched a saturation bombing attack on Germany's *'Florence on the Elbe'*. An exercise repeated by the USAF on the 14th which was, ominously enough, Ash Wednesday. Following the two day blitz, the German city of Dresden lay flattened and beyond recognition. Continuing to deflect attention from Jonathan Teale, further performances on the world stage saw Churchill, Roosevelt, and Stalin sharing top billing at 'The Yalta Conference', whilst still unconfirmed reports placed the Russians forty miles from Hitler's beleaguered Bunker in Berlin.

Elizabeth's diary closed down February by drawing comparisons between Alan Carter's Welshman and her own newly acquired 'magical provider'. *Delicate Doris* was reportedly proving to be someone whom suppliers could not, or dare not, refuse. Elizabeth, *said her diary,* had been advised to turn a blind eye to 'special arrangements' which had seen *Strife and Strumpet* regulars gastronomically satisfied once more, and the re-opening of the convalescent home's grapevine channel.

As the ninth day of March had dawned on Elizabeth's new regime, news was received that the London based Smithfield market she fondly remembered, had been struck by a V2 rocket, reportedly suffering appalling damage and the loss of many civilian lives. But as Elizabeth had been tuning in to Les Brown's rendition of *'My Dreams Are Getting Better'*, another kind of bomb had landed closer to home. Evidently marring her preparations towards celebrating Matthew's first birthday, had been the sense of unease reprised in the diary entry which told of the badly timed arrival of Katherine Swan's second letter.

Once again, the writing on the envelope differed to that of Katherine's scrawl on the single page it contained.

"Let *me* read it," said Mary, snatching the missive before she could be stopped, "I can censor anything unsuitable. I *will not* have your day spoiled by that selfish little cow."

Elizabeth smiled as she watched her friend scan the single sheet of paper.

"She says, and I quote," began Mary, "She's fed up with staying at Tom Ball's brother's place because the brother's wife doesn't like her. She says she's tired of having to save up coupons every time she wants something she doesn't have to put on a plate."

Elizabeth saw Mary's face darken as she silently read on, and then her friend raised her head and sounded strained when she spoke again.

"I thank God that you took Matthew away from this woman, Elizabeth. Listen to what she says at the end here," said Mary, lowering her head again to the letter. "*Still, it looks like this bloody war is over, so we can all have some fun soon. You'll be pleased to know that Tom now has a son. He wanted it called David if it was a boy, so that's what he's got and that's what's he's called. That's it,*" said Mary, sounding aghast, "That's just how it ends. She doesn't ask about *you*, or *Matthew*, or say anything pleasant at all for that matter. This is just a list of complaints."

"And no mention of when her son was born," remarked Elizabeth, "But I suppose I should write to congratulate her, don't you think?"

"Poor little beggar drew the short straw with *her*, no matter when he was born," said Mary.

A later diary entry recorded the writer's pleasure that Matthew's first birthday party had been briefly attended by a busy quartet comprising Mary Reynolds, Peter Corder, Jonathan Teale, and *Delicate Doris*. According to the diary, Matthew had slept through his first three visitors but had come awake to the kitchen aromas emanating from *Doris*. The diary's month of March closed lamenting the death of David Lloyd-George, and the village grapevine's report that another V2 rocket had struck London's East End with devastating effect.

Chapter Seventeen

The English are paralysed by fear. That is what thwarts and distorts the Anglo-Saxon existence. Nothing could be more lovely and fearless than Chaucer, but already Shakespeare is morbid with fear. Fear of consequences. The consequences of action.
(D.H. Lawrence)

Surrey, England, Carshalton apartment of Andrew Teale, Monday evening, 13th Jan 1992

She'd been caught napping. Clutching to her chest the cushion she'd been using as a pillow, her tone of voice resonating with tiredness and anxiety, Jenny Murray impatiently acknowledged Andrew Teale's return to their apartment.

"Are *you* okay? You're back sooner than I expected. How was he? How did he react?"

"Coffee would be fine, thanks," he responded, a second before deflecting the thrown cushion and capitulating to her obvious concern. "*I'm* fine, and apart from toothache," he paused to shrug his shoulders, "or maybe because of it, *he* seemed sharp enough."

A partly mollified Jenny headed for the kitchen, trailed by a wholly contrite Andrew.

"It really didn't take long," he continued, "to outline what we'd found and your recommended order of reading." He paused, "He seemed preoccupied as I laid it out for him."

"*Hardly* surprising, surely," retorted Jenny as she busied herself with cups, "Before *you* arrived on his doorstep, all he had to worry about was finding a traitor in his boardroom."

"He didn't mention that," said Andrew, frowning as he resumed, "But you're right of course, the man had a full enough plate before *we* added to it."

"*We?* Don't include *me* on your guilt trip; I'm just the innocent collator."

"Who agreed," responded Andrew, his frown deeper now, "that he should be shown what had been found, *and*, on brief reflection, *traitor* sounds very melodramatic."

"Yes, I agreed," she admitted, making eye contact as she added, "And what else can you call someone who takes Matthew's coin whilst betraying his trust."

"Now you sound positively biblical," responded Andrew, smiling now, "But I take your point."

"Well God help the man," said Jenny, "when he's finished reading those diaries, and *you* sound smug, legal boy."

"What, exactly, has found its way under *your* saddle? Why are you having a go at *me*?"

"I've been having second thoughts," confessed Jenny, "He doesn't know that *we know* what we thought was *all* that he had done." She took a deep breath before resuming, "*But*, when he has read those diaries he's going to realize that he didn't in fact *really* know what he was doing, and, when *that fact* hits him, will there be enough of a man left to *cope with that* as well as what he *thought* was his main problem before he was handed those bloody diaries?"

Running his fingers through his hair again, Andrew was suddenly conscious of the fact that this time it was *he* who was filling his lungs with air before slowly blowing it back out again as he replied, "Yes, I hear what you're saying, Jenny. If *he* falls apart, the company will be in serious trouble."

Jenny watched him worry his hair, and wondered if he was thinking about his late father's misguided judgement bequeathing him a potential professional disaster.

"And yours truly," resumed Andrew, quietly, "representing Teale and Lewis, will have been the cause of it."

In that moment Jenny Murray was reminded of just one of the reasons why she loved the man standing before her. She smiled as she embraced him and whispered in his ear, "Who could resist a man who would take the rap for his collator?" She stood back and gently punched his shoulder as she added, "If Matthew starts to fall apart, you'll just have to be on hand to hold him together. *Capiche*?"

Jenny saw the smile begin on his lips and reach his eyes as he replied, "It's a done deal, Delilah."

Chapter Eighteen

History is, indeed, little more than the register of the crimes, follies, and misfortunes of mankind.
(Edward Gibbon)

The Chantal Cheval Convalescent Home, Carshalton, Surrey, England, April... through to end of August 1945

As without fanfare the moon continued to orbit the earth, each of the following five Lunar divisions of 1945, telescoped within Elizabeth's diary, contrastingly appeared to have been competing for the *'Tumultuous Month of the Year'* title.

April entries mentioned the formation of the 'United Nations'. *Another title which,* according to one of the more literal village 'wags', *would probably prove to be an unfortunate misnomer.*

A diary page recorded the Ministry of Health circular regarding the national return of evacuees. Large numbers of mothers with new babies, along with older children, were now being returned to their already hard-pressed communities. Some of the older children had been away from their homes and families since 1939. The circular warned of the likely impact upon such things as rationing and accommodation.

The death by cerebral haemorrhage of America's President Roosevelt was noted, and a question mark stood alongside the name of Harry S. Truman. Two harrowing paragraphs on an April page told of Elizabeth's radio shocking her as it brought to her ears Richard Dimbleby's broadcast from a German concentration camp in a place called Belsen.

With Adolf Hitler's reported suicide, and a grapevine-confirmed entry that Italy's Mussolini had been hanged in the street by a mob, Elizabeth could have been forgiven for imagining no more dramatic end to her April diary pages. But as a postscript in her neat hand bravely showed, with barely hours of the month remaining, cruel fate had demanded a late inclusion. At the behest of a widowed mother bearing a letter from Simon Rawlings on behalf of her son, a convalescent bed had been urgently provided. No diary could ever have conveyed Elizabeth's sadness as she'd stood at the bedside looking down into Alan Carter's blue eyes which had shown no sign of recognition.

In line with the Creacey expansion plans, a May diary entry recorded the purchase of a Sussex building destined to become *The Chantal Cheval Home for Palliative Care*. Peter Corder, noted the diary, had been sounded out with a view to eventually managing it.

On a war-related entry; the sturdy 'Vine' had reported that in the French town of *Reims*, led by Field Marshal Alfred Jodl, the German High Command had unconditionally surrendered. Mentioned on another May page, was the reported announcement of VE day.

The village grapevine had been quick to point out that whilst one war was ostensibly over, another war was still going on in Japan. But at that time, as was noted within her diary, Elizabeth was more focused on her own battle to restore to health the traumatised Alan Carter. *It was*, she boldly committed to print, *a battle she was determined to win.*

Towards the month's end, as Elizabeth sat outside writing of the euphoria sweeping the country, Mary Reynolds wistfully gave voice to an opinion.

"Perhaps the future can be glimpsed with more certainty," said her friend.

"Well at least we'll know if it's going to rain," responded Peter Corder.

Elizabeth smiled, realizing that Peter's caustic comment sprang from the fact that since the announcement of VE day, newspapers had been allowed to print weather forecasts for the first time in five years.

Elizabeth's June, July and August diary pages were short on words but could hardly be described as lightweight. Entries covered June newspapers bombarding readers with facts and opinions on the nationwide absence of housing stock, qualified by Elizabeth as the seeming bone of contention in the lead up to forthcoming government elections. Commenting briefly on the published manifesto of an ageing Churchill's Conservative party, Elizabeth had evidently singled out his declared obligation to fulfil his government's plans for the treatment and rehabilitation of war-disabled servicemen and women. Attached to her diary page was a carbon copy of the letter she'd written to Winston Churchill inviting the great man himself to visit the convalescent home.

A July diary page recorded the Labour party's landslide election victory. As July busily neared its close in the convalescent home, Elizabeth's own daily visits to the bedside of Alan Carter were still going unrecognized. She wasn't sure whether or not Peter Corder was just trying to cheer her up, but *he* had voiced his own confidence in a successful outcome to the care and attention Carter was receiving.

She had grown used to her thoughts on Peter Corder always producing a mix of emotions: He was an excellent Doctor; a seemingly tireless worker; a good manager; wonderful with baby Matthew; was always considerate towards her; and he made her laugh a lot. Whenever she talked about these thoughts with Mary, who'd gone beyond subtle some time ago now, her friend had said *'What you're talking about is first class husband material'*.

A late July evening, and the trio were relaxing with a drink before going their separate ways to bed when Peter started chuckling to himself.

"What's so funny that can't be shared?" queried Mary.

"I've been thinking about the reason our domestic staff have all been having a laugh today."

"Which is?" joined in Elizabeth.

"It's this new officially entitled 'Mass-Observation Research Programme' "

"We have a pamphlet somewhere, but I haven't read it yet," said Elizabeth, "The title sounds very portentous. Why are they laughing about it?"

"It's a programme," began the smiling Peter, "seemingly inspired by a government declaring itself, and I quote; *anxious to discover the public view on a wide range of subjects.*"

"Laudable stuff," opined Mary, "but I imagine they could find better ways to spend their time, and the public's money."

"I repeat," said Elizabeth, "Why are they laughing about it?"

"A research team has apparently been to the village," replied Peter, still smiling, "and were reported to have left in a daze following their encounter with *Strife and Strumpet* regulars."

And on that qualification, the trio had laughed their way to individual sleeping quarters.

Whilst the village grapevine was reportedly claiming it had beaten the national press with the news that the Russians were trampling all over Poland's soil, Elizabeth closed down her July with a diary entry praising Winston Churchill. Despite his overwhelming general election defeat, the great man himself had actually telephoned to accept *her gracious invitation.*

An August diary page despairingly recounted that despite the ongoing potency of her special licence, rationing was continuing to bite into attempts by *Delicate Doris* to obtain and provide the necessary balance of foodstuffs required for the home's patients and staff. Jonathan Teale's visit was recorded, with his projected opening date for the Sussex home given as January 1946. Also noted were his comments on the country's domestic turmoil in the aftermath of war; '*A domestic turmoil which, in view of the high number of divorce cases being handled by my own office alone, could only be measured in the imagination.*'

Elizabeth also recorded the generally expressed disbelief surrounding events in Japan. She wrote of the collective inability to conceive the seeming power of Atomic bombs dropped on Hiroshima and Nagasaki, and her entry noting Japan' surrender was noticeably bereft of joyful exclamation marks.

Modestly conveyed by a brief August diary entry, the visit of Winston Churchill had seemingly been made with surprisingly little ceremony. Accompanied only by his wife, Clementine, and the obligatory bodyguard, the democratically deposed wartime leader had spent almost two hours at the convalescent home. But, as was noted, within the first ten minutes Churchill had informed her they shared a mutual friend in the shape of Simon Rawlings and that he'd been requested to visit the bedside of a patient named Alan Carter.

A closing entry was dedicated to the memory of Churchill sitting at the seemingly unresponsive Carter's bedside, and talking. Not about battle campaigns, or lost elections, but about music.

Churchill was quoted as having said; *'I'm not speaking to the damaged soldier, but to the man who has been and could be again.'* Witnessing this empathy with her patient had brought back to Elizabeth, the memory of Carter's virtuosity on the piano.

Chapter Nineteen

For secrets are edged tools, and must be kept from children and from fools.
(John Dryden)

The Chantal Cheval Convalescent Home, Carshalton, Surrey, England, Sunday 21st and Monday 22nd December 1945
Despite the amount of progress and levels of achievement attained over the past year, Elizabeth had found the early months following the cessation of war particularly hard to bear.

Witnessing men returning to their families, she'd constantly thought of how it could have been for herself and Jack. Pouring her heart out in her diary had been steadily helping her come to terms with a life without him, but the closing down of her emotional conduit for the previous three months had re-awakened the longing for what she had been denied. The fractured right arm had now healed, but the pain in her heart was still felt.

Nevertheless her 26th birthday had been celebrated with her friends and colleagues, the Surrey home was running smoothly, the Sussex home was on course for its January opening, Alan Carter was slowly recovering, and, as Mary had been reminding her, she could be thankful that young Matthew was healthily happy.

She was totally unprepared for the phone call from Simon Rawlings four days before Christmas, and immediately consented to his request to come and see her the following day. She had thought of him often, and now welcomed an opportunity to thank him for all that he had done for her. She was startled by the realization that it had been almost two years since she'd seen the man who had made it possible for her to have Matthew.

"Perhaps he might be persuaded to stay over until Christmas," she said to her friend.

"The man is quite likely to have a family of his own to spend Christmas with," replied Mary.

Suitably chastised for not having thought of that, it was then agreed that Elizabeth would be left undisturbed for her meeting with Rawlings the following day.

Simon Rawlings arrived the following morning and Elizabeth was immediately struck by the change in his physical appearance. In addition to noticeable weight loss, he was no longer ruddy-complexioned or chubby-cheeked and his eyes looked tired in the pale looking face. Knowledgeable these days about the variety of uniforms used to cover differing branches of the military tree, she made no comment upon recognizing that the one now worn by Rawlings revealed him to be a full-Colonel in the service of his country's Intelligence Corps. She instead briefly thought of Jack, and of Alan Carter, and mothballed uniforms, and questions which had never been answered. Once inside the lounge of the annexed-cottage, her visitor went straight to where Matthew sat propped up in his day-cot.

"He's a fine looking little chap," said Rawlings, smiling as he spoke.

Elizabeth had seen the smile, but had also seen something else in the tired looking eyes, "There's nothing wrong, is there?" she queried, anxiously adding, "About Matthew, I mean."

"Good gracious, No," he responded instantly, "Absolutely nothing at all. You need never worry on that score," he assured her.

Relieved, she invited him to sit down. But he seemed not to hear, and instead paced to the window with its view of the grounds.

"Lovely spot you have here," he said, sounding wistful.

"Yes, it is," she replied, moving to stand beside him. As she watched him the thought came to her that the last man to enter this cottage wearing an army uniform had been Alan Carter; when he'd come to telephone the man beside her now. "You could look in on Alan Carter whilst you're here," she quietly suggested.

She saw the uniformed shoulders stiffen and the tired eyes which refused to meet her own narrowed in the pale face as he replied.

"I imagine I'm the last person he would want to see."

At a loss for words, Elizabeth could only stare. His response had surprised her so much that in that instant she decided not to divulge any of the never-forgotten information entrusted to her by Carter. *'Not until I hear what this man has come to say to me,'* she thought.

"The Chantal Cheval Convalescent Home," said Rawlings, turning to her now as he smiled, "Thoughtfully chosen name. You're idea, obviously," he quietly added.

"Well the legacy stems from her, after all," she responded, adding firmly, "And I know that Jack would have approved."

Rawlings nodded his head in seeming agreement before smiling again with his question, "Any tea in this paradise?"

"Yes of course. I'll put the kettle on. You sit down and relax."

She left his side and moved into the kitchen, but had hardly started her task before she was aware of his shape filling the open doorway.

"Sorry I've come so close to Christmas. Must be a busy enough time for you without me landing on your doorstep at such short notice."

"That's perfectly all right," she assured him, glancing over her shoulder to add, "I've wanted to thank you again, anyway, for your help with Matthew. And for all the other extraordinary things you've done for me since. Milk and sugar?"

"Both, if you can manage."

She turned back to her task, conscious of him remaining rooted in the doorway. As she busied herself with cups she wondered how she could ever really thank him properly for everything; silently concluding she could never thank him enough.

"I have to leave for Germany tomorrow and I may be there for some time. I wanted to speak with you before I go."

"It's about Jack, then, is it?" she asked, feigning calmness, and his answer seemed to pierce her shoulder-blades.

"Yes, It's about Jack," replied Rawlings, quietly.

The boiling kettle provided Matthew's cue and from the other room he began some attention-seeking noises.

"I'll see to him," volunteered Rawlings, quickly moving away from the doorway.

Conscious of the man's restlessness seeking release, Elizabeth remained where she was and completed the tea-making preparations. She carried the tray-laden offerings back into the lounge where Matthew, watched by the smiling Rawlings, was quietly and happily trying to separate a Colonel's cap-badge from its housing.

"Please choose a chair and sit down, Colonel," she politely commanded.

Proffering a quick grin in response, Rawlings made his choice and sat down but elected to sit forward in the chair to take the cup she gave him. He didn't look in any way relaxed.

"So what is it you have to tell me?" she asked bluntly, seating herself opposite him.

Rawlings shifted to perch even further forward on his chair and for a second she imagined he might fall to his knees. His words came to her hesitantly, as if gingerly feeling their way across the space between an obviously tense speaker and a seemingly relaxed looking audience.

"I'm afraid I haven't told you... the complete truth about Jack, and I feel... well, never mind how I *feel*... I've *wanted* to tell you... from the beginning really... I've wanted to, for Jack's sake." He paused, then his voice became firmer as he quietly added, "I feel you have the right to know what a brave man your *fiancé* was. And you should know the reason he gave his life."

Elizabeth rose abruptly from her chair and took three paces to where Matthew now lay asleep. The Officer's cap was clutched in his tiny fingers and she gently removed it from his grasp, wordlessly returned it to Rawlings, and moved to stand again at the window. She looked out at the grounds but saw other things as she spoke."I could never really accept the idea of Jack shuffling paper, as he said he did." She turned away from the window to see that Rawlings held his cap in his hand and wore the look of a man uncertain as to whether or not he was about to be dismissed. "Do you have a family of your own, Colonel?"

"Yes I do," replied Rawlings, clearly surprised by the deflection, "My wife Laura and I have a son. Gordon is seven now," he ended, a smile now battling his frown of uncertainty.

Elizabeth merely nodded and moved away from the window to sit down opposite him again, and she faced him squarely as she addressed him. "You've been uncomfortable since you arrived. Is it because you lied to me about Jack? Or is it because you cannot decide how truthful you should be *now*?"

Rawlings slowly bent to place his cap on the floor before lifting a hand to stroke his chin as he replied, "Bit of both, really," he confessed, "I've always held myself responsible for Jack's death, you see."

"*No*, Colonel, I do *not* see," she rebuked.

"I phrased that badly, I apologise. Let me explain how it was," he said quietly.

Her head bowed, she steeled herself to listen as Rawlings began by telling her he was a senior officer of S.O.E. He explained what the acronym stood for and verbally sketched the part his organization had played in the war. She lifted her head in surprise when he told her that *before* the war with Germany had been officially declared, Jack and his mother had contacted S.O.E. in London to offer their services.

"We'd already known of Chantal, of course. She did a lot to upset the Germans before she came over here to see us," qualified Rawlings.

Elizabeth remained silent, remembering Jonathan Teale's account of Chantal.

"They both wanted to go back to France to organize resistance," continued Rawlings, "and we jumped at the offer because Chantal had many friends still in important positions at that time. We persuaded them to operate within different groups in the same region, and Chantal went over first, to *Bordeaux*. Jack was to follow soon after but we had problems setting things up for him and it was a few months before *he* actually became operational."

"What about Scotland?" she interjected, forcing self-control, "and Jack's letter?"

"Jack didn't want you to know where he would be," replied Rawlings, sounding unperturbed by the change of direction, "or that he would be in any kind of danger. He wrote *that*, and other letters to you, before he left that last time. My organization arranged for the one you received to be posted from Scotland. It was standard procedure, I should just mention."

Elizabeth saw now in her mind's eye the figure of Jack at the writing table in the Knightsbridge apartment that long ago Sunday morning. She recalled now the sheets of paper he had carefully ensured she didn't see too closely. Meanwhile she could now almost *feel* Rawlings measure his words as he took his narrative back to where she'd interrupted him.

"Chantal quickly became an invaluable agent. She was a brilliant organizer, and many of our early successes were due to the information she supplied us with. She built up and controlled what became a highly effective network of her *own* people and some of ours."

She watched as Rawlings rubbed a hand over his face before the tired looking eyes met her own again as he resumed, "And then she was betrayed," he quietly revealed. "We knew from our own people that certain members of her network, notably among them group leaders, harboured resentment because they were forced to take orders from a woman. Group leaders were hard to replace, so Chantal just had to live with their obstructions from time to time."

She saw Rawlings edge further forward on his chair, and found herself doing likewise.

"Her network had become a top priority target for the Gestapo," continued Rawlings, "and they'd put a high 'dead or alive' price on Chantal's head."

She was now close enough to hear his intake of breath as he paused.

"Two of her group leaders came under suspicion when Chantal was, we believe, seized by the Gestapo from a supposedly safe location where the three of them had arranged to meet."

This time it was Rawlings who abruptly rose and walked over to the window whilst Elizabeth, completely still by contrast, waited and watched as he visibly gathered himself.

"*Claude Dubois* and *Henri Lecroix* were the two group leaders scheduled to meet Chantal, but neither of them admitted to actually being with her when she was presumably captured. *Dubois* claimed he'd got the date of the meeting wrong and hadn't even attempted to be there. *Lecroix* said he'd arrived late, in time to see the Gestapo storm the meeting place."

Elizabeth immediately pounced on the words she had isolated, "You *believe* she was seized. You say she was *presumably* captured...," he stopped, surprised by Rawlings imperiously waving away her words as he began walking back from the window.

"Semantics, Elizabeth," he curtly responded, "We know she went there, and she's never been seen since," he ended in a hard-edged tone of voice.

She silently watched him retake his seat. His tone had taken her aback but she quickly reminded herself that this was a man who evidently had controlled people like Jack, and Alan Carter, and the ferocious Welshman, and no doubt countless others, so she shouldn't be surprised to hear steel in his voice. Alan Carter's words suddenly resurfaced in her mind; *'Jack used to refer to him as the dependable Dubois...,'* and then Rawlings cut into her recall by reaching out to clasp her hands with his own, and the memory of Jack was clear for an instant before Rawlings began speaking again and his words were emerging slowly.

"When Chantal went back into France, and for operational reasons in some quarters, she still used her late husband's surname of Sands... "

"*Sands...?* But I...," tried Elizabeth, but Rawlings had obviously anticipated her reaction because he held her hands tightly now as he pressed on over her startled interjection.

"We didn't want any confusion with regional communications over there," he hurriedly qualified, "So we gave Jack the operational name of Matthews."

"But why lie to *me*?" she protested.

"You've got to understand," insisted Rawlings, "that Jack had lived in his world for almost four years with the name of Matthews before he met you. It was a second skin to him by then."

Elizabeth saw Rawlings study her as he paused, and instinctively knew he was allowing time for his explanation to germinate in her mind. A mind suddenly recalling Jonathan

Teale's hesitant pronunciation of *Matthew S. Matthews* and beginning to realize that her solicitor would have known about this. She was about to voice her thoughts when Rawlings pre-empted her.

"Jack had conditioned himself to automatically giving his name as Matthews. So once he'd *told* you that name, he couldn't just casually produce another one the next time he saw you."

She stared at Rawlings, hearing his words but seeing Jack introducing himself on a Hammersmith dance floor.

"But there was another reason," continued Rawlings, "why the name of Sands had to be concealed during those times."

"*What* other reason?" she snapped, pulling her hands free of his grasp.

"Chantal was an exceptionally brave woman," responded Rawlings, "but we had to assume the Gestapo would have... learned from her... of her son, Jack."

Rawlings stopped and she saw him watching her through eyes that were narrowed, as if they were peering at her through a microscope to observe the effect of his words. And then she suddenly grasped their horrible meaning. "You mean she was... *tortured?*" she managed to ask, feeling herself almost choke on that last dreadful sounding word.

Rawlings didn't flinch as he responded, "We had to assume so, and few can prevent themselves breaking under such treatment. We had to protect Jack, so we drummed it into him to forget the name Sands."

"What," she couldn't stop herself asking, "do you think happened afterwards... to Chantal?"

"*Some* of her network were rounded up before they could be warned. *Dubois* and *Lecroix* were among the few who remained at liberty. *Dubois,* in fact, later move to Jack's group."

"You haven't answered my question," she persisted, "What happened to Chantal?"

"We just don't know, Elizabeth," he finally conceded, adding softly, "Dead, certainly."

Rawlings rose to his feet again and moved back to the window, and, like a moth seeking contact with the flame, Elizabeth moved to stand beside him.

"What a deviously complicated world you describe, Colonel," she said, glancing at him and seeing the familiar signs of stress etched on the pale and drawn face, "No wonder you look so... so weary," she carefully chose to end.

"I've had to write a lot of letters to wives and mothers," he quietly began, "but I've never been able to tell them how it really was for those whom they'd lost. *This* encounter isn't exactly easy duty, but it's certainly preferable to my usual prevarication. And it's high time *you* started calling me Simon," he added, before turning to face her as he paused.

She heard the anger behind the still quietly spoken words he used to continue, "What guts me is that so many good men and women have been lost. They all paid the highest price to preserve," he waved a hand to indicate the peaceful scene outside the window, "all of *this* for *us*, and no one will ever really know how they chose to make the final sacrifice."

Suddenly needing the support, Elizabeth slowly moved back to her chair. Rawlings remained at the window, staring outwards into the past as he began speaking again.

"We were unable to prove beyond doubt that Chantal had been betrayed, but suspicion naturally fell upon *Dubois* and *Lecroix*. The amount of operational activity involving them both was limited from that time onwards. They both realized this, of course, and naturally resented the slur upon their names, and protested their innocence to anyone who would listen."

She watched him turn to face her, and with his back to the window his face was in shadow as she heard him continue.

"Which made life even *more* difficult for *our* agents who were trying to hold things together. I sometimes thought that the work of people like Jack and Alan Carter should have been given to Lion tamers with a degree in diplomacy. Honestly, Elizabeth, you wouldn't *believe* the number of conflicting political factions they had to contend with. The same factions who, even as I speak, are still fighting over their perceived to be rightful piece of the French pie. The *Lecroix* family, for example, will probably emerge with a large portion of that pie; they're still very influential in political circles."

Sensing there was more to come, Elizabeth remained silent as she watched Rawlings retake his seat opposite her.

"But of course mud sticks, and the Chantal business might have remained stuck where it was at that point had it not been for Jack."

Instinctively steeling herself once more, she watched his face as he continued, "So successful had *he* been in his operational region, he'd become a kind of legend to his network. Jack had inherited his mother's organizational flair, and, having widely expanded his area of operations, he was by then controlling a group of networks which were causing great damage to the German war machine over a considerable area. Someone had dubbed him *L'ombre*, and we used that as his radio codeword. The name had even spread to the extent that the Gestapo very badly wanted the man they too were then also calling 'The Shadow'."

Taking her by surprise, he stopped to ask if she wanted him to continue.

"I want to hear it all," she replied firmly.

"So with my blessing, Jack set up a special operation involving the networks of four regions. He briefed the group leaders personally, and separately, in their own areas. Two of those leaders were *Dubois* and *Lecroix*. Jack had never met *Lecroix* before, but both of them were given false details of a June rendezvous they were told Jack himself would attend. And then finally, *and without my blessing,* to both of them he revealed the fact that he was the son of Chantal Sands, *nee* Cheval."

Transfixed by his narrative, Elizabeth couldn't hold back the interjection, "What happened?"

Rawlings shook his head, "The rendezvous never took place. Which finally," he added in a tone edged with bitterness, "brings me back to why I blame myself in part for Jack's death. I was the one who ordered his return home in May of '43. I was having second thoughts about the size of the operation he'd planned, as well as being angry about him having revealed his identity. So I used the excuse of needing a face-to-face meeting in order to clarify certain aspects of the operation. Otherwise he would never have left his networks."

Elizabeth thought she saw the pain of remembrance in the tired looking eyes looking at her now, and a heavy sigh prefaced his next, quietly spoken words.

"Then of course he met *you* at the end of that month of May. As I've hopefully proved to you by now, Jack wasn't just a colleague of mine, he was a very close friend. So before he went back to France he spoke to me at length about you. About what you meant to him. I gave him my word that I would help you if anything happened to him."

"Why do you blame yourself for...?" began Elizabeth, only to be interrupted.

"While Jack was back here in London, the Germans were having considerable success against the networks he'd left behind him in France. They were badly hit, and they lost many good people. By the time Jack got back to them, morale was very low."

She watched him pause, and was conscious of his weighing his words again before he resumed, but his voice was firm.

"It's an acknowledged fact in our business, that the longer an agent is away from the centre of things, the more he or she loses that edge which is vital to survival. Before Jack even attended a rearranged rendezvous with *Dubois* and *Lecroix,* he was picked up during a random papers search in a cafe. The sort of thing which wouldn't normally have presented him with any problem; he was always professionally disguised and his papers were flawless. But as was later confirmed to us in London, the Gestapo had something they had never possessed before. When they picked Jack up in that cafe, the Gestapo had a detailed description of his disguise and knew his real identity."

Elizabeth's thoughts raced as she faced Rawlings, and the words were out before she could stop them, "It was *Lecroix,*" she declared, "You said earlier that Jack had never met him before he arranged the rendezvous." She paused, then emphatically added, "It was *Lecroix* who provided his description to the Gestapo."

Rawlings suddenly smiled across the space which separated them as he responded, "You could have been one of *us,* Elizabeth. You may very well be right, but we'll never know."

"What became of *Lecroix*? And *Dubois,* for that matter?" queried Elizabeth.

Rawlings released another of his sighs before replying, "I'm afraid I don't know. Things were pretty chaotic over there after Jack was taken, and we lost track of a few French people for one reason or another."

She then saw something indefinable in the man's eyes a moment before he leant forward and once again clasped her hands in his own. She instinctively braced herself.

"But what I *do* know is this," he resumed, "I mentioned earlier that few can prevent themselves breaking under torture, but Jack was one of those very brave few. *Not one* of his own network, the *Créon* network, was targeted in the aftermath of his capture. He died protecting them."

Concerned now as to how she would react, he continued to hold her gaze, watching her closely as she sat unmoving for several moments. Until she suddenly stirred and utterly surprised him by smiling as she spoke.

"I realize," she began quietly, "it cannot have been easy to have told me everything."

Rawlings looked away from her tears as the quiet voice continued, "I don't think you should blame yourself about Jack. If he hadn't come back to London on your orders, I would never have met him. So you see, I have *you* to thank for *that. As well as* all you did to ensure that Matthew would have a future with me, and all that you've done since to help me carry out Jack's wish that I should fulfil my dream of running a convalescent home."

Rawlings produced a pristine white handkerchief which he placed in her hand as he spoke, "Don't be too hard on young Teale. He was ordered to conceal things from you and the official secrets act left him with no choice other than to obey." He paused, "Can't have been easy for him. As I recall, my impression then was that he was rather smitten by you," he ended.

Elizabeth chose not to comment, thinking back to her 'discovery' sessions in Jonathan's London office and realizing now just how much had been held back from her. She didn't like the thought that he hadn't trusted her enough to tell her the truth. She forced her thoughts to change direction and focus on the man before her *now*.

"Will you be looking in on Alan Carter before you leave?"

"I understand he's coming along well," replied Rawlings, smoothly adding, "I wouldn't want to get in the way of the remarkable progress you've made with him."

Elizabeth was silent for a moment, weighing up how he'd phrased his reply, his words more or less confirming her suspicions that Churchill's memorable visit owed more to the man before her now than her own letter of invitation, and that one of Carter's now frequent visitors was in fact from 'the world of Rawlings'. Nonetheless, it had been generally agreed that the young woman had worked wonders on Alan Carter, encouraging his use of the piano which had been generously gifted to the home by 'an anonymous benefactor'.

"Since Mister Churchill spoke to him," said Elizabeth, "and shrewdly left us with the key to unlock Alan's love of music, yes, he's coming along well."

She saw the Rawlings smile preface the attempt to disguise his satisfaction, and she reached out to touch his arm as she added, "And gifting us the piano was very thoughtful of you, Simon. As was engineering Churchill's visit," she declared, squeezing his arm with affection, "Mister Churchill must think highly of you," she paused, adding firmly, "As indeed *I do*. You have more than honoured your word to Jack, and for that I shall be eternally grateful to you."

She saw the Rawlings smile openly revealed this time as he responded, "One of my government moles told me about your letter of invitation to the great man. *He* gave his time, and *I* gave the piano. Carter deserved both; he's a good man. And I *was* right, Elizabeth, you *could have been* one of us." He paused, the smile fading as he added, "Jack was a rare man, and he chose an exceptional woman. Thank you for what you've said."

She could feel the tears again but smiled through them as she responded, "A rare man? Yes, Simon. Yes he was, I believe," she voiced from the heart.

Cheerfully taken in hand by Mary Reynolds, who had been briefed to avoid the bedside of Alan Carter, Simon Rawlings was given the grand tour of the convalescent home. Mary later swore that when he'd been presented with a cake by *Delicate Doris*, the man's eyes had widened at the size of the Head Cook as much as his mouth had visibly salivated at the sight of the cake.

Later that day, Elizabeth once again found herself standing in the driveway preparing to say Goodbye to someone to whom she owed so much.

"Can you tell me," she asked, "if the Welshman made it back safely to his Narberth?"

"Oh," replied Rawlings, "*He* made it okay. Hitler didn't have enough Germans to stop him."

They shared a chuckle at that, and then he lightly kissed her cheek and promised he would keep in touch when he returned from Germany. Rawlings climbed into his car and she watched him drive off and was moved to wave after the man, suddenly remembering how she had last seen Jack drive away that night so very long ago, suddenly unable to lose the image in her mind's eye of being unable to move as he'd driven off , suddenly feeling she couldn't move now. *'It's easy once you take the first step,'* Jack had said to her.

Elizabeth turned to take the first step back towards the cottage, and her son, Matthew.

Monday 25th March to end of April 1946

Three months after the Rawlings visit, Elizabeth Creacey issued specific instructions to her solicitor, Jonathan Teale: He was to make contact with the French solicitors his predecessor, Arthur Freemantle, had dealt with on behalf of Chantal Sands, *nee Cheval*.

Through his French counterparts, Jonathan was to find out if a particular two former 'Resistance' members were still alive. Jonathan was supplied with the barest details: He was told that the first man was named *Henri Lecroix,* progeny of an 'influential' family, and that the second man was named *Claude Dubois*. Both men, he was coolly informed, would have been known to have operated in the *Bordeaux* region of their country during the war. The bemused Jonathan's instructions included the proviso that if *Dubois* could be found, a question should be put to him. The question was *Would he agree to meet La Veuve de L'ombre?*

When Jonathan's dictionary provided him with the translation, 'The Widow of The Shadow', he was left no less bemused.

As Elizabeth's re-commenced diary entries informed, much had transpired since she had received what the now fully briefed and equally supportive Mary Reynolds and Peter Corder had jointly entitled *The Rawlings Revelations,* and the first quarter of a new year was now a memory. In Sussex, The Chantal Cheval Palliative Care Home was fully operational and consuming much of Corder's time. But even for Elizabeth, the months had passed faster than seemed possible. An experience exhaustively shared by those following in her wake.

"Creacey's Cavaliers are either turning into Creacey's Crocks, or time itself is just making us feel too slow to keep pace with developments," Peter Corder was heard to wearily remark.

Matthew's second birthday had invited Mary's observation that His Lordship seemed to be the only one with time to celebrate a birth date, and *Delicate Doris* had reported that the *Strife and Strumpet* was undergoing renovation, rendering the grapevine inactive.

As the month of April drew to a close, Elizabeth took a telephone call from Jonathan Teale and listened to his mission report:

"Both *Henri Lecroix* and *Claude Dubois* are still alive. They both, in fact, reside in the *Bordeaux* region of France. I have translated the *Dubois* reply to your question, which reads as follows:

La Veuve de L'ombre will always be welcome in the house of Dubois.

He requests that the widow be asked to send a photograph, along with her travel plans, to the address he has provided."

"Just read the address to me, please, Jonathan," said Elizabeth, and when she'd finished writing down the given address, the voice in her ear sounded frustrated.

"Am I to take it that this concerns someone in your convalescent home, Elizabeth?"

"Yes, it does," she replied truthfully, "Thank you for your assistance. I'll deal with the follow up myself. Goodbye, Jonathan," she ended, disconnecting before he could respond.

Elizabeth looked down at the address she had transcribed, and took a deep breath as her thoughts turned over in her mind: *'So she now knew where she had to get to. Having already* partly *briefed Mary Reynolds and Peter Corder of her intended plans; arranged for the reliable Mrs Bruce to reside at the Surrey cottage and look after Matthew; she was now immediately able to begin her own necessary personal preparations for her journey into the unknown.'*

Chapter Twenty

Sow an act, and you reap a habit
Sow a habit, and you reap a character
Sow a character, and you reap a destiny.
(Charles Reade)

North-West France, Port of Dieppe, Saturday, June 1ˢᵗ 1946
Everywhere Elizabeth looked she could see the bustle of movement associated with busy sea-port activity. In the final moments of approach the noise had reached her ears, and, as she gingerly made her way down the ship's gangplank, the cacophony of sound was now almost deafening. Over the blare of horns; shrill intermittent whistles; and clatter of iron-wheeled carts being man-handled over cobble-stoned ground, her hearing picked up a variety of languages being used to shout what she assumed to be instructions of one kind or another.

Her periphery vision took in bulky shapes criss-crossing the space between *terra firma* and undulating sea, as her carrier vessel began its synchronised unloading and loading of its assorted cargo. Swirling around her, a freshening breeze buffeted darting seagulls and brought to her nostrils the pungent smells of engine-oil on sea water and what she thought must be fish.

She stepped onto French soil for the first time, on the first morning of June, to be greeted by the short and powerfully built looking figure of *Claude Dubois*. Instantly identified by his holding aloft her own photograph, the Frenchman also sported a large moustache and a beaming smile of welcome. She quickly judged him to be a man in his mid-to-late thirties and he was, she realized, accompanied by an older white-haired man who also smiled at her as he relieved her of her suitcase. The trousers and shirts worn by both men, she discreetly observed, were clean but obviously well-used.

Using thankfully understandable English, the gravel-voiced *Dubois* rapidly introduced the taller and thinner man as *Louis Bardot*, explaining as he did so that his companion was unable to speak and that he had also served under Jack's command. The white-haired man bobbed his head and smiled through the introduction and then turned on his heel and began walking away.

"Please follow me, *Madame*," said *Dubois*, already moving as he spoke.

To the sounds of numerously muttered *'Pardonner Moi's*, *Sorry's*, and *Scusi's'* she was led and bumped through a multi-national throng of people until finally she saw the white-haired *Bardot* ground her suitcase beside a stationary vehicle. Through her involuntary burst of laughter she could see the pained expressions on the faces of her hosts, and she had to quickly explain the reason for her amusement. *Louis Bardot* beamed apparent understanding, whilst *Claude Dubois* chuckled as the three of them clambered aboard the converted ambulance.

Dubois confirmed to her that their destination was his home village of *Créon*.

"It lies to the South-East of *Bordeaux*," he said, "and will take us about eight hours to get there, but *Louis* and I will share the driving. *You, Madame*," said the gravel-voice, "can sleep in the back whenever you wish."

What was obviously an old seat from something else had been squeezed into the front cabin, and, as they set off with the silent *Louis* behind the steering wheel, she was comfortably perched between the two Frenchmen. Quickly sensing the tension on either side of her, and wondering if it was because they had a woman as a passenger, she was now very glad she'd sensibly opted for the non-provocative black slacks and plain wine-red sweater under her lightweight dark-coloured jacket. *'Surely it can't be,'* she thought, *'my style of dress which is making them uncomfortable.'*

Her thought was diverted by *Louis Bardot* winding down his window, and the rich mix of sights and sounds and aromas assailed her senses as the ambulance was slowly and carefully manoeuvred through the bustling Port area. Startling her, his hands expressively chopping the air, *Dubois* commenced a running commentary on the underlying reasons behind the passing scenes of activity. Telling her of the efforts currently being made to bring into his country the much needed materials required to restore not only damaged buildings and infrastructure, but also shattered lives.

"But alas, *Madame,*" growled the Frenchman, "We have lost much that can never be restored."

Elizabeth immediately found herself struggling to decide upon a response. Wondering if *Dubois* was referring to his country in general, or his own shame at having been branded a traitor and losing his good name, or even her own loss of Jack. Realization of his *faux pas* was suddenly reflected on his now reddened face, and she saw the *Dubois* moustache quiver with what she perceived to be embarrassment. At the same time, with *his* face registering obvious disapproval of his countryman's choice of words, *Louis Bardot* slapped a hand to his forehead in what she took to be a gesture of *Gallic* dismay.

An awkward silence might have developed into something more difficult to recover from had she not instinctively applied the balm of diversionary dialogue. She calmly began to relate her privately rehearsed, and carefully edited version of what Simon Rawlings had told her about the fate which had befallen Jack and his mother, Chantal. *'What she was leaving out could be discussed at a time of her choosing. And this was certainly not the time',* she silently told herself.

With his head of closely cropped hair, *Claude Dubois* had been providing nods of affirmation throughout her recital but now surprised her by turning to her with tear-filled eyes.

"There are many, *Madame,* who will always remember what Chantal and her son did for them. I myself could never repay the debt I owe your husband, *Madame.*"

Once again she stopped herself from correcting the Frenchman. Something had stopped her before, also, when he'd been addressing her as *Madame,* and now she realized that she rather liked the idea of being thought of as *Madame,* and she also liked the sound of the words *your husband, Madame.* Just at that moment, and taking her by surprise, *Louis Bardot* reached to squeeze her hand and she imagined she could see in his eyes the words he couldn't speak. Moved entirely by instinct, she grasped a hand of each of the men and raised them to her lips and her quietly voiced *'Merci,'* followed by *'Vive the friends of L'ombre,'* was received by a smiling *Dubois* who then hugged her and a *Bardot*-initiated blare of the ambulance horn which made her jump. The earlier tension she'd felt in the cabin was instantly dispelled, and, as she sat for a while in *companionable silence,* she suddenly felt very close to Jack in reliving the line from his poem.

With their transport finally clear of the Port and on the open road, Elizabeth was tentatively asked about children so proudly produced from her jacket the several photographs she'd brought with her. *Dubois* roared his approval when he heard she'd named her son Matthew, telling her he knew that Jack's father had borne the same name. She might have pursued this disclosure had not the Frenchman began speaking about his own son, *Pierre.* A son who was, they discovered, the same age as Matthew. The trials and joys of parenthood were then mutually expressed for some time thereafter, intermingled, to Elizabeth's delight, with recounted anecdotes concerning Jack and his former comrades.

As the kilometres sped by, Elizabeth warmed to the man who referred to his memories of Jack with such obviously genuine respect. However, she noted, following his earlier enigmatic comment regarding the subject of loss, and her own recital about Chantal and Jack, the man logged in her diary as *The dependable Dubois,* had carefully refrained from saying anything else which might have invited further discussion on the subject of betrayal.

They had passed through *Tours,* and were into the *Loire* valley when *Dubois* announced it was time for a break. The ambulance was brought to a halt beside some farm buildings, where a woman could be seen taking in washing from a line. *Dubois* engaged the woman in rapid French before telling Elizabeth with a shy looking smile that *'If Madame wishes to... powder the nose, you can accompany this woman.'*

When Elizabeth returned from the welcomed hospitality of the farmer's wife she found both Frenchmen busily engaged but seemingly relaxed, so she assumed they'd also managed to relieve themselves in her absence. She saw that *Bardot* had obviously just finished topping up the petrol tank from a jerry-can, and *Dubois* was pouring into mugs what she realized was soup. She was invited to sit on the ground with her hosts, so with backs against the ambulance, and with soup-filled mugs and plate-held bread and cheese, the trio sipped and munched contentedly whilst she calmly told the men only part of the purpose behind her visit. The Frenchmen ate and drank as they listened until she had finished.

"*Que c'est bon*," said *Dubois* to *Bardot* as they exchanged clearly approving looks. *Dubois* turned to her as he continued, "We will be honoured, *Madame*," said the gravel-voice, "*Louis* and myself, to assist you with all the necessary arrangements."

Elizabeth acknowledged the pledge with a warm smile, whilst also silently reminding herself that she mustn't wait *too long* before declaring her full intentions to the Frenchman. Gratefully accepting the post-meal suggestion that she should try to sleep on this next leg of their journey, she clambered into the back of the ambulance and wearily collapsed onto the makeshift bed which, she sleepily recognized, had obviously been thoughtfully prepared for just this eventuality. But sleep was refusing to come easily.

Her conscience was troubling her, adding to her tiredness, pushing its way to her forebrain and forcing the reflective thoughts. Before leaving England, all her preparations had been fuelled by the impulsive thought that once in France she would, with the help of Jack's former comrade, find and confront *Henri Lecroix*. Now that she was actually here and had met the outwardly genial *Claude Dubois* and his mute companion, she realized that both men, in their different ways, still clearly carried the scars of their wartime existence.

Her adjoining and now equally sobering thoughts centred around her fresh perception of *Claude Dubois*. Because before she could confront the man she was convinced had betrayed Jack's mother, *how could she broach with Dubois a subject which he seemed at pains to avoid, and, if she did so, what effect might it have on the man?* She fell asleep pondering the wisdom of her intentions.

Elizabeth was awakened to be told she'd slept for four hours and that they had arrived at the *Dubois* family home in the village of *Créon*. Gallantly assisted by the smiling *Louis Bardot*, she emerged from the vehicle to find herself in a small courtyard. *Dubois* was in the act of carrying her suitcase inside a two-level stone-built farmhouse which had smoke lazily spiralling from its roof-chimney, and the whole edifice was bathed in early evening light.

Elizabeth turned her head towards where the sudden and unmistakable sounds of bovine livestock could be heard emanating from a barn standing off to her right, and from one of the several outbuildings she could see, came the squawk of chickens. The farm was on high ground, she realized, and in a valley below where she now stood she could see the twinkling lights of other habitation. As she began trailing the silent *Bardot* towards the main house a shooting star blazed across the night sky, and her still tired mind conjured thoughts of biblical omens. They reached what looked to her like a new front door, just as it opened to reveal a smiling *Claude Dubois* with his arm around a petite slim-bodied woman whom Elizabeth guessed to be in her thirties. The woman wore a clean white blouse over a black skirt and her short dark hair gleamed with health under the light spilling from an inviting looking interior behind where she stood. *'She must think I look an absolute mess',* thought Elizabeth.

"Welcome to our home, *Madame,*" said the now very formal sounding gravel voice, "Permit me to introduce *ma femme, Lucille,*" he ended, his deep voice filled with obvious pride.

"*Le jeune femme est fatigue, Claude!*" exclaimed the tiny woman, unceremoniously bundling her husband aside and moving forward to kiss Elizabeth's cheeks as she continued in English, "I'm telling the fool that you are exhausted. Elizabeth, is it not? Come inside, *Cherie,* I love your hair, would I suit the long hair, do you think? I am preparing the food, but first you would like to freshen up, *Oui?*"

Instantly liking *Lucille Dubois,* the warmly welcoming and wiry looking bundle of energy now linking arms and leading her inside, Elizabeth had a fleeting glimpse of a large sprawling lounge area, together with her tantalising scent of something good cooking in a kitchen she couldn't yet see. Her bubbly hostess began steering her up a wooden staircase.

"Everything is prepared for you, *Cherie,* come, let me show you."

The woman's energy was already transmitting itself to Elizabeth, who was smiling as she was led through another obviously new door and shown into a room which took her breath away. A gleaming mahogany-hued wardrobe, ornate dressing table and chair, together with a huge and magnificent looking four-poster bed and some other smaller pieces of furniture, were all comfortably contained within the deceptively spacious room. A large warmly coloured rug lay over a richly dark wooden floor, and, high above it all in their clearly original state, knotted Oak beams traversed the ceiling.

"What a *wonderful* room," acknowledged Elizabeth.

"*Oui,*" responded the Frenchwoman, her face openly displaying her pleasure at the observed reaction, "I have prepared this room especially for you, *Cherie.*"

Something in the woman's voice sharpened Elizabeth's attention as *Lucille* quietly resumed, "Not much has changed in this room. This house used to be the home of *Chantal Cheval.* This was her bedroom, and your own husband was born in this room."

Elizabeth could actually feel the blood drain from her face, and the Frenchwoman moved quickly to her side and guided her into a chair beside the bed.

"Breathe deeply, *Cherie,*" said *Lucille,* "It is a shock, *Oui?* But something," she added firmly, "you should know, *n'est pas?*"

Nodding her head and managing what she knew must be at best a wan looking smile, She watched as *Lucille* moved to a small table and poured water from an earthenware pitcher.

"I was too hasty, *Cherie,* I should not have told you so soon."

"I can often be impulsive myself," confessed Elizabeth, "and I'm glad you told me now." She accepted the proffered drink and gratefully sipped the fluid as her hostess spoke again.

"In the event of his death, your husband arranged for this house to become *Claude's.*" She paused, holding Elizabeth's gaze as she added, "But we did not learn of this until after the war."

Elizabeth could feel her circulation improving and was about to speak, but was pr-empted.

"*Claude* has told me that they used this house many times, your husband and mine, for their meetings during the war. Your husband often slept in this room, *Claude* has told me."

Reactively glancing at the four-poster bed, Elizabeth was again about to speak when *Claude Dubois* entered the room with a child in his arms. She rose slowly from the chair, but managed a brighter smile as she was introduced to the boy named *Pierre*. When the child was proudly passed to her, she hugged him and longed for Matthew. She allowed *Lucille* to gently relieve her of the child and watched as he was passed back to his father. With his face now being examined by the tiny fingers of his son, the man was being *shooshed* from the room by his wife, who, in the act of following him, turned back to her as she spoke.

"We can speak privately later, *Cherie,* if you wish," she said, winking an eye, "But for now, I will leave you to freshen up while I rescue the vegetables. You will find clean towels in the bathroom which is behind the door just here," she indicated, "opposite your room."

Left alone, her head filled with thoughts of Chantal and Jack having used the very room she now found herself occupying, she slowly unpacked and placed various items of clothing in the beautifully crafted wardrobe. Memories of *Gerrard Laporte* drifted through her mind. She was suddenly stilled by the heartfelt poignancy of a scene before her. The selected skirt and blouse she would wear to dinner, now lay beside her current diary on top of the sumptuous looking bed in which Jack's entry into the world had taken place. Sighing deeply, she gathered up her toiletries for the trip to the bathroom.

A little later, newly washed and dressed, feeling refreshed and more clear-headed, she descended the wooden staircase and followed the sounds of conversational French until she found the kitchen. Cheerfully greeted by the assembled gathering, comprising her host and hostess and a smiling *Louis Bardot*, she was immediately captivated by the atmosphere in the warmly inviting kitchen. She was informed that baby *Pierre* was asleep whilst being gallantly ushered by *Claude Dubois* to one of the chairs surrounding a circular wooden table. A table upon which stood flowers, several bottles of red wine, colourfully patterned crockery, sparkling wine glasses, and various bowls of obviously hot and attractive looking food. The kitchen area itself was large and spotlessly clean looking and flames swirled around a log burning fire at one end of the room.

Wine glasses were immediately filled and raised in salute, and Elizabeth blushed as she sipped her wine to *Claude's* words of welcome and his wife's expression of her delight at being told what their visitor intended to do whilst in France.

Whilst the ensuing meal she shared that evening with the *Dubois* family and *Louis Bardot* was an enjoyable affair, it also served to add to her already conflicting emotions. Emotions in turmoil; she hadn't been entirely honest with these decent people, and tonight she would be sleeping in the bed in which Jack had been born. Then, as the men were still showing no sign of ending the evening, her eyes were met by those of a perceptive hostess who announced it was time to allow their guest to retire.

"You go up, *Cherie,*" said *Lucille,* "I will bring you a cognac, and *these two,*" she declared whilst elbow-nudging her husband, "can do the washing up."

Bidding the men Goodnight, Elizabeth retraced her route back to the bedroom. With every step she took on the staircase, thinking that *this was where Jack would have trod on the occasions he'd slept her.* Regaining the bedroom, she left the door open and sat down to compose herself for the arrival of her hostess. A moment passed in the quiet room before the impulsive thought came to her that she would like to show *Lucille* the poem that Jack had written. She retrieved her handbag and extracted the folded sheet of paper, carefully unfolding the much handled poem and staring down at the familiar words *For You... For Us... For Life...* and the sound of approaching footsteps brought her head up.

Lucille Dubois entered the room balancing a tray which Elizabeth could see held two small glasses of amber liquid, together with two cups giving off the almost forgotten aroma of freshly made coffee.

"I cannot remember when I last tasted freshly made coffee," she told her hostess, rising to join the woman by the dressing table beside the window.

"And *I forgot*," confessed Lucille as she positioned a small table near the bedside, "to ask if you actually *like* cognac?"

"I've never tried it," admitted Elizabeth, accepting the proffered drinks and placing them on the table before sitting down.

"I have interrupted your reading, *Cherie?*" asked *Lucille* as she sat on the bed.

"No, not really. I've read it many times. It's a poem which was written for me by Jack, soon after we met...," she hesitated, "I just wanted to show it to you, I still do, but first, *Lucille*, I would like to say," she paused to offer a tentative smile, "to explain more fully... to be more honest with you as to why I'm here in your country."

Without waiting for a response, and speaking quickly, Elizabeth confirmed the integrity of her previously declared intention and then divulged the second of her twin objectives. At the dinner table her hostess had warmly endorsed the first objective, but her response now to the second one was less than positive.

"My husband no longer speaks of this," began *Lucille*, "because he is ashamed. *Chantal* and her son were respected by many people, and *Claude* is ashamed because there are those in *Créon*, and beyond, who still wonder if he betrayed them. *Claude* is ashamed of his inability to prove them wrong, and he is ashamed of his failure to restore the good name of *Dubois*."

Elizabeth suddenly realized that the woman was welcoming the opportunity to speak about something which had obviously impacted upon *her* as much as her husband.

"Finding *Lecroix* is not the problem, Elizabeth," stated the now bitter-sounding woman, "The abominable man lives here in *Créon*. But even if you confronted him, what would it achieve? When you have accused him, he's not likely to confess to you, and when he learns that you are here under this roof, he would make trouble for *Claude*. Your Simon Rawlings was correct, Elizabeth, The *Lecroix* family *is* an influential one."

In the pause that followed Elizabeth saw the woman inhale deeply before resuming, "And things are difficult enough here as it is. My husband's parents were natural born farmers, but we lost them to the war. *Claude* is not the farmer his father was but he *is* trying, and I know he will succeed if... "

Elizabeth was fixed with a steely look as the woman abruptly paused before continuing, "No one dares to cross *Henri Lecroix*. His family controls most of *Créon's* main suppliers, and a word from them could even make people afraid to buy our stock. If *Henri Lecroix* used his influence against my *Claude*, it would probably ruin us."

"*Lucille*, I would do nothing which could bring harm to your family," declared Elizabeth.

"I'm relieved to hear you say that, *Cherie,* and your other objective is an admirable one."

Elizabeth was silent, her thoughts awash with a mixture of disappointment, frustration, and self-imposed embarrassment.

"Had our roles been reversed, Elizabeth, I too would have attempted what you have set out to do. So you must *not* feel as embarrassed as you look, *Cherie,*" said the perceptive woman.

Elizabeth smiled as she replied, "We have wasted your coffee. It has gone cold."

"No matter," dismissed the woman, "You can try your cognac while I read your husband's poem. If you're not too tired?"

"No, I'm not tired now." She paused, made up her mind quickly, and continued, "*Lucille*, Jack and I were never married. He wanted to wait until after the war."

"*Pah!*" retorted the woman as she picked up the poem, "A piece of paper may make it legal, but it does not necessarily make it a marriage of the heart."

Elizabeth received a warm smile as the woman continued, "*Claude* has told me of your convalescent home named after Jack's mother. You must have loved him very much, and in your heart he is still alive, *Oui?*"

"*Oui,*" replied Elizabeth, feeling inestimably sad behind her smile.

"So try your cognac," suggested *Lucille*, "Toast your love, and I will read this poem of yours."

She tentatively sipped from her glass as her hostess began reading. The cognac was warming her insides, stimulating her thoughts as she looked around the room, '*Chantal must have had so many thoughts in this room...,*' and then suddenly she was aware of *Lucille* frowning down at the poem she was holding up to scrutinise.

"Is there something...?" she began, but was interrupted.

"This is so... so beautiful, Elizabeth," said *Lucille*, her frown deepening as she looked up and began visually scanning the room, "But this mark that Jack has made at the end," she added as she rose to her feet, "this shape that looks like a lazy letter S. I have seen this shape before, in this room," she qualified, "When I was preparing the room for you, *Cherie*. I remember thinking... "

As the woman abruptly broke off, Elizabeth followed her gaze to the Oak wood beams traversing the ceiling.

"It's on *one of the beams*," declared *Lucille,* emphatically, "I remember now, I remember thinking... what an odd place to find such a mark."

"I can't see anything," said Elizabeth, also on her feet now and scanning the aged beams.

"No, you won't," agreed *Lucille*, "Not from here, but it's there," she said, picking up Elizabeth's chair, "I was cleaning the ceiling light when I saw it."

Elizabeth watched as the woman positioned the chair and mounted it, and then saw her hand reach out and touch a section of beam.

"It is here, *Cherie*," said *Lucille,* quietly, "Just as in Jack's poem."

Elizabeth saw the woman slowly trace her finger over the discovered shape and then heard the gasp of surprise.

"It *moves*, Elizabeth. There is a small compartment here, and there is something inside it."

Lucille's hand emerged brandishing what appeared to be a small piece of paper. She stepped down from the chair and presented the find to Elizabeth, who stared wordlessly at what she realized had been folded over several times to reduce its size.

"Only *Chantal*, or Jack, could have put it there, *Cherie*," said a clearly excited *Lucille*, "So you must be the first to look."

Seemingly ignoring her own statement, the Frenchwoman stood at Elizabeth's shoulder as the piece of paper was slowly unfolded to reveal an unrecognized writing hand. The message, however, unmistakably identified the writing hand's owner.

Cherie... I have been betrayed... Not much time left... they won't get me... I'm using a bullet... Au Revoir Cherie. My son, Lecroix is the traitor!

The strangled sound of *Lucille's Mon Dieu!* echoed around the bedroom of Chantal Cheval.

In the immediate aftermath of reading Chantal Cheval's final words, the first response of a visibly transformed *Claude Dubois* had been the growled statement;

"She must have expected Jack to find this."

And in the silence which had followed that statement they had all paused to wonder, from their individual perspectives, *what might have been... if only.*

Radiating energy and purpose, *Claude Dubois* had been on the verge of immediately leaving to seek out former 'Resistance' members. Tempering her husband's adrenalin rush with liberal doses of common sense, *Lucille Dubois* had reminded him of the potential ramifications inherent in such a premature reaction. Thus it was, thanks to *Lucille's* intervention, some little time later an emotionally drained but more rational quartet re-assembled around the kitchen table to drink coffee and chew over thoughts. Initial shock had given way firstly to realization that they now possessed proof of their past collective suspicion. Reluctantly acknowledged however, was the fact that possession *'per-se'* did not mean the good name of *Dubois* would be quickly restored. It would take *time* to arrange for photographs to be taken of the proof they possessed, and *time* to circulate those photographs to those who mattered. It would take *time* to then arrange the meetings needed to discuss how best to proceed, and yet *more time* to implement whatever judgement would be decreed. And understood without question was the expectation that *Henri Lecroix* would use that time to commercially ruin *Claude Dubois.*

In Elizabeth's mind, *Lecroix's* revealed to be current title of Deputy Regional Controller, together with his family's influence, made such an outcome inevitable. "Does it sound callous," she said into a pensive silence, "to say that at least she was not subjected to Gestapo torture?"

"No *Madame*, It does not," *Claude Dubois* quietly responded, "And the method by which she chose to deny them is an explanation, less painful to the imagination, as to why they failed to obtain from her the names of so many she could have given."

It was on that note that they decided to sleep on their turbulent thoughts. *Louis Bardot* made his exit, the *Dubois* couple disappeared into a downstairs room, and Elizabeth remounted the wooden stairs to the scene of their discovery. Abandoned in the excitement and now reclaimed, the remainder of the cognac brought to her earlier was carried and sipped as she restlessly moved around the room. Memories of that long ago night in London's Knightsbridge apartment flooded her mind as she touched things which she imagined would have been handled by Chantal and Jack. She stood at the foot of the four-poster bed and visualised Jack being born, and baby Matthew, lying then unnamed, on the Knightsbridge bed.

She undressed, slipped into pyjamas, and sat down with her diary at the small table under the window. As she began her painstaking entries, all around her she could feel the presence of Chantal and Jack. Sleep did not come easily that night.

The following morning Elizabeth arrived apologetically late for breakfast in the kitchen. To hear herself being cordially greeted and forgiven by *Claude Dubois*, her sole companion. Her meal was efficiently prepared whilst she sleepily occupied the circular table in solitary splendour, and, betwixt and between Creacey yawns and *Dubois* banter, it was explained to her that *Lucille* had left earlier that morning with *Pierre* in his pram and Chantal's fateful missive in her purse.

As her man-sized breakfast was finally served to her, it was further explained that one of *Lucille's* old *paramours* still carried a torch for her.

"But more importantly," *Claude* cheerfully added, "he owns a good camera and has his own darkroom, and will keep his mouth shut."

Following breakfast, over her second cup of coffee, Elizabeth raised the subject of her first objective. They began amicably discussing the arrangements to be made for the memorial stone she was commissioning to honour the memory of Jack, and his mother Chantal.

The Frenchman told her of the stonemason, *Francois,* a former 'Resistance' fighter, who would prepare the stone. They agreed that the memorial's location should be accessible to *Claude* so that it could be frequently tended, and her genial host said that he would personally escort her to some places which he thought bore potential. Elizabeth smiled as the *dependable Dubois* told her she was welcome to stay until she herself had selected the place she considered suitable. The light-hearted banter between them was resumed as together they tackled the washing up, and continued afterwards on their journey by ambulance to *Claude's* local bank. The bank manager was suitably impressed by Elizabeth's proffered financial credentials, and the arrangements to transfer sufficient funds to the *Dubois* account were officially concluded to the satisfaction of all parties.

Throughout the entire morning, from kitchen to bank and back again to kitchen, Elizabeth had silently marvelled at the change in *Claude Dubois.* It was, she thought, as if overnight he had shed one skin and grown another. He positively glowed with energy, and her own spirits were being lifted and carried along by his infectious mood.

Back at the farmhouse; her mission reportedly accomplished, *Lucille* was once more in residence. She made them tea as her husband bounced baby *Pierre* on his knee, and she answered Elizabeth's questions. Freely given answers, which now added to Elizabeth's store of knowledge the fact that in addition to Alan Carter and *Gerrard Laporte,* the life of *Claude Dubois* had also been saved by Jack.

"I owe your husband," said *Lucille,* "everything you see before you, *Cherie.*"

It was on the second full day of her stay in France that Elizabeth's innate respect for the sanctity of life and her abhorrence of violence, clashed with irrevocable consequences. Giving no hint of what was to come, the day began innocently enough with breakfast and lively conversation around the circular table in the *Dubois* family kitchen. Where it was revealed that *Lucille's* torch-carrying old *paramour* with the precious camera and private darkroom had promised fresh prints within two or three days. Demonstrably unable to sit still for even two or three minutes, *Claude Dubois* rushed Elizabeth through her second cup of coffee and into the converted ambulance before she'd had time to brush her teeth.

They had travelled a few picturesque kilometres south of *Créon*, to the neighbouring village of *La Sauve-Majeure*, when she knew she had found her location for the planned memorial stone. The village itself, peacefully basking now in early morning sunlight, ranged across a valley nestling between two majestic looking mountain peaks, and, as the ambulance approached one end of the village, she saw the weather-bleached stonework of an obviously old and tiny church. Drawing nearer still, she saw the sign which proclaimed it to be *The Church of Saint Pierre.*

Her transport coasted to a halt beside the church and she looked again at the twin peaks, their symbolism not lost to her as she thought of Jack and Chantal. Informing a silently watchful *Claude* that she would like the memorial stone to be *somewhere here,* the Frenchman smiled and told her that *Lucille* had named their son after *Saint Pierre.*

"To atone for the sins of the father, she said," growled *Dubois* in mock-indignation.

They both laughed at that, but, when the laughter had subsided, Elizabeth's hand was firmly gripped and the gravel voice softened as it said, "*Madame* has chosen well."

Her instant delight in his remark was intuitively jarred by her sensing *something else in his voice*, but he was already exiting the vehicle and she followed suit, trailing behind him on their approach to the church, wondering if her imagination was simply over-reacting.

Entering the church quickly proved to be unnecessary; standing now in its doorway was a black-cassocked elderly man clutching a crumpled paper bag. Elizabeth couldn't decide how old he might be, but *could* see that he had once been a tall man whose shoulders were now stooped with age, and he smiled at her as he was introduced as *'Father Dupont'.*

Covering the parts of a bony looking frame she couldn't see, displaying to her woman's eye all the signs of wear and tear, his cassock bore the marks of countless repairs. On his head she saw the mottled veins that defied concealment by the wisps of snowy-white hair, but his brown eyes still sparkled with life-force and the friendly voice was firm as he invited them to join him on a stone bench which stood just outside the church.

As Father *Dupont* listened to the story of her quest, around Elizabeth's feet two small birds began their hopping game of 'finders keepers' as they competed for the breadcrumbs being thrown from the crumpled paper bag.

"I knew *Chantal Cheval* well, my child," disclosed the priest, "And, of course, her son."

The look on the priest's face made her hold her breath as she saw him flick a glance at *Claude Dubois,* and then the brown eyes re-focused on her as he spoke again.

"My heart, and my church, says yes to you, my child."

She watched as he paused to further crumple the bag with a force which surprised her, and she saw the brown eyes re-directed towards *Claude Dubois* as he resumed, "But alas, as that *coquin* beside you knows only too well, you must obtain the permission of our high and mighty Deputy Regional Controller, *Monsieur Henri Lecroix.*"

Her own glance at the so-called *rascal* took in his shamefaced expression and his *Gallic* shrug of acknowledgement to the priest's announcement. She gazed off over his now lowered head, to the twin peaks standing regally in the background, before once more facing the alert brown eyes of Father *Dupont.*

"Well, gentlemen, we will just have to go and obtain his permission, won't we?"

Father *Dupont* accompanied them on the journey back to *Créon.* Once more perched between two Frenchmen in the front cabin of a converted ambulance, Elizabeth's thoughts comprised an unsettling mix of satisfaction and growing trepidation. Satisfaction at having found both proof of *Henri Lecroix's* treachery and a fitting location for the memorial stone: Trepidation stemming from thoughts of what might lie ahead of her. She was suddenly reminded of a similar turmoil, a long time ago, when she'd paced up and down outside the Nurse's Gate waiting for Jack. Wondering *then*, what the future might hold for them. Wondering *now*, how the past might influence the present.

As part of her mind began considering an answer to the priest's gently probing question as to how she and Jack had met, her thoughts were running at a tangent. *'I am finally about to confront the man who betrayed Jack's mother, and provided the Gestapo with sufficient identification for them to capture Jack. I will be facing the man who robbed Jack of his life, myself a husband, and Matthew a father. But instead of flourishing photographed proof of his crime against humanity, and exacting legal and moral retribution, I will be expected to plead for his permission to erect a memorial stone to those he himself had condemned.'*

Her answer to the kindly priest delighted him but also fuelled further questions, and she told herself it was the inner tension which caused her to reveal far more than she'd intended. By the time they had reached the outskirts of *Créon* she was imagining this must be how the priest's flock felt following a visit to his confessional booth. In addition to her dance floor introduction to Jack, Father *Dupont* now knew of the existence of baby Matthew, and had learned all about the *Chantal Cheval Convalescent Home* in Surrey and its Palliative Care sister in Sussex.

All too soon the ambulance was brought to a halt on the edge of *Créon's* village square. Now that they were stationary, it was hot inside the vehicle, but, even as *Claude Dubois* wound up his window, neither of them immediately moved to disembark. As the trio remained immobile behind the ambulance windscreen, on either side of Elizabeth's vision the village square cafes were busy with lunchtime activity. Evidenced by the colourfully dressed and fully occupied outdoor tables, the square presented a mixed scene of relaxed looking customers and bustling servitude. Directly ahead of her, on the opposite side of the square and dominating its surroundings, stood an imposing looking *Chateau*. The building's frontage was heavily scarred with what she recognized as the unmistakable signs of bomb damage to some of its upper floor verandas. There was, thought Elizabeth, a peculiar *stillness* about the building which contrasted starkly with its current foreground.

"They have more money than the Pope," said the familiar gravel voice, "but every Franc is a prisoner to them."

Seemingly unperturbed by the religious reference having been made in a tone of disgust, Father *Dupont* merely chuckled before calmly giving voice, "True, my son, true." He then turned to Elizabeth and added, "What you see before you, my child, is the current home of our regional masters. *Lecroix* has his office in there."

"The rat never travels far from its nest," growled the gravel voice.

Elizabeth's uncomprehending look was gently dealt with by the priest.

"The Gestapo commandeered the building during the war," he explained, adding quietly, "This is where *we think* they brought *Chantal,* and where we know they brought her son."

Elizabeth felt as if her heart was in her throat, and, as she stared at the *Chateau* with newly opened eyes, the full import of the priest's words struck home.

"You said, *We* think?"

"Oh yes," replied the priest, calmly adding, "Someone had to keep the faith with *coquins* like the one beside you, my child."

Elizabeth's questioning stare towards the other Frenchman was answered by a shoulder shrug and calmly delivered words.

"It is as he says," acknowledged *Dubois,* "The white-haired heavenly goat beside you actually went in there and tried to get Jack out with kind words."

"Sometimes," said the Priest, smiling into Elizabeth's eyes, "words are all that we have."

She couldn't stop her now indignant sounding words coming out, and nor did she want to, "*Claude Dubois,* shouldn't we be telling Father *Dupont* something?"

"No reason we should not," came the growled assent.

The Priest listened without interruption as she appraised him of what had been found, what it had confirmed, and where it was now. "Holy Mother," was his finally succinct response but into the small silence which followed, he was more verbose. "And of course, my child," he said, holding Elizabeth's stare, "If you delay seeking permission for the memorial stone, and *Chantal's* words are brought into the light of day, it could take forever to... "

"Precisely," interjected Elizabeth, exercising her own succinctness with a small smile.

"Glory be, my child," said the Priest as he returned her smile, "You could be a scheming Frenchwoman lurking behind that sweet English smile."

Disturbing her focus, Elizabeth's mind instantly conjured the memory of another time and place, and a Welshman's compliment *apropos* dual nationality. "Well?" she queried, suddenly now impatient, "Shall we get on with it?"

"And she is also," growled the gravel voice, "as bossy as my wife."

Nevertheless it was *Dubois* who reached the ground first, offering his hand to assist Elizabeth's own disembarkation from the vehicle, smiling as he linked arms with her to silently follow Father *Dupont's* approach to the foreboding looking *Chateau*. One of the building's two arched front doors was open, and, as the Priest made to lead the way inside, an elderly couple emerged and squeezed between the trio in their obvious haste to leave. The man was stiff-faced and the woman was crying, noticed Elizabeth.

Once inside the *Chateau,* the Priest led them over a bare wooden floor and past naked walls revealing the faded outlines of where framed canvasses would have hung. Signalling their arrival at what had obviously been designated as a reception area, further unmonitored progress was now prevented by an austerely dressed and officious looking female barrier seated at a table and armed with both typewriter and telephone.

As Father *Dupont* addressed the unsmiling woman, Elizabeth feigned disinterest in her coldly unwelcoming surroundings. Trying not to think of how Jack would have felt when he'd been brought here. In attempted distraction, she forced herself to imagine how this place might have looked in its past; to when it would not have been a place of torture and death; to when it might just have been a warm family home; with framed depictions of a possibly proud history adorning its walls; a place echoing the sound of children's laughter, instead of the clack of typewriters and angry voices she could hear coming from somewhere.

Elizabeth watched now as in response to the Priest's words the miserable looking woman spoke into her telephone, relaying their presence to the man who had never left her thoughts since Simon Rawlings had first brought him to her attention six months ago. She felt strangely disembodied as she and her French companions were escorted up seemingly endless stairs which made her think of Bart's hospital, before reaching the ancient building's top floor. Then she just felt numb as the unspeaking escort finally deposited them outside a door and casually indicated they should enter what she now knew to be the business domain of *Monsieur Henri Lecroix*, Deputy Regional Controller and proven traitor. Without any hesitation or apology to the others, this time *she* was first over the threshold. She found herself standing just inside an apparently empty room.

Dupont and *Dubois* were still behind her as a light breeze caressed her face where she stood. Wide open French windows led her eye-line to the bomb damaged veranda fronting the village square and suddenly she had her first sighting of *Henri Lecroix*. Discourteously still seated on a veranda chair and imperiously beckoning them closer to his presence, he was younger looking than she'd expected. *'He looks no older than me'* was her first thought. *'He has a long lifetime ahead of him'* was her gut-wrenching second thought.

She could now see that, even seated, *Lecroix* was clearly a tall man. He wore a coal-black suit and matching tie over a white shirt, and the ensemble covered a lanky looking frame. She also saw that his sharp featured face was unflatteringly pockmarked with what she recognized as shrapnel damage. She stepped towards the veranda, and stopped as a large black cat suddenly materialised from within the room and began rubbing itself against her, obstructively twining its way around her legs. *Claude Dubois* moved past her and she heard the barely contained anger in the gravel voice.

"So, *Lecroix,* still short on manners, I see. A gentleman would stand for a lady, but a communist sinner like you should always hedge his bets anyway and stand for a Priest."

"Calm down, my son," said the Priest as he moved past Elizabeth to flank *Dubois*.

Elizabeth disentangled herself from the cat and moved forward to join the men now crowding the veranda. She saw *Lecroix* lazily rise to his feet as he spoke.

"But of course, my dear *Dubois,* I keep forgetting that you foolish romantics think you rule the universe and must teach us all how to behave."

Elizabeth immediately didn't like the tone of his voice. The silky smoothness irritated her and made his words sound deliberately offensive. The patently arrogant man had still not in any way acknowledged her presence as he now leant back against the veranda balustrade, and she saw the black cat move under his outstretched legs as he spoke again now.

"I've already reduced *one* woman to tears before *you two* arrived," he scornfully continued, "*She* was another of your romantics, *Dubois.* And since the Priest is here, I presume this one you both have in tow is about to beg for something more interesting." He paused, smiling as he resumed, "Or have you come at last to confess your own sins, *Dubois,*" adding with a sneer, "Or is she simply another sacrifice, perhaps?"

Three men and a cat moved almost at once, but an impulsive Elizabeth Creacey was faster than all of them. Father *Dupont* was struggling to prevent *Claude Dubois* reaching his target as with the beginnings of alarmed surprise replacing the sneer, the *Dubois* tormentor was pushing himself upright as the startled cat became entangled around his ankles.

With the frightening speed of an angry snake, Elizabeth used a clenched fist to strike the pockmarked face of *Henri Lecroix*. All the emotive hatred harboured over the past six months powered the blow which made him stagger backwards as the cat screeched and clawed at his legs. *Lecroix* was overbalanced now, still attached to the cat, teetering on the edge of the bomb damaged balustrade, and adrenalin raged through Elizabeth's body as she pictured Jack's face and Chantal's fate. She struck again, and the tall figure of *Henri Lecroix* toppled over the balustrade and fell to the village square below.

For Elizabeth, the next several hours passed in a blurred mix of weeping and officialdom.

Understandably shocked into almost total silence, a trembling *Madame* was mercifully shielded from much of the ensuing questioning thanks to the protective presence of *Claude Dubois* and the eloquent testimony of a readily believed Father *Dupont.* Watched by a large and impassive looking black cat, the attending officials expressed their sympathies that *Madame* should have witnessed such a terrible thing. Clearly grateful for such a credible witness as a Priest, the local *Gendarme* officer together with the superior of the late *Henri Lecroix,* both agreed with the presented *most unfortunate accident* scenario.

In response to the opportunistic Father *Dupont,* official assurances were received that unconditional approval would be granted to *Madame* for the placement of a memorial stone at her chosen location. *Madame* was then steered from the scene by a serenely mannered Priest and a suitably subdued *Claude Dubois.* She was driven back to the *Créon* farmhouse and handed over to the quietly briefed *Lucille Dubois,* undressed with her assistance, and plied with cognac until she fell into the forgiving arms of *Morpheus.*

Elizabeth awoke to darkness, and her memory of another time. She lay perfectly still, silently recalling the immediate aftermath of her very first encounter with Simon Rawlings, her mind replaying the scenes of her reaction to his contrived version of Jack's death. Long ago scenes, which were now intermingled with new ones, clashing with those on the veranda of a building in which Jack's death had probably really occurred.

After a while, she rose from the bed and moved to the table by the window. Silently thanking *Lucille's* thoughtfulness as she poured water from the earthenware jug. She located her diary journal and sat down with it at the table. Denied Father *Dupont's* confessional booth, she began instead to write in her diary.

One week later, in the picturesque village of *La Sauve-Majeure,* the memorial stone was positioned in the grounds of the thirteenth century church of *Saint Pierre.* The following day, Elizabeth Creacey, the *Dubois* family, *Louis Bardot,* and a host of former 'Resistance' fighters, attended the memorial service. The infant member of the *Dubois* family slumbered unaware whilst the adults watched and listened in respectful silence as Father *Dupont* read a dedication to the memory of Jack and his mother.

Standing at the scene, Elizabeth felt strangely at peace with herself; instinctively knowing that she was also laying to rest a part of herself along with the memorial stone. She would return here to this shrine, she knew, but had decided that whenever she did she would do so alone. Matthew should not, she had decided, be brought here to stand in the shadow of a man whom he had never known. Her son should not be force-fed knowledge of the horrors which had been inflicted upon Jack and Chantal. The definitive decider being that young Matthew should remain unseen by the surviving members of the influential *Lecroix* family, who were far from satisfied by the outcome of recent events.

"Perhaps, Elizabeth," *Lucille Dubois* had said only yesterday, "you will now meet someone else with whom you can share a life."

She looked again at the words *Francois* the stonemason had carved at her request:

> *In Memory of Jack and Chantal Sands*
> *Who Gave All*
> *That We Who Remain*
> *Might Have Something*
> *Might Have Life.*

Elizabeth Creacey felt then in her heart that there could never be anyone else. Two days later she bade *Au Revoir* to *Lucille Dubois* and her son *Pierre,* and climbed aboard the converted ambulance with *Claude* and *Louis* for the return trip to *Dieppe.*

Photographed copies of Chantal's final words had now been sent to those that mattered, and *Bordeaux's* regional equivalent of the Carshalton village grapevine was confidently expected to do the rest. So the good name of *Dubois* was in the process of being restored, and her driver was a currently happy man.

Tacitly deployed to the *Justifiable* file since its occurrence, the unforgettable incident at the infamous *Chateaux* had not once been referred to aloud by its principal participants. At one stage Elizabeth had thought that perhaps the Frenchmen had simply chosen to convince themselves that they had in fact witnessed an accident. She had dismissed that theory when later reminding herself that these were men who had lived with violent death for several years, therefore knew the difference between accidental and intentional. For her own part, talking to Jack in her diary had left her conscience completely free from internal reproach.

When she later warmly hugged *Claude Dubois* before boarding her ship at *Dieppe,* the Frenchman's gravel voice made its best attempt to whisper in her ear, "*Vive La Veuve de L'ombre.*"

Chapter Twenty-One

I never travel without my diary. One should always have something sensational to read in the train.
(Oscar Wilde)

1946 to 1949 extracts from Elizabeth Creacey's diary, and her 1949 visit to France

Having once been described by Winston Churchill as '*A modest man with much to be modest about*', began the diary entry on Clement Atlee, the country's current Labour government leader. The entry which Mary Reynolds had been allowed to peek at and which she and Peter Corder were now dissecting.

"In spite of the bolstering 1946 American loan and 1947 Marshall Aid," opened a critical Peter, "the so-called 'modest man' is presiding over a Britain bankrupted by six years of war and fronting a massive extension of State control over individual lives up and down the land."

"Did you know," riposted the knowledgeable Mary Reynolds, "that Atlee was a first world war Major and that he refused to serve under Neville Chamberlain in his political life?"

"No, I didn't know that," replied Elizabeth, busy feeding Matthew and wishing she hadn't let her friend peek at the diary entry.

"A principled stance," continued Mary, "which unarguably helped secure the 1940 Conservative government premiership of none other than *your* friend, Winston Churchill," ended Mary.

"Atlee was as surprised as anyone else," said Peter, habitually trying to outshine Mary in the political knowledge stakes, "when Churchill's wartime prestige failed to deliver the expected post-war electoral victory."

"But the so-called modest man donned the mantle of power and has gone on to confound his critics," said Mary, adding in a superior sounding tone, "Not forgetting his own party's attempts to replace him with a more charismatic figure."

"The support of an influential Union leader made sure that they failed," said Peter, struggling to hold his own now, "and Ernest Bevan earned himself a spot in the Foreign Office for *that*."

"Ah well, since you mention appointments, young Peter," said Mary, "I think Atlee demonstrated his disarming political guile by appointing one of his fiercest critics, Herbert Morrison, to the Home Office, *and*," added Mary, smiling as she delivered her points-winning *coup de grace*, "revealed a modest man's boldness with his contentious appointment of Aneurin Bevan to the Department of Health."

"I've got better things to do than stand around here debating politics with an ignoramus," declared a defeated Peter Corder, "I'm going back to Sussex now, Elizabeth. I'll be in touch," he added prior to making his dignified exit from the cottage.

"You're a wicked woman, Mary Reynolds," said Elizabeth, "Teasing the poor man like that."

"Listen to *you*," retorted Mary, "The *poor man* doesn't know whether he's coming or going whenever he's around you."

"It *has been* difficult at times," admitted Elizabeth, "He's such a nice man, and he has been so generous with his time when it comes to Matthew."

"Well it's certainly not your money he's interested in," said a sad sounding Mary Reynolds. Elizabeth's diary entries continued to record the ongoing stewardship of the convalescent and palliative care homes and a growing son; the latter being greatly aided by the now permanent residence of the faithful Mrs Bruce. Logged within the diary was the July '46 crisis of bread and flour rationing which had severely challenged the resourceful *Delicate Doris*.

Also recorded was the nostalgic 1947 note that Hammersmith's poignantly remembered bandleader, Lou Preager, had teamed with someone called Jimmy Leach to hit the music charts with 'An Apple Blossom Wedding'. Following her return from France in 1947, another entry penned that year said that she had fondly remembered the industrious *Gianfranco* when learning that *Alcide de Gasperi* had formed a new government in Italy. A 'grapevine-reported' entry on the opening day of 1948 told of the dramatic Berlin airlifts commencing to counter the Soviet blockade. Another entry, made that year upon her return from France in July, said that the flour rationing had thankfully come to an end.

At the start of Elizabeth's 1949's diary, as the journal's earlier question-marked name of Harry S. Truman was beginning his first full term as America's President, Peter Corder was again in conversation with Mary Reynolds.

"Philip Hench and Edward Kendal," opened an excited Peter, "two Bio-Chemists, are showing motion pictures of patients treated with a Cortisone compound which has enabled them to *run* after being bedridden for years with Arthritis. Isn't that *fantastic?*"

"It certainly sounds fantastic," responded Elizabeth, smiling at the man's enthusiasm, her mind more on Matthew's upcoming fifth birthday.

"I think if you read the reports which have followed that," said Mary, "you'll find that the descriptions of the side-effects cause one to pause before getting too excited."

"The village grapevine has seemingly caught the 'Show Business' bug," announced Peter, clearly intent upon avoiding another debating defeat by switching the subject matter.

"How so?" asked an aware and amused Elizabeth.

"They're talking about the first USA-entitled 'Emmy' awards ceremony for the new craze of television programming. The ceremony was held at a Hollywood Athletics Centre, and apparently took place before an audience of six hundred people."

"Sounds exciting," said Mary, "The Americans are so forward thinking."

"The ceremony had no television coverage!" revealed Peter, delighted that Elizabeth had been present to hear his 'Reynolds-deflating' punch-line.

Obviously delighting Elizabeth, and presumably every other woman in the land at that time, was the news relayed by her March entry that clothes rationing had been lifted.

Rivalling factions within Carshalton's 'Vine' hierarchy were evident in Elizabeth's April entries. One faction had loftily claimed its report on the formation of The North Atlantic Treaty Organization, founded to provide opposition to the Soviet Union, by far outweighed in gravitas the other faction's 'Show-Biz' news that the first non-USA production to win an Academy Award for 'Best Picture of 1948' had gone to Lawrence Olivier's production of Hamlet.

An entry made in April of '49 referred to Simon Rawlings and his 1945 trip to Germany.

Alongside the entry on the man who regularly kept in touch, she had inserted a magazine cutting bearing the title 'Nuremberg Trials held by the United States of America under Control Council Law Number10'. It made for sobering reading: *'Telford Taylor, Chief of Counsel for the trials held at Nuremberg, notes that decisions appertaining to who should be indicted were based on whether or not substantial evidence was available suggesting the perpetration of 'criminal conduct under accepted principles of international law'. These Nuremberg trials were carried out for the punishment of crime, not for the punishment of political or other beliefs, however mistaken or vicious. Consequently, in the selection of defendants, the question of whether a given individual was or was not a 'Nazi' in a political or party sense, was immaterial'.*

In the ongoing battle for 'Vine' supremacy, the 'serious news' faction reported that a year after the creation of the State of Israel, Golda Meir had been appointed as her country's first Ambassador to Moscow. Elizabeth amusedly penned the other faction's tart follow-up report that quoted 'Look' magazine as saying that Radio was doomed and that Television would overtake it within three years.

Watched by Mary Reynolds, Elizabeth was choosing from her closet the underwear she would pack for her annual June trip to France. Her radio was broadcasting a variable selection of opinions on the news which had scandalised the established Lawn Tennis world. An audibly heated body of contrastingly outraged and delighted panellists were arguing over an American female tennis player, reportedly Press-headlined as 'The Gorgeous Gussy Moran', who had evidently been featured on the front page of London's Daily Express five times in a single week.

"For wearing lace-trimmed panties on a Wimbledon tennis court," confirmed Mary. "Teddy Tinling, the man who designed *her* underwear, is a former Wimbledon umpire and player turned *couturier*. Did you know," she added, chuckling, "that in 1948 he created a *colour*-trimmed dress for one of the Wightman Cup team. That's why the club has introduced its 'all white' rule."

"No, I didn't know that," replied Elizabeth, gazing forlornly at her own unexciting underwear.

Mary Reynolds departed to answer the call of duty and as Elizabeth continued her packing, two fresh news items on the radio caught her attention and sent her thoughts back to the past. The first news item was on a strike by British Dock workers which had closed a number of Ports. Thankfully noting that her own intended Port of departure would be unaffected, she was reminded of the crippling labour strikes during her London trip to see Thora Silverthorne. All too evident *then*, she thought now, had been the contrasting ways in which the power of a union body could be brought to bear on authority.

The second news item of interest told her that the new novel written by George Orwell was entitled 'Nineteen Eighty-Four', and she smiled now as she recalled the author's unwitting part in a patient-nationality fracas on Bart's Harmsworth Ward.

To complete her packing she placed in her suitcase for continued perusal, the newly published third volume of poetry written by John Ciardi. Entitled 'Live Another Day', reading it had reminded her of Jack's power to convey with words the future he had wished for them both. With only final briefings and the usual difficult partings to get through now, she closed her suitcase and left the room in search of her son and Mrs Bruce.

Collected once more at the ever changing landscape of *Dieppe* by the seemingly *never* changing *Louis Bardot* and the now clean-shaven but still *dependable Dubois*, Elizabeth happily settled herself between the two Frenchmen for the now very familiar journey aboard the now very *un*familiar transport. As *Louis* beamed and started up the obviously new truck, the *Dubois* hands began their expressive gesturing as the gravel voice regaled her with news of the burgeoning *Dubois* family vineyards.

She smiled as she listened: Over the previous two years, using the money she had eventually persuaded him to accept, the once reluctant farmer had become an enthusiastic newcomer to the world of grapes and the financial rewards stemming from their end product.

Reflecting now upon the Frenchman's conditional acceptance of the money which had enabled him to start his new business, she remained convinced that Chantal herself would have approved of some of her legacy passing to one of her own countrymen who had faithfully served with her own son, Jack.

Lucille and *Pierre* were both fine, she was told between bursts of commercial reporting.

"The 'heavenly goat', *Dupont,* is also fine," growled the gravel voice, "He has a young Priest helping him now."

Her son Matthew was as usual sincerely enquired about, but all *Claude Dubois* really wanted to talk about was the wonderful wine the family vineyards would be producing to provide *Madame* with a healthy return on her investment. She felt *Louis* nudge her and turned to see his expressive eyes roll upwards towards the bushy white eyebrows in feigned despair. She gave *Louis* a conspiratorial smile, but willingly braced herself to continue listening to the torrent of ideas pouring from the man she'd come to regard as the brother she'd never had. She listened with an inward chuckle, silently telling Jack that *this* particular journey with his former comrade was evidently not destined to be made in *companionable silence.*

Now routinely allocated the room in which Jack had been born and in which Chantal's message had hidden in wait, upon her arrival at the *Créon* farmhouse a weary Elizabeth was soon tucked up in the four-poster bed. She fell asleep wondering what Matthew's reaction would be to the gift she planned on giving him when she returned from this trip.

The next morning, following warm hugs and a hot breakfast with the people she now looked upon as her extended family, the bubbly five-year-old *Pierre* departed with his smiling father and she and *Lucille* were left as the sole occupants of the kitchen. Dressed in a flared light blue skirt and white blouse, eyes sparkling in the smiling rosy cheeked face, the Frenchwoman radiated *joie de vivre.*

"*Yesterday* I did *today's* paperwork, *Cherie,* so we can have the time together to talk about anything and everything, *Oui?*"

Elizabeth smiled with the thought that *Lucille* was the same vibrant bundle of energy; clearly enjoying her new and multi-faceted role within the vineyard business, but still always eager to discuss and *critique* their respective country's latest scandals or fashions. Not to mention constantly comparing the individual progress of *Pierre* and Matthew. Experiences and insights in *that* minefield were endlessly traded with the express purpose of helping them, as *Lucille* was wont to say, *'to simply keep up with the little monsters, Oui?'* But her hostess also liked to be kept up to date on the subject of *who was doing what to who.*

"So, *Cherie,* is there at last a new man in your life?"

She couldn't stop the grin; *Lucille* was never slow to reach this point of the social compass, but normally would have been fielded by evasion. This time she decided to surprise. "Actually, there are two men in my life. But not quite in the way you're probably thinking of. Nothing has actually... happened. And I doubt that it ever could."

"*Mon Dieu! Two?* You are the dark horse, Elizabeth. Tell me *everything, Cherie.* Who are these men? Why has nothing happened? Is there something wrong with them? Why do you have this doubt that you speak of?"

Elizabeth smiled at the barrage of questions as she held up a hand to stop them coming.

"One is named Peter Corder. He's the Doctor who helped me start the convalescent home, and he still works with me. The other one's name is Jonathan Teale, and he's my Solicitor."

"Both professional men," voiced Lucille, "That is good, *Oui?* They are, how do you English say? Men of means, *Oui?* Are they both handsome? Are they both in love with you, *Cherie?*"

"The answer to all of that, is yes," she replied, smiling.

"Ah, so you don't know which one to choose? Is that your problem, *Cherie?*"

"No, *Lucille,* that's not my problem. If I even *have* a problem. It's just...," she trailed off, suddenly doubting the wisdom of having engendered this conversation in the first place.

"Don't start regretting your need to talk, *Cherie,*" said Lucille."Sometimes it helps to *hear* the words we use to think about the things which are in our hearts."

Elizabeth stared at Lucille as she absorbed those words; she'd forgotten how perceptive the Frenchwoman could be. She smiled as she responded now, "I have a friend I talk to, another Nurse, her name is Mary. She has been reminding me that I'm hurtling towards a 30th birthday. She tells me that any other single woman might conceivably consider herself fortunate to be the subject of attention from two prospective suitors."

"So far, I would agree with this Mary, *Cherie.*"

"*But,* as my mother would have said, *'Therein, my dear, lies the rub'.* Because I don't think of myself as *single.* I see myself as a working mother, raising the kind of son myself and Jack would have... *should have...* raised together. I think of myself as the wife whose prospective husband was cruelly taken from her. The same intended husband whom *Lucille Dubois* unerringly perceived at our memorable first meeting *to be still living in my heart.*"

The Frenchwoman was suddenly at her side, making no attempt to stop the tears which were running down the rosy cheeked face.

"*Jacques* can still live in your heart, *Cherie,* but you have a *big* heart, *Oui?* You don't have to live the rest of your life without sharing it."

"I share it with Matthew," replied Elizabeth, adding with a smile, "And with the wonderful *Dubois* family."

"What about this Peter, and the other one, Jonathan?"

"The professionally erected barriers have so far prevented my defences from being breached," she replied, shaking her head as she continued, "In Jonathan Teale's case, his own busy legal practice occupies a great deal of his time. And I can't erase the memory of his once having deceived me. Albeit under threat, but it's always there at the back of my mind."

The Frenchwoman merely nodded her head; she and *Claude* had been made aware of Elizabeth's so-called 'discovery' sessions with a Solicitor who had hidden the truth.

"And Peter, *Cherie?*"

Elizabeth smiled, "Peter has come closer to unlocking the door to my heart than any other man since Jack. But our very proximity acts as a deterrent. My father used to say...," she broke off, hesitating, unsure whether she should continue.

"*Cherie,* don't do this to me. What was it your father used to say?"

"He used to say, with a twinkle in his eye, '*Elizabeth, my dear, you will always stand tall alongside your professional colleagues, and you may even choose to rise above them, but you must never lie down with them.*'

When *Lucille's* laughter had subsided she nodded her head with the words, "Your father was a wise man, *Cherie.*"

Apart from occasionally growling discontent with his country's still turbulent political scene, *Claude Dubois* was an obviously happy man. As with all her previous local trips, regardless of how busy Elizabeth ever found him to be, he always insisted upon personally taking her wherever she wanted to go. On this occasion, the impeccably behaved little *Pierre* accompanied them on such trips, subsequently gaining frequent mentions in the *Créon* evening diary entries.

Over the period of her current stay, several visits were of course made to *La Sauve-Majeure.* Where, in the clearly well-tended grounds of *The Church of Saint Pierre,* she would sit beside the memorial stone with its view of the symbolic twin peaks, and chat with the increasingly frail but still ever-alert and welcoming Father *Dupont.* On one of those occasions, when consulted on a matter of specific importance to *La Veuve de L'ombre,* the wise old Priest was particularly careful with his response.

Very early the following day, with her now traditional French escort party, Elizabeth began the journey back to *Dieppe.* The day after that, she woke up in England.

Chapter Twenty-Two

There is always a moment in childhood when the door opens and lets the future in.
(Graham Greene)

Carshalton, Surrey, and West London, England
With 1949's July beginning upon her return to England, Elizabeth Creacey immediately issued specific instructions to Jonathan Teale. He was tasked to successfully complete his given mission before September, which was when his client's son, Matthew, was scheduled to commence his formal education.

No longer 'a one-man-band', the ambitious Jonathan now led a fully staffed office dealing with a growing number of commercial clients and his firm had earned itself a reputation for efficiency. Nevertheless he alone handled Elizabeth Creacey's commercial *and* private business, and so, always glad of an opportunity to communicate with her, it *was* therefore the frustrated legal suitor himself who eventually telephoned to report that his given objective had been satisfactorily achieved.

At which point Elizabeth had belatedly appraised Mary Reynolds and Peter Corder on the idea she'd taken with her on her recent trip to France. She then told the astonished duo of her consultation with Father *Dupont,* and of the subsequent instructions to Jonathan Teale which had now been completed and legally ratified. Then she sat down with her five-year-old son and gently told him of the surprise she'd arranged for him.

Young Matthew thought it was a super terrific idea, better even than the junior artist's colouring box he'd been angling for. When his mother attempted to explain why, she got all flustered and he honestly thought he would never understand 'grown-ups'. It all sounded pretty normal to him. After all, he reasoned with child-like simplicity, *some of his comic-book heroes had two, so why shouldn't he?*

Still bearing the unknown but now recognizable hand on the envelopes, Elizabeth had continued to receive infrequent letters, frequently unfinished, from Katherine Ball. Which she had always replied to with news of herself and Matthew. Contrastingly; Katherine's often abbreviated letters rarely mentioned the boy, David. Her last letter had been almost entirely about Tom Ball's new job of 'commercial traveller', though typically she'd neglected to mention what Tom was actually selling. Instead she'd briefly gushed about *what fun it was* to accompany Tom in the company-provided automobile. Elizabeth's last letter of reply to one of these frustrating communications, advised Katherine that she had recently changed her name by deed-poll.

That September of 1949, as an excited Matthew Creacey-Sands enrolled at his new school, Elizabeth's diary logged the fiscally shell-shocked village grapevine's far from sterling news that the nation's currency had been devalued by the 'modest' Clement Atlee.

A later entry that month, on the 23rd, recorded the announcement by America's President Truman that his administration '*had evidence of an atomic explosion having occurred in the USSR in recent weeks*'. Elizabeth's neat hand conveyed her memory of the horror felt by herself and others at the time of Hiroshima and Nagasaki; and expressed her current disbelief that mankind had replicated the means by which such horror could be unleashed.

The diary also noted that; clearly still financially reeling from the devalued currency, some aggrieved village grapevine subscribers had expressed '*their possible understanding as to what might have motivated the eleven US Communist Party leaders convicted of advocating the violent overthrow of the US government*'. An immediate follow-up entry on behalf of those possibly more 'financially cushioned' subscribers reported their disassociation with such irresponsible remarks.

Whilst the handwriting on envelopes containing Katherine's letters was familiar now, though still unidentified, Elizabeth was surprised at how bulky the envelope was this time. Inside she found her own last letter, still sealed and marked *Returned Unread*. An accompanying note was written, realized Elizabeth, in the same hand which had addressed all of Katherine's previous envelopes. The writer of the note was Tom Ball's brother, Charles, and the message was brief:

Dear Elizabeth, I regret to inform you that Tom and Katherine have been killed in an automobile accident. If you would like to attend the funeral...

The jarring note from Charles Ball informed her that his own sibling had already been laid to rest, and supplied her with the directions which would guide her to the imminent second ceremony. Ironically noting the West London district destined to provide her former room-mate's final resting place evoked bittersweet memories of both the area itself, and a fatefully shared introduction to another of its then happier venues.

Afterwards Elizabeth could never really have explained, even to herself, why she chose to take Matthew with her to Katherine Ball's funeral. Held in a small time-worn place of worship badly in need of restoration, the Hammersmith church service itself was a bleak affair. Witnessed in embarrassed silence for the most part by herself, Tom Ball's brother, Charles, and Lilly, his wife. And a man from Tom's former office whose name Elizabeth hadn't caught at the muttered doorway introductions. All in all a sadly meagre congregation, slightly swelled by two visibly uncomfortable small boys who, between the occasional shy glances they exchanged with one another, were shuffling feet in their natural impatience to be somewhere, anywhere, else.

With the burial ceremony's words of homage mostly swept away by a noisy swirling wind, they were quickly concluded by a minister clearly anxious to escape the inclement weather. The shivering representative of Tom Ball's former colleagues delivered his verbal condolence before hastily disappearing, and the remaining group gravitated towards the front of the church to form an awkward gathering of strangers now braving the elements.

Observing the tall, grey-faced and delicate looking figure of Charles Ball, Elizabeth was reminded of the man having been hospitalised at the time when Katherine had met his brother.

She judged Charles to be in his mid-to-late forties, clearly underweight for his height, and her trained eye told her she was looking at someone to whom prolonged ill-health had thus far been a fact of life. She saw the warmth in his unexpected smile, which she returned as she reminded herself of the man's selfless act of addressing Katherine's mail to her over the years.

Presenting the opposite side of their married coin to Elizabeth's quiet study, the wife of Charles Ball was a short robust looking woman whose 'don't mess with me' tough facial features reawakened images of the fearless East London females last encountered within the environs of Bart's hospital as visitors. Illness would never have dared to trouble *them*, any more than it would the woman before her now, thought Elizabeth.

She saw Lilly's gaze dwell on the limousine and driver which had been seen to bring herself and Matthew, and now waited to take them home. She suddenly felt embarrassingly ostentatious, and wished now that she'd told her driver to wait somewhere out of sight. In an attempt to deflect the woman's focus, she remarked that at least David had not been in the fateful car with his parents. Only to hear Lilly's hard-edged tone of response cutting through the blustery wind.

"Fat chance of *that* but yes, thank God he's safe."

She saw that her surprise at the woman's tone of reply had been seen by Charles, who smiled at her as he explained,

"The boy has spent most of his time with us, Elizabeth."

"More of a mother to him than *she* ever was, God rest her soul," said Lilly, sniffling.

Elizabeth now realized that Charles was a practiced foil to his wife's cutting edge, as he smiled again to soften Lilly's words whilst explaining that his brother and Katherine had only ever been interested in having *fun*, as they'd called it.

"Which basically resulted in him being ignored by his parents," Charles quietly qualified.

"Never heard anybody *moan* so much about having fun," rasped Lilly.

Charles then explained how Elizabeth's last letter had lain unopened because Katherine had been away for weeks with Tom in the car. "I knew your address, of course," he shyly added.

"Shouldn't speak ill of the dead," said Lilly, proceeding to do so, "But she was a lazy cow who would write down her moans and groans and then couldn't even be bothered to send them."

Contrasting the biting tone which had delivered the words, Elizabeth saw how Lilly Ball's tough looking facial features softened as she hugged David to her legs and used her threadbare coat to shield the boy from the wind. The woman's voice also changed as she spoke to the child, and Elizabeth saw too the love etched deep in the face that defiantly looked back at her. Trying to forget the fact that only *she* knew that the woman being maligned had given birth to both children now standing in their presence, she asked the couple if they had children of their own.

"Only David," replied Charles, quietly.

"He'll be fine with us," Lilly emphatically stated.

Throughout the verbal exchange between adults, the two boys, each head filled with its own jumble, had continued their shy and silent observations of one another. *Matthew only knew that the dead lady had been a friend of his mother, and he wanted to get back to the limousine. He'd left a sketchbook there, and maybe he could draw this funny church before the car drove off. The boy called David seemed okay. Funny clothes, though.*

David Ball thought the boy called Matthew must be very rich. He could sense his mother was troubled by the way she held on to his shoulder. He didn't know why she was upset, the lady she was talking to seemed nice. He'd hardly known his Auntie Katherine, so he wouldn't really miss her. He wondered what it would be like to ride in a big fancy car like Matthews'

Elizabeth looked at the couple; Charles with his quiet dignity; Lilly with her strength, and knew that the boy David would never want for love. The grey-faced man held out his hand and smiled as he said his farewell, and she smothered a sob as, unbidden, the two boys politely shook hands and smiled at one another. She led Matthew back to the limousine whilst telling herself it was the wind which was causing her eyes to water.

On the day following Katherine Ball's funeral, Elizabeth issued specific instructions to Jonathan Teale. Without disclosing the source, he was to arrange for money to be sent regularly to

Charles and Lilly Ball of Hammersmith. Elizabeth gave him the address he would need, and appraised him of the reason behind her intentions. They then discussed and agreed the amount which the couple would receive. Finally, she tasked Jonathan to find out if there was some unobtrusive way she could be kept informed on the progress of David Ball.

A week later, as she listened to Jonathan's sooner-than-expected telephoned report, she found herself thinking that the Solicitor might himself have employed some of the methods which could have been taught at the 'Simon Rawlings School of Subterfuge'.

"I've arranged for the company that employed Tom Ball to write to his brother, Charles. The letter will inform Charles Ball of the existence of an insurance policy found in their offices and belonging to his late brother. The letter will further advise that the policy document has been passed to Tom Ball's designated Solicitor, namely myself."

"What happens then?" she queried.

"I will then eventually contact Charles Ball to explain to him that the policy was constructed to provide monthly income until David Ball reaches the age of twenty-one. I will explain that the insurance company is also a client of mine and has authorised my own practice to manage this arrangement. When the money starts to arrive each month, I would imagine the Ball family won't be over concerned as to who is issuing the cheques."

"You're probably right," she agreed, and thought she could hear his sigh of pleasure.

"I have engaged *Ramsay and Shields,* a reputable firm, who in addition to their investigative work, also provide the form of report service you seek. Elizabeth Creacey-Sands will henceforth receive twice yearly reports on the progress and well-being of David Ball."

"You've been brilliant, Jonathan, well done and thank you," she acknowledged, and she definitely heard his sigh of contentment this time.

Evidently reminding her of the Bart's Harmsworth Ward benefactors, towards the end of the year Elizabeth's diary journal told of the Daily Mirror having become the UK's best selling newspaper. But the entry chosen to close down 1949 was the one joyfully relaying the Carshalton village grapevine news that the 'Time Magazine Man of The Year' was none other than the venerable... Winston Churchill.

Chapter Twenty-Three

The present contains nothing more than the past, and what is found in the effect was already in the cause.
(Henri Bergson)

Redhill, Surrey, England, Home of Matthew and Alicia Sands, Tuesday, 14th January 1992

The re-packed Pandora's box lay at his feet as Matthew Sands heard the dawn chorus of birds telling him he had lost a night's sleep. He sat perfectly still, thinking of all the other things he had lost, slowly coming to terms with what he had found.

He silently acknowledged that it was certainly easier now, though no less surprising, to realize the commercial ramifications referred to by Andrew Teale. A Frenchman named *Pierre Dubois,* seeming architect of Compass's current European problems, was on the Board of the French company with which Compass Designs sought to merge. In the box now benignly lying at his feet, an attached note from Andrew Teale had told him that *'Pierre Dubois is resident in Bordeaux and is known to be the only son of deceased parents Claude and Lucille Dubois.'*

So it seemed pretty clear-cut, he told himself, that his very own *problematic Dubois* was the son of the *dependable Dubois* featured in Elizabeth Creacey's diaries.

"So where do I go from here?" he murmured to himself, remaining exactly where he was as his thoughts attempted to provide an answer. *'I could confide in this Pierre Dubois guy, tell him who I really am, and reveal everything about my mother. I could explain about my father...'*

His thoughts jarred then, and he stared back into the past which the diaries had revealed to him. He might very well now know *who* his mother had been, but he hadn't *known* her at all. And his father had apparently been someone called *Larry!* So

314

how in the hell, he wearily wondered, could he continue to claim otherwise? Then again, what was to prevent him from continuing to present a false claim? To do so simply required him to conceal the 'real mother' card and play to a Frenchman's ignorance of the truth. And keep on playing for an Englishman's dishonestly hoped-for beneficial response.

'Yes,' Matthew silently concluded, 'Easier, certainly, to see the commercial ramifications alluded to by Teale. But not so easy to see the methods he should employ to handle them.'

Ignoring the stiffness in his joints, and the throbbing in his mouth, he continued to muse. Andrew Teale had said his client, yours truly, would hopefully understand the motives behind the decisions taken by Elizabeth Creacey, and others, all those years ago. Perhaps he would in time, he reflected, but right now he was struggling with the concept.

He hadn't put *everything* back in the box, and, as he looked at it again, he recalled how Elizabeth had cherished the framed head and shoulders sketch of the man he'd believed to be his father. He remembered now that after her funeral, Jonathan Teale had told him the sketch *has gone with your mother* and he'd imagined that to mean it had been buried with her. He realized now that Jonathan had chosen his own method to bury *everything* connected with that period of their lives.

His train of thought suddenly jumped stations: *'Would taking him with her to Bordeaux have made any difference?'* He'd always believed her annual visits to be *just that*, yearly visits to a place she'd enjoyed. *'Some time on her own'* she'd said. Why, he wondered now, had she chosen to suspend the lie yet deny herself the opportunity to reinforce it by taking him with her? Pushing *that* thought aside were other revelations he must face up to now, and when Andrew Teale had said *personal*, not even *he* had realized just how personal those revelations were. He wryly recalled now that only two nights ago, he'd wished Elizabeth had been alive seven years ago to help him through that nightmarish period. Realizing now, that if she *had* been alive, what she might have prevented had he spoken to her at the time.

Matthew Sands sat perfectly still, thinking that in time he could probably come to terms with being *born a bastard*, but, given the inclusion of David Ball in his thoughts, he just didn't know how he would cope with the newly-found knowledge that he had behaved like one.

Later that unforgettable morning, Matthew Sands finally surrendered himself to the oral attention of a masked man. The Dentist peered into his mouth and told him the roots were dead and a new filling was needed. Perhaps spurred by this prophetic diagnosis, Matthew decided right there and then how he would handle his new-found lineal knowledge.

Later still, when the Dentist had carried out his recommended procedure and the effects of the anaesthetic had worn off, Matthew telephoned the overseas company and eventually spoke to *Monsieur Pierre Dubois*. They conversed awkwardly, but finally agreed to meet the following day in France's capital city of Paris.

Chapter Twenty-Four

The words God, Immortality, Duty, pronounced with terrible earnestness, how inconceivable was the first, how unbelievable the second, and yet how peremptory and absolute the third.
(George Eliot)

The Diary Journals of Elizabeth Creacey-Sands, 1950 through to 1965

Elizabeth's diary journals continued to faithfully record and commemorate selected events as they unfolded in her life. Never absent from their pages was *The Chantal Cheval Convalescent Home* and its Palliative Care sister in Sussex, the demands of both on her time undoubtedly responsible for the markedly shorter entries throughout.

That both homes were now firmly established and thriving was, *if any future reader of these journals with little or no business experience chose to believe,* entirely due to the indefatigable Mary Reynolds and the dedicated Peter Corder and their respective care teams. Any future reader possessing personally acquired business acumen, would of course see between the lines. Such a reader would recognize the unceasing commitment of a founder who had sacrificed a personal life upon the altar of business life.

But when writing of her care homes, Elizabeth's entries rarely used the word *business.* Instead the reportedly increasing demands of officialdom upon her time, seemingly resulting in endless nocturnal paperwork, were countered by the logged passages on the *vocational* pleasure she derived from easing the suffering of her patients and their relatives. The personal sacrifices had obviously been painful ones, notable among them her expressed regret at the apparent lack of time spent with the growing Matthew Sands. Frequent entries on her son proudly spoke of his emerging artistic talent, evidently evoking once more the memory of his birth-mother and the then-named Katherine Swan's sketching of Jack's portrait.

Obviously retaining her links to the now Carshalton *Town* grapevine, an early 1950 entry told of the excited reporting that in President Harry Truman's USA, a Brinks Boston Express office had been robbed by masked men of almost three million dollars! Penned within 1950 entries was mention of Elizabeth and Mary's joint acceptance of a theatre invitation from Jonathan Teale. Mary's words had been noted as; *'He knows this is the only way he can get close to his target.'* Apparently both women had enjoyed Anna Neagle's performance in the musical *Maytime in Mayfair*, though Jonathan had slept through the scenes displaying 1950's fashions.

In May of 1950 the delight of *Delicate Doris* and many others was recorded by the news of rationing being lifted on a range of items which had included canned and dried fruit, treacle and syrup, jellies and mincemeats, chocolate biscuits, and petrol. In September of that year, to the reported relief of Mary Reynolds and her nursing staff, the rationing of soap was also ended. And beside an end of year entry saying she couldn't believe she was listening to Bing Crosby and Gene Autry singing *Rudolph The Red-Nosed Reindeer,* was a line ending with three exclamation marks. The line read; *I've just celebrated my 31st birthday!!!*

Evidently matching Elizabeth's own pleasure, the Carshalton Town grapevine's joy of 1951 was logged by its 'Show Biz' faction's news that Teddy Johnson and Theresa Brewer's rendition of *'Longing For You'* was aptly combining with the political faction's announcement of the venerable Winston Churchill's return to London's number Ten Downing Street.

Frequently mentioned were the visits to *Las Sauve-Majeure,* where the *dependable Dubois* accompanied her to watch as she laid fresh flowers beside the memorial stone. A 1952 entry conveyed her sadness at the news of Father *Dupont's* death, and described with neatly penned eloquence his funeral service which she had attended.

Delicate Doris re-appeared in a May1953 entry, no doubt sharing the domestic delight of UK womenfolk at the news that the rationing of sugar and butter had ended.

Management changes featured in a 1954 entry: Peter Corder handed over the Sussex home to a qualified replacement, returning to Surrey *'Where'*, he was quoted as having said, *'he could personally ensure that the female contingent of the Creacey-Sands Cavaliers, did not continue unabated in the undoing of all his earlier good work.'* A 1955 entry logged Winston Churchill's replacement at Ten Downing Street, her appendage remarking that at least Anthony Eden came from the same political party.

The professional pace and weight of commercial life was evidenced by the sparsely covered journal pages over the next few years. However, happily commented upon throughout *all* of the passing years, were the received regular reports on David Ball. Evidently presenting episodic pictures of a normal boy enjoying a healthy and well-cared-for life.

Then in 1958 a clearly amused Elizabeth wrote that she'd been listening to her radio broadcasting someone called Conway Twitty singing *'It's Only Make Believe'* as the news had reached her that Jonathan Teale was to be married to Violet Edwards, a woman he had reportedly met in a public library. The subsequently attended and diary-logged wedding ceremony had apparently been a happy affair. In stark contrast to the 1960 entry, which told of Violet having died giving birth to the son Jonathan had apparently longed for.

1961 entries included mention of that year's visit to France, and her delight that the *Dubois* family vineyards had successfully spawned commercial offshoots which had proved *Claude Dubois* to be an astute businessman. The latest addition to his growing interests had apparently been a fledgling firm of commercial office designers.

Written with obvious difficulty, were the 1962 entries recording the accumulative effects surrounding the tragic loss of two stalwarts in a single month: Firstly, the cheerfully reliable woman who had only ever been addressed as *Mrs Bruce*. Commemorated in diary pages as the person who had reminded Elizabeth of Jack's account of Chantal, when *she* had kept alive for Jack the memory of his father. Because, as with Chantal, Mrs Bruce had ensured that Matthew always received the attention denied him by an absent parent, whilst never allowing that parent's absence to be misconstrued, nor the parent herself to be dismissed from the mind.

And secondly lost to Elizabeth in that painfully recorded 1962 month, Mary Reynolds, her irreplaceable friend and colleague. Mercifully passing away in her sleep.

Later in that same year, unsurprisingly perhaps, a journal entry confirmed that following her consultation with a still equally bereft and weary Peter Corder, Elizabeth had successfully concluded the combined sale of the Surrey and Sussex homes. Peter was reported as planning to go into private practice and Elizabeth would return to London and the Knightsbridge apartment.

And then appeared the simply written entry which said she'd been listening to the Beatles on her radio and singing along with *I Want To Hold Your Hand* as Peter Corder arrived at the Knightsbridge apartment with the results of recent tests. A simply written but devastating entry which said that the Cancer had been found in her body. The entries continued in their painstaking way until 1964, when the diary recorded Peter Corder's news that her condition was terminal. Evidently made as her radio was broadcasting news of Winston Churchill's death, the very last entry, in January of 1965, was a single line in homage to her past:

'My dearest Jack, I have finished the race.'

County of Surrey, England, Carshalton Gardens of Remembrance, 1965

From several global starting points the men from vastly differing backgrounds and walks of life, who for their varied personal reasons had loved and admired the woman known as Elizabeth Creacey-Sands, came together under a grey Carshalton sky to pay their last respects.

Using what inner strength he could summon up to support the young man at his side, a grim-faced Peter Corder stood with his arm around the pale looking Matthew Sands. The visibly aged quartet of Arthur Arkwright, Alan Carter, Simon Rawlings, and *Claude Dubois* stood together; all unashamed of the tears they shed. Standing alone was Jonathan Teale, inconsolable at the loss of the woman who had been an integral part of his life for twenty-one years.

On behalf of Matthew Creacey-Sands, as willed by Elizabeth Creacey-Sands, the following year Jonathan Teale sold the Knightsbridge apartment. He also took it upon himself to cancel future reports from *Ramsay and Shields* on the progress and well-being of David Ball.

Chapter Twenty-Five

Now that I do know it, I shall do my best to forget it.
(Arthur Conan Doyle)

Carshalton, Surrey, England, Offices of Teale & Lewis Solicitors, 1977

It should have been just another 'business as usual' day for Jonathan Teale. It became something else when he arrived at his desk, checked his mail, glanced at the morning newspaper and found himself staring at the name *David Ball*. Presenting him with an unwelcome dilemma and plunging him twelve years back in time. To when he'd been sorting through the private papers of Elizabeth Creacey-Sands after her death. To when he'd found the diaries, and had brought them to the privacy of his office.

'*To preserve her recorded thoughts and her secrets, and to protect young Matthew*', he'd told himself then. And partly, he uncomfortably admitted now, to comfort *himself* at that time. A time when he'd needed *something physical* to sustain his memory of her. He automatically glanced now towards the filing cabinets, the recollection of his past behaviour suddenly making him feel resentful of this unexpected development.

He sat at his desk considering the implications of the information he now possessed, quickly reaching the conclusion that nothing positive would be gained by either party were he to speak out now. Memories of Elizabeth swirled within his mind, and he wondered briefly what *she* would have thought of this current revelation. Sighing heavily, he removed the relevant page from the local newspaper before picking up his pen and scrawling *No Action* across the article on David Ball's appointment to the well known company named Compass Designs. He rose to his feet clutching the article and his professionally ingrained *modus operandi,* garnered from years of noting down informational facts and storing them somewhere for future reference, took him to the cabinet drawer where he kept the wooden box. Resolutely closing down his thoughts, he secreted the article beside the rest of the memorabilia in the box, and firmly closed the cabinet door on his links to the past.

Chapter Twenty-Six

Everything ends this way in France. Weddings, christenings, duels, burials, swindlings, affairs of state – everything is a pretext for a good dinner.
(Jean Anouilh)

Hotel Faberge, Paris, France, January 15th, 1992

Located a stone's throw from shops displaying designer-labelled temptations and within easy access of the Charles de Gaulle airport, the *Hotel Faberge* was reputed to have been purpose-built for the tourist trade. Unfortunately its original owners had neglected to factor in to their profit forecasts, the long and unforgiving wartime memory of a *Concierge* and his staff. Consequential *Gallic* indifference to the service and creature comforts made available to German and American visitors had severely dented shareholder expectations. Sold off in the 60's to an Anglo-French consortium, the *Faberge's* somehow seductive blend of old world style and new world glitz, coupled with an in-house *Chef de Cuisine* of four-starred renown, had quickly turned it into a favoured meeting place for food *connoisseurs* and local businessmen seeking to impress prospective clients. Both were often identical.

The two men facing one another across a coffee table in the hotel lounge, had of course met once before. On that occasion they'd been separated by a Boardroom table and had been surrounded by British and French colleagues. Ostensibly all of them had been attempting to produce a successful formula for the meld of their two companies, but on that particular day something other than the translation minefield had lain under the surface of discussion. The undercurrent of commercial resistance had been *sensed*, but not until his return to England had the feeling been confirmed. Matthew Sands had been informed that

Pierre Dubois, 'The Main Man' on the French Board, was turning lukewarm towards the proposed merger.

Despite the vastly different setting on *this* occasion, the invisible barrier of cautious reserve was still in place between the two men as Matthew, using the deflection of a waiter placing their coffees on the table, studied anew the appearance of the sturdily built *Pierre Dubois.* Endorsing the mistaken impression he'd formed at their first meeting, what Matthew saw sitting opposite him was a physically powerful looking man perhaps more suited to 'sports' than business. But subsequent research had told Matthew how false that impression had been; opposite him was a business brain every bit as powerful as the physique.

The Frenchman's neatly trimmed moustache separated a firmly set mouth and thinly sculpted nose, and, as with their last encounter, brown eyes in the florid face betrayed nothing of the man's thoughts. The dark hair on a heavy boned skull was cropped short and a sheen of perspiration covered his forehead, and his strong looking neck was unfettered by any formal tie. Over the man's cream coloured shirt, a well tailored dark suit disguised what Matthew deduced was probably, *as with himself,* a waistline which had suffered from lack of exercise.

The previous day, during the telephoned request for this meeting, he knew that he'd aroused the Frenchman's curiosity by mentioning the name *Claude Dubois.* Now, with the coffee waiter gone and having already made the decision to *honestly present* the reason for his visit, and *himself,* the time had arrived to satisfy that curiosity. As the stiffly polite and visibly puzzled Frenchman listened, he nervously related what he had learned from the wartime diaries of Elizabeth Creacey-Sands. When finally he ran out of words there was a moment's silence, and then the reaction of the Frenchman proceeded to astound.

Pierre Dubois stood to round the coffee table, and, misinterpreting the action, *he* also rose to his feet. Then the Frenchman was enthusiastically embracing him, smiling broadly as he declared he was *holding a brother.* Retaking his seat, the burly Frenchman then went on to tell an astonished listener of how, on some of Elizabeth's visits to *La Sauve-Majeure,* he had joined his father in accompanying her to the memorial stone of *L'ombre* and *Chantal*.

Listening to the Frenchman actually voicing the names, Matthew was momentarily lost in remembrance of the words which he now knew Elizabeth had commissioned to be carved upon the memorial stone. In his vision now the hands of *Pierre Dubois* were being used to emphasise words, and the voice of the animated Frenchman was eloquently brushing aside Matthew's earlier expressed reservations concerning birthright.

"But *of course* they were your parents, *Matthieu*. The one who saved my own father's life twice; the second time giving his own life to do so, was also the man who enabled the woman he loved to raise in freedom her son. The same man who gave *my* mother her husband back to father the child you see before you now. But sadly, *Mon Ami*, his life was one of the many paid as the price of the peace you and I have both lived to enjoy, *Oui?*"

The Frenchman broke off to signal a passing waiter before turning again to Matthew, "And as for *your* mother, *Matthieu*, who else but a true mother gives her life to raising a son and to honouring the love of a man whose name she chose to give you?"

The waiter arrived to receive *Pierre's* rapidly delivered instructions before Matthew was verbally assailed once more. "You English," he began, waving his hands in the air as he continued, "are so uptight about emotions, *Matthieu*. Truly you were blessed to have had such a mother who was loved by such a man."

Perhaps it was the freedom from toothache, coupled with the Frenchman's reaction-induced release of tension, which suddenly brought the tears he was unable to stop. Embarrassed, he tried blinking them away but then the Frenchman surprised him yet again. *Dubois* had rounded the table once more and was crouching to deliver another bear-hug of an embrace as he spoke.

"No, let them flow, *Mon Ami*. From tears, comes strength. Every woman knows this, which is why *they* are often so much stronger than we mere men, *Oui?*"

The waiter reappeared bearing drinks and Pierre beamed, "But after tears, *Mon Ami*, must come the *cognac*," proclaimed the smiling Frenchman.

As the tray of drinks was placed on the coffee table, Matthew could see that the waiter was ignoring him with studied politeness. The astute waiter departed, balloon brandy glasses were jointly lifted, gently clinked together, and he swallowed some of a very fine *Remy Martin*. With the second swallow of the smooth cognac, Matthew felt his reserve melting in the warm afterglow. So he told *Pierre Dubois* of the even more personal dilemma presented to him by Elizabeth's diaries, and qualified the potential impact which disclosure could have upon his troubled marriage.

In the time-honoured tradition of bar-room and coffee lounge confessionals the world over, *Pierre Dubois* dutifully listened. Interjecting only to offer sympathetic comments or to re-fill their brandy glasses. Then, as he saw the Frenchman initiating yet another transaction with the professionally discreet waiter, he realized that lunch was being ordered so composed himself sufficiently to change the subject. He asked about the memorial stone for Jack and Chantal Sands, and *Dubois* obligingly described the location of *La Sauve-Majeure* and explained some of the history connected to its ancient church of *Saint Pierre.*

"Where my own parents are buried, *Mon Ami*," disclosed the Frenchman.

"I would like to see it," said Matthew, hearing himself add, "On my next trip, perhaps?"

"*Certainement, Mon Ami*," responded *Pierre,* rising to indicate Matthew should accompany him, "You must bring your wife. Meet my *own* family. Stay for a while, *Oui?*"

Over lunch and several cognacs later, he asked *Pierre* why he was opposed to the merger and the Frenchman replied without hesitation.

"Despite the information fed to us by your disloyal Finance Director, I'm *not really* opposed to it, *Matthieu*. The merger would be good for both our companies; I see that behind the lies of your traitor. I just think it should be directed from France." He paused to slap one of his dark-suited thighs, "Why not by *you, Mon Ami?* From what you have told me, it might be a good thing for you and your wife to get away from the bad memories of England,

Oui? And it would, how do you say?, give space to the brother who must not know he is the brother, *Non?*"

His arm was gripped as the Frenchman continued, "I would personally support this idea, *Mon Ami.* You would be good here in France for our business. It's a *good* idea, *Oui?* It is *such* a good idea, it deserves another *cognac,* I think."

Matthew was almost rendered speechless by both the proposal, and the revealed identity of the traitor who had sat beside him in his own Boardroom. Even as his brandied-brain was preparing to receive another of *Pierre's* toasts, it managed to get a response through to his vocal cords. "*C'est une idée magnifique, Mon Ami.*"

As the Frenchman roared his approval, Matthew threw back another cognac and wondered if Alicia would agree.

In his window-seat on the plane back from Paris, Matthew's befuddled mind was still filled with thoughts of Elizabeth Creacey's diaries and the analysis of *Pierre Dubois.* He gazed out the window and silently reviewed his situation, thinking that *Pierre* had been 'spot-on' with his remark about Anglo-Saxon emotions. He had indeed been fortunate in having Elizabeth Creacey for a mother, and, as the diaries proved, she had *been* his mother from the first week of his life. For all of that life up till now he'd imagined the man in the sketch to be his father. The man his mother had rarely spoken about. A man he'd never known. The man his mother had considered worthy of being the father of her son.

'*So what was different?*' The answer had to be *Nothing.* So scratch *born a bastard,* that wasn't what his mother had seen when she'd looked at him on that bed in the Knightsbridge apartment. '*What of his half-brother?*' Another man he hadn't known, albeit a successful one but still just another man among many in Compass Designs. A man who'd also grown up with people who'd taken the place of birth-parents. A man who'd made his own life, with his own family. '*I can't undo what I did, and what would the man gain from the truth?*' The answer was, again, *Nothing.* As he obeyed the *Fasten your seat-belt* command, he decided that was precisely what he would do. *Keep it all tightly belted up and free from spillage.*

He also decided to stop off at the office on the way home.

County of Kent, England, Offices and workshops of Compass Designs, 15th January, 1992

Transferred from his car, awaiting a decision on its fate, the wooden box stood now before him on his desk. Wondering just what he would ultimately do with Teale's box and its contents, Matthew was tiredly checking through his business mail when he suddenly remembered an altogether different type of letter. *'Another blast from the past,'* he thought.

On impulse, he began rummaging in one of the desk drawers: *'She had written to him during that dark time seven years ago. Telling him about the pregnancy. Telling him other things too. Things which had comforted him at the time, so he'd kept the letter.'* He found the wallet he'd discarded when Alicia had given him a new one, and following through on the impulse he extracted the letter and began reading as the intercom on his desk buzzed for attention.

"Ah Matthew, glad I caught you. Can you spare a moment, here, now?"

"Sure," he replied to his Chairman, "Be right there."

He slowly rose from his desk, wearily thinking that now was as good a time as any to give Stanley Crane the bad news and the good news. As he left his office, his mind busy composing what he would say, he was only vaguely aware of the familiar figure in the corridor.

Still mentally composing in his tired head, he didn't see where the figure went.

Redhill, Surrey, England, Home of Matthew and Alicia Sands, Evening, 15th January, 1992

"Paris?"

"*A fresh start,*" emphasised Matthew.

"You mean we just leave? *Everything?*"

"No. We take what we want. What we can use," he paused, "We leave what we don't need."

Alicia looked around her where she stood, and over her shoulder Matthew could see the garden.

"What we don't need," she echoed.

"We need," he said, selecting his words with care, "to put this place behind us."

"We don't need *this place*?" she riposted, arching an eyebrow.

"We don't need the memories," he responded quietly but firmly.

Alicia came towards him and her smile looked tentative as she replied,

"Have they been... all bad? No, don't answer that," she ended quickly.

Alicia reached out and put her arms around him, and her face betrayed her surprise when he squeezed in response.

"We got lost, didn't we." she softly stated.

"I let it happen," he confessed, "I won't let it happen again," he promised.

"In Paris?" came with Alicia's smile.

"A fresh start," repeated Matthew.

Chapter Twenty-Seven

I felt as if I was walking with destiny, and that all my past life had been but a preparation for this hour and this trial.
(Winston Churchill)

County of Kent, England, Offices and workshops of Compass Designs, Early February, 1992
Responding to the ringing telephone, David Ball, Compass Designs' Sales and Marketing Director, could never have imagined that the incoming call was about to shatter his life. An all too familiar voice sounded stressed in his ear.

"David, has Cross spoken to you yet?"

"About what, exactly?"

A brief pause ensued and the quickly exasperated David used it to glance at his watch. *'I could do without the mystery quiz,'* he thought.

"David, I'm really sorry," resumed the voice in his ear, "I would have preferred to do this face to face but I know you're about to take a meeting, and I'm already running late for one myself."

"So...?" invited David, his eyes now caught and held by his anxious looking secretary on the other side of the glass separating their offices. The voice in his ear regained his focus.

"So you should avoid Cross until you and I have had a chance to talk privately." Another pause was too brief to allow a response, "I need to explain myself," said the voice.

"I routinely *try* to avoid Cross. Listen, can this keep? I shouldn't *be* here." The word *No* was terse in his ear and then the voice switched to rapid speech.

"Cross has copied something he shouldn't have seen. A letter from your wife to myself. It's about Susan and Gerald, and about Gerald's father... "

"What about me?" interjected David, not bothering to suppress the exasperation now.

"No, David, I'm sorry," the voice hurriedly resumed, "About Gerald's *real* father. *Christ*, it shouldn't *be* like this but you had to hear it from me first. If Cross gets to you, David, before we can speak properly, you shouldn't blame Susan. Give us both a chance to explain."

Stunned into shocked silence by the callers last words, David Ball could only watch as his worried looking secretary entered his office. There was no sound in his ear now as the questions he couldn't seem to articulate swirled around in his head. The source of the call was unimpeachable, which made this all the more surreal. He briefly struggled for self-control and then realized he'd lost it as he clumsily re-cradled the phone to vent upon his secretary.

"What the hell do *you*...?" he began, stopping himself, instantly regretting the angry vocal tone *and* the act of cutting off his caller.

"Your meeting," interjected the clearly startled woman, "You're late... " She stopped abruptly, obviously shaken, then turned on her heel to retreat from the office.

Common sense kicked in with its urgent commands: '*Placate secretary **later**, call **him** back **now**'* and he punched in the numbers and listened to the voice again. Only this time it was on tape, telling him to leave a message. Inwardly raging at the sound of normality, he re-cradled the phone for a second time and felt his blood pressure pounding its own warning message.

Mentally cursing his squandered opportunity to make sense of the call, he continued to sit at his desk. Consciously ignoring the now desperate looks coming from his secretary. '*So what now? What the hell am I supposed to make of **that**? No point in charging about looking for him, and I don't have the time in any case.*' His preoccupied gaze fell on the framed group smiling brightly at him from a corner of the desk. He must have looked at it countless times before, yet now had the weird feeling he was seeing for the first time the photograph depicting Susan, his wife of fifteen years, happily flanked by their ten-year-old daughter Christine *and Gerald.* Snatches of the voice he'd just terminated echoed in his ear again, and his hands were trembling. *'Not **now**,'* he thought, *'Lose control **now** and I lose the ballgame.'*

Seeking refuge in his past; his disjointed thoughts flickered between ***now*** and past years of domestic juggling and personal sacrifices; pausing at commercial triumphs which had propelled him to his current position. The man he'd just been told to avoid now threatened his advance. *'So what kind of weapon,'* he wondered, *'has the bastard now been gifted?'*

Caroline Prout was observing David Ball through her own side of the glass partition. Knowing her boss as she did, she could readily see that something to do with the telephone call she'd caused him to abort had seriously upset him. Deftly capturing escaping saliva with her handkerchief, she worried a damaged lip with her teeth as her thoughts went into overdrive.

The 'Compass' betting pool currently had it down to a two-horse race between David Ball and the Finance Director, Harold Cross, as to who would become the company's new UK Managing Director. The outgoing incumbent, Matthew Sands, was moving to France as a result of the recent merger with the French company. The general consensus was that Sands would be a hard act to follow, but the general knowledge was that Ball would be hard to beat. Leanly good looking (the typing pool had unanimously agreed he was 'early Gregory Peck') and exuding a magnetism which still attracted women he seemed to ignore, her charismatic boss was the ladies favourite and looking good in their eyes for the mantle of MD successor.

More pragmatically, the male contingent of the betting pool's participants were saying that their money was safe on a horse which could overcome hurdles and go the distance. Pointing out that the forty-four year old David Ball had already spent the last fifteen years of his life ruthlessly clawing his way up the 'Compass' corporate ladder.'

Fifty-nine year old Caroline Prout knew all about hurdles and 'going the distance'. She'd been forty-one when her husband had survived the car crash which had condemned *him* to life in a wheelchair, and herself to a life of 'Carer'. She'd been forty-two when she herself had contracted the Bell's Palsy which had paralyzed one side of her once attractive face, and forty-three before her widower-brother had moved in with them for the company and to help with Care duties. With the change had come an extra mouth to feed and an arrangement had been agreed upon by the trio. So Caroline Prout had been forty-four when she'd plucked up the courage to submit her application for the secretarial post at Compass Designs.

Caroline sighed now at the indelible memory of her life-changing introduction to the man on the other side of the glass partition. *She had never forgotten the initial telephone call from the man who was labelled 'ruthless' by some people within 'Compass'. The man who had complimented her on the handwritten and typed presentation of her previous experience. The man who had politely told her he knew he was flying in the face of employment law by confessing he liked to hear the voice of a prospective secretary before actually meeting her. The man who had said she had a lovely voice and had invited her to attend a formal interview.*

She had duly faced an interview panel comprising Stanley Crane, Matthew Sands, Crane's own secretary, Moira, and David Ball. The man now labelled as ruthless had ignored the then obvious doubts of his fellow panellists, and had praised her courage whilst brushing aside the apology for not having mentioned her disability. The same so-called ruthless man who had seen behind the facial disfigurement to the skills she possessed and had smiled as he'd offered her the job. Employment which had breathed new life into her self-esteem and had provided the much needed income. Employment which had seen David Ball happily changing titles throughout the past fifteen years, but steadfastly refusing to change his secretary. The man who laughed when his managing director now frequently asked if she could be 'borrowed'. The 'ruthless' man who had taken the unasked for time to deal with Social Services and had negotiated the extra benefits for her husband. The 'ruthless' man who had unfailingly presented her with flowers and chocolates on her birthdays, and made her want to hug him whenever he kissed her on the cheek which most people tried not to look at.

Still watching her boss and having decided she would give him a few more minutes before braving another entrance, Caroline Prout had instinctively reached the conclusion that this unexpected behavioural 'blip' must have something to do with

Harold Cross. On her desk now, complete with photographs, was the galley-proof of the new 'Compass' promotional brochure. She looked at Harold Cross's photograph as she allowed her thoughts free reign again.

She knew that, as with most sales executives, David Ball had learned to live with love-hate relationships when it came to accountants. With Cross however, she also knew that despite David's earlier clenched-teeth efforts, their commercial couplings were entirely loveless affairs.

Caroline stared down at Cross's image; which, she thought, even a professional photographer had failed to make appear flattering: *The Financial Director was a tall man, with permanently stooped shoulders which caused his clothes to droop awkwardly on his slender frame. A narrow-shaped and jutting-boned skull was crowned by thinning black hair slicked back from a forehead which met dark and perversely bushy eyebrows. Sunken cheeks flanked a hooked nose which supported the heavy-framed glasses he habitually wore, and which fronted eyes constantly seen darting from side to side.*

As she looked at the photograph; she couldn't stop the smile escaping with her thought that she didn't disagree with the description (birthed in the typing pool) that Harold Cross physically resembled a Vulture who'd seriously fallen out with its Tailor. The smile vanished when she remembered that the man had his supporters in his current battle with her boss.

She'd been present at their most recent clash concerning a marketing initiative for a series of promotional videos designed to heighten the UK market's awareness of Compass Designs. David and his team were convinced the idea was a winner, but the so-called 'Calculator Cross' had argued for continuance of more traditional techniques which were, in his then expressed view, less costly.

'We would be left scrabbling for UK business,' David had asserted.

'Depends upon who is conducting that business,' Cross had icily responded.

Caroline re-directed her thoughts to her boss's first instruction earlier today: The tactical invitation to dinner this evening at

David's home had been warmly accepted by Stanley Crane; who'd confirmed he would be accompanied by his wife, Iris. Wondering now how Harold Cross could possibly have upset her boss at this stage, she finally decided the time had come for her to re-enter the Lion's den.

Still disturbed by the call he'd received, David's reverie was finally broken by his insistent secretary. He rose behind the desk, fleetingly wishing that *he* could gather his thoughts as effectively as *she* did now the notes and charts needed for the meeting. His gaze fell once more to the family photograph, and fragmented snatches of the familiar voice instantly forced their reprise: *'About Gerald's real father... mustn't blame Susan... give us both a chance to explain.'*

Fighting back the wave of anger threatening to engulf him, he hurriedly left his office. The normally hectic pace of Compass Designs production life was currently at the 'frenetic' level, with busy 'Graphics' teams aggressively vying for space and facilities to complete projects within all-important deadlines. As he passed through the milling scenes of activity, contrastingly punctuated by those managing to convey an oasis of creative calm, David turned his thoughts to the meeting he was about to attend. A meeting which would provide the needed feedback in order to clarify some issues he would raise with his Chairman. He would, he reckoned, score a few points over dinner tonight... *Dinner tonight!*

David's stride faltered, along with the crowded thoughts now struggling for prioritised release. His first urgent thought was that Susan knew nothing of his earlier decision to invite Stanley Crane to dinner this evening. He'd told his secretary *he* would phone to let his wife know, but had forgotten to make the call. His second and nagging thought was that he still had to somehow persuade his wife to play the part of willing hostess. His third and unwelcome thought was the fact that he knew Susan wouldn't be *at all* willing, because she disliked the Chairman's wife, Iris. His final thought, unbidden and utterly crushing, was *'What happens in any case when I confront Susan about our son?'* His mind froze on the words *our son*.

He was trying to imagine what he would say to Susan when he suddenly became aware he was standing outside the office where his meeting was to be conducted. *'I'm not ready for this,'* he told himself. *'Get a grip, Ball,'* he silently responded, *'Get in there, do the business, and get out. Deal with the other stuff later,'* and then the door was abruptly opened from inside and he found himself facing his Sales Manager, Harry Parker.

"Ah, there you are, David, I was just coming to get you."

'The words had been delivered with a hint of rebuke,' thought David. But he banished *that* thought and replaced it with, *'Paranoia I **don't** need.'*

Bald head gleaming under fluorescent lighting, familiar easy smile in place on the chubby red face, Parker's medium height build was encased in conventional suiting which covered one of the innumerable jazzy waistcoats favoured by the man. Harry had been one of David's own appointments, having poached him from a competitor, and was an important component of the plan to beat Harold Cross to the MD spot.

"Are you all right, David?"

Parker's eyes, realized David, had narrowed in a show of sudden concern. "Never better," he replied, forcing himself to continue on into the room. Wherein he smiled his greetings to the assembled 'Marketing' team and willed the need to focus. But within the first fifteen minutes he was aware of the sharply surprised looks he was drawing from Harry Parker. Normally used to witnessing the persuasive extraction of any sought-after informational feedback, today the Sales Manager was seeing an impatiently interrogative Director. Which of course was causing those being questioned to become defensive, which in turn was aggravating what should have been a convivial meeting.

Throughout this period of verbal tennis, David's mind was in unaccustomed turmoil. Twice he'd considered leaving the room to phone Susan. Rejecting the idea firstly for fear of 'losing' the meeting entirely, and then because he'd figured it would be better to face her when they eventually spoke to one another. Finally, in an obvious effort to dispel the growing tension in the room, someone made a jocular reference to *'The Title Race'* and the impending announcement of a winner. David used the moment to close the meeting, and, declining diplomacy, brushed aside Harry Parker's offer of 'a private chat.'

He decided not to return to his office, instead making for the company's car-park. Within minutes he was driving towards an unpredictable outcome to the unavoidable confrontation he seemed destined to have with his unsuspecting wife.

Chapter Twenty-Eight

*They tell you, when you get angry, count to five before
you reply. Why should I do that? It's what happens **before**
you count to five that makes life interesting.*
(David Hare)

Compass Designs building, same day... February 1992
The building housing the creative hearts and minds of Compass
Designs, stood alongside its bricks and mortar companions
forming an industrial estate on the outskirts of Kent County's
town of Maidstone. Set apart from the company's warehousing
facilities, the four-level main building's sprawling ground floor
comprised a reception area; the fabrication division; a transport
office; and toilets. The first floor held the typing pool; dedicated
'Graphics' offices; and additional toilets. In addition to the
ubiquitous toilets, the second floor contained the offices of the
Sales Manager; the Marketing team; and a room used by the field-
sales force whenever they touched base. The third floor had been
given over to the canteen and its kitchen staff, and the fourth floor
supported the Boardroom and executive dining room, together
with the En-suite offices of the Chairman; Managing Director;
Sales and Marketing Director, and Financial Director.

The quartet of fourth floor secretaries were currently huddled
in the executive dining room: Officially convened over tea and
biscuits to correlate executive diaries, and *un*officially joined
together for the regular discussions concerning their personal
lives and to exchange individual versions of the latest office gossip.
Today; one of them 'trumped' the other three with the excited
recital of her boss's morning behaviour. She was uninterrupted
as she told of her overhearing Harold Cross informing Matthew
Sands, *'in the most malicious of tones,'* that he was in possession of
a copy of a letter which he intended showing to David Ball.

The late afternoon sky was still permitting natural light to play into the office of Matthew Sands, who was attempting once more to reach the woman by telephone. He had returned as fast as the motorway traffic had allowed, only to be told by David Ball's secretary that her boss had already left the building and that his mobile phone still lay on his desk.

The woman wasn't answering and he reluctantly re-cradled his phone. He was still appalled at the consequences of his past carelessness, silently cursing anew the timing and disruptive agenda of the opportunistic Harold Cross. He was also now ashamed and embarrassed by the 'dog's breakfast' he'd made of his earlier call to David Ball. He still couldn't believe he'd allowed himself to blurt things out in the way that he had. He glanced at his watch, an idea hastily forming itself in his mind, *'I'll phone Alicia now, tell her I'm going to be late, then I'll try the other number again before speaking to Stanley Crane and that bastard Cross. Maybe I should ask David's secretary how he reacted to my call'* was an afterthought as he picked up the phone again and stabbed down at numbers as he strangled Harold Cross in his mind.

On a daily basis; Caroline Prout filtered all manner of telephone callers targeting her boss. So she knew the sound of legitimate urgency when she heard it, and she'd heard it moments ago in the voice of Matthew Sands. But she had refrained from properly answering his concerns about her boss. Nor had she felt able to divulge her knowledge of the existence of a letter, a letter which she was beginning to believe might be the reason for Matthew Sand's concerns.

Caroline sighed; it was so unlike David to have left the building without firstly letting her know where he was going, and he'd never before gone without his mobile phone. *'Everyone else is acting out of character today, so why shouldn't I?'* she thought, having decided to pay an unannounced visit to the office of Matthew Sands to find out what was going on. She would do so once she delivered these papers to the second floor.

'Okay,' thought Matthew, *'that's Alicia partly briefed but completely happy to spend an evening in her garden. A quick word with Stanley now, and then beard that bastard Cross in his den.'*

He rose purposefully from behind his desk and instantly realized the need to relieve his bladder. *'You can't even hold your water anymore, Sands,'* he told himself, smiling ruefully as he made for the en-suite bathroom.

Fifteen years of habitually avoiding exposure to other 'Compass' personnel in the confined space offered by elevators, instinctively took Caroline Prout to the marble stairway on her fourth floor. The descent to the second floor was managed with ease; and the papers were duly handed over to the intended recipient. Sighing resignedly whilst telling herself the exercise would do her good, she began her climb back up the stairs to the fourth floor.

The product of a loveless marriage, long ago broken on the rocks of divorce proceedings, Harold Cross had spent his lonely formative years distrusting personal relationships. Instead learning to love the less demanding ledger-form of life. He had rapidly acquired fluency in the language of balance sheets, and his single-minded approach to a career non-dependent upon commitment to a personal life had brought its own rewards which didn't have to be shared. He had journeyed friendless along his chosen road, and had liked it that way.

He had crossed the Rubicon to an early side-path of embezzlement and had tasted power for the first time with his amorally engineered dismissal of a 'suspected' and unsuspecting accounts manager. Harold had never learned how to cultivate friends, but that had never bothered him. He effortlessly attracted enemies but that didn't bother him either; he knew how to deal with *them*. Seated now in his office a few yards along the corridor from the 'Checkmated' Matthew Sands, he sighed contentedly as he reviewed his latest Rubicon crossing. Victory was in sight, and, ironically, the merger he'd initially opposed had been his ally.

Harold Cross smiled to himself as he reviewed the current situation: Unwilling to rock the French boat, and singing from their own self-interest hymn sheet, the Venture Capital duo conditionally appointed to the 'Compass' Board had persuaded Stanley Crane to accept *their* interpretation of his Finance Director's 'misconstrued indiscretions'. Thus negating the stigma of 'Traitor' which Sands had sought to attach to the name of Cross.

Having happily exchanged 'Judas handshakes' with the 'VC' duo beforehand, he was of course aware of the motivation behind their support. By encouraging him to contest Ball and potentially replace Sands, they foresaw his appointment to MD status as their own route to more 'hands-on' control over the future direction of a merged Compass Designs. His new partners in the power game were even now lauding his; *quote;* 'Innovative financial strategies'. But *he,* of course, had always known that wouldn't be enough to tip the scales in his favour. Just as he now knew he had *more than enough!*

He carefully inserted his copy of the revealing letter inside the 'Creacey' diary journal he'd stolen from the wooden box. Clutching his plunder he rose from behind the desk, once more wishing that he'd fully appreciated what the box had contained. *'Had I done so,'* he thought, *'I would have taken more than one of the informative diary journals.'* Whilst sometimes privately conceding to himself that he wasn't really cut out for the commercial 'heel-on-throat' tactics so glibly depicted by his television screen dramas, at this particular moment he *was* congratulating himself on having located the hidden underbelly of not just one, but two opponents. Discoveries he fully intended to expose.

Regretfully feeling all of her fifty-nine years, Caroline Prout continued her steady ascent to the fourth floor level.

Matthew Sands emerged from his office to see Harold Cross coming towards him. Seemingly heading for the elevator, the clearly startled looking man turned on his heel and made for the stairway, and, as he did so, Matthew recognized the diary journal clutched by the man. *'The bastard must have nicked it from that damned box,'* was his instant thought, quickly followed by *'Which one? What has he seen?'* and his spontaneously shouted "Hold it, Cross, I *want* you," came a second before he charged after the man.

Caroline Prout heard the voice of Matthew Sands and her eye-line took in the heads and shoulders of two moving figures on the fourth floor level as nine marble steps remained between her and the corridor's floor.

In response to the shouted command, Cross turned to face him again and Matthew slowed to walk the remaining paces separating them. His anger began spilling over even as he caught sight of the familiar figure reaching the top of the stairs. "So, you *bastard,* as well as having threatened to destroy David Ball's marriage, you stole that diary and I want it back *right now.*"

Caroline Prout found herself staring at a rear view of Harold Cross who stood a few paces in front of her. She froze where she stood, the words she'd heard ringing in her ears, the realization crystal clear now as to what had upset David. And then the man who was apparently bent upon destroying the person who had done so much for, was speaking. She heard *his* words and felt her own fury bubbling inside her.

"I rather think," began a disdainful sounding Cross, holding aloft the diary he held, "that once *this* is in the public domain, it will in fact *prove* that *you* are the only *real bastard* here, Sands."

Propelled by a murderous rage, Matthew Sands was moving even before his tormentor had finished speaking. The *lightning-speed* thought of the pain Alicia and Susan would suffer by the intended action of this creature before him, powered the single blow which was delivered to the taller man's midriff. His fist connected with a force which drove the oxygen from the lungs of Harold Cross, who wheezed in obvious agony as he spun away to stagger towards the stairway.

A sudden *thought-flash* of the boy Gerald's life being torn apart and *another thought-flash* of Elizabeth Creacey's private thoughts having been read by such an invader, carried Matthew after the man who'd drawn level with a shocked looking Caroline Prout and was slowly straightening up. In Matthew's mind the word *witness* was too late to stop his second punch which he knew instantly had damaged the man's ribcage, then he saw Caroline Prout snatch the diary from Harold Cross as the man began his headlong fall down the unforgiving marble stairs.

Clutching the diary to her chest, David's secretary wordlessly stood beside him as they both looked down at the now stationary figure below them. The unnatural angle of the man's neck told its unmistakable tale; Harold Cross was very definitely dead.

Matthew turned his eyes towards the sound of voices and saw the other fourth floor secretaries approaching at pace. *'Attracted by the noise, I suppose,'* he thought dully, trembling now in the aftermath of his anger-fuelled action, his adrenalin spent. The enormity of that action, and its likely additional consequences, was already beginning to sink in when suddenly in his disbelieving hearing was the melodious voice of Caroline Prout addressing her peers.

"I'm afraid," began Caroline Prout, "there has been a terrible accident, ladies. Mister Cross seemed to have a fainting spell. Mister Sands tried to catch him, but couldn't prevent the poor man falling down the stairs."

And on the words *terrible accident,* Matthew was momentarily lost in the memory of his mother's recorded role in another *accident,* witnessed by *Claude Dubois* in a French *Chateau.* Milling around him now, on the fringes of his memory-jarred distraction, and despite his not having uttered a single syllable, it was quickly apparent that the fourth floor secretaries were quite prepared to immediately accept the word *accident* from one of their sisterhood. One of the secretaries left with the declared intention of *reporting the accident* to the police. A second one moved off saying she would telephone the Chairman *about the accident,* and the woman who didn't seem at all upset by the loss of her boss went away with the promise to return with cups of tea. *'Just what you both need after a nasty accident,'* were her departing words.

In the course of waiting for the summoned police, *'nasty accident'* was the scenario jointly honed by Caroline Prout and Matthew Sands upon those other Compass personnel coming across the scene in the course of their duties. By the time the police *did* arrive, they could have chosen from any number of employees who would have related the fateful event as if they themselves had recently witnessed it at first hand. Both completely at ease with the anticipated arrangement, Matthew and Caroline were separated for the taking of statements. Given statements which, now sculpted by practice, were found to be individual pieces of a perfectly fitting jigsaw.

Brought from his home by the news, Stanley Crane appeared in time to hear the attending police doctor confirm that the injuries sustained by the late Harold Cross were entirely consistent with those to be expected from rapidly falling flesh and bone impacting upon the solid surface and lethal edges of marble stairs. The 'Compass' Chairman looked on dry-eyed as his now former Finance Director was carried away in a body-bag, and Matthew knew that Stanley would shed no tears for a man he'd wanted to be rid of since learning of his treachery.

Contrasting his older and seemingly bored Sergeant, the police Inspector *'was very young looking,'* thought Matthew, *'Obviously one of the 'fast-track' graduates they were churning out these days,'* he silently deduced. Which initially worried him, imagining that the officer's youthfulness would be allied to a keenness to find something which others had missed. But the man was readily believing Caroline Prout's version of events and Matthew realized he couldn't have wished for a more credible 'witness'. He found himself imagining Elizabeth Creacey must have felt the same way about Father *Dupont* all those years ago in France.

When asked by the Inspector if the object she still clutched to her was of relevant significance, Matthew heard Caroline Prout calmly explain that she had been on her way to return the diary to Mister Sands when she had been caught up in *his attempt to save that poor man.* The bored looking Sergeant seemed to perk up on learning that the *poor man* had no dependants needing to be informed and consoled. *'He wants to get out of here and go home to the wife,'* thought Matthew.

He and Caroline were advised of the need to observe the formalities: Their presence would be required at the police station tomorrow in order to verify and sign their typed statements, whilst both were reassuringly told *now* by the satisfied Inspector that the forthcoming Coroner's Inquest would undoubtedly deliver its *Accidental Death* verdict.

Later, when the official circus had closed notebooks and departed; when Stanley Crane and the other fourth floor secretaries had disappeared; when Matthew felt like a limp rag and was now fully appreciating what strength his mother must have possessed to endure, and to have survived, the immediate aftermath of her own rage-fuelled experience; the two collaborators were left in sole occupancy of the fourth floor.

Caroline Prout remained at his side. *'As if,'* thought Matthew, *'they were now joined at the hip by their collusion.'* The silence they now shared was both blissful and suddenly awkward as she chose that moment to hand him the diary without saying a word. Neither of them so much as glanced at the marble stairway as she gave him a twisted smile and nodded acquiescence to the invitation to his office for *a proper drink.*

Inside his office; he seated Caroline in front of his desk and moved to the drinks cabinet whilst silently marvelling at her seeming composure in the wake of all that had happened. His glance around the spacious office sharply reminded him that had it not been for this woman's intervention, he would probably now have been languishing in a police station's cell instead of standing here in comfortably familiar surroundings selecting his best brandy and two glasses. *'I wouldn't have survived a murder charge,'* he told himself as he moved back to the desk.

Matthew was suddenly unable to prevent the comparison and his mind conjured the unbidden image of Elizabeth Creacey *not having survived her own experience.* He stared at Caroline Prout as he tried to imagine what his life would have been like without the woman who had been protected by Father *Dupont;* and simply *couldn't see any life at all.* A swiftly cold wave of relief washed over him, snapping him from his mental gymnastics, making him shiver whilst soberly crystallizing the magnitude of his debt to his brother's secretary.

"The first thing I want to offer you," he began, still standing as he poured them both measures of brandy and realized he was trembling again, "is a heartfelt thank you." He handed her the drink and looked down at the ravaged face as he continued, "Which suddenly feels like a woefully inadequate thing to offer, given the circumstances."

The woman looked up at him; her tears beginning with her response, "The *circumstances,* to use *your* word, simply demanded I do nothing less than I did."

Matthew watched as she then swallowed down some brandy and he saw that the hand which took his proffered handkerchief to her tears was trembling as much as his own.

"I really don't know," said Caroline as she wiped away tears, "how we managed to get through that, *but I'm very glad that we did*," she ended firmly.

"Why *did* you help me? *Why* did you risk being...?" His questions were waved away by his own handkerchief and Caroline Prout's firmly voiced interjection.

"I heard what you said to him, and I was *not going to allow* that odious man to bring any harm to David Ball and his family. And neither did I want *you* to be punished for also trying to prevent that happening."

Moved by the woman's words, he reached down to grip her shoulder. She instantly acknowledged the gesture by covering his hand with her own free one and he suddenly realized she was now squeezing the same hand which had formed a lethal fist only a short time ago.

"Are you going to be okay?" again sounded lame in his ears, but he watched her drain the brandy glass a second before her reply continued to surprise.

"I've given birth to three children, and lived to bury one of them. I've coped with an invalid husband for seventeen years, and battled with Bell's Palsy for sixteen years. Yes, Mister Sands, I'm going to be okay." She smiled her twisted smile, "But thank you for asking. And your own earlier expressed thank you is *not at all* inadequate," she emphasised whilst holding out her empty glass, "May I have some more brandy? I think it's helping the aftershock."

Using the desk as a formal barrier between himself and this obviously formidable woman was no longer acceptable in his mind, so Matthew positioned another chair in front of the desk and sat down to replenish her drink. "What with aftershock and brandy-chasers," he said, injecting lightness into his tone, "maybe I should drive you home, when you're ready."

"I'll call my brother," she replied, "He lives with us, and he'll be happy to collect me." She smiled, adding, "He'd also be happy to meet *you*, if he got the chance, if *you* wouldn't mind?"

"Of course not. But why...?" began Matthew.

"As children," interjected Caroline, "my brother and I used to visit our father when he was convalescing after the war. He was in The Chantal Cheval Convalescent Home in Surrey, and they transformed a very sick man into one well enough to be returned to our mother. My brother and I once met your mother, Elizabeth Creacey-Sands, and we both remember her as the woman who helped make our childhood a happier one because of what she did for Dad."

Astonished, Matthew stared at the woman as she sipped some more brandy before smiling again as she resumed talking.

"It was one of the reasons I applied for a job here," she revealed, "I knew you worked here and imagined it would be nice to work for you, in a roundabout way."

"You never said...," he began, only to be interrupted.

"No, I never did. As time passed here I didn't want to be seen as currying favour. And besides, with David Ball, I found myself working for a man I admired. A man who has privately done so much to help me and my husband over the years. A man who speaks highly of you, Mister Sands, even though," she paused to chuckle, "he's after your job."

Matthew swallowed some brandy as his thoughts performed somersaults inside his head. He was back in a Paris hotel with *Pierre Dubois,* being offered a formula to save his marriage; back in the diaries of Elizabeth Creacey and remembering her recorded inspiration behind the naming of the convalescent home; back in a French *Chateau* as Elizabeth Creacey disposed of *Henri Lecroix*; back at the top of the marble stairs looking down on Harold Cross; back again now with the daughter of a man who had been helped by Elizabeth Creacey, and who had now saved from disaster the adult versions of the two children in Elizabeth's history; back to the realization that the problem still remained as to what he could do to redress the content of his telephone call to David Ball a seeming lifetime ago.

'Christ,' he thought, 'Can this day possibly get any weirder?' He gazed at the woman before him, "I just don't know what to say, and I certainly don't know how I can ever repay... "

"Oh, I don't think," interjected Caroline once more, "we need say anything more, ever again, about what has transpired here today. And as for payment," she smiled her crooked smile, "I think we've both already had all that we could have wished for, wouldn't you say?"

The telephone call to Caroline Prout's brother eventually resulted in Matthew being introduced to Samuel Prout, a man in his late sixties, who was calmly told by his sister that an office 'incident' had caused her to have one brandy too many and it had been deemed wiser for her to be driven home.

Upon departure, the elderly brother shook Matthew's hand with the strength of a teenager and told him to remember Elizabeth Creacey with pride. For her own farewell, Caroline Prout offered her hand but Matthew refused it and instead took her in his arms. He told the blushing woman to take a few days off, and that he'd square it with her boss.

"Certainly *not*. I wouldn't dream of it," she briskly responded, "David will need me at my desk, and *that*, Mister Sands, is where I shall be."

Watching her being driven away, Matthew was left with the thought that whilst the Bell's Palsy had severely affected the 'Trigeminal' one, there was absolutely nothing wrong with the rest of Caroline Prout's nerves.

Chapter Twenty-Nine

I keep six honest serving-men
(They taught me all I knew);
Their names are What and Why and When
And How and Where and Who.
(Rudyard Kipling)

A25 trunk road linking Surrey and Kent Counties
Further leaked extracts from the soon to be published Tomlinson report on the future of the London health service, have provoked political controversy today. Sections of the report will apparently question the future viability of the renowned Saint Bartholomew's hospital. Since its foundation in eleven twenty-three, Saint Bartholomew's, or Bart's as it's commonly called, has successfully prevailed in the eye of many storms, including the historical turmoil during the dissolution of the monasteries and the Great Fire of London in sixteen sixty-six...

David Ball reached out to switch radio stations and the tears surprised him, coming suddenly, forcing him to steer into the side of the road and brake the car. Replacing the news now was the distinctive voice of John Lennon fronting the Beatles composition *'In My Life'* and for some inexplicable reason David was reminded that the last time he'd wept like this had been when he and Susan had watched his Aunt Lilly being laid to rest beside her beloved Charles.

As he groped for tissues he was further reminded of Lilly's old gramophone with the broken stylus, because certain words were now insistently scratching their disjointed reprise across his mind. *About Gerald's real father... A letter from your wife... You mustn't blame Susan... A letter from your wife... About Gerald's real father... Give us both a chance to explain...*

In My... y... y... y... life, I've loved them all... He felt the fresh tears begin as Lennon ended his song but there was anger mixed with the bewilderment as he blew his nose and silently raged. *'I have loved all my family,'* he told himself, *'How could she have lied about such a thing?'* He took a deep breath, wiping his eyes as he finally allowed the admissions to surface from his thoughts, *'I shouldn't have hung up on the man. I should have demanded a meeting. And I should have gone looking for Cross.'* He exhaled with the silent confession that he hadn't wanted to confront *either* man because he hadn't wanted to find himself facing the truth.

Homeward bound traffic continued to *Whoosh* past him and the sound, regular and mooted, was having a calming effect on him. His thoughts slowed and began to sort themselves out into some semblance of order. *'I must tell Susan about the dinner and overcome the expected objection. It's essential that I stay on track for tonight's meeting. I must somehow, never mind how, get through the dinner. Only then, when Stanley Crane and his wife have left, can I confront Susan about Gerald.'*

With a last relieved thought that the children were not due back until tomorrow from an arranged 'sleep-over' with friends, a dry-eyed and resolute David Ball restarted the car and his journey home.

Sundridge, Surrey, England, Home of David and Susan Ball

Wanting to leave the driveway clear for his expected guests, David Ball parked his company Volvo beside Susan's Mini in the double-garage which stood beside their detached bricks and mortar proclamation of... *'Of what?'* he tiredly wondered, *'Of having successfully avoided more snakes than life's other players while climbing the ladders? Or of being the proud possessor of a crippling mortgage?'*

He continued to sit in the car, comfortable in the warmly familiar cocoon, the voice of Lilly Ball in his head; *'Any fool can have fun, David, but fun alone won't put bread on the table and money in the bank. But hard work will. You work hard, David, and the good things in life will be your reward.'* He shook his head and used a hand to rub his tired eyes, wondering how many times the Volvo had transported him from the office to here on 'auto-pilot'.

Leaving him with no memory of the journey in between. It was always alarming and he always told himself he wouldn't allow it to happen again, but of course if frequently did. Usually it was a business problem 'driving the car' but this time it had been fifteen years of matrimonial weights and measures which had brought him here with the debilitating thought that he wasn't sure which way the scales were balanced. With a weary sigh he forced himself to get out of the car.

The front vestibule of their home was, as usual, immediately welcoming. So many times before, he reflected, he had paused here to symbolically divest himself of what Susan had entitled his *stressed executive persona* and allowed the warmth to relax him. But he knew he couldn't relax this time. This time he would need to retain the invisible armour of wariness. Despite the vestibule's furniture and plants skilfully blending to create a disarming illusion of spaciousness, it was actually quite a small area. Reminding him anew that Susan's interior decorating, admired by all their friends, was her special talent. It was here in the welcoming vestibule that Susan came to meet him, smiling as she offered her embrace, the surprise obvious in her voice.

"Hello Darling, you're not usually here this early."

David did his best to smile at his wife's greeting. Standing almost as tall as his own six-feet height, her finely boned facial features were framed by the long dark hair which gleamed and fell to her shoulders. Susan's trim figure was casually dressed in black Ski-pants, over which she loosely sported a white cheesecloth shirt. He looked into the sparkling blue eyes and tried not to wonder if they would tell him when she lied. "No," he finally replied, "I need, *we need* to talk."

As he drew her through the hallway and into the lounge, Susan smiled and asked him if he'd already heard about the promotion. "No, not yet," he replied, glad of her lead, "But that's what we need to talk about."

"Well *I'll* fix us both a drink while *you* start," she breezily responded whilst moving purposefully to the drinks cabinet.

Glancing around him quickly he was immediately struck by how cosy and peaceful the lounge was without the presence of noisy and disruptive kids; the scene now making him uncomfortable with the fact that he was about to change its whole ambience. His glance took in Susan's rippling back muscles under the shirt and he realized she was bra-less and he suddenly felt himself hardening with desire. *'Christ, get a grip, this is no time for that,'* he told himself.

"I've invited Stanley Crane and his wife to dinner. They're coming here, tonight."

He watched Susan's back stiffen before she turned, open-mouthed, to face him as he rushed on, "I need to get him on home ground and it's my last chance to get some important points across before the appointment decision is made."

"Well," opened a now grim-faced Susan, "you already know I can't *stand* his wife," then her face brightened as she added, "Anyway, why can't we just take them *out* to dinner? *You* can choose the restaurant, so you'll still be on your own ground," she ended on a triumphant sounding note.

"It's not *just* that, Sue," he retorted, "and *you* know it. We haven't had them here for ages, not since you quarrelled with Iris, and I have to... *we* have to... show them that we can all get along with one another." He ran a hand through his hair, suddenly irritated by the circumstances which prevented him broaching the subject he *really* wanted to discuss.

"You're going to be," he resumed, unable to stop his voice rising, "seeing a lot of Iris if, *No, when* I get the job."

"There's no need to shout," objected Susan, her tone suddenly icy, "Just what sort of miracle am I supposed to produce for this dinner? And what time are they coming?"

"Not for hours yet," he replied quickly before glancing at his watch and feeling his stomach lurch, "Well, two hours, actually." He tried to smile but couldn't make his facial muscles relax enough, then he watched his wife go from glacial to volcanic in a heartbeat.

"Why couldn't you have phoned to let me know?" she erupted.

"Do *you*," he snapped back, "*tell me* everything I should know?" and his already fragile composure shattered as he heard himself savagely spit out the addition, "Have *you* always told me *everything I should know* at the right time?"

Trembling with his own emotion, he saw Susan physically recoil but couldn't tell whether it was from his facial expression or his words. Then she burst into tears before running into the kitchen and slamming the door behind her. Silently cursing his inept handling of the encounter, he moved to the drinks cabinet and poured himself a glass of wine as he listened to the sounds of his wife crashing about in the closed-off kitchen. *'I should be the one crashing about,'* he told himself, gulping at the alcohol he couldn't really taste through his anger, *'But I suppose I should try to calm her down.'*

As he moved towards the kitchen his glance fell on the framed picture of Gerald and Christine, tripping the memory of the day he'd brought Susan and their son from the hospital to this very room. He stopped moving, but his thoughts didn't, and he felt again the onset of unexpected and uncharacteristic tears. *'What the hell is it with these tears?'* he asked himself uselessly, abruptly turning away from the kitchen door to make his way upstairs, wearily deciding to wash his face and put on a clean shirt. He was buttoning the fresh shirt in the bedroom when he realized he hadn't washed and he needed a shave. He sat down to remove the clean shirt, telling himself *'I'd better get my act together if I don't want to blow this meeting with Stanley Crane.'*

Some thirty minutes later, shaved, washed, and freshly dressed, he descended the stairs feeling marginally better equipped to face Susan. As he crossed the lounge, bracing himself for the kitchen, the telephone rang and he actually *felt* his heart skip a beat. He picked up the phone along with the now wryly perceived thought that perhaps crying outbursts and frayed nerves meant he wasn't in such good shape after all. In response to his polite query, the anxious sounding voice of his company Chairman was suddenly in his ear.

"David, I'm sorry to call at such short notice, but would you and Susan object to my bringing an extra guest to your dinner table this evening?"

Before a reply could be formulated, Stanley Crane coughed his embarrassment over the line before continuing, "I should have alerted you sooner, sorry, but you know how it goes. Only it's Matthew Sands, you see. He knew we were meeting this evening, *and*, having apparently failed to get hold of you himself, rang *me* earlier to say it was important that he be given an opportunity to speak with you as soon as possible."

"Don't worry, Stanley," he replied, striving for a calmness he didn't feel while his heart pounded in his ears, "That's quite all right. I'm sure we can cope with that." The pounding in his ears was replaced by the sound of a dog barking, quickly deciphered as Stanley Crane's burst of laughter prefacing his resumption.

"I told Matthew it takes more than an extra dinner guest to rattle David Ball."

David knew that the short pause which followed was inviting response but when none was given, the company Chairman pressed on regardless.

"Of course the situation here," continued a now solemn sounding voice, "has radically altered since Matthew first called *me*. This promotion business somewhat pales in the light of what has happened. Nevertheless I *did* see Matthew briefly when the police had finished with him, and he repeated the request to be included at your table. Despite his ordeal," Crane enigmatically ended.

"What the hell has been happening?"

"What? Oh, good gracious me," responded Crane, sounding flustered, "I just assumed that you knew, old chap. Harold Cross was killed in an accident earlier today inside the Compass building. Anyway," continued a now brisk sounding Chairman, "we can tell you all about *that* when we get to your place, but I'm glad to hear that Matthew's request doesn't pose a problem and I'd best let you get on now. See you later, David."

David re-cradled the phone and stood perfectly still. Staring towards the kitchen door behind which he could hear Susan moving about. He could feel the sweat on his body attacking the crisply clean shirt, and his rising blood pressure was stoking the heat in his veins and dancing across his eyeballs as the thoughts bludgeoned his forebrain. *'Harold Cross is dead. The 'How' is academic, but since there's nobody else in the frame for the post then my appointment is a sure thing. Which completely negates the need to dazzle Stanley Crane with last minute ideas. Which makes this damned dinner date pointless!'*

He felt his skin prickling as the thoughts kept coming; *'Matthew Sands is coming to dinner. The man whose job he coveted. The man who'd phoned him this morning and had inferred, more than inferred, that Gerald's real father was someone else. The man who had a letter from Susan. The man who had asked that they should both be given a chance to explain...'* He sucked in oxygen as he glanced at his watch; which told him that a little more than an hour remained before people would arrive. He must now tell Susan there would be an extra guest for dinner, but he couldn't seem to move. He remained rooted to the spot while his thoughts raced unchecked; *'It must be true. A man in his position has no reason to invent such a thing. Had they continued to see one another?'* He stood, trembling anew, fighting to suppress the image of Susan and Matthew Sands making love. Trying to clamp down on the question, *'Where had they done it?'*

He drew in another deep shuddering breath and forced his legs to propel him into the kitchen, to find Susan busy with flour and milk. She looked up when he entered, her face beginning to register a tentative smile which froze when she saw the stricken look he knew he'd failed to conceal. Her voice was a tonal mix of concern and alarm.

"David, what is it?"

David looked at his wife; she held a bottle of milk in one of her flour-covered hands and perspiration glistened on her anxious looking face. He could feel the warmth of the kitchen; the comfortable warmth of a familiar scene, and he could also feel the heat in his own face as he choked out the words, "Susan," he began, swallowing the lump in his throat, "I just took a call from Stanley Crane and... "

"Don't tell me," she interjected, "they've bloody cancelled."

"No, they haven't cancelled. He rang to ask if he could bring an extra guest to dinner."

He saw her slam down the milk bottle and her single word *What?* sounded like a gunshot. He drew a deep breath and returned fire. "Susan, it's Matthew Sands who is coming and...," he saw her eyes react and his voice shook as he went on, "Matthew phoned me this morning. He said he had to tell me something before I heard it from someone else." He paused, trying to create saliva inside his dry mouth before continuing, "He actually told me that I'm not Gerald's real father. He said that he has a letter from you and that I should give you both a chance to explain." Into the silence which was already beginning to tell him what he didn't want to know, he gathered himself to add, "A letter from *you* which says *what*, exactly? That it's true? Susan? *Is it true?*"

Susan's eyes didn't lie to him after all, he saw now, and that bitter realization combined with her stunned looking silence, removed any vestige of doubt he'd attempted to harbour. Her face had crumpled and he saw sudden tears on her cheeks which she attempted to wipe away with a flour-streaked hand before reaching for a cloth. She used the cloth to wipe her hands then covered her face with it for silent seconds whilst he stood transfixed. His stomach churned as he suddenly felt the desire to comfort her, and, at the same time, an urge to strike her. She removed the cloth from her face and locked eyes with him, and, when she finally spoke, her words served to snap him out of his partly violent thoughts.

"We need to talk, obviously, but first I need a drink," she announced tersely, moving briskly past him to re-enter the lounge.

As he slip-streamed behind his wife, David's mind reeled. He knew this was happening but couldn't believe it was happening to *him*. He suddenly felt as if he was having one of those 'out-of-body' experiences he'd read about and that *he* was up there on the ceiling looking down at a David Ball he didn't know who was following a woman *neither* of them knew. She went straight to the drinks cabinet and he watched her pour two drinks, one of which she silently proffered and *he* mutely accepted. Then she sat down, stared briefly into her drink, and her next words immediately brought him down from the ceiling and pinned him to the floor.

"What happened; happened once only, years ago. You probably don't even remember that period of our lives. It was one of several times you chose not to be with me. I love you, David. I always have, really, even though you've tested my love on many memorable occasions."

He opened his mouth to protest but she waved aside the unspoken defence.

"No, let me finish," she resumed firmly, pausing only to down some of her drink, "You were always away somewhere or other in those days, making the next deal for mother Compass, building our future, you said." She paused once more and her shoulders dropped, then straightened again as she looked him squarely in the eye and continued, "It wasn't really *our* future you were building, David, it was your own."

He heard in her tone the echoes of past bitterness as she went on relentlessly, "Oh, sure, I've materially benefited from your work, from your success, but that's not quite the same thing as building a life together... "

"Of *course*," he interjected heatedly, "*we* built our life together. *I did what...* "

"Oh please *don't*," interrupted Susan, "say you did *what a man has gotta' do.*" She paused, flashing a brief mixture of smile and grimace as she added, "Sorry, couldn't resist that."

Off-balanced by her flippancy and trying hard not to think of impending guests, he was forced to listen again as Susan fired off more verbal bullets. "Christine was only three when she had that viral infection. She was very ill and I was at my wit's end and all alone in that awful flat we used to live in. *You* were in Manchester and I phoned you and pleaded with you to come home."

Susan rose to her feet, and, as David surprisedly registered the fact that her glass was empty, her steely voice penetrated his senses once more.

"You said you couldn't leave."

He watched her approach the drinks cabinet, his beleaguered thoughts somersaulting between the past and the present, wondering vaguely if she always drank like this when he wasn't here, and then she looked over her shoulder as she continued speaking.

"You said you would call Matthew. Remember?"

As Susan looked at him questioningly, his memory bank flooded enough to provide the recall; *'Yes, he had been at the closing stages of a marathon negotiating session when she'd called him at the hotel. Unable to leave, he'd called Matthew and had asked him to 'look in on his girls...' '* His reverie was broken by the now quietly damning voice.

"Matthew came round to the flat and was marvellous. He dismissed the Doctor's instructions to keep Christine in bed at the flat, and instead put her and myself in his car and drove us straight to the hospital."

"Hospital? You never told me she was in hospital," he protested, and saw the blue eyes regarding him calmly as she replied.

"No, that's right, I never told you." Suddenly muttering 'kitchen' she rushed from the room.

David remained where he was; motionless; stuck in the past with his one-sided memory of the period Susan had referred to. As he strove in vain for further recall, she re-entered the lounge and, as if interpreting his thoughts, seamlessly re-opened her dialogue even as she strode back to her discarded drink.

"You were gone for four days that time, and even your goodnight calls were short affairs. But I'd grown used to that. For the first and only time when you were away on business, I called you, because of my concerns about Christine. And you didn't even call me back that evening to find out how your own daughter was," she stated quietly whilst holding his stare.

Feeling mentally punch-drunk now, David desperately dredged his memory and was only too aware of how composed his wife appeared to be as he heard himself croak the words, "I must have called."

"You didn't," she responded flatly.

Then he saw the blue eyes narrow as she spoke again. Bewildering him, her tone actually softened but the words seemed to pierce every fibre of his body.

"I remember hating you then. Christine was confined for twelve hours," she paused, her voice firming as she resumed, "Matthew wanted to phone you, but I wouldn't let him. He brought Christine home eventually. He and I talked for hours."

He saw her colour slightly as she glanced away from him before continuing, "His wife was away, they'd been going through a bad patch. I was miserable, and fed up with the company widow routine."

Susan faced him again and his splintered mind registered the fact that her blue eyes no longer sparkled but still held his attention as she went on, "We comforted one another. He stayed one night, almost eight years ago, and frankly had he not done so at that time I would probably have left you there and then. It was Matthew who persuaded me to stay. He helped me remember the reasons I'd married you. He genuinely respected you, even then. He wanted to try explaining to you *why* it had happened, but I made him swear not to. Strange as it may sound to *you* now I thought him an honourable man, so I can only assume something he couldn't control has forced him to tell you now."

He watched the slim shoulders being shrugged in the pause and heard her sigh.

"That incident from the past is the reason I've cried off so many invitations to your 'Compass' social functions," she qualified, shaking her head as she sat down again, "I didn't want to run into Matthew. Silly really, I suppose, after all these years. But it was *my* way, however misguided, of keeping faith with *you*."

Susan rose to her feet again and deftly plucked his empty glass from his grasp. He couldn't recall drinking anything as he numbly watched once more her pilgrimage to the drinks cabinet. He saw fresh drinks being poured for them both and then she suddenly stopped what she was doing and he heard her voice break as she spoke.

"Anyway I knew Gerald was Matthew's child, and I told him in a letter because I wanted him to know. I wanted him to know that night had produced something which neither of us needed to feel ashamed of."

David watched as she abandoned the drinks and returned to her seat. She bowed her head in her hands whilst he stood as if carved from stone and tried to think; to think of something rational to say. But all he could manage was, "All these years."

Susan looked up at him, nodding fiercely through her tears as she responded, "Yes, *all these years,* and you have *both* of the children to thank for them. Gerald was a mistake but I was determined to love him *as ours,* and *I have,*" she emphatically declared, "and he and Christine have been the glue in this marriage. You've worked hard, David, and built a career, but you seem to have been brainwashed out of enjoying the fruits of your labours. Spending time with your family has never been your top priority, and your family should be the best fruit you'll ever taste. I know you've never been unfaithful, but God how I've wished sometimes it *had been* another woman instead of a bloody company behind all the broken promises to *me, and* to the children. *You* haven't had to pick up the pieces, *but I have.*"

In the pause which followed, he wordlessly watched her attempt to control her trembling.

"And now," continued Susan, "Ironically, *I'm* going down the same stupid blind alley. I hardly see this place while I'm decorating interiors for other wives with husbands who never see *their* bloody homes."

David continued to watch as she covered her face with her hands, muffling her words, "Such a pointless, vicious circle. I sometimes dread to think what will be there for us when the children are grown up. When they're no longer *here* for *us.*"

Susan rose to her feet to stand directly in front of him. "I still love you, David, but in my heart I will always be grateful to Matthew Sands. Because if it hadn't been for him, our marriage might have ended and we wouldn't have *had* the past seven or eight years. Whatever we've allowed them to do to us, at least we've had them together. For some of the time anyway," she ended softly.

As his mind wrestled with the import of Susan's words, and the images they conjured, the heavy silence was broken by the startling sound of the ringing doorbell. He glanced at his watch and heard himself gasp the words, "Half an hour early!" but Susan was already rushing headlong into the kitchen and he was still rooted to the spot when the doorbell rang again.

Chapter Thirty

Whoever wills the end, wills also (so far as reason decides his conduct) the means in his power which are indispensably necessary thereto.
(Immanuel Kant)

David Ball opened the front door and there they were; the 'all-invited', and, at that particular moment, the completely unwelcome trio of Stanley and Iris Crane and Matthew Sands. The usual hearty greeting sounds emanated from Stanley and Iris as they crossed the threshold and David heard his own voice calmly explaining away Susan's temporary absence with a brief and fabricated tale of 'kitchen misadventure'. If Matthew Sands spoke at the point of entry, David wasn't aware of it. He studiously avoided eye contact with the man as he ushered the group into the lounge; showed them to chairs; offered drinks; mixed and finally handed them drinks, whilst vaguely wondering how much alcohol he himself had already consumed.

Continuing his charade of attentive host, he subjected himself to an exchange of views with Iris Crane on the subject of house-plants, whilst registering from the nearby cross-talk that Matthew had arrived outside his front door at the same time as the Chairman and his wife. Through the smokescreen of polite chatter with Iris, he observed that Stanley Crane was his usual urbane self; evidenced by the full head of white hair above the plump sun-lamped face and the light-grey suit skilfully tailored to comfortably cover his medium-height and overweight body. Hard of hearing these days, the 'Compass' Chairman tended to shout rather than speak and had a disconcerting habit of silently mouthing the words as he lip-read what others were saying to him. Saying something to Stanley *now*, and unusually for the man now being lip-read, Matthew Sands was wearing a tired looking suit and appeared to be in need of a shave. Beyond that brief surreptitious appraisal, David continued to ignore his cuckolding Managing Director.

Sartorially speaking, judged David as he now eyed the chattering object of his feigned attention, everything about Iris Crane was showroom neatness. He'd never seen her in anything other than a trouser suit, and, crowned by her usual coiffeur hairstyle, tonight's well-filled offering on show was a two-tone blue. The woman his wife couldn't stand had a habit of jerking her head from side to side as she spoke, making David think of a stalking bird listening for worms, and her voice had a piercing tone which he himself normally found grating after listening to it for a while. It wasn't hard to understand why Susan would have clashed with her, he silently conceded, because apart from everything else a caustic tongue normally came with the Iris ensemble.

To his mixed feelings of relief and surprise, Stanley and Matthew seemed content to continue engaging one another in small talk as opposed to enlightening their host on the subject of Harold Cross. His relief was briefly enhanced when Susan emerged from the kitchen to rush past the group saying, '*Sorry folks, can't stop, running late, need to change,*' and his now heightened awareness of his wife's current predicament, along with his own hard-earned knowledge of her normal moods, *in normal situations,* was instantly in conflict with his already crowded thoughts.

Susan had just airily breezed through the room smiling radiantly at everyone, including himself, and had left behind the impression that the only thing on her mind was what she would be wearing when she returned to dine with a relaxed looking group of friends. Knowing that his wife was perfectly aware of how *abnormal* this situation had already become, was compounding his difficulty in coming to terms with the fact that there was more of the evening still to come. Meanwhile, Susan had left behind a chuckling Stanley Crane; a silent Iris; and a thoughtful looking Matthew Sands. And a husband with what was beginning to feel like an inane grin on his face. An inane grin which he quickly removed when he saw that Matthew was directing his thoughtful looking expression to *him*, before the question was bluntly voiced.

"Where are the children?"

Only four words had been used to pose the not unexpected question, nevertheless something in Matthew's voice caused David to pause.

"Perhaps he's forgotten where he put them," came Iris's caustically voiced suggestion.

"That will do, Iris," reprimanded Stanley.

Ignoring Iris, David openly gave his attention to Matthew Sands. What he saw was a face which, he wryly thought, could almost have been a mirror image of the one he himself had shaved earlier: The man looked exhausted and careworn. Defying immediate interpretation however, was the inflection which had been put on the four-worded question. A subtle inflection which when coupled with Susan's words on the questioner, *still hammering in his head,* was inducing the now bewildering thought that *'He should surely be feeling something other than empathy with this jaded looking man before him.'*

He couldn't prevent the reflection that he had shared many meetings with the Managing Director he had come to admire and had sought to emulate. He had marvelled at the man's commercial stamina and outwardly relaxed negotiating skills. He had become familiar with the man's mannerisms and had learned to listen for, and decode, the messages hidden behind the public utterances. But Matthew's present appearance and demeanour surprised him. The man's body language silently conveyed a tension he'd never witnessed before and the normally impassive facial features now displayed the distress signs of strain, revealed in part by the reddened eyes now holding his own in silent communion.

"He *has* forgotten," sniped Iris.

Breaking eye contact with Matthew and spreading his response between Stanley and the irritating Iris, he was in the act of explaining where the children were when Susan reappeared. Watching her smile as she finally greeted everyone properly, he thought she looked wonderful and then he heard Matthew remark upon the green dress she now wore.

"David's surprise," responded a delighted sounding Susan, "when he got back from Scotland last month, and I just adore it. He has the wonderful knack of being able to choose things I like."

He rose to his feet, physically steady but mentally reeling from the compliment's source, ands was further surprised when Susan closed the space to link arms with him.

"Can you keep our guests happy a little while longer, darling? I just need to finish off in the dining room," she added with a smile.

David saw Susan raise an eyebrow to him as Iris stood up announcing that *she* would help, and off went the women leaving a now male-dominated room. He reflexively offered fresh drinks but Stanley held up a practically full glass.

"Do relax, David, our drinks are fine," assured Stanley, turning to Matthew and increasing the volume, "Why don't you put this poor man out of his clearly obvious misery?"

He saw Matthew's nodded agreement preface the man's action of leaning forward in his chair, and recognized the mannerism intended to give emphasis to his words.

"David," began Matthew, his voice firm, "this is a bit unorthodox, but we want you to know *now* that the 'Compass' Board will be receiving my strong recommendation to appoint *you* as the new UK Managing Director."

"And *I* can tell you, David," chipped in Stanley, "that the majority of the Board will take great pleasure in ratifying the appointment."

"Quite apart from the fact," resumed Matthew, "that the job's yours on merit," he qualified with a brief smile, "your protagonist, Harold Cross, overplayed a bad hand before... "

As the man hesitated, David thought he saw pain in the reddened eyes holding his own.

"Before," repeated Matthew, "meeting with his unfortunate accident."

David saw the flicked glance to Stanley then his own eyes were firmly re-engaged as he heard the quietly added words, "Which is why I called you this morning."

David saw Stanley's puzzled look signalling he was about to shout, but at that moment Iris reappeared to declare that the dining room was now ready for occupation. The men rose to follow the woman, and, trailing alongside Matthew, he wondered what else might have been disclosed had it not been for the interruption. He placed a hand on Matthew's shoulder, stopping the man in his tracks. "What the hell happened to Cross?" he asked quietly, and read the body language he knew so well and saw the lie before he heard it.

"He accidentally fell down some stairs and broke his neck," said Matthew, "Leave it at that."

David stood perfectly still as Matthew continued walking on and into the dining room. Now questioning his own instincts and hearing the same unbelievable answer in his mind. *'Whatever had happened to Cross had been no accident!'* He recalled now Stanley's remark about Matthew's *ordeal* as another stunning thought silently voiced itself, *'Well however Matthew engineered the so-called accident, it would appear that he has got away with it!'*

Beginning again his approach to the dining room, he briefly examined his own feelings on the demise of Harold Cross and wondered if his seeming ambivalence was simply due to his previous dislike of the man, or because he now had more pressing matters on his mind. *'How can I possibly hope to conduct any useful form of dialogue with Matthew Sands in front of Stanley and his wife?'* He also wondered just how long this nightmare scenario would last, and how it would end. Then his thoughts took another mind-twisting turn when he entered the dining room. *'This is surreal. This is certainly a celebration scene I'm looking at, but just what, exactly, should I be celebrating?'* Nevertheless, knowing the limited and trauma-filled time Susan had been given to prepare everything, he gazed appreciatively at the table presentation his wife had managed to conjure.

Commanding 'centre-table' directly under the room's chandelier, an amber-coloured glass vase held red and yellow roses. Beside the flowers, catering to red or white taste, stood uncorked bottles of wine. His admiring gaze took in almost regimentally exposed areas of the maple-wood table proudly gleaming their reflections of shining steel cutlery and silver cruets and the flickering flames from strategically placed table-top candles. Burgundy woven placemats lay beneath the richly patterned Royal Doulton soup bowls which Susan was busy filling from a shimmering silver soup tureen, and 'Compass-designed' black granite coasters supported sparkling crystal wine glasses. His reaction was spontaneous.

"Darling, this looks absolutely wonderful," he exclaimed, and was rewarded with Susan's very 'aware' smile as the others in turn chorused their appreciation.

David and Susan positioned themselves at opposite ends of the oval-shaped table, with Iris on David's right and Matthew to his left. Stanley was happily captured between the two women and already giving the soup his full attention. Iris was chattering to Susan as they attempted to find table-space for bread rolls, and Matthew turned to quietly address him.

"As you can imagine," he began, his *sotto voce* delivery clearly intended for his host's ears alone, "I've been clearing my desk of personal effects. *You* know, the sort of things we somehow never seem to take home for one reason or another. A few days ago I came across such an item. An old... umm, report of sorts, which relates to you and me."

David curbed his impatience as the man paused to sample his soup. The women were still chattering as they ate.

"Of course it should have been destroyed a long time ago," resumed Matthew, "But there it was. Anyway, David, so far as I can recall of that time, I got called to a meeting as Cross was, shall we say, in the vicinity of my office. He must have seen the... umm, information then, and couldn't resist the temptation to try using it as a lever against both of us. And, for whatever reason, he chose today to make his move."

Matthew re-addressed his soup as the quizzical looking and lip-reading Stanley shouted, "What information are you referring to?"

"Oh nothing that need concern *you*, Stanley," responded Matthew, calmly, "Just an old marketing strategy David had outlined," he qualified, before immediately turning back to his host, "So I thought it best to alert you this morning," he ended quietly.

Whilst still struggling to control his conflicting emotions, David nevertheless felt that his professional instincts remained sufficiently intact. Instincts still keen enough to cut through Matthew's verbal subterfuge and allow a grudging appreciation for the way in which the man was countering the proximity of Stanley and Iris by using a form of coded language to address his morning phone call and his presence here this evening. Although equally mindful of other ears, and lip-reading eyes, he still couldn't prevent his honest response.

"Your call certainly came as a shock."

"I made a complete mess of that call," acknowledged Matthew, "I hadn't planned on ambushing you like that, sorry. Anyway, I *had* intended teaming up with you to defuse the situation. I thought that by standing together against him, we would have nullified whatever damage he sought to do."

Whilst automatically decoding those words as the man paused, David was in no doubt this time that he was looking at pain in the reddened eyes.

"But of course," resumed Matthew, "as a result of the accident, the situation has changed. With Cross no longer posing any threat in the public domain, you and I can hopefully deal privately with whatever problems remain."

David stared at the man, wondering how he should respond to him, but then the sometime lip-reading Stanley shouted his intervention.

"So, David, one of your first priorities will be to find a replacement for Cross."

He ignored Stanley and toyed with his soup whilst digesting his thoughts, then he heard Matthew politely addressing Susan.

"It's good to see you looking so well, Susan. I tried reaching you by phone earlier. I wanted to ask for your invitational blessing rather than rudely crashing your dinner table as I *have* done. My belated thanks, Susan, for allowing me this opportunity to see you both."

David saw the man turn back to him, smiling as he spoke his still encoded words, "It has been a long time since I've spoken to Susan and of course had *you* been here when I phoned, we might have arranged to do this differently."

He numbly managed a nodding smile and glanced at Susan who was now listening to Stanley complimenting her on the soup, and he saw the strained smile with her response.

"You old flatterer, I hope you enjoy your next course of overcooked chicken."

Saying it was time to bring Stanley his poultry, Susan rose from the table as Matthew, still flying diplomatic flags realized David, began speaking quietly to him again.

"I'm glad that we've kept matters under public radar. But I'm aware my calling you has obviously been a disturbing factor, and I'm hoping you can forgive that, David."

With what David silently acknowledged as impeccable timing, Susan returned at that point pushing a hostess trolley. Iris Crane uncharacteristically began chatting pleasantly to her hostess about the benefits of heated serving trolleys. *'Stanley has had a word with her about behaviour before she got here,'* he thought. As plates were switched and the main course dishes appeared to collectively voiced praise, he used the camouflage of the table's activity to contemplate, and decode anew, everything Matthew had said to him. Throughout that fast-moving mental exercise, still resonating in his mind was Susan's earlier and dramatically expressed summation of both their marriage, and the man now seated to his left. A man he should, at the very least, resent. Instead of turning out to be the man to whom he apparently owed the saving of his marriage, without his even having been aware of the circumstances which had almost destroyed it! Accepting a plateful of the chicken dish without really seeing it, and not giving a damn what Stanley or Iris might make of his words, he directly addressed Matthew Sands.

"You seem to have thought it all out, but then you've had more time than I to do so."

"Leaving aside the business connection," Matthew instantly replied, "Your friendship means a great deal to me. So yes, I *have* considered carefully what I wanted to say to you."

'Give the guy his due, he doesn't miss a beat,' thought David. The small silence following Matthew's words was suddenly broken by Stanley proposing a toast to the Chef, and, when the toast had

been made and the glasses were being downed, his eyes were found by Susan's as she raised her glass once more.

"And to friendship," began Susan, "and mistakes that can...," she trailed off, floundering.

"Have unexpected, but beneficial results," completed Matthew, quietly, "I'll drink to that."

Susan's laugh sounded nervous as she lowered her wine glass, and her eyes.

"Some mistakes," resumed Matthew, smoothly, facing David as he spoke, "can be like that, of course. One-off things, unplanned, and yet producing nothing but good."

David's eyes were being steadily held by Matthew's own, and for a crazy second he thought he saw something new in the man's face; *'Something which brought back a tantalising glimpse of the past. Something his mind was reaching for... '*

"What, exactly, are we talking about here?"queried Iris, her tone both caustic and piercing.

"Respect. Love. Friendship. Human frailty. All those everyday things," responded Matthew.

As the patently confounded Iris glowered, her equally bemused looking husband shouted, "David, I haven't quite followed the conversation thus far, and Iris and I seem to be the only ones doing justice to Susan's splendid meal, but I understood you to have some points you wanted to discuss with me over dinner. So, mine host, do you think we might now hear them?"

"And understand them, even," added the caustic Iris.

Ignoring Iris's barbed comment, David suddenly realized how very tired he felt. His earlier planned reasons for the dinner lay redundant in his mind like the food growing cold on his plate. *'Like so much waste and no longer relevant,'* he admitted to himself. Still in his head, Susan's clarity-inducing words had replaced the salesman's mind-games he'd lived to play, and, as he stared at his plate, he remembered she'd said that she still loved him. Vaguely aware that the commandingly raised hand of Matthew Sands was the only thing keeping Stanley and Iris quiet, and beyond caring about the stares directed towards him, he briefly recalled now a medley of other, warmer, times he had shared with Susan. Before his scheming ambition had frozen those times out. Distancing him from what it was all supposed to be about, as Susan had pointed out in devastatingly effective fashion.

He looked across the table to his wife, the woman he lived *with* and *for*, the woman who had stood by him through all the lean times. The woman without whom he knew his life would be meaningless. The mother of their children, *'Yes, damn it, she was right, they're **our** children. And I'm looking at the woman who has **made** them ours. '* Feeling suddenly clear-headed, he knew that the decision he'd reached was the right one. So when he addressed the clearly impatient Stanley, it was with the voice which had always been able to hold its audience and close the deal.

David smiled at the 'Compass' Chairman, "I'm glad you've been enjoying your meal, Stanley, and yes I do have some things to say to you. To all of you, in fact." He paused, making eye contact with Susan as he resumed, "I'm now withdrawing my application for the position of 'Compass' M.D.", he calmly stated.

As the group stared at him with varying expressions of shock and surprise, he delivered the rest of his bombshell, "I am in fact resigning from Compass Designs. I'm going to take my wife on an overdue second honeymoon, and, when we get back, see how she feels about having me as a partner in her own interior decorating business."

Into the short but palpable silence following his declaration of intent, firstly came Stanley's loudly spluttered "What on earth?" which was quickly overtaken by Susan's incredulous sounding "Darling, do you really mean that?" His own *'Yes, I do,'* was emphatic.

The eyes of Matthew Sands were being made even more red by his rubbing them as he voiced *his* response, "You'd make a good MD, David, is there any way I could persuade you to change your mind?"

"I won't be changing it," he replied, "My finances will change, but not my mind," he added with a quick glance towards a still shocked looking Susan.

Still obviously struggling to come to terms with what he'd heard, Stanley's shout this time was an angry one. "Just where does this leave *us*? The company can't just lose two senior men in one day. I mean, *What **is** going on,* Matthew?"

Matthew Sands blew air through his pursed lips, grinned quickly at his host, and delivered a brisk reply to his Chairman. "We're losing a good man is what's going on, Stanley, but we don't have to lose our heads. *I'll* stay on this side of the pond till we find a replacement for *me*. David's Sales Manager will step up to the S.D. plate as planned and *he'll* choose his own replacement, and the 'Head-hunters' will be told to pull their fingers out and produce shortlists from which we'll appoint a new M.D. and F.D. Calm down, Stanley, we'll manage."

Stanley Crane seemed to be somewhat appeased by the outline of a damage-limitation plan, whilst his wife, obviously muddling the roles of guest and hostess, again surprised by offering to make coffee for everyone.

"Bugger the coffee," shouted Stanley, "I need a whisky."

As the flustered Iris followed Susan's directions to bottled spirit, Stanley Crane rounded on his host.

"All a bit bloody sudden, isn't it?" bawled the clearly bewildered Chairman.

"Yes, I suppose it is," replied David, calmly adding, "I only began to consider it tonight."

The Compass Chairman's face displayed his obvious disbelief, but David held the man's gaze as he began qualifying his decision. "Try looking at it this way, Stanley. For reasons which needn't concern you, tonight I've been forced to examine my life from someone else's perspective. Someone I respect. I've been quite rightly made to see that my life has *been* your company for the last fifteen years. Naturally there *has* been a constructive by-product, *your* Compass Designs has enabled *me* to realize my own ambitions, but at what price? I was so focused on keeping *your* company afloat, Stanley, I didn't even realize that I was steering my own marriage on to the rocks."

He leant back in his chair as he continued, "I've been successful within the company, and both you and myself have benefited from that. But what's the point of that kind of success? To make money? Sure, that's a given. But from a personal point of view, once you've *made* the money what's the point of the performance if at the end of the day there's no applause from the audience that really matters. Because *that* audience, not you and your shareholders, Stanley, has been ignored to the point where it has ceased to care."

He came forward again in his chair to emphasise his conclusion, "Now I know that to your ears this might all sound like something taken from a Hollywood film script, Stanley, but the fact is that my wife and I have given half of *our* lives to *me* and *your* company. Now I want to give the other half of *mine* to Susan, and our children."

Not yet ready to seek out Susan's eyes, David then turned to Matthew and thought he saw understanding on the tired looking face returning his scrutiny without flinching. He was suddenly reminded of the office gossip which said that Alicia Sands had never been the same since losing a child, and he heard again Susan's voice saying *'His wife was away, they'd been going through a bad patch,'* and he reckoned that Matthew, like himself, had probably also paid a price over the odds to be where he was now. Caroline Prout's opinion on the man now before him had first been voiced long ago, had often been repeated, had never altered, and remained memorable: *'The mother who raised him to manhood would still be proud of him today,'* Caroline had said.

"But whether it's success or failure, Stanley," he continued, ignoring the Chairman and staring into the face of the man he knew he could never bring himself to hate, *'How could I ever hate the man who stopped Susan from leaving me?'* he silently reasoned, "we end up being indebted to someone, and the time has come for me to repay *my* debt to my wife." He smiled into the reddened eyes of Matthew Sands and softly mouthed, "A one-off mistake?"

"Yes it was," acknowledged Matthew, quietly adding, "The circumstances at that time... "

"I'm a bit more aware of some of those," interrupted David, pausing before resuming hesitantly, "It's a bit... difficult... to say exactly what I would...," he broke off, looking away from Matthew to finally meet Susan's eyes with his silent plea.

"Matthew," said Susan, "We each of us know it happened a long time ago, but I think David is trying to say...," she faltered, then recovered to firmly add, "We're both still very grateful, Matthew, for what you did for Christine, aren't we, darling?"

Susan's own eyes were twinkling again, noticed David, encouraging his own smile as he faced Matthew squarely with the words, "I'm belatedly glad to thank you for *that*," and once again he thought there was something indefinable in Matthew's eyes which challenged comprehension as the man proffered his hand and quietly responded.

"We both have a lot to be thankful for, David, and everything you've said tonight could also be applied to me. We've both put up a good front, but we could be brothers under the skin."

Puzzled by Matthew's choice of words, David clasped the proffered hand whilst a patently perplexed Stanley Crane looked on. Susan was suddenly on her feet, moving to reach him while his hand was still being gripped, bending down to embrace him, kissing him as Iris returned saying she could only find Rum and Stanley shouted, "Just the thing for *this* sort of do."

Susan Ball moved back to her seat; wiping tears from her eyes and uncaring of the mess she knew she was making of her make-up. Brimful of emotion, her ears filled with the sound of a pounding heart which she thought might burst at any moment, she imagined everyone must notice her trembling but a quick glance at the table's occupants told her no one was reading her body language. A heartfelt sigh; travelling from deep within her and escaping from her body, was one of contentment. She attributed it to the tremendous relief of her long-held secret finally being known to, and accepted by, the husband she loved.

She thought of Gerald, the boy whom they *both* loved, and glanced at Matthew Sands, who, together with David, was re-engaged in placatory conversation with Stanley Crane. She saw Matthew look at David and was suddenly startled by her perception that it was the kind of look she might have associated with *'a benignly smiling older brother figure'* she thought, *'presiding over a relaxed family get-together, instead of the life-altering experience this evening has turned out to be.'* And then their eyes met. He smiled warmly, giving every appearance of a man at peace with the world, and she returned the smile and thanked him with her eyes. *'I really hope,'* she thought, *'that Alicia has learned to appreciate the kind of man she has.'*

She saw David rise from his chair; saw him casually grip Matthew's shoulder as he moved past him towards the standard lamp which stood off to one side of the dining table. She saw Matthew's pleased look of surprise at the gesture before the table was bathed with fresh light, and she was suddenly overwhelmed by the thought that the shadow of the past had finally been removed from the future path of her marriage, and her son, Gerald.

Chapter Thirty-One

In my end is my beginning.
(Motto of Mary, Queen of Scots)

Bordeaux region of France, August 1992
In the picturesque village of *La Sauve-Majeure,* in the obviously well-tended grounds of the ancient church of *Saint Pierre,* the couple stood together before the memorial stone dedicated to Jack and Chantal Sands, *nee Cheval.*

"Having read the diaries and *then* to come here, seems so fitting, somehow," said the quietly voiced woman.

He squeezed her hand in response. Thinking now that he finally understood why Elizabeth Creacey had chosen not to bring him here as a young boy. Apart from her fear of reprisal from the *Lecroix* family, and her wish to protect him, she would have known that he could never have understood *then* what it meant to lose someone you loved. He could never really have *shared* with her, such a deeply personal experience.

Glancing around him, picturing her here all those years ago, he instinctively felt that she would have approved of his being here *now*. Now that he *had* shared, with his wife, the terrible pain of loss. Now that he *had* experienced, like Elizabeth Creacey-Sands, the way in which love could drive one person to take the life of another. Now that he had done all that he could to redress his past mistakes.

His thoughts touched upon Susan and his brother, David, and recalled now the surprised delight of the man when he'd been given the very substantial 'Golden Goodbye' bonus. Ostensibly presented as coming from Compass Designs, and reminding Matthew of her own past machinations, he knew that Elizabeth Creacey-Sands would have approved of his using a part of his legacy to provide for the man she herself had provided for all those years ago when that man had been a boy.

Matthew Sands drew Alicia closer to him as he whispered, "Happy?"

"Very," she replied simply.

The couple turned away from the memorial stone and Matthew thought that next week would probably be the right time to show her the brochure in his pocket. The brochure of hope which an understanding *Pierre Dubois* had given him. Matthew felt strangely confident that Alicia would like the idea of adopting a French child, and *Pierre* had the connections who could smooth the way to making it possible.

As they began retracing their steps to where he had parked the car, Matthew Sands could see that ahead of them the light was changing. From behind one of the valley's magnificent twin peaks, the morning sun was steadily emerging to begin lifting the shadows from the path upon which he and Alicia walked.

Lightning Source UK Ltd.
Milton Keynes UK
UKOW05f2236301214

243811UK00001B/8/P